SPARTAN

DR VALERIO MASSIMO MANFREDI is an Italian historian, journalist and archaeologist. He is the Professor of Classical Archaeology at the Bocconi University of Milan, and a familiar face on European television. He has published nine novels, including the bestselling Alexander trilogy. He is married with two children and lives in a small town near Bologna and is currently at work on a screenplay for a major Hollywood studio.

Valerio Massimo Manfredi

SPARTAN

Translated from the Italian by Christine Feddersen-Manfredi

PAN BOOKS

FOR GIULIA AND FABIO

First published 2002 by Macmillan

This edition published 2003 by Pan Books
an imprint of Pan Macmillan Ltd
Pan Macmillan, 20 New Wharf Road, London N1 9RR
Basingstoke and Oxford
Associated companies throughout the world
www.panmacmillan.com

ISBN 0 330 49102 4

Originally published 1988 in Italy as *Lo Scudos di Talos* by
Arnoldo Mondadori Editore S.p.A., Milano

1 3 5 7 9 8 6 4 2

A CIP catalogue record for this book is available from
the British Library.

Typeset by SetSystems Ltd, Saffron Walden, Essex
Printed and bound in Great Britain by
Mackays of Chatham plc, Chatham, Kent

PART ONE

My guest, it is difficult for man to stave off
what the gods have willed, and this is the worst
of human pains: foreseeing many things and
being powerless to change any of them.

Herodotus IX, 16, 4–5

1

MOUNT TAYGETUS

HIS HEART FULL OF BITTERNESS, the great Aristarkhos sat watching his son Kleidemos sleep quietly within the paternal shield that served as his cradle. Close by, in a little bed suspended by four ropes from the ceiling beam, slept his older brother Brithos. The silence that enveloped the ancient house of the Kleomenids was suddenly broken by the rustling of the oaks in the nearby forest. A long, deep sigh of the wind.

Sparta, the invincible, was shrouded in darkness; only the fire that burned on the acropolis shot red flares into the black clouds of the sky. Aristarkhos shivered and pushed aside the cloth covering on the window, staring into the sleeping countryside beyond.

It was time to do what had to be done; the gods had hidden the moon and darkened the earth. The clouds in the sky were swollen with tears.

He took his cloak from the hook on the wall and threw it onto his shoulders, then bent over his tiny son. He lifted him up and slowly drew him close to his chest as the little one's wet nurse suddenly stirred in her sleep.

Aristarkhos stood uncertainly for a moment, hoping for something that would force him to put off this tremendous act. Then, reassured by the woman's deep breathing, he braced himself and left the room by the atrium, dimly lit by an earthenware oil lamp. A gust of cold wind invaded the courtyard, nearly extinguishing the weak flame. As he turned to close the heavy oaken door behind him, he saw his wife Ismene standing there like a mysterious divinity evoked by the night, pale, her eyes shining. A mortal anguish was painted on her face; her mouth, taut as a wound, seemed to contain an inhuman suffering. Aristarkhos felt his blood freeze within his veins, and his legs, sturdy as pillars, turned to straw.

'It was not for us . . .' he murmured with a cracked voice, 'it wasn't for us that we generated him. It has to be tonight. I'll never find the courage again.'

Ismene's hand reached towards the bundled child and her feverish eyes sought her husband's. The little one woke up and began to cry. Aristarkhos lunged out of the door, escaping into the countryside. Ismene, poised on the threshold, watched the man flee into the night, listened to the faint wail of her child . . . tiny Kleidemos, stricken by the gods while still in her womb. Born a cripple and condemned to death by the terrible laws of Sparta.

She closed the door and slowly walked to the centre of the atrium, pausing to consider the images of the gods to whom she had always brought generous offerings before the child was born and to whom she had continued to pray, over these long months, to instil strength into that stiff little foot. In vain.

She sat at the hearth in the centre of the huge, bare room and unwound her long, black braids, pulling her flowing tresses over her shoulders and breasts. Gathering up the ashes at the base of the great copper tripod, she spread them over her head. By the tremulous light of the oil lamp, the statues of the gods and the Kleomenid heroes stared at her, their immutable smiles carved into cypress wood. Ismene soiled her beautiful hair with ashes and slowly gouged her face with her fingernails as her heart turned to ice.

*

Aristarkhos fled across the wind-battered fields, his arms clutching the small bundle close to his chest. His cape whipped around him, animated by Boreas' powerful breath. He trudged up the mountain, struggling to open a path through the thick undergrowth of blackberry bushes and shrubs. Sudden flashes of lightning cast frightening shapes onto the ground. The gods of Sparta were far away in that bitter moment; Aristarkhos had to proceed alone among the dark spectres of the night, among the evil creatures of the forest who lie in wait for the traveller and drag up nightmares from the bowels of the earth.

Freeing himself from the grasp of a large bush, Aristarkhos found the trail and stopped a moment to catch his breath. The little one cried no longer, hoarse from his long wailing. Aristarkhos felt only the convulsive movements of tiny limbs within the bundle, like those of a puppy enclosed in a sack, waiting to be thrown into the river.

The warrior lifted his glance to the threatening clouds that filled the sky. He murmured an ancient oath under his breath, and then started off along the steep path as the first heavy drops of rain fell with dull thuds against the dust. Past the clearing, the bushes surrounded him again, the branches and the thorns clawing at his defenceless face as he held the bundle against his chest.

The rain, dense and heavy now, penetrated even the blackberry bushes, and the ground became spongy and slippery. Aristarkhos fell onto his knees. He was soiled by the mud and the dead, rotten leaves and cut by the sharp stones that jutted up along the steep and narrow footpath. Calling up the last of his strength, he reached the first of the great mountain's wooded summits, and entered an oak grove that rose in the middle of a clearing of thick, low cornel and broom.

The rain pelted Aristarkhos, but he continued his slow, unfaltering walk on the soaked, pungent moss, his hair pasted to his forehead and his clothing drenched. He stopped before a gigantic holm oak, older than the ages. Aristarkhos fell to his knees between the roots and deposited the small bundle within the huge hollow trunk. He paused a moment, grimly biting his lower lip, watching the small flailing arms of his son.

Water streamed down Aristarkhos' back, but his mouth was dry, his tongue stuck to his palate like a piece of leather. That which he had come to do was done. His son's destiny was now in the lap of the gods. The time had come to silence forever the voice of his blood. Rising to his feet slowly, with immense effort, as if carrying the mountain upon his shoulders, he returned the way he had come.

The fury of the elements seemed to have spent itself as Aristarkhos descended among Mount Taygetus' abrupt crags. A light fog rose, spreading between the trees, covering the dripping bushes, skimming the footpaths and the clearings. The wind continued in stiff breezes, shaking the water from the foliage. Aristarkhos shuddered with every breath; his muscles cramped violently in the cold. Stumbling down the mountain, he left the forest behind him and reached the plain. He stopped again, for just a moment, and directed a last sombre glance at the mountain peak.

The glimmering waters of the Eurotas river ran through the damp fields before him, illuminated by the moon, whose frigid rays cut a broad gash between the clouds. As he began to cross the river's wooden bridge he heard a sudden noise on his left. Aristarkhos turned sharply: the faint moonlight revealed a horseman, his face hidden by a helmet, sitting erect on his steaming mount. The emblem of the royal guard flashed for an instant on his burnished shield.

Sparta . . . Sparta already knew! At a sharp blow of the rider's heels, the horse reared and began its gallop, disappearing with the wind, far off in the fields.

*

'Krios, Krios! In the name of the gods, won't you stop for a moment? Come back here, you rascal!' The small mutt paid no heed; trotting decisively down the footpath, he splashed through the puddles as the old shepherd followed him, swearing, with his uncertain step. The little dog headed resolutely towards the trunk of a colossal holm oak, howling and wagging his tail.

'Damn you!' grumbled the old man. 'You'll never be a shepherd's dog . . . what is it this time? A porcupine, that's what it'll be, or a baby blackbird . . . no, it's too early in the season for the blackbirds. By Zeus and Hercules, could it be a bear cub? Krios, are you set on my ruin, you little beast? His mother will show up and kill us both.' The old man finally reached the point where Krios had stopped. He stooped to pick up the dog and turn back, but suddenly stopped still, bent double. 'It's no bear cub, Krios,' he muttered, calming the dog with a rough caress, 'it's a cub born of man. He is not even a year old!'

'Let's see,' he continued, unwrapping the bundle, but when he saw the little one, numb from the cold, barely moving, a dark, grave expression passed over his face. 'They've abandoned you. Yes, you were left to die ... with that leg you'd never have become a warrior. And now ... what shall we do now, Krios?' he said scratching his beard. 'Shall we abandon him, too? No. No, Krios, the Helots don't behave this way, we Helots do not abandon children. We'll take him with us,' he decided, gathering up the bundle from the hollow of the tree. 'And you'll see that we can save him. If he hasn't died yet, it means that he is strong. Let's go back now, we've left the flock unguarded.'

The old man set off towards the house as the dog joined a flock of sheep at pasture nearby. He pushed open the door of the cottage and entered. 'Look what I've found for you, daughter,' he said, turning to a woman past her youth who was intent on curdling a great vessel of milk. The woman, with expert movements, lifted the curd with a cloth and hung it from a hook on the ceiling beam. Drying her hands in her apron, she curiously drew closer to the old man, who had laid the bundle on a bench and was carefully unwrapping it. 'Look, I've just found him in the hollow of a big holm oak . . . it's one of them. They must have abandoned him last night. Look at his little foot, see? He's not moving it. That's why they did it. You know, when one of them is born with some defect, they just leave him to the wolves! But Krios found him and I want to keep him.'

The woman, without speaking, went to fill a bladder with milk, tying one side to create a swelling and pricking it with a pin. She brought it to the lips of the little one, who began to suck slowly at the warm liquid, and then more avidly.

'Ah, I said he was strong,' exclaimed the old man with satisfaction. 'We'll make a good shepherd out of him. He'll live longer than if he'd remained among them. Doesn't great Achilles tell Odysseus in the Underworld that it is better to be a humble shepherd in the land of sun and life than a king among the shadows of the dead?'

The woman stared at him, her grey eyes veiled with a deep sadness. 'Even if the gods have stricken his leg, he will always remain a Spartan. He is the son and the grandson of warriors. He will never be one of us. But if you wish, I will feed him and help him grow.'

'Of course I want you to! We are poor and fate has made us servants, but we can give him the life that was taken from him. And he will help us in our work; I'm getting old and you have to do almost everything yourself. You were denied the pleasure of marrying and having children, my daughter. This little one needs you, and he can bring you the joy of being a mother.'

'But look at his leg!' said the woman, shaking her head. 'Perhaps he'll never be able to walk, and our masters will have given us only another burden to bear. Is this what you want?'

'By Hercules! The little one will walk and he will be stronger and more clever than the other boys. Don't you know that misfortune makes men's limbs more vigorous, their eyes more piercing, their minds quicker? You know what must be done, my daughter, you take care of him and never let him want for fresh milk. Steal the master's honey if you can, without letting him know. Old Krathippos is further gone than I am, and all his son thinks about is the young wife he sees once a week when he can leave the barracks. None of the family cares any more about the fields or the flocks. They'll never notice another mouth to feed.'

The woman took a large hamper and arranged some sheepskins and a woollen blanket inside. On these she rested the child, exhausted and full from his meal, already nodding with sleep.

The old man stood a moment to watch him and then returned to the flock. Krios greeted him joyously, barking and jumping at his feet.

'The sheep! You're to stay with the flock, not with me! You dumb little mutt . . . do I look like a sheep? No, I'm no sheep; old Kritolaos, that's who I am, foolish old man. Away from here, I said! That's it, bring back those lambs headed for the ravine. A deranged goat would do a better job than you!'

Thus muttering, the old man reached the field where his flock was grazing. The valley opened wide before his gaze, divided by the silver ribbon of the Eurotas river. At the centre of the plain glittered the city of Sparta: an expanse of low houses covered by small terraces. On one side rose the massive acropolis; on the other, the red-tiled roofs of the temple of Artemis Orthia. On the right, one could make out the dusty road that led towards the sea.

Kritolaos contemplated the beautiful countryside, resplendent with the dazzling colours of early springtime. His heart was elsewhere; his thoughts went back to the ancient times when his people, free and powerful, occupied the fertile plain: the old times, preserved in the stories passed down by old men, when the arrogant Spartans had not yet succeeded in taming his proud and unfortunate people.

The sea breeze ruffled the old man's white hair. His eyes seemed to search for distant images: the dead city of the Helots on Mount Ithome, the lost tombs of the great kings of his people, their trampled pride. Now the gods sat in the imposing city of their oppressors. When would the time for honour and revenge return? Would his tired eyes be allowed to see it?

Only the bleating of the sheep, the sound of servitude, reached his ears. His thoughts returned to the little one that he had just snatched from a sure death: who was his family? The mother with the womb of bronze who had torn him away from her own breast? The father who had delivered him to the wild beasts of the forest? Was this the power of the Spartans? The pity that had moved him: was it only the weakness of a servant, of a defeated race?

Perhaps – he thought – the gods mark out a destiny for each people, as they do for each man, and we must walk down that pathway, without ever turning back. What it is to be a man! Poor mortals, prey to sickness, to misfortune, as leaves are prey to the wind. But yearning to know, to judge, to listen to the voice of our hearts and our minds, yes . . . The tiny cripple would become a man: to suffer, perhaps, to die, certainly, but not at the very dawn of his life.

The old man knew in that moment that he had changed the course of an already marked destiny. The little one would become an adult and he, Kritolaos, would teach him all that a man needs to know to step along the pathway of life, and more! He would teach him what a man must do to change the course of the destiny that has been assigned him . . . the destiny of a servant.

A name. The little one needed a name. Certainly his parents must have prepared a name for him, the name of a warrior, son and grandson of warriors, the name of an exterminator. What name could one servant give to another? An ancient name of his own people? A name to remind him of the dignity of an age long past? No, the child was not a Helot, and the brand of Spartan blood could not be cancelled. Yet he was no longer a son of Sparta. The city had disowned him.

Kritolaos thought of one of the old stories that the children would beg him to tell on many a winter night: *In a time very long ago, when the heroes still walked on the roads of the earth, the god Hephaistos had fashioned a giant, all of bronze, to guard the treasure of the gods that was hidden in a deep cave on the island of Lemnos. The giant moved and walked just as if he were alive because in the hollow of his immense body, the gods had poured a miraculous liquid that animated him. The liquid was sealed with a cork, also of bronze, hidden at the bottom of his heel so that no one could see it. So, the weak point of this colossus lay in his right leg. His name was Talos.* The old man half closed his eyes. The boy's name would remind him of his misfortune. It would keep his strength and his anger alive within him. His name would be 'Talos'.

*

The old shepherd rose, leaning against the crook that was worn down where his large callused hand always gripped it. He rejoined his flock. The sun began its descent into the sea, and wisps of smoke rose from the cabins scattered among the mountains; the women were beginning to prepare meagre dinners for their men returning from work. It was time to round up the flock. The old man whistled and the dog began to run around the bleating sheep who clustered together. The lambs leaping across the fields ran to hide under their mothers and the ram moved to the head of the flock to lead them to the pen.

Kritolaos herded the animals in, dividing the males from the females, and began to milk, collecting the steaming liquid in a large jug. He dipped in a cup and brought it with him into the cottage.

'Here we are,' he said, entering. 'Here is some fresh milk for our little Talos.'

'Talos?' repeated the surprised woman.

'Yes, Talos. This is the name I've chosen for him. Thus I have decided, and thus it must be. How is he? Let me see . . . oh, he seems much better, doesn't he?'

'He slept most of the day and just woke up a short while ago. He must have been exhausted, poor creature.

He must have cried for as long as he had breath! Now he can't utter a single sound. That is, if he's not mute, on top of everything.'

'Mute? Absolutely not! The gods never strike one man with two clubs . . . at least that's what they say.' Just then, little Talos let out a confused cry. 'See, he's not mute at all. No, I'm sure this little rascal will have us jumping with his shrieks!' Saying this, he drew near to caress the little one lying in the wicker chest. Immediately, the baby grabbed the shepherd's knobbly index finger and held it tightly.

'By Hercules! These legs aren't doing too well but we certainly have strength in our hands, don't we? That's it, that's it: grip tight, little one! Never let what is yours slip from your hands, and no one will be able to take it away from you.'

From the cracks in the door penetrated the rays of a dying sun. They touched upon the old man's white locks and cast golden reflections of amber and alabaster on the little one's skin, and on the poor, smoke-blackened furnishings of the cottage. Kritolaos, sitting on a bench, took the baby on his knee and began eating the simple meal his daughter had prepared. The bleating of the sheep reached his ears from the pen. And from the edge of the clearing, he heard the deep sigh of the forest, the consuming hymn of the nightingale. It was the hour of the long shadows, when the gods dispel the pain in men's hearts and send them purple clouds that bring the soothing calm of sleep.

But down there, on the plain, the noble house of the Kleomenids had already been swallowed up by the cold shadow of the tremendous mountain. From the wooded peaks of the sullen giant, anguish and pain descended upon the valley. In their marital bed Aristarkhos' proud wife stared with glassy eyes at the ceiling beams. In her heart the wolves of Taygetus howled, her ears resounded with the sharp grating of their steel jaws, and their yellow eyes lit up the darkness. Neither the strong arms nor the broad chest of her husband could console her, nor would the tears come to wash the bitter pain from her heart.

*

Limping on his bad leg, Talos urged the flock along the flowered banks of the Eurotas river, his crook held tightly in his left hand. A light wind sent waves through the sea of poppies around him, and the sharp odours of rosemary and mint spread through the air. The boy, soaked with sweat, paused to refresh himself with the river water. The sheep were oppressed by the heat as well, and lay down under an elm whose sunburned branches provided a little shade. The dog curled up near the shepherd boy, wagging his tail and softly yelping. The boy turned to pat his matted fur, clotted with oats and lupins. Krios nudged closer to his young master and licked his misshapen foot as if it were a painful wound.

The boy watched the little dog with deep calm eyes, occasionally ruffling the thick fur on its back. His gaze became suddenly troubled as he turned towards the distant city. The acropolis, scorched by the sun, rose from the plain like a disquieting ghost trembling in the sultry air, thick with the deafening screech of the cicadas.

Talos drew a reed flute, a gift from Kritolaos, from the pack strapped across his shoulders. He began to play: a fresh, light melody spread among the field poppies, mixing with the gurgling of the river and the song of the skylarks. Dozens of them flew about him, rising dazzled towards the flaming sun and plunging down as if thunderstruck to the stubble and the yellowed grasses. The voice of the flute became suddenly muffled like that of a spring gushing in the darkness of a cave in the deep womb of the earth.

The soul of the little shepherd vibrated intensely to the primitive music of his instrument. Occasionally he laid down his flute and looked out in the direction of the dusty road that came from the north, as if waiting for somebody.

'I saw the shepherds from the highlands yesterday,' the old man had said. 'They say that the warriors are returning and with them many of our men who served in the army as porters and muleteers.' Talos wanted to see them; for the first time he had brought his flock down from the mountains to the plain so as to see the Spartan warriors he had heard described with so much anger, with disgust, with admiration . . . and with terror.

Krios suddenly lifted his snout to sniff out the still air, and growled.

'Who's there, Krios?' asked the young shepherd, suddenly springing to his feet at the edge of the river. 'Good boy, quiet now, there's nothing wrong,' he said, trying to calm the animal. The boy strained his ears, and after a while seemed to hear a far-off sound; a sound of flutes like his own but very different, joined by a deep rhythmic noise like distant thunder. Soon after, Talos distinctly heard the rumble of a multitude of footsteps treading the ground, reminding him of the time the Messenian shepherds had passed with their herds of oxen. Suddenly from behind the hill on his left he saw them appear. It was them: the warriors!

In the shimmering air, their outline was confused yet formidable. The sound that he'd heard came from a group of men who advanced at the head of the column playing pipes, accompanied by the rhythmic roll of drums and the metallic sound of kettledrums. It was a strange music, unchanging, haunting, made up of taut vibrant sounds that awoke an extraordinary longing in the boy, an uneasy excitement that made his heart beat crazily.

The hoplites came behind them, foot soldiers with legs sheathed in bronze greaves, chests covered by armour, faces hidden by the sallets they wore on their heads, decorated with black and red crests. Their left arms carried great round shields adorned with fantastic animals, monsters that Talos recognized from Kritolaos' stories.

The column advanced with measured step, raising up dense clouds of dust that covered the crests and the banners and the warriors' curved shoulders.

When the first ones came close to him, Talos felt a sudden pulse of fear and an urge to flee, but a mysterious force from the depths of his heart nailed him to the spot.

The first ones passed so close that he could have touched the spears that they leaned on as they walked, if he had just reached out a hand. He gazed into each face to see, to know, to understand what the shepherds had told him. He saw their staring eyes, stinging with sweat behind the grotesque masks of their helmets, blinded by the blazing sun; he saw their dust-covered beards, he smelled the acrid odour of their sweat . . . and their blood.

Their shoulders and arms were bruised. Dark clots of blood stained their hands and sweaty thighs, and also the tips of their spears. They advanced, impervious to the flies that settled avidly on their tortured limbs. Awed, Talos stared at the fantastic figures who marched past him to the endless cadence of that strange music as it became increasingly distant, unreal, absurd, like a nightmare.

The sensation of an unexpected, oppressive presence suddenly shook the boy and he wheeled around: a wide chest covered by a storied cuirass, two huge hairy arms as full of scars as a holm oak that a bear has used to sharpen its claws, a swarthy face framed by a raven beard, sprouting its first white bristles, a steel hand tight around the hilt of a long ashwood spear shaft. Two eyes as black as night that shone with the light of a powerful and tormented will: 'Keep that dog back, boy. Do you want a spear to split apart his bones? The warriors are tired and their hearts are vexed. Call him off, his barking is annoying us all. And go away yourself, this is no place for you!'

Talos drew back, dazed as if awakened from a dream. He called the dog and walked away, leaning on his staff to ease his limp. After a few steps, he paused and slowly turned his head; the warrior stood immobile behind him with an astonished expression. He stared at the boy in wild and amazed pain. His shining eyes fixed the boy's deformed foot. Biting his lower lip, the warrior was shaken by a sudden tremor, his thighs of bronze were unsteady as reeds. It lasted but a moment; the man covered his face immediately with the great crested helmet, took up the shield emblazoned with the figure of a dragon, and joined the end of the column as it curved down the road.

The tension that had gripped Talos suddenly abated and he felt a hot stream of tears rise from his heart. They filled his eyes and ran down his cheeks until they wet his bony chest. All at once he became aware of a tremulous calling from the path that led down the mountain: it was old Kritolaos, struggling along as fast as his old age and aching legs would let him.

'Talos, my son!' exclaimed the distressed old man, hugging the child, 'Why did you do it, why did you come here? This is no place for you! You must never come here again, do you understand? You must promise me ... never again!'

The two of them turned back down the path as Krios rounded up the sheep, driving them towards the mountain. On the distant plain, the long column was entering the city: it seemed like a wounded serpent hurrying to shelter.

Stretched out on his straw bed, Talos couldn't sleep that night. He couldn't drive that intense, suffering gaze out of his mind ... that hand that gripped the spear as if wanting to crush it. Who was the warrior with the dragon on his shield? Why had he looked at him in that way? That strange music that had awakened so much emotion in Talos' heart continued to play in his mind. At last, the late hour closed his eyelids. The warrior's eyes melted into darkness, the music became slower and then as sweet as a woman's song, caressing his tired heart until sleep settled his head to rest.

2

THE BOW OF KRITOLAOS

'Listen carefully, my boy,' said the old man, considering young Talos with his clear, penetrating gaze. 'You know well that a bird with a broken wing will never be able to fly again.' Talos listened to him intently, sitting back on his heels on the ground next to Krios. 'But a man is different. You are agile and quick, even though your foot is lame. But I want you to become stronger and surer in your movements, even more so than the other boys. The staff that you grasp in your hand will be like a third leg for you and I will teach you to use it. It will seem strange at first, and will take all the determination you've got to make it work, but that staff can do much more than just support you as you walk, as it has until now. You'll learn to use it to pivot your body out in any direction, gripping onto it with one hand or both, as need be.'

'What's wrong with the way I walk, Kritolaos? Are you saying that I'm not quick enough for you? I can catch up with any sheep that wander away from the flock, and in the long marches to pasture, I hold up better than Krios, and he has four legs!'

'I know, my boy, but you see, your body is becoming crooked, like a piece of green wood left out in the sun.'

Talos scowled. 'If we let that happen, you'll be more and more limited in the ways you can move, and when your bones have become stiff and inflexible, you won't be able to depend on your strength any more.

'Talos,' continued the old man, 'your foot was damaged when the midwife pulled you too forcefully from your mother's womb. Your father, Hylas, was killed by a bear on the mountain, and I promised him before he closed his eyes that I would make a man of you. I've succeeded, certainly: your spirit is strong and your mind is quick, your heart generous, but I also want you to become very strong, and so agile that nothing will seem impossible to you.'

The old man fell silent for a moment, eyes half closed as if searching for other words in his ancient heart. He laid a hand on the boy's shoulder, and slowly went on. 'Talos, answer me honestly. Have you returned to the plain to see the warriors, even though I've forbidden you?' The boy lowered his eyes, twisting a stalk between his fingers. 'Yes, I know,' continued the old man. 'You have returned. I'd imagined as much, and I know why.'

'If that's so,' interrupted the boy with a scowl, 'tell me, grandfather, because I don't.'

'You're fascinated by their force and by their power. Perhaps your heart is not that of a simple shepherd.'

'Are you making fun of me, Kritolaos? What else can we be but servants and the shepherds of other people's flocks?'

'That's not true!' exclaimed the old man suddenly, and for a moment his eyes blazed with a fierce and noble light. A hand like the claw of an old lion gripped the boy's wrist.

Talos was amazed and perplexed. The old man slowly pulled away his hand, and lowered his eyes and his head – the gestures of one who has been forced to learn obedience. 'No, it's not true,' he resumed in a more subdued tone. 'Our people have not always been servants. There was a time when we dominated the mountains and the valleys as far as the western sea. We ruled the plains as far as Cape Taenarum, raising herds of fiery horses. Nestor and Antilochus, the lords of Pylos and Ithome, fought alongside Agamemnon under the walls of Troy. When the Dorians invaded these lands, our people fought with great valour before submitting. The blood of warriors flows through our veins: King Aristomenes and King Aristodemus—'

'They're dead!' burst out the boy. 'Dead! And all those warriors that you're talking about with them.' His face was distorted with anger, the veins on his neck bulged. 'We are slaves, servants, and always will be. Understand, old man? Servants!'

Kritolaos stared at him, saddened and surprised. 'Servants,' repeated Talos, confused, lowering the tone of his voice.

Talos took the hand of the old man, who was silent and bewildered by the boy's rage. 'How many years ago,' continued Talos in a softer voice, 'tell me, how many years ago did the things you're talking about happen? The glory of your kings is forgotten. I know what you're thinking, I know my words are a surprise to you because I've always listened to your stories. They're beautiful stories. But I'm not a little boy any more, and your dreams make my heart ache.' A long silence fell between them, broken only by the bleating of the flock in the pen nearby.

Suddenly the old man stood up, straining his ears intently.

'What is it?' asked Talos.

'Do you hear them? Wolves! They howled like this the night that you— were born. But it's not the mating season yet. Isn't that strange?'

'Oh, let them howl and let's go inside. It's raining, and nearly dark.'

'No. Did you know, Talos, that the gods sometimes send signs to men? It's time you knew. Take my cloak and a torch and follow me.'

They started off towards the forest that loomed at the edge of the clearing. The old man chose a tortuous path amidst the trees, followed by the mute, pensive boy. After nearly an hour of this silent march, they reached the foot of a protruding cliff covered by a thick mantle of moss. At the base of the cliff was a pile of rocks which seemed to have tumbled down from the mountain.

'Move those stones,' ordered Kritolaos. 'I don't have the strength to do it myself.'

Talos obeyed, curious and impatient to uncover the old man's mystery. The rain had stopped and the wind had died down. The forest was immersed in silence. Talos worked energetically, but his task was not easy. The rain-soaked stones, covered with greenish, slimy moss, slipped through his hands, but the boy continued resolutely. By the light of the torch that the old man held, Talos caught sight of an opening underneath. He moved the last of the rocks away – they had been covering an underground passage! Peering into the darkness, the boy could make out irregular stairs covered with grey mould.

'Let's go in,' said Kritolaos, nodding towards the entrance of the tunnel. 'Help me,' he added, 'I don't want to break my leg.'

Talos started down first and reached up to help the old man, who leaned on the boy so as not to lose his footing. The two of them continued down the rough steps carved in the rock, and came to the opening of a small cave. The dripping ceiling was barely high enough for a man to stand up straight. The cave seemed empty at first, until Kritolaos, moving his torch, lit up one of the corners and revealed a great wooden chest reinforced with bronze plates. The old man lifted the latch and chipped away at the pitch sealing the lid with the point of his knife.

'Open it,' he ordered Talos, who had been watching him astonished.

'What's in the chest?' asked the boy. 'Some kind of treasure you've kept hidden?'

'No, Talos, there are no riches here. Some things are far more precious than gold and silver. Open it, you'll see.'

The old man handed him the knife. The chest's lid was well sealed, but Talos succeeded in forcing it. He shot Kritolaos a questioning look. The old man nodded; Talos struggled to remove the lid and leaned it back against the cavern wall. He shone the torch inside the chest.

What Talos saw left him speechless: a splendid helmet of bronze crowned with wolf fangs set into the metal, a heavy bronze cuirass decorated with tin and silver, an amber-hilted sword enclosed in its sheath, embossed thigh-guards and greaves, and a great shield with the head of a wolf, all looking as though they'd just been forged.

'It's incredible,' gasped Talos, not yet daring to reach out and touch. 'But this is impossible! This chest has been closed up for who knows how long, but look at this armour: it's perfect!'

'Look closer, touch it,' ordered the old man.

The boy stretched out his hand to touch the resplendent weapons. 'Grease!' he murmured. 'Covered with grease. Did you do it, grandfather?'

'Yes, I, and others before me, for a very long while. That sack, too, was soaked in grease before being closed. Open it,' Kritolaos said, pointing to a dark bundle that the boy, blinded by the armour, had not noticed. Talos worked excitedly to open the rigid, wrinkled sack, and drew out a huge bow, completely covered with a layer of ram's fat.

'Excellent!' exclaimed Kritolaos. 'It's still in fine shape. It could strike again if guided by an expert hand.' His eyes glittered. 'By an expert hand,' he repeated, turning to the boy with a sudden flash of tremendous determination in his eyes. 'Your hand, Talos!'

The old man's lean and bony arm, mapped with blue veins, extended the immense bow towards the boy. Talos gazed at it as if hypnotized, not daring to touch it. 'Take it, boy, it's yours,' Kritolaos urged.

Talos took the amazing weapon into his hands. It was made of an animal's horns, smooth and polished. The handgrip was wrapped in a thin sheath of silver embossed with a wolf's head. The deep indentation on the right showed how many arrows had been shot from that weapon, with great force. Talos was pervaded by wild emotion, a thousand thoughts wheeling through his head. A strange essence seemed to emanate from that old bow and flow into his body, making him shake like a reed.

'Whose bow is this, Kritolaos? Whose are these weapons? I've never seen anything like them. Not even the warriors down on the plain had anything like this. This bow isn't made of wood.'

'You're right, Talos. It's made of horn.'

'But animals with horns this long don't exist!'

'You're right, they don't. At least not in our country. The animal who provided these horns ran ten or more generations ago on the distant plains of Asia. The bow was given to us as a gift by a lord of that land.'

'But who . . . who did it belong to?'

The old man had a solemn, almost noble, expression. 'This is the bow of King Aristodemus, lord of Pylos and Ithome, sovereign of the Messenians, heir of Nestor, shepherd of peoples.' He lowered his white head for a moment, then gazed again at the boy, who stood before him with widened eyes and parted lips: 'Talos, my boy, I've waited so long for this moment—'

'What moment, Kritolaos, what do you mean? I don't understand. It's as if my mind were full of smoke.'

'The moment in which to pass on the King's bow. I am the last custodian of these weapons, preserved so jealously for generations. These are the symbols of the pride of our people, the last remembrances of our freedom. The time has come for me to entrust you with this terrible and precious secret. I am old, and my days could soon come to an end.'

The boy gripped the horn bow, and stared with bright eyes at the armour. Suddenly he raised his eyes to meet Kritolaos' gaze. 'But what am I to do? I don't know anything about our people. Weapons are made for fighting, aren't they? Aren't they, Kritolaos? I'm a cripple and I'm just a boy. Close up that chest again. I can't, I don't know how. You shouldn't have shown me those weapons, it's useless. No one will ever use them again.'

The old man rested his hand on the boy's shoulder. 'Calm down, Talos, calm down. There are still so many things that you don't know and that you must learn. It will take time, but one day someone will wear that suit of armour. When he does, King Aristodemus will return to his people again and restore their lost freedom. The gods already know his name. Now, take that bow. I'll teach you to use it to defend yourself, and to live with this secret even after I'm gone. The bow will be your faithful companion. It will save you from wolves and bears. And from men, Talos. From men as well.'

'Why would I be in any danger from men? I've never hurt anyone. Who cares about the life of a crippled shepherd?' Talos asked morosely.

'There are things I can't tell you yet, boy. Be patient, one day you'll know. Now close that chest, it's time to go.'

Talos set down the bow. Lowering the lid of the chest, he glanced once again at the weapons glowing with a sinister light under the flickering torch light. He suddenly reached out his right hand to the sword's hilt.

'No, Talos, stop!' cried out the old man, startling the boy. 'Don't touch that weapon!'

'You scared me! Why shouldn't I touch it? It's only a sword, even if it did belong to a king.'

'To a great king, Talos. But that doesn't matter,' grumbled Kritolaos, as he hurried to shut the chest himself. 'That weapon is cursed!'

'Oh, you and your silly superstitions!'

'Don't joke about this, Talos,' responded the old man, gravely. 'You don't know. With that very sword King Aristodemus sacrificed his own daughter to the gods of the Underworld, to win victory over his enemies and freedom for his people. A futile act. No one has ever since dared to grip that sword. You must not touch it!'

The chastened boy took the torch from the old man in silence and traced it along the borders of the chest, melting the pitch to seal it once again. They left the cavern, and Talos replaced the rocks at the entrance, camouflaging them with moss so that they seemed undisturbed. He ran to catch up to Kritolaos, who had already started down the path. The old man's torch was reduced to a flaming stub.

They walked in silence until they reached the edge of the clearing. The pale light of the setting moon revealed their cottage. Krios' yelping greeted them.

Kritolaos tossed away the butt of the torch and paused, turning to Talos. 'Some day a man will come to take up that sword, Talos. It is written that he will be strong and innocent, moved by such a strong love for his people that he will sacrifice the voice of his own blood.'

'Where are these words written? Who said them? How do you know?' asked Talos, searching for the old man's eyes, hidden in the shadows. 'Who are you, really?'

'One day you will come to know all of this. And that will be the last day of Kritolaos. Let us go now, the night is almost over and our work awaits us tomorrow.' He strode towards the cottage. Talos followed him, tightly holding the great horn bow, the bow of Aristodemus, King.

*

Talos lay on his straw pallet, wide awake in the dark; a thousand thoughts tumbled through his mind. His heart pounded like it had that day down there on the plain, when that mysterious warrior had spoken to him. He sat up and stretched a hand towards the wall, reaching for the bow that Kritolaos had given him. He gripped it tight with two hands: it was polished and cold as death.

Talos closed his eyes and listened to the furious beating of his heart, the hammering of his burning temples. He lay down again. His eyes, still closed, saw a city, fortified with powerful ramparts, crowned with towers, built with gigantic boulders of grey stone on top of a desolate mountain. A city shrouded in a cloud of dust.

Suddenly a violent wind came up, clearing away the thick fog from the parched fields. Warriors appeared, the same he had seen on the plain. There were thousands of them, encased in gleaming armour, their faces hidden by helmets. They advanced from all directions, encircling the seemingly deserted city. Springing out from behind rocks, bushes, holes in the ground like phantoms, they were urged onward by the obsessive drumming that came from nowhere. As they advanced, their ranks became tighter, more compact. They fell into a march. Their shields, close one against the other, became a wall of bronze. Like an enormous, monstrous pair of claws, they prepared to close their grip on the deserted city.

As the extraordinary circle closed, Talos felt his throat tightening so that he could not breathe. As much as he tried, he could not open his eyes or release his hold on the horn bow that burned into his numb fingers.

Suddenly a frightening, fierce cry exploded like thunder from within the city. The walls were alive with a multitude of warriors, different from the others. They wore strange armour and carried immense shields of oxhide. Their helmets, also of leather, did not cover their faces. Talos saw the faces of men, of young boys, of old men with white beards. From below, hundreds of ladders were being placed against the walls, thousands of the enemy soldiers were climbing up from all directions, their weapons in their hands. In silence they scaled the city's walls.

The crowd on the bastions suddenly parted and a gigantic warrior appeared on the highest tower. His burnished bronze armour completely covered his body. From his side hung an amber-hilted sword. Talos felt his eyes dim and his heart slow to match the beating of the drum. He looked again towards the scene that seemed to be fading. The warrior held the lifeless body of a young woman, draped in black. A black drape, a rose of blood on her breast, a cloud of blonde hair, beautiful . . . how he wanted to touch that hair, caress those delicate, pale lips . . . Talos, the cripple.

The drum sounded again, louder, always louder. The bronze warriors poured over the walls like a flooding river overflowing its banks. Their swords tore through the great shields of oxhide, pierced the leather cuirasses. They advanced, endlessly, hundreds of them, towards the man still standing on the highest tower. The great warrior lay down the girl's fragile body and lunged into their midst, whirling his amber-hilted sword. Attacked from every direction, he disappeared and re-emerged like a bull among a pack of wolves.

Silence. Smoking ruins, demolished houses. Dead, all dead. A blanket of dust carried by a warm, suffocating wind covered the martyred bodies, the dismantled walls, the falling towers. A solitary, motionless figure sat on a smoke-blackened mass. An old man, bent over, with his face hidden in his hands, hands full of tears. The white head lifted . . . a face devastated by pain . . . the face of Kritolaos!

★

Kritolaos' face, illuminated by a ray of sunlight, was above him. The old man was saying something, but Talos couldn't hear him at all, as if his mind and his senses were still prisoners of another world. Suddenly, the boy found himself sitting up on his straw pallet as Kritolaos said, 'It's time to get up, Talos. The sun has risen, we must bring the flock to pasture. What's wrong with you, boy? Didn't you sleep well? Come on, the fresh air will do you good and the cold spring water will wake you up. Your mother's already poured milk into your bowl. Get dressed and come to eat,' he added, leaving.

Talos shook himself. Still dazed, he held his head between his hands and looked slowly around him for the bow: nothing! The bow had disappeared! He searched under the pallet, among the sheepskins that lay piled up in a corner of the room. Could it all have been a dream? he thought. No, impossible ... but what, then? Dumbfounded, he moved aside the hanging mat that separated his sleeping place from the rest of the house and went to sit before the bowl of milk that his mother had poured.

'Where's my grandfather, mother? I don't see him.'

'He's gone out already,' answered the woman. 'He said he'd wait for you with the sheep at the high spring.'

Talos quickly downed his milk, put a piece of bread in his pack, took his staff, and hurried to the place his mother had indicated. The high spring flowed from the mountain not far away from Talos' cottage. The shepherds of Mount Taygetus used this name to distinguish it from another that spouted at the large clearing at the edge of the forest, where they usually brought the animals to drink in the evening before closing them in their pens. Talos crossed the clearing quickly and entered the forest. He started along the high path and soon saw Kritolaos in the distance, driving the flock along with the able help of little Krios.

'Grandfather, listen, I—'

'I know, you didn't find the bow.' The old man smiled and opened his cape. 'Here it is, boy. In good hands, as you can see.'

'By Zeus, grandfather! I could have died when I didn't find it this morning. Why did you take it with you? And why didn't you wait for me like the other mornings?'

'I didn't want you asking questions in front of your mother.'

'So, she's not to know about any of this?'

32

'No, your mother knew well where I took you last night and what you saw, but she mustn't know anything else. A woman's heart can be easily troubled. Now follow me,' he said, starting up along the path again, covering the bow with his cape. They walked along together until the boy broke the silence.

'Why did you take that bow, grandfather? Why do you keep it hidden?'

'The first question is reasonable. The second is only silly, Talos.'

'All right, the Helots are forbidden to carry weapons. This is a weapon.'

'Let's say, a very unusual weapon.'

'Right, but will you at least answer the first question I asked you?'

'Yes, son, you have a right to the answer,' said Kritolaos, stopping in the middle of the path. Krios had already understood where they were headed, and stubbornly continued to drive the sheep in the direction of the small grassy clearing near the high spring. 'I want you to learn to handle this weapon with the same skill as the great Ulysses.'

'But how could that ever be, grandfather? You are so old and I—'

'You must only believe in yourself,' reprimanded Kritolaos. 'As for me, don't think I've become this old doing nothing.'

They had reached the small grassy clearing where the flock was already grazing under Krios' vigilant eye. Kritolaos looked around; his gaze searched the peaks of the surrounding hills to assure himself that they were completely alone. He threw his cape to the ground and held out the bow to Talos.

'So I'm too old, is that it?' he asked with a smile. 'Listen well, greenhorn,' he continued, winking, 'who taught the great Achilles to use his weapons?'

'Old Khiron, the centaur, if I'm not mistaken.'

'That's exactly right; and who taught the great Ulysses to use his bow?'

'The father of his father in the forests of Epeiros.'

'Good!' laughed the old man, satisfied. 'I thought that as your beard was sprouting, your mind was going soft. As you can see, it's the old man's experience that allows an ignorant and presumptuous young one to become a man worthy of his name.'

Talos rubbed his chin; it seemed too much to call those sparse little hairs a beard. He gripped the bow firmly in both hands with a suddenly serious expression.

'Not like that, by Hercules! That's not the stick you use to push the goats into their pen. Pay attention: look here, this part covered with silver is the handgrip, which must be grasped firmly in your left hand.' The boy nodded, imitating what he was taught.

'Very good,' continued the old man. 'With your right hand you must pull taut the cord that will shoot the arrow forward.'

'But there is no cord here,' protested the puzzled boy.

'Of course not! If there were, this weapon wouldn't be worth anything. The bowstring is attached only at the moment when you want to use the bow, and then must be taken off again. If this weren't done, the bow would become curved and lose all of its flexibility, and thus its power. Don't worry, here's the bowstring,' he said, rummaging in his pack. 'It's made of corded gut. I've been preparing it myself for many weeks without your knowing.

'Now we shall attach it to the bow. Watch carefully: you prop one end of the bow on the ground behind your left leg, being sure to keep it in a vertical position with your left hand. Like this, you hook the cord to the ring at the bottom, and then attach the other end to the hook that's jutting out on the top part of the bow.'

'But it won't reach!'

'Of course it doesn't reach. If it did, the bow wouldn't have any force. It would be too flexible, and your arm wouldn't be long enough to string it. To be able to hook the cord, you have to curve the bow with all your strength, leaning your whole body onto the upper horn that you're grasping with your left hand. At the same time, with your right you must extend the end of the cord until you can slip it over the final ring, into the right hook. Simple, no?'

'It's easy for you to say, grandfather,' replied the boy, panting as he tried to carry out Kritolaos' instructions. 'This thing is hard! It just won't bend, and then . . .' continued Talos, unhappily abandoning his efforts, 'and then, you mean to tell me it takes all this work just to fix the cord? Damn it, grandfather, if I really had to defend myself against an enemy, as you say, he could easily cut me to pieces while I'm standing here like an idiot with this thing that won't bend. I don't think you should have counted on me, old man. Maybe you're like Khiron or the father of Laertes but I'm not the great Achilles, or brave Ulysses. I'm Talos, the cripple.'

'When you're finished feeling sorry for yourself,' burst out Kritolaos, irritated, 'and when you've stopped whimpering like a little girl, I'll tell you some more things you should know. To begin with, here's one: stop thinking that everything can be learned easily and immediately. All difficult things require willpower, and learning to use this bow is certainly not an easy task. It's not muscles that are lacking, it's your faith in yourself. Now let's stop this small talk, take the bow and do as I've told you!'

The tone of his voice was so commanding that Talos didn't consider even the smallest objection. He swallowed the knot that he felt rising in his throat, and grasped the upper horn of the bow with his left hand, pulling the cord with his right. He clenched his teeth, drawing on all his force. Painfully straining his muscles, he began to pull with a constant, continuous effort.

'Yes, boy, like that, grip tight!' Kritolaos instantly heard his own words echoing in his mind. He saw a small hand reaching up to squeeze his index finger from a rough cradle, the distant light of a sunset that entered through a crack in the door, the long shadows. The image suddenly faded as he saw Talos' face dripping with sweat, the expression of triumph in his reddened eyes. He had conquered the great horn bow! Talos grasped the bowstave in his left hand, and his right touched the string that vibrated with a low hum.

'Is this what you meant, grandfather?' Talos asked smiling. Kritolaos' look was full of emotion and amazement. 'You've strung the bow of Aristodemus,' he said with a tremor in his voice. The boy looked at the gleaming weapon, then lifted his eyes serenely to his grandfather's, filled with tears.

'The bow of Kritolaos,' he murmured.

*

Many months had passed since the day Kritolaos had begun to teach Talos to use the bow. Every day, the old man had demanded increasingly intense training from the boy. The incredible perseverance of the old master overcame even Talos' occasional discouragement. By the end of autumn, when the first cold winds blew up from the mountains, the boy had become quite agile. His arms, stretched by constant exercise, had become brawny and muscular. His physique was well developed; although he was just a little over sixteen, he seemed much more a man than a boy.

Kritolaos, on the contrary, was in quick decline. It seemed that the energy that was blossoming in the boy's limbs must have been draining from Kritolaos' tired bones. The effort of continuous concentration had rapidly exhausted the old man's spirit. As the days passed he became increasingly fretful, hurried by his fear of not finishing the task he had begun. This very fear seemed to feed the endless attention needed to direct and guide the boy, protected from prying eyes in some hidden valley or solitary clearing.

Talos' exercises were progressively more difficult; Kritolaos had taught him to make arrows, to balance them perfectly, and to shoot with great precision and power. The bow itself, rigid at first because it had not been handled for so long, had repeatedly been on the verge of breaking. Talos had greased it thousand of times and warmed it by the fire, so that it gradually became more elastic.

The moment of his final test approached; the test that for Talos represented a kind of initiation, his passage into manhood. He was excited and enthusiastic about his constantly growing prowess, but at night, stretched out on his straw pallet, he often remained awake thinking. It was hard to understand what the old man was aiming for with this continuous and even brutal drilling. He had taught Talos to use his staff as well as the bow. And Talos had learned to bend the cornel crook to his will, while exploiting its formidable power. Certainly, defending the flock from thieves and from wild animals was a valid reason for wielding such weapons; but that couldn't explain everything. Talos continued to puzzle over this problem without coming to an answer. Also, he was very worried about Kritolaos' rapid decline. The old man was stooped over, his legs had become very unsteady. Sometimes the light in his tired gaze seemed to be going out.

3

THE CHAMPION

THE DAY THAT KRITOLAOS had chosen for the final test arrived: clear but very windy.

The old man and the boy woke up very early and quickly reached the high spring. Talos threw off his cloak and washed himself in the chill spring water. At Kritolaos' signal, gripping the bow, he put the sheepskin quiver over his shoulder and walked forward about thirty paces. The old man stood near a young cornel tree, straight and slender. He took its topmost branch and curved it downward so that its tip nearly touched the ground. He turned to Talos.

'Careful!' he shouted. 'When I let go of the branch, I'll count to three, and you let fly. All right?'

'Yes,' replied Talos, reaching for the quiver. Kritolaos had made the test as difficult as possible: the boy had to hit a small, rapidly moving target, calculating the speed and direction of the wind. Talos looked up at the leaves of the trees and again at the target, which seemed incredibly small: a twig at this distance! He chose a long, rather heavy arrow, and slowly put himself into position to shoot.

'Here we go!' shouted Kritolaos, releasing the slender branch and moving quickly aside. The tree whistled like a whip, swaying rapidly. Talos held his breath. He followed the target's movement for a second, gripping the bow lightly with his left hand. He shot; the heavy arrow, perfectly balanced, flew through the air with a muffled roar. It tore through the tree's bark and ended up in a nearby field.

'I failed, damn it!' raged Talos, running towards the still-moving target.

'By Hercules, my boy, you hit it! You got it, I tell you!' The old man marvelled, still watching the tree. 'Great Zeus, from thirty paces, in movement, and with this wind.' He turned towards the breathless boy. 'You got it, understand? What did you expect, to nail it straight through the middle? Talos, do you know what this means? In a few months . . . you've done this just in a few months!'

The old shepherd shook with emotion, his knees trembled. It was evident that he had anxiously awaited this moment.

'Wait, help me to sit down, my boy. My knees won't hold me up. Come here, sit next to me. There, good. And now listen to me, boy: you will become a great archer, as great as Ajax Oileus, like Ulysses—'

Talos laughed heartily. 'Don't get ahead of yourself, grandfather! Don't you think that toothless mouth of yours is opened too wide? It was just luck!'

'Impertinent little bastard!' exclaimed Kritolaos, his eyes rolling upwards. 'I'll break this staff on your rump. You'll learn to respect your elders!'

Talos tumbled sideways to escape the stick that the old man jokingly threatened him with, then jumped to his feet and ran towards the forest. He called to his dog, 'Here, Krios. Run! Come on, old thing, catch me!'

The animal flung himself after its young master, wagging its tail and barking. It was a game they had played many times. He hadn't yet caught up to the boy when Talos stopped suddenly, paralysed: behind a leafy beech tree stump stood a man, unmoving, wrapped in a heavy cloak of dark wool, his face half covered by a hood. He paused a moment, staring at the boy. Then he snatched up a bundle of twigs and hurried away along the path. Meanwhile Kritolaos, panting, had reached the boy. Obviously disturbed, he gripped Talos' arm.

'What's the matter, grandfather, haven't you ever seen a wayfarer?'

Kritolaos continued to stare in consternation at the hooded figure rapidly moving away. The old man put the bow to Talos. 'Kill him,' he commanded.

'Have you've lost your mind, grandfather? Why should I kill him? I don't even know who he is, he hasn't hurt me or anything.'

'He saw you using the bow. He's not one of us, he's a Spartan. You must kill him. Now, while there's still time.' The old man's voice betrayed his fear.

'No, I can't,' Talos replied calmly. 'If he attacked me, maybe I could shoot him, but not like this; he's unarmed, and has his back turned to me.'

Kritolaos didn't speak another word that whole day, despite Talos' efforts to cheer him up. He seemed terribly discouraged, as if all of his hopes, his very reason for living, had been rubbed out in a single moment. The following days were full of anxiety for the old man: he kept a close watch even at pasture, and hardly dared to let his young charge practise with the bow. When he did allow it, he sought out distant, out-of-the-way places: he acted as though they were being watched, spied upon; every noise startled him, made his eyes brim with tears. Talos became very worried.

Days passed, months. Springtime was almost over, and nothing untoward had happened. Kritolaos seemed reassured, but his health was quickly declining. Some days he didn't even go out to pasture. He sat on his stool for long hours; men from nearby farms going to work or to pasture with their sheep stopped to talk to him. They all seemed strangely troubled, as if they knew that Kritolaos' end was at hand. In the evenings, Talos returned alone with the flock and little Krios. After finishing his tasks, he would sit at his grandfather's feet and talk with him for hours. Talos reported his progress with the bow, which he still carried with him. Sometimes he was gone for several days at a time, when the pasture was far away, and slept in a crude hut made of branches, twigs and leaves.

One day, as springtime was ending, Talos was on the slopes of Mount Taygetus, not too far from his home. Kritolaos hadn't felt well the night before, and Talos didn't want to be too far off. His mother could easily reach him if she needed to, or send someone after him.

It was almost noon, and hot. Talos sat under a tree, looking towards the plain where the silver olive trees glimmered. Behind him was a long stretch of road that came from the north and appeared deserted. Talos had heard from friends of his who were servants in the city that important things were about to happen. The sailors of Gytheum, who brought the fish to market, had seen an immense fleet coming from the east during the night: hundreds and hundreds of ships with long bronze rostra ploughing through the waves. A great king had sent them from his empire beyond the sea, to wage war on Athens.

Talos had only very vague ideas of what went on away from his mountain. He had heard Kritolaos speak of the other nations of Greece, but he had never seen anyone except the people of Taygetus and the warriors of the city. Talos wondered why that great king would want to declare war on such a small city as Athens. Why would he come with all those ships, if what the sailors of Gytheum said were true? He thought of how much he'd like to see a ship. He'd heard that there were some so big that all the people of a whole village could fit inside, but that couldn't be true. Anyway, there was something strange going on: squads of warriors were departing almost every day, both along the north road and the sea road. Many of the Helot shepherds and farmers were afraid that a great war was about to break out; if so, they would have to accompany the warriors to serve them and carry their weapons.

As Talos was absorbed in his thoughts, his gaze lost over the plain, it seemed to him that he could see something moving far off, on the road that came from the north. Slightly bigger than a black speck in a cloud of dust. He strained to see: yes, someone was arriving on the road from Argos. Someone running alone under the sun in the direction of Sparta.

Talos stood up, anxious to see better, and began to

make his way down the side of the mountain towards a small spring that flowed near the road. The man seemed to be carrying nothing but a small bundle, tied behind his shoulders: the short chiton that came just to his groin and the dagger hanging from his belt meant that the runner was a warrior.

He was quite close now and Talos could see him very well. When he reached the spring, the man stopped. He was covered with dust and sweat and breathing strangely, blowing air loudly out of his mouth, and swelling up his huge torso rhythmically. With the water he washed his face, his arms, his legs. Then, removing his chiton, he graduually washed the rest of his body gasping at the freezing mountain water.

Talos smiled. 'Cold, isn't it?'

'Ah, yes, boy, it's cold but it's good for me. It strengthens the muscles and awakens the energy in these weary limbs.'

The man, nearly naked, had an extraordinary build: thick arms, a wide chest, long, nervous legs. Talos looked at him closely: he had to be a warrior, but what country did he come from? He had a curious, sing-song way of speaking, and a manner of doing things that inspired confidence. In fact, Talos was amazed at himself for having spoken so spontaneously to a man who was obviously a warrior. The stranger got dressed again.

'Is Sparta far from here?' he asked.

'Not very. If you keep running like you were just now, you'll be there in no time. There, see: the city is behind that curve in the road, you can't miss it. But what are you going to do at Sparta? You're not Spartan. You must come from far away,' he added, 'I've never heard anyone speak like you, not even the Messenian shepherds or the fishermen who come to the market from Gytheum.'

'So, then, you were watching me. Spying on me?'

'Oh, no, I was just up there tending my sheep and I happened to see you running from such a long way. Won't you tell me who you are and where you come from?'

'Of course, boy, I'm Philippides of Athens, winner of the last Olympics. And you?'

'I'm Talos,' replied the boy gazing straight into the stranger's eyes.

'Just Talos?'

'Talos the cripple.'

The stranger was struck silent for a moment. 'What happened to your foot? Did you fall on the mountain?'

'No,' replied the boy calmly. 'My grandfather Kritolaos says that the midwife who pulled me from my mother's womb was too rough. But I'm wasting your time; don't you have to go?'

'Yes, Talos, I should go, but if I don't rest a bit, my heart will burst: I left my city three days ago at dawn.'

Talos looked at him, astonished. 'That's impossible! I know for sure that Athens is beyond the sea. You couldn't have got here on foot!'

'That's just how I got here. Philippides doesn't tell stories, boy. Yesterday before dawn I was at Argos.'

'It's not that I don't believe you, but my grandfather Kritolaos told me that it takes nearly a week to get to Athens from here.'

'Your grandfather Kritolaos must know a lot of things.

Maybe he even knows who Philippides is,' said the athlete, smiling.

'I'm sure he must know your name. He spoke to me about the Olympics once. He told me about the valley where the athletes compete. The river that flows there has its source not far from here, in our mountains. And so,' he continued, 'you've made it here in just three days. Your mission must be a very important one.'

'It is. Not only for me, but for all of the Greeks,' he said, suddenly serious, a shadow passing across his green eyes.

'I think I know what it's all about,' said Talos. 'The fishermen of Gytheum said that the King of the land of the rising sun has sent hundreds of ships full of soldiers to plunder the islands.'

'Not only the islands,' said the athlete darkly. 'They've already landed on the continent. They're as thick as locusts, and they've set up camp on the beach, just a little over two hundred stadia from Athens, at a place called Marathon. All of our warriors are down there, but they'll never suffice to push back that multitude. At night their fires are as numerous as the stars in the sky. The prows of their ships are as tall as towers. They have thousands of horses, servants, carts . . .'

'You've come to ask for help from the Spartans, haven't you? They will never agree to it; my grandfather Kritolaos says that the Spartans are awesome warriors, the best, but they are dull-minded, and can't see past their own noses. Besides, their city doesn't have walls, you know. They'd never be willing to abandon it, or leave it unprotected. That's another stupidity: if they'd only build walls around the city, a few of them would do to protect it, and the warriors could go to meet any danger instead of waiting until it reaches the banks of the Eurotas.'

'You are very wise, Talos, for such a young boy, but I hope you won't mind too much if your grandfather has made a mistake for once: about the stubbornness of the Spartans. They must listen to me. If they allow us to be destroyed, it will be their turn tomorrow and there won't be any Athens to help them.'

'I know. It's too bad that you don't have to convince me. I'd be willing to fight at your side if I could. Your words are so straightforward and persuasive. Are all the Athenians like you?'

The athlete smiled. 'Ah, there are far better men than me.'

'I don't believe it,' said Talos, shaking his head. 'You won the Olympics.'

'That's true, my boy, but in my city it's not only muscles that count. No, the mind is far more important, and our citizens always try to choose the wisest men to govern the city, not the strongest.'

'Do you mean that in your city the people choose who will govern them? Don't you have kings?'

'No, Talos. We did once, a long time ago, but not any longer.'

'How strange your city must be!'

'Yes, maybe, but I think you'd like it there.'

'I don't know. Do you think there is anywhere a slave could be happy?'

The athlete stood up, gazing sadly at the boy. 'I must go, now,' he said, but instead of walking away, he turned to Talos, taking off his leather armlet decorated with copper studs, and handed it to the boy.

'This is for you, Talos. I wore it at the Olympics, but I don't think I'll be needing it any longer. Remember Philippides every now and then.' The athlete tightened the belt that lay across his hips and set off running towards Sparta. Talos stood speechless for a moment, and then took off after the athlete, already so far away.

'Champion! Champion!' Philippides stopped a moment and turned around. 'Good luck!'

The athlete raised his right arm in a wide salute, and began running. He swiftly disappeared into the blinding rays of the sun.

*

The Athenian sat wrapped in his white pallium before the noble Aristarkhos, who was attentively listening to his words.

'I thank you for your hospitality, Aristarkhos. The nobility and valour of the Kleomenids are well known even in Athens and it is a great honour for me to sit at your table.'

'The honour is mine, Philippides. My house is proud to receive the champion of Olympia. You triumphed over the best of our youth and the Spartans respect such a worthy adversary. I regret that my table is so sparse; I have no refined dishes to offer you. I know that you Athenians often joke about our cooking, especially our black broth. As you can see, I have spared you its acquaintance.'

'I'm sorry about that, Aristarkhos, I'd have been quite curious to taste it.'

'I'm afraid it wouldn't have been a very pleasant experience for you. I still remember the face of Aristagoras of Miletus when he tasted it at a dinner our government hosted in honour of his mission to Sparta eight years ago. A mission that, as you well know, met with very little success. He asked our kings to send five thousand of our warriors to support his revolt against the Great King of the Persians. Five thousand warriors meant the bulk of our military forces: to send them across the sea was a risk that we couldn't take.'

'Indeed, you refused him any aid, contrary to what we in Athens decided to do. We're still paying for that gesture. But at that time the assembly felt that all possible aid should be sent to the Hellenic cities that had rebelled against the Great King.'

'Should I conclude that you judge our government's refusal of Aristagoras' request negatively?'

'Not exactly, Aristarkhos,' said the Athenian, realizing that he had pushed his sensitive host too far. 'I appreciate that it wasn't easy for you Spartans to make such a far-reaching decision.'

'That isn't the point, Philippides. At first, that man seemed to be moved by noble ideals: he decried the conditions of the Greek cities in Asia under the Persian yoke. It seemed that his only desire was to liberate them. In his speech in front of the assembly of the equals, he spoke with such vehemence that our warriors were fascinated. You know that we Spartans are not used to such eloquence: we are simple people of few words, but we are not fools. The ephors who govern our city along with our kings were well aware of Aristagoras' attempt to subjugate the island of Naxos, which was populated by Greeks, using Persian troops. It was a bid on his part to gain favour in the eyes of the Great King Darius, who was then in Thrace fighting the Scythians across the Ister river.

'The inhabitants of Naxos repelled the attack and the Persian officers laid responsibility for the failure on Aristagoras. Terrified as he must have been at the thought of having to face the ire of the Great King, he took advantage of an incident between Persian and Greek officers, and proclaimed a revolt. He was supported, naturally, by the Asian Greeks. This certainly demonstrated that they desired to be liberated from the Persians, but Aristagoras was only acting in his own personal interest. If he cared so much about the freedom of the Greeks, why did he try to subjugate the island of Naxos? We have good reason to believe that he set off the revolt against the Persians solely in order to shield himself from the anger of King Darius when he returned from his expedition against the Scythians.

'You must admit . . .' he continued, pouring wine into his guest's cup, 'you must admit that it's not easy to trust a man who's caught in such a difficult situation, and yet insists that he is animated only by his passion for freedom. But I'm telling you things that you know better than I do.'

'Certainly, I'm acquainted with the situation,' answered Philippides, 'but, please, continue. I'm interested in knowing your thoughts on the matter.'

'Well,' Aristarkhos went on, 'the equals present in the

assembly may have been convinced by his pleas, but the fact is that the final decision rested with the ephors and the kings, and Aristagoras had made quite a bad impression on them, apart from what they already knew about the man. I remember an episode that will make you smile: one day by chance I found myself at King Cleomenes' house, where Aristagoras was a guest. He had just got out of bed, and must have been cold, you see, because in the house of the king they wait until sunset to light the hearth. Well, there he was, sitting with his hands under his mantle, as one of the servants was lacing up his boots. The king's little daughter, who was only six years old at the time, pointed her finger at Aristagoras and exclaimed: 'Look, daddy, our foreign guest has no hands!' I swear to you that I myself had to turn aside and cover my mouth so as not to burst out in laughter. In short, the man who presented himself as the leader of a revolt couldn't even lace his own shoes without help!'

'So we Athenians were too credulous regarding Aristagoras,' said Philippides with a bitter smile.

'Oh no, my friend, that was certainly not the meaning behind my words! I do not wish to criticize the action taken by Athens, which was undoubtedly quite generous. The decision to send ships and troops was certainly not solely a response to Aristagoras' request. After all, racial ties unite you to the Ionians who settled in Asia, and it is understandable that you would want to help them.

'Our refusal at that time depended largely on our natural diffidence: it seemed to us that Aristagoras wanted to involve us in a futile venture that only his own ambition was responsible for,' concluded Aristarkhos.

'I can understand what you mean to say, but the substance of the matter is that the Persians are now in Greece, endangering the liberty of all Greeks,' his Athenian guest replied.

The Spartan was pensive, pulling at his beard with his left hand. 'I realize full well', he said, 'how useless it is to recriminate past events now. We Spartans could say that if Athens had not interfered in Asia, we would not have the Persians in Greece now. You Athenians could claim that if Sparta had intervened in Ionia, the expedition would have met with victory.'

'I see your point, Aristarkhos, but the situation at the present is desperate: Sparta must absolutely intervene at our side. United we can win, divided we can't but lose. Today, danger is impending over Athens and the cities of Attica, but tomorrow it will be the turn of Corinth, then Argos, and even Sparta itself. The King of the Persians has hundreds of ships ready to set thousands of warriors ashore at any point in Hellas.'

'Yes, the argument you made today in the assembly; undoubtedly a convincing speech.'

'Do you think so?'

'Certainly. If I know my people, I'm sure that your words had the right effect. Your government made an excellent choice in sending not a politician or an orator to Sparta, but the champion of the Olympics. The Spartans are more inclined to believe in personal valour than in elegant rhetoric.'

'So you think that tomorrow I'll be able to bring the promise of your immediate military intervention to Athens?'

'You will probably obtain a pact of alliance. As far as any immediate intervention . . .'

'Well then?' asked Philippides anxiously.

'I'm afraid you'll have to wait until the full moon, when the festival of the goddess Artemis will take place. The assembly of warriors will meet then to approve the decisions of the ephors. This is the law.'

'That's absurd!' exclaimed the Athenian. Quickly, noting his host's expression darken, he added, 'You must excuse me, but asking me to wait for the full moon is the same as giving a refusal. The Persians can attack at any moment.'

Aristarkhos rubbed his forehead. 'You could close yourselves up inside the walls and hold out until we arrive.'

'And abandon the countryside to be pillaged and destroyed? Dozens of villages have no fortifications, and even if they had, there would be no hope of resisting. Don't you know what happened in Eretria? The whole island of Euboea was put to fire and sword and in the end the city itself was forced to capitulate. The entire population was enslaved. No, Aristarkhos, there will be no second chance here. We must stop them on the shore, but we can't do it alone. I just don't see how we can do it alone,' Philippides repeated, disheartened. He fell into silence, his head in his hands.

'I understand all this,' answered the Spartan, rising to his feet and pacing nervously back and forth across the room. 'But, on the other hand, these are our laws.'

'Then there is no hope.'

'Listen, Philippides, tomorrow I will speak in favour of your request to send our army immediately. I can do no more than this. But at the worst, it's only a question of gaining time. The full moon is not so far off; in a little more than a week we could be side by side at Marathon. Believe me when I say that this is sincerely what my heart wishes.'

'I do believe you,' said the champion, warmly gripping the Spartan warrior's hand, 'and this is a great comfort to me. I hope that your words will be heeded; I am sure that together we can defeat the enemy, and then it will be my honour to return your generous hospitality. Now I must ask you to excuse me, I'm very tired and would retire. I pray that the night brings counsel to you, Aristarkhos, and to your fellow citizens, in whose hands rests the destiny not only of your own country, but that of all Hellas.'

'May the gods' wisdom be with us,' said Aristarkhos, rising to accompany his guest to his room.

*

'Brithos! Brithos! Hurry, our men are on their way back! You can see the vanguard from the road to Argos.'

'I'm coming, Aghias, wait up!'

The two boys ran along the road that crossed the centre of the city in the direction of the northern port. They got past a crowd of women, old men and children thronging on the main road, and managed to find a good vantage point. Having been informed by a messenger, the ephors were already at the gate awaiting the army's arrival.

'Look, Aghias,' said Brithos to his companion, 'there's the head of the column, and there's the king!'

King Cleomenes advanced on a black thoroughbred,

surrounded by his escort. The king's rather curved shoulders and greying hair revealed the weight of his years.

'It's strange,' said Brithos to his friend, 'I don't see my father; as a relative to the king, he should be at his side.'

'No reason to worry,' Aghias reassured him, 'there was no battle, so there couldn't have been any fallen; that's what the messenger told the ephors. They said that our warriors arrived after the Athenians had already won the battle. The field of Marathon was still covered with Persian bodies. We'll soon know more. Look, the king is meeting the ephors. The herald will be making a public announcement in the square this afternoon.'

The boys drew closer to the column of warriors entering the city, who broke ranks as they met family and relations waiting for them.

'There's my brother Adeimantos,' said Aghias, pointing to a hoplite of the rear guard. 'Let's go hear what's happened. Surely he'll be able to tell us about your father. 'Look,' he added, 'your mother's arrived too, with your nurse. They must be worried.'

Abandoning their observation point, the two boys ran together towards Adeimantos, who at that moment was stepping away from the ranks and removing his heavy helmet. Aghias nearly tore it from his hands.

'Give us your weapons to carry, Adeimantos, you must be tired.'

'Yes, we'll carry them home for you,' echoed Brithos, slipping the shield from his left arm.

The group moved towards the western section of the city, where Adeimantos' house was. The warriors had been allowed to return to their own family homes instead of to their respective barracks, as was usually the case.

'Where's my father?' Brithos asked immediately. 'Why didn't he come back with you? The women of my house are troubled.'

'Don't worry,' answered Adeimantos, 'your mother will be notified immediately by one of the horsemen of the king's guard. Your father decided to stay to participate in the funeral of a fallen Athenian warrior.'

Meanwhile, they had arrived home. The returning warrior was greeted joyfully by his family. He loosened his armour and sat down, waiting for one of the women to prepare his bath.

'Do you know who it was?' asked Brithos curiously.

Adeimantos frowned. 'Remember that Athenian champion who came to Sparta to ask for our aid?'

'Of course,' replied Brithos, 'he was our guest when he stayed in the city.'

'The champion of Olympia?' asked Aghias.

'Yes, exactly,' answered his brother. 'When the battle was over, the defeated Persians returned to their fleet to attempt a surprise attack against Phaleros, the port of Athens, which they thought was unguarded. But Philippides, the champion, had been sent by the Athenian commander to announce victory and to warn the city's defending forces. He covered the two hundred and fifty stadia from Marathon to Athens without ever stopping, after having fought the entire morning on the front line. It cost him his life. He arrived in time to bring his message, then he collapsed to the ground, dead from exhaustion.'

The two boys were silent, fascinated and struck by his words.

'He was a great and generous man; his was a warrior's and a champion's death. The Greeks will remember him!'

Brithos nodded thoughtfully and rose to his feet. 'I must be going home,' he said. 'My mother's alone and she'll be waiting for me. See you tomorrow at the training field,' he added, turning to his friend. Leaving the house of Adeimantos, Brithos walked quickly down the road towards the northern gate from which he had entered. At the gate, he turned right towards Mount Taygetus, in the direction of his own house, which was nearly at the foot of the mountain.

At the side of the road, he noticed a small crowd of old men, women and children. They were the families of the Helots who had followed the Spartan army as servants and baggage carriers. The joy of these people was tremendous. Many of them had seen their loved ones depart with great fear and anguish. They had heard terrible things about the Persian army, and even though the Helots were not used in combat, there was reason for worry. If the enemy had won, at best their men would have been captured as slaves and taken far away. The poor wretches would have had no hope of ransom or of bargaining with the Persians, since their families had barely enough to survive. The news of frightening Persian massacres on the islands added to their terror. They had heard that entire populations had been deported to distant countries with no hope of return.

Young Brithos watched them with a sense of contempt.

People who thought of nothing but saving their own squalid lives didn't seem worthy of being called human beings. At the same time, the embarrassment of the futile intervention at Marathon weighed upon Brithos, as on the whole warrior caste, quite heavily. The unthinkable and striking Athenian victory obscured the prestige that the Spartan military forces had always enjoyed. It seemed to Brithos that those wretched Helots were delighting, even if they dared not show it, in their masters' embarrassment.

As Brithos drew nearer, the excited voices fell silent, and every gaze dropped to the ground save one: that of a boy a little younger than he, who looked him directly in the eye with a strange expression, then took off in the direction of Mount Taygetus with a curious rolling gait.

4

THE SHIELD

THE LAST PART OF that tumultuous year passed uneventfully for the mountain people. They returned to their monotonous existence, punctuated only by the passing seasons and their work in the fields.

Talos had become a strong young man and, as he was often out on his own, he began to seek the company of other young people. The remote position of his grandfather's cottage, near the high spring, had kept him separated from other children throughout his childhood. But the Helots were used to living such isolated lives in the fields and pastures because the Spartans had always prevented them from gathering in villages. Only the old men recalled the ancient times when the Helot people had their own cities, surrounded by walls and crowned by towers.

They told of the dead city, abandoned on Mount Ithome, in the heart of Messenia. The towers, crumbled and corroded by time, now served as nests for crows and sparrowhawks. Figs and wild olive trees had sunk their roots among the dilapidated houses.

But beneath those moss-covered ruins slept the ancient kings. The shepherds who passed with their flocks during the seasonal migrations had strange stories to tell. On the night of the first full moon of spring, they said, eerie flashes of light pulsed through the ruins, and a great grey wolf could be seen wandering among the fallen walls. And if the moon disappeared behind a cloud, a lament would be heard, coming from beneath the earth, from deep within the mountain: the cry of the kings, prisoners of *Thanatos*.

Talos listened fascinated to these marvellous stories, but he considered them imaginings – fables told by old men. His thoughts were occupied, instead, by the work that needed to be done and by his daily tasks: it had become his responsibility to deliver their produce to the family of old Krathippos. He knew that they could continue to live untroubled as long as nothing was lacking in the home of their Spartan master, down in the valley.

On his daily journey from the mountain to the plain he often met up with a Helot peasant who farmed another stretch of land near the Eurotas river that was also the property of Krathippos. The elderly peasant, Pelias, was a widower. He had only one daughter, and had been finding it quite difficult to carry on his work in the fields alone. And so Talos sometimes brought his flock down to the plain and entrusted it to the care of Pelias' daughter, Antinea, while he took care of the heaviest and most pressing chores himself. He sometimes stayed several days in a row on Pelias' farm.

'It seems that you have forgotten where you live,' teased Kritolaos. 'We see you so rarely here! It wouldn't be, by chance, little Antinea infusing you with all this new enthusiasm for working in the fields? By Zeus, I wanted to make you into a shepherd, and here you are becoming a farmer!'

'Oh, stop that, grandfather,' Talos replied brusquely. 'That girl doesn't interest me at all. It's poor old Pelias that I'm worried about. If I weren't there to help him with the toughest jobs, he could never manage on his own.'

'Naturally,' replied Kritolaos. 'I know that you have a good heart as well as strong arms. It's only that I have heard that little Antinea is becoming very pretty indeed, that's all.'

In fact, Pelias' daughter was beautiful. She had long blonde hair and eyes as green as grass moist with dew. Her body, although forged by the hard work of the fields, was lithe and graceful, and Talos was often distracted from his work as he saw her pass with her quick step, carrying an earthenware pot full of spring water on her head.

But that wasn't all. Sometimes he tried to guess the shape of her breasts and the curve of her hips under the short chiton that she wore gathered at the waist with a cord. And this threw his normally serene spirit into such confusion that he was quite brusque with her, almost rude. He was afraid that she could read how he felt plainly on his face, and he did everything he could so as not to be discovered. And yet, he couldn't help but watch her as she bent down to gather a sheaf of dry grass for the animals and her thighs were bared: a sudden blaze rushed to his head and his temples throbbed madly.

What confused him the most was that Kritolaos didn't need to guess at anything: he seemed to know Talos' every thought. It was unbearable to be considered a young ram in heat! So, at times Talos preferred to set out alone to listen to the skylarks and blackbirds or to lay traps for the foxes in the forest.

Was this what it meant to become a man? Yes, this, but so much more: mysterious sounds resonating within, sudden tremors. Wanting to climb up to the highest peaks, to let out a yell and wait for it to echo back from far off pinnacles. Tears in your eyes when the sun at dusk sets fire to the clouds, like thousands of lambs, fleece in flames, grazing in the blue and then dissolving into the darkness. Your chest swelling with the melody of the nightingale and the raucous shrieks of the sparrowhawk. A desire for wings with which to fly far away over the mountains and over the valleys glittering with silver olive trees; over the rivers, between the willows and the poplars in the scented silent night, by the pale light of the moon . . .

These were the things that Talos, the cripple, felt in his heart.

★

One day, Talos was bringing his sheep down from the mountain to Pelias' house so he could lend the old farmer a hand. The great feast of Artemis Orthia, when the young Spartiates would be initiated as warriors, was drawing near. Krathippos' house had to be put in order and decorated, the wood for the hearth had to be prepared, and a lamb had to be slaughtered for their banquet. Talos had left home at the first rays of dawn, taking the path that led to the plain. He emerged from the forest just as the sun was rising above the horizon. Suddenly he heard yelling from a nearby clearing.

'Come on, Brithos, grab her! Hey, don't let her get away, you slow-moving oaf!'

'Get over here, yourselves, then. This little savage runs like a hare and scratches like a cat!'

Talos sensed immediately what was happening. He shot out of the forest and burst, running, into the field where several horses were grazing next to a stream. Their masters, all young Spartans, had encircled Antinea who was now at their centre, terrified, her clothing ripped and her hair dishevelled. Goaded on by his companions, the youth named Brithos circled close around the girl as she drew back, clutching her torn clothes to her breast.

'Hey, Brithos, let's see if you can tame this little filly, too!' shouted a boy with reddish hair and freckles, with a vulgar laugh.

'Leave her alone!' bellowed Talos, hurling himself into the centre of the circle, moving close to the trembling girl who clutched at his side.

'What have you done, Talos?' she sobbed. 'They'll kill you.'

'Friends,' shouted Brithos, recovering from the shock of the sudden apparition, 'the goddess Artemis has shown us her favour today by sending us not only a fawn, but also this goat!'

Talos felt his blood boil in his veins and pound at his temples. He grasped his cornel staff with two hands, standing firmly on both legs.

'Oh, but he's dangerous,' sneered another. 'He has a stick! Let's be careful not to get hurt or we won't be able to take part in the initiation.'

'So, who's going to take care of him?' asked a third boy.

'I will,' shouted the boy with the red hair advancing behind Talos, who reeled around to face him.

'Oh, but he's lame!' yelled another. 'It doesn't count, Aghias, too easy!'

'That's all right,' said the red-haired youth, continuing his advance towards Talos. 'I'll take him bare-handed.'

The Spartan flung the javelin he held in his right hand to the ground and lunged forward. Talos dodged him and pivoted on the staff which he had planted forcefully in the ground. He tripped his adversary and drove his heel into the back of the young Spartan's neck, knocking him senseless. Talos immediately returned to his guard, gripping his staff in both hands.

An astonished silence fell among the group. The boy they called Brithos, their leader apparently, turned livid with anger. 'That's enough!' he shouted. 'Duels are for warriors. Let us squash this miserable louse and get out of here. I'm tired of these games.'

They rushed upon Talos as a group, veering to avoid the staff that he wielded in the air with deadly precision. Two of the Spartans fell, struck directly on their sternums, twisting in pain and vomiting. The others were upon him, wildly clubbing him with the shafts of their javelins. Talos struggled furiously, howling like a wild beast, trying in vain to break free as his adversaries rained down kicks and punches onto his stomach and back. They nailed his shoulders to the ground, and one of the boys drove his knee into Talos' chest.

'Move over!' commanded Brithos. The other boys scrambled aside, panting heavily. Brithos raised his javelin to deliver the mortal blow. Talos, shaken by tremors, stared up at him, his swollen eyes full of tears. Brithos faltered, and in that moment Antinea, who had been paralysed with terror, threw herself with a cry onto Talos' body, covering it with her own. Brithos, furious in his rage, stood a moment as if transfixed. He stared stupidly at the girl's back, which was shaking with sobs. Slowly, the youth lowered the javelin.

'Pick up those idiots,' he said to the other boys, pointing to his two battered companions still on the ground, 'and let's get out of here.'

The boys reached their horses and took off towards Sparta. Brithos was thinking of that gaze that had caused him to falter. These eyes ... he'd seen them before, staring at him, but he didn't remember where, or when. He remembered, without knowing why.

*

It seemed to Talos that he was waking from a deep sleep. Sluggish limbs were racked with piercing cramps. A sweet, warm touch, the throbbing body of Antinea, awakened life in his shivering skin. Slowly, his swollen eyes opened. He saw the girl's face soiled with his own blood, lined with tears, as Antinea caressed him, quietly sobbing. Her small rough hands moved through his matted hair.

'Talos, you're alive,' she managed to say, as if she couldn't believe her own words.

'Looks like it,' he muttered under his breath. 'But I don't know for how much longer. They massacred me, those bastards.'

Antinea ran to the stream, and soaked a corner of her chiton in the cool water. She crouched next to Talos and wiped his disfigured face, his tumid mouth and eyes.

'Can you stand up,' she begged, 'or should I call my father?'

'No, don't,' he answered. 'I'm all bruised, but I think I'm still in one piece. Help me, that's good. Hand me my staff.'

The girl gave him the staff and Talos used it to brace himself. His left arm around Antinea's shoulders, he lifted himself to his feet, painfully stretching his limbs. They started out slowly, stopping often to rest, and reached Pelias' farm when the sun was still high. Alerted by the barking of his dog, Antinea's father stepped out into the courtyard. Shaken by the scene before his eyes, he ran towards them.

'In the name of the gods, what has happened?' cried the old man. 'What have they done to you?'

'Father, help me, quickly,' gasped the girl, weeping. 'Talos defended me from some Spartan boys. It's a miracle he's alive.'

They laid him out on a bed, covering him with a woollen blanket. The violent fever brought on by the ferocious beating racked his trembling body with convulsions.

'Please,' he begged in a feeble voice, 'don't let my family know about this. It would kill them.'

'Stay calm, my boy,' Pelias reassured him. 'I'll send word that you'll be staying with us for a few days to help me prepare the feast and gather the hay. As soon as you're better, you'll be able to invent some story. You'll say that you fell into some crevasse.'

'Yes, all right,' murmured Talos, his eyelids dropping.

Pelias watched the boy with tear-filled eyes, then turned towards his daughter, whose gaze still betrayed the fear she felt. 'Go put on another dress,' he said. 'There's not much left of the one you have on. Then come back here and don't leave his side for an instant. I must go into town to our master's now. The feast will take place in two days and I've still got quite a lot to do.' He disappeared, closing the door behind him and leaving the house in darkness.

Talos, exhausted, had fallen into a deep sleep. He moaned weakly, turning in his bed. Every small movement made Antinea start, and she moved closer to Talos to better see his face in the dim light. She then returned to one of the benches, and sat there with her hands folded in her lap. When Pelias returned it was almost dark.

'How is he?' he asked in a low voice, entering.

'Better, I think. He's sleeping peacefully and his fever seems lower. But just look at how swollen he is!' replied the girl. Pelias opened the window a crack, and a little of the glow of dusk entered the room. His face tightened in sadness as he saw Talos' distended features, the boy's chest covered in bruises, his skinned and bloodied arms. The old man's hands tightened into fists. 'Damn them,' he muttered between his teeth. 'Damn them! And to think that they're the offspring of the most noble families of the city: Brithos, son of Aristarkhos; Aghias, son of Antimakhos; Philarkhos, son of Leukhippos . . .'

'How did you find out their names?' asked Antinea, shocked.

'From our friends who serve in their families. Some of those damnable bastards came back in bad shape and the truth has leaked out, even if they did try to make the others believe that it was some accident that happened during their military drills. That boy Talos, he hit hard! Even though he was alone! It's strange, I never would have believed it; he is strong, but how could he have knocked those young warriors to the ground? All those boys do is train and wrestle and fence all day.'

'I don't know, father. It was amazing. You should have seen how he used that staff,' said the girl, indicating the cornel crook leaning against a corner of the room. 'He swung it around so incredibly fast, and with so much strength! If they hadn't all jumped on him together, they couldn't have beaten him like they did.'

Pelias was very thoughtful for a moment, staring at the shiny cornel rod, then he gripped it with his hands. 'Old Kritolaos,' he murmured, 'no one else . . .'

'What did you say?' asked the girl.

'Nothing, nothing my daughter. I was only talking to myself.' He put the staff back in its place, then sat down next to the bed where Talos lay sleeping. 'Now the boy is in real danger, though. They could kill him at any time.'

'No!' cried out Antinea.

'Don't you realize what he's done? Not only has he dared to rebel, but he even managed to strike down some of the Spartans. They don't need that much of a reason to kill a Helot. Fortunately, he hasn't been recognized yet, but it won't take them long to find out who he is. They saw that he was lame.'

Antinea twisted her hands, and anxiously watched Talos' face. 'We have to help him escape immediately, hide him somewhere!'

'And where, my daughter? A fugitive Helot can't get very far, and in any case, where could we possibly hide him? Any family who protected him would be exterminated as soon as the Spartans found them out.'

'Then, there's no hope?'

'Calm down, daughter, we'll find a solution. For the time being he's safe. No one saw the two of you come here. At least, I hope not. And then, there is a thread of hope.'

'What do you mean?' blurted out Antinea.

'You told me that Talos was on the ground, and that one of the boys had raised his javelin to run him through, isn't that so?'

'Yes, that's right.'

'But he didn't do it.'

'That's true, but I'd thrown myself on him then, I covered him with my body. The Spartans don't kill women.'

'I don't think that's it. If that boy with the javelin hesitated, there could have been a reason. A reason that escapes us at the moment, but one that was good enough to stay his hand. In any case, if he had wanted, he would have had his companions drag you off, and he could have easily killed Talos. So if he didn't do it, it was of his own will. And if he didn't kill him in that moment, when he must have been foaming with anger, it's improbable that he would kill later in cold blood.'

'But what about the others?'

'From your description, the boy must have been Brithos, the son of noble Aristarkhos, the last offspring of the Kleomenids. If he doesn't want it done, you can be sure that the others won't do anything. For now, in any case, we have time. Everyone in the city is busy preparing the initiation ceremony for the new warriors, which will be taking place the day after tomorrow at the temple of Artemis Orthia.'

Old Pelias drew near to Talos, observing his face more closely. He touched the boy's hair. 'Poor boy,' he murmured. 'Courageous as a lion. He doesn't deserve to die; not even twenty years old yet!' He turned to his daughter: 'Go, prepare something to eat, so there'll be something when he wakes up.'

Antinea suddenly remembered that she hadn't eaten all day, and went to prepare a modest dinner. She called her father when it was ready, but the old man seemingly had to force himself to eat. They went to bed early, drained by the day's events.

On his bed, Talos was still deep in a slumber filled with frightening nightmares. His throat was parched and his temples pounded. He saw, in rapid succession, Brithos' face lit up in anger, the sinister glimmer of the javelin tip suspended like a death sentence over his head, the faces of the others spinning around him in a frightening vortex. Their mocking laughter echoed louder and louder in his head. 'It doesn't count, Aghias, he's lame! He's lame! He's lame!' repeated the screaming voices, ten times, a hundred times, louder and louder.

Talos woke up, crying out with anguish in the middle of the night, his forehead dripping with sweat, his heart beating madly. Before him, softly illuminated by the moonlight, was Antinea. Her hair looked like silver, diffused like a light cloud around the soft oval of her face.

Her short dress was a little girl's gown that didn't reach her knees. She placed the lamp that she was holding on a bench and sat on the edge of the bed. Talos, caught between sleeping and waking, couldn't seem to come to his senses. Antinea reached her small rough hand up to his forehead and began slowly to dry his sweat with the edge of the woollen cover, in silence.

Talos watched her with a trembling heart, but that cool hand, on his chest now, seemed to call him back from his nightmare. Antinea's face became slowly clearer in the near darkness. Her eyes – full of anxiety and infinite sweetness – caressed his saddened spirit, his shaken mind. He saw her face come closer, slowly, he felt her hair brush his chest like a warm wave, her lips rested on his thirsty mouth. No longer was the odour of blood filling his nostrils. Talos, the cripple, smelled the sweet scent of hay, of ripe grain, of wildflowers and dreamed in his heart of Antinea's golden skin, the perfume of her breast . . . for the first time.

*

As the cocks' cries spread over the countryside, Antinea left the stable carrying a heavy jug of fresh milk.

Her father Pelias had already gone off towards the city. He was bringing the first fruits of the fields to his master's house to decorate his table on the great feast day. Two large sackfuls hung from the saddle of his ass. The girl leaned backwards against the door to open it, entered the cottage and placed the jug on the ground. She filled a cup with steaming milk; it was time to wake Talos so that he could eat. She quietly entered the room where he slept. A ray of light brightened the room, revealing the straw pallet still stained with blood: empty! Antinea felt suddenly faint. Realizing that he couldn't have got far, she rushed outside.

She ran towards the wood near the stream, but there was no trace of him. She turned towards the mountain, but decided immediately that Talos couldn't have gone that way; he would never return to his family in that state. There was only one possible explanation: Talos must have gone to Sparta! The one place that both she and her father had forbidden him to go at any cost.

She returned wearily to the farm, weeping by the time she reached the door. She sat on a stool for a while in thought, then suddenly understood what she must do. Antinea stood up and put on a long cloak which fell from her head to the ground. She started off for the city with her quick step, noting the crowds that were gathering along the streets and in the squares.

Antinea's intuition had not failed her: Talos had been roaming about on his unsteady legs for some time in the city, hooded to hide his face from the throngs filling the streets that led to the temple of Artemis Orthia. The great sacrifice and initiation ceremony for the new warriors was about to begin.

Many Perioeci – people of the middle caste: farmers and shopkeepers – had come with their families from the outlying fields, and there were also quite a few Helots. Some were certainly there in the service of their masters; others, attracted out of curiosity, had come to witness the cruel initiation rites. All at once, from the end of the square in front of the temple, a roll of drums could be heard along with the sound of pipes. A sound Talos remembered well – he had heard it for the first time when he descended the mountain to the banks of the Eurotas to watch the returning warriors.

The crowd opened to allow the court to pass. First came the priests wrapped in white robes, their heads bound with long woollen bands that fell to their shoulders. Next came the heralds and the temple servants. A short distance behind them followed the divisions of equals, warriors dressed in crimson cloaks and tunics covered with polished armour, their helmets crowned with high horse-hair crests.

Talos, half hidden behind a column, felt a shiver run down his spine as he watched them march in perfect order with their measured step. He saw himself as a boy, on the edge of that dusty road, before a warrior who fixed him with sorrowful eyes. The equals began to wheel, arranging their ranks into four rows all around the square. They stopped, still as statues, shield against shield, hands gripping long shining spears. At the end of the column came the royal guard with their scarlet crests rippling in the wind, their great shields decorated with the insignia of the city's most illustrious families. On one of those shields, Talos saw a dragon with shining scales of copper. The boy's heartbeat quickened; he tried in vain to search for the face of that warrior, hidden behind the helmet's mask. Behind them, the two kings: Cleomenes on his black stallion and Leotychidas in the saddle of a Corinthian sorrel, their armour richly adorned and their great mantles falling to cover the hindquarters of their steeds. Finally came the supervisors of the barracks and, behind them, the youths who aspired to become *eirenes*, men and warriors who would defend the power and honour of their city.

Taking their places, the two kings signalled to the heralds, who sounded the trumpets for the beginning of the sacrifice. The steaming blood of the slaughtered animals dripped on the pavement and a pungent odour spread through the square as their entrails were placed to burn on the fires of the altar. The great moment had arrived: the doors of the temple were flung open. The five ephors emerged and went to take their places among the elders. The first of these raised his right hand, and the heralds called out the names of three young candidates: Kresilas, son of Eumenes; Kleandridas, son of Eupites; and Brithos, son of Aristarkhos.

Talos started; although physically exhausted, he felt a shock coursing through his limbs. He realized that he had come just for this. That boy Brithos, whom he had never seen before, had been about to kill him. Maybe he would kill him yet. Talos had to know the outcome of this test.

The priests pronounced the ritual formulas and the servants stepped forward to strip the boys of their clothing and hold their arms fast. The whipping began to the tune of the pipes. The spectators were struck silent. The boys stiffened at the first lashes, all of the muscles of their bodies contracting in a single, wrenching spasm. Then, exhausted, they abandoned themselves to the pain, shaking uncontrollably as each blow fell.

Talos moved up among the crowd, grinding his teeth in pain from the jabs and shoves of the spectators. He finally reached the first row, lined up to watch the frightful rite. His eyes rested mercilessly on Brithos' tormented body. Brithos continued to stand upright, whereas the other two boys called with him to the test had begun to bend their knees. The cool, strange music of the pipes went on, measured by the cracking of the whips as the boys' bare backs were flogged.

Kresilas was the first to fall. The servants immediately ran to help him up and to carry him out of the sacred enclosure. Next was Kleandridas. Although they all passed the test, each tried to hold out as long as possible to demonstrate his superiority over pain. Brithos alone remained. He ground his teeth, his hair was plastered to his forehead, his chest drenched with sweat. His eyes were glassy, but he remained standing.

Talos lowered his eyes to the ground in disgust. When he lifted them it was to see Brithos crumble to his knees and then to his hands, his head swinging between his shoulders. Talos felt an acrid joy invade his spirit, poisoned by the desire for revenge. The servants came towards Brithos to lift him, but he motioned them away.

He slowly lifted his head and chest to look at the crowd before him. Talos lowered his hood, uncovering his battered face. Brithos blinked several times to clear away the tears and the sweat from his eyes, and recognized the boy before him. They glared at each other for long moments with eyes full of ire, of challenge . . . of admiration.

*

The bloody rite went on until all the youths had passed the initiation trial. Their shoulders were then covered with the crimson cape of the *eirenes*, and each new warrior received a shield adorned with the great 'lambda' which stood for Lakedaimon, the ancient name of Sparta.

'Which one of these youths will someday receive the shield of the dragon?' Talos asked himself. The fathers of the *eirenes*, one by one, put down their weapons. Each warrior left his post on the square, and went towards the priests to receive the shield which he then delivered to his own son. Talos eagerly watched as the warrior of the dragon lay his weapons on the ground and left the lines of the royal guard of King Cleomenes. He proudly gave the shield . . . to Brithos!

Talos was deeply shaken. That long-ago emotion of his childhood was re-awakened in his soul, and clashed fiercely with his hate for Brithos, his resentment, his wounded pride, his fear.

'Are you mad? You must want to get yourself killed!' breathed a voice in his ear. It was Pelias, warned by Antinea. He had been searching for Talos, only to find him among the crowd watching the initiation rite.

'Don't worry, Pelias,' Talos responded calmly. 'I've already been recognized, but nothing has happened. I don't know why, but nothing has happened.'

'But why expose yourself so foolishly to such fatal danger?' reprimanded Pelias.

'Don't ask me why. I wouldn't know how to answer. I had to do what I did. What I do know is that it's never possible to escape your destiny; it's better to face it.'

Antinea took him gently by the hand. 'Let's go, Talos, please let's go now. You're still so weak, you're tired.'

Talos pulled up his hood and followed Pelias and

Antinea. They turned off the main road and entered one of the many alleyways that formed the dense and intricate network of the old city. They emerged in the square of the other great temple, the one dedicated to Athena, called the House of Bronze. They turned behind the massive construction, and proceeded among the low white stucco houses until they reached the road for Amyclae. It was not long before they had reached Pelias' farm.

5

KRYPTEIA

In Aristarkhos' home, there was great feasting that day: Brithos, the son of the noble warrior, had become an *eiren*. He would stay with his family only one more week before entering the military barracks as a member of the twelfth *syssitia*, the company he would join at table. The members of his *syssitia*, fifteen men in all, were part of the third of the four great battalions which composed the Spartan army at that time.

For ten long years they were to be his family; he would eat and sleep with them, returning to his father's home only for special occasions. Ismene, his mother, had prepared herself long ago for this separation. Like every Spartan mother, she knew that she had brought her son into the world first for his city, and only secondarily for herself and her husband.

She was accustomed to him being away; during the various stages of his initiation Brithos had lived for long periods of time outside of his home with his companions under the supervision of the *paedonomus*. These trainers prepared the boys to endure fatigue, cold and hunger and to confront pain without a whimper. Brithos had won the admiration of the whole crowd present at the flagellation trials by surpassing all limits of endurance. They were sure that the youth would become, without a doubt, one of the strongest and most courageous warriors of Sparta.

Despite all this, Ismene could not share in her husband's serene pride. The loss of her other son had left an indelible mark on her. Although she had been prepared since childhood for the possibility of losing a son for the honour and well-being of her country, the realization that Brithos was the only one left to her filled her with gnawing apprehension. Her son's fiery nature would always push him forward in a risky situation, and their country was now nearer to war than peace. She watched him as he packed his things, assisted by his nurse and one of the servants. Only six days after the trial he had already recovered, and was moving about easily. Ismene herself had prepared the unguents to cure the bruises and wounds that the flagellation had left on his back.

It was time for her husband to give Brithos the special gift that tradition required on such an occasion. Ismene heard him calling his son from the outer courtyard: 'Brithos! Don't you want to see your father's gift?'

The boy stopped his packing and went outside.

'Here is my gift for you, son,' said Aristarkhos. From behind a corner of the house came a servant trying to control a superb Laconian Molossian hound on a leash.

Brithos, glowing, warmly grasped his father's hand. 'Only noble Aristarkhos could have thought of such a precious gift. Thank you, father; he's really splendid! I've never seen such a beautiful dog.'

'He's already fully trained. I've had my best man raising him for three years on our farm in Tegea.'

'You've been rash, father,' teased the boy. 'What if I hadn't lasted at the trial?'

'Oh, in that case, I would have kept him for myself; he certainly wouldn't have gone to waste. Let me tell you, though, that I was certain that the son of Aristarkhos would be the best, and I wasn't wrong. The king himself complimented me on your superb performance, but you needn't have pushed yourself so far, Brithos. Your mother suffered terribly in that square: she's a proud woman, but a woman she is,' said Aristarkhos, looking away.

'Oh, father, you know well that a warrior can't let himself be influenced by such things.'

'Yes, son, that may be true, but remember that a real warrior is a real man and that a real man has strong limbs, a quick mind, and also a heart: without any one of these things the armour that covers you is no more than an empty shell.'

Brithos contemplated his father in silence, taken aback by his words.

'Well then, son,' continued Aristarkhos, 'Aren't you going to take your gift? Here . . .' he said, taking the leash from his servant, 'This is Melas. I've named him for the colour of his fur. It's rare to find a Molossian with such an intensely black coat.'

The gigantic dog, as black as night, approached Brithos and sniffed his hand.

'See?' Aristarkhos smiled. 'It seems he already knows that you are his master. I think you'll become good friends. But now, go to your mother, spend some time with her. Tomorrow you will enter the *syssitia* and you won't have another chance to enjoy her company for the next couple of years.'

The next day, at first light, Brithos awoke and ate a frugal meal with his parents. He then put on his armour and bid them goodbye; the time had come for Brithos to leave home. He crossed the great atrium, and bowed his head in respect to the images of the Kleomenid heroes. He unbolted the door that led to the outer courtyard where a Helot servant was waiting for him with his bags. In that moment he heard his name called. 'Brithos . . .' It was his mother, standing before the hearth.

The youth turned back towards her. 'What is it, mother?'

'I have something to ask you, if I may,' answered Ismene.

'Ask me freely,' said Brithos.

'Do you remember the day of your test?'

'Of course.'

'After you had fallen to the ground, on your knees . . .'

'What about it?'

'The servants wanted to lift you but you waved them away. You stayed that way . . . for just a few moments. You seemed to be staring, intensely, at someone in front of you . . .' Brithos wrinkled his forehead. 'Who was he?'

'A Helot.'

'A Helot?'

'A Helot. A cripple.'

He turned and crossed the atrium again. His hobnailed boots resounded on the hard stone as he closed the heavy oak door behind him. Ismene remained staring at the ashes of the hearth, her dark eyes brimming with tears.

*

Talos was worried that his prolonged absence might distress his family, and so convinced his host that he could stay no longer.

'I have to go, Pelias, my mother will be getting anxious and my grandfather Kritolaos will be unbearable. That old man is as crafty as a fox; he'll have a thousand questions ready for me, and he'll make me fall into some trap for sure. Believe me, it's better that I go, for your sake as well. If nothing happens you'll see me returning soon.'

'Yes, maybe you should go, my boy. But be careful, watch out for yourself. Are you sure that you feel well enough? It's a long walk, and the mountain trail is very steep. Shall I come with you?'

'No, Pelias, if you came with me, it would just stir up suspicion. My grandfather, you know . . .'

'Yes, I know, Kritolaos is an old fox. Then may the gods go with you, Talos. I will not forget what you did for Antinea. If you should ever need anything, you know that you can trust me. My door is open at any moment, and that little that I have—'

'Oh, Pelias,' Talos interrupted smiling, 'don't say such things. All I really did was to take a bit of beating.'

He walked alone down the path that led to Mount Taygetus, having said goodbye to Antinea.

'I'll come with you up to the wood,' she had said.

'No, you stay here. Don't leave your house at all, not

for any reason.' He touched her hair. 'Don't worry, Antinea, and don't be afraid for me. Nothing can happen on the mountain.'

He set off, disappearing into the olive trees that spread out at the base of Taygetus. He hurried along the road, hastened by an uneasiness that he couldn't really explain. He had been gone from his house for many days now, and even though Pelias had sworn to him that his family had believed his story, he still felt uncertain about keeping such a big secret from Kritolaos.

Besides, he was afraid of what might still befall him. Trying to cope without his grandfather's advice and experience made him feel very alone. For him, Kritolaos was beyond doubt the wisest man on earth. What would happen in the days, or the months, or the years to come? He knew of men sentenced to death by the Spartans who survived for a long time, only to have their terrible destiny finally catch up with them. He remembered the hooded man they had seen at the high spring on the day when Kritolaos had tested the boy's skill with the bow. Most likely, Sparta knew about that too. But, then, why hadn't they reacted? What were they waiting for? He had gone into the city, shown himself in the square. Surely he must have been recognized, and yet nothing had happened.

He thought of what he had heard about the dreaded *krypteia*, the secret forces of the Spartan army. The Helots of the mountain said that they would stalk anyone they considered dangerous and would think nothing of elimi-nating him, without mercy, without warning, in the darkness of the night, in the middle of the forest. He had sometimes heard the word whispered, charged with terror, over the lifeless body of a Helot found in the wood or in a cabin.

Kritolaos had told him once of a peasant from the plains who, pursued by the *krypteia*, had escaped to Messenia with the help of the mountain shepherds. The relentless revenge of Sparta reached him four years later in a tavern at the port of Methone. Suddenly the wood which had always seemed protective and secure to Talos – in which he had found himself many times face to face with a wolf or a bear without trembling – seemed hostile and fraught with danger. He felt hunted, certainly followed. Talos drove away these thoughts and quickened his pace, trying to calm down. How he longed not to be so alone at that moment! Even the company of little Krios would have lightened the weight in his heart.

Antinea. How strange, he still couldn't understand what had happened to him. It was like some kind of magic and now her face and her eyes were always appearing in front of him; he dreamed of her rough peasant's hands, her bare feet, her golden hair. But his feelings for her could not wash away the rest. He thought of the wretched peasants of the plains, crushed by responsibility for their families and perpetually exposed to the cruelty of their masters.

He thought of Pelias who would have borne their abuse of his daughter without protest, so that worse things would not follow. He remembered his own struggle against the young Spartans and felt full of pride. No, he would not bend: if he had made his masters taste dirt, maybe he wasn't born to be a slave. He thought of the great horn bow and of the cursed sword that lay under the earth: what did Kritolaos expect of him? What did he want him to do? It was time to find out: he would ask him.

With all these thoughts, Talos had nearly reached the end of his journey. He left the wood behind him and entered the great mountain clearing.

He stopped to look at his land, his home which appeared in the distance with its rugged straw roof and its pen for the flocks. In just a little while Krios would run up to him, barking and wagging his tail in welcome. Talos began walking through the fields, soon noticing that there was a small group of people gathered in the courtyard of his house: mountain shepherds, it seemed, but Krios was nowhere to be seen. What could have happened? He hurried into the courtyard. His dog approached him slowly, its eyes veiled with cataracts. One of the men took his arm. 'Talos,' he said, 'your grandfather Kritolaos . . .'

The youth froze. 'What has happened?' he asked anxiously.

'He's not well.'

'Do you mean that he's dying?' The man lowered his head.

Talos opened the door and entered; he crossed the room with the hearth and moved aside the hanging mat that separated it from the other room where Kritolaos was lying on his pallet. His mother, sitting on a stool, watched him in silence, her eyes full of tears. A ray of sunlight illuminated the simple bed, the old man's gnarled hands, his tranquil eyes that seemed to search for distant truth. Talos fell to his knees next to the bed and took that cold hand into his. The old man turned his head towards the boy.

'I knew that you would come,' he said hoarsely. 'I was waiting for you, I couldn't have closed my eyes without seeing you.'

'What are you saying,' interrupted Talos with a tremor in his voice. 'You've been ill other times, you'll soon be on your feet again and we'll go together to the spring.'

'No, Talos; last night I heard *Thanatos* settling on the roof of this house. My time has come.'

Talos passed his hand through Kritolaos' snow white hair. 'What foolishness, old man, I'll go up to the roof and beat off *Thanatos* with a stick. I won't let you go. There are so many things that you still have to teach me!' He felt a knot closing his throat: 'Will you leave this baby sparrow alone, Kritolaos?'

The old man looked at him with dimmed eyes. 'Kritolaos is tired,' he said as he struggled for breath, 'he's going to join his ancestors. This baby sparrow . . .' He began again, approximating a feeble smile. 'No, I see a young wolf now.'

Talos felt the old man's hand weakly grasping his own. 'I know everything,' said Kritolaos. 'I knew that one day it would happen.'

'What do you know?' asked Talos, drawing closer so as not to miss a sound of the dying old man's words.

'Your struggle on the plain.' The old man stared at the contusions still quite visible on Talos' face and arms. 'Talos, listen: they will come, you know, they will come, you must be ready . . . The bow . . . the bow of the king must not fall into their hands.'

'Yes, the king's bow is safe. Don't talk now, you're tiring yourself.'

'It's no use, Talos, this is the last day of Kritolaos, remember?'

Talos saw the dim underground chamber in his mind's eye, the weapons gleaming in the torchlight.

'Talos, my boy, tomorrow I will not see the light . . . I'll be leaving with the last rays of the sun. You are the keeper of the weapons of King Aristodemus. Of the sword . . . sacred . . . and cursed.'

Talos felt a chill run along his spine. He squeezed the bony hand more tightly, his eyes veiled with tears, his heart swollen.

'This old man . . .' continued Kritolaos, his voice weaker still, 'this old man is the last leader of his people, Talos. Talos, one day our people will shake off the yoke, and the city . . . the dead city will rise again on its ruins . . . That will be the day of the test . . . the final test.'

Kritolaos spoke with great effort, his bony chest rising, wheezing in agony. 'Listen to me . . . Talos . . . listen; on that day a man blind in one eye will come to you. He can remove the curse from the sword of the king . . .'

The old man's gaze searched for the light of the sun that entered through the shutters: like distant music the chirping of the cicadas was carried on the glaring light. Talos touched his chilly hands and leaned his head upon the old man's chest. 'Don't go away, grandfather . . . don't go,' he implored with a broken voice. 'How will Talos, the cripple, be able to—'

'No,' protested the dying man, 'no . . . Talos the Wolf . . . the sword . . . of the king.'

Talos felt Kritolaos' heart stop. He saw him give up his life on the humble bed, the white head resting on its side, eyes fixed on nothingness. Talos passed a hand over his forehead, closing his eyelids, and then stood up in the centre of the silent room.

Even the chirping of the cicadas had stopped in the still air and only the dull buzzing of the flies could be heard: the flies, companions of *Thanatos*.

He left the room, slowly pushing aside the straw mat. His mother had collapsed, weeping, into a corner. He turned to the shepherds, to the men of the mountain:

'Kritolaos is dead,' he said. 'Let us pay homage to Kritolaos!'

The dark foreheads of those men were lowered in silence. A huge bearded man advanced towards Talos, and laid a hand on his shoulder.

'May Kritolaos be honoured!' he said.

Then, turning to the others: 'And honour to Talos the Wolf!'

In that moment Talos met his mother's gaze. Her grey eyes, drained of tears, were full of sorrow and surprise.

★

'He must die!' shouted Aghias angrily. 'What that bastard has done is intolerable. And I cannot understand why you insist on covering for him. If it weren't for you, we'd have finished him off already.'

'Aghias is right,' intervened Philarkhos. 'We have to get rid of him, and soon. Above all, because he could be dangerous.'

Brithos sat in silence, besieged by his companions. Suddenly he rose to his feet. 'Dangerous?' he asked in a voice heavy with irony. 'A lame Helot? Warriors of Sparta, are you certain that you aren't losing your minds? Flapping around like a flock of frightened geese because a crippled shepherd caned you, ruining the fun you had planned with a peasant girl stinking of the stable and of cow dung!'

'Don't joke about this,' interrupted Philarkhos, livid with rage. 'You know very well what our law says. If we allowed those bastards to rebel against us, we'd have a revolt on our hands in no time. The Helots are a continuous peril for Sparta, and you are aware of that. Didn't you see how he used that staff? Someone must have taught him some military technique. There's something very strange about this whole thing.'

'What an imagination you have, Philarkhos!' Brithos shot back. 'All shepherds know how to use a staff; they have to defend their flocks from wolves and chase foxes out of the chicken house. Even if what you say were true, that the cripple has been supposedly trained by someone, that's even more reason not to kill him. Listen to me now,' he added, leaning a hand on the shoulder of his angry companion, 'and you too, Aghias, and all of you, friends, use your brains if you can. If it's true that there is something suspicious in the way that shepherd handles his staff, some kind of military training behind it, if I understand you right, we certainly won't solve any mysteries by killing him. Dead people, as we all know, don't talk, do they?'

The others fell silent, dominated, as usual, by the personality of the son of Aristarkhos.

'The day of our initiation,' he continued, sitting down again in the circle of his companions, 'we proved that we were among the strongest young men of Sparta. Now we are also members of the *krypteia*, which means that our superiors believe that we are capable of using our minds, and not only our fists. This story is something that I'll take care of, but in my own way. Can you say that you've ever seen me tremble, or back away from any type of challenge? During all this time that we've been training together, you've seen me do much more than pin to the ground a lame Helot bastard armed only with a stick.

'On the other hand, if we notify our superiors and inform them of our intention to eliminate that shepherd, we'll have to give some explanation, won't we? Because he's probably at the service of one of the families of our city. Do you think that it would be cause for honour, you wolves of Sparta, that a Helot cripple made you taste dirt using only a shepherd's crook?'

The boys lowered their gazes to the ground.

'Without counting the fact,' continued Brithos relentlessly, 'that when you've gone and killed him you'll never know whether you are able to get the better of a broken shepherd. What I mean is, fighting him on equal terms!'

'Brithos is right,' said one of the youths. Then, turning to him, 'All right, Brithos, but what do we do next?'

'That's it, Euritos, help me to convince these stone heads!' He thought a moment, and then went on. 'Listen, friends,' he said, softening the tone of his voice, 'I'll handle this with the help of two or three of you, no more. We'll make that bastard understand that he should never even dream of rebelling, and we'll make him wish that he never thought of playing the hero. We'll take care of him once and for all.'

Aghias stood up. 'As you wish, Brithos. The reasons

that make you want to save the bastard's life are more than good enough for me. I do have the feeling, though, that there's another reason that only you know, and that you're not telling.' He threw on his cloak and slammed the door behind him.

'Yes, maybe there is another reason,' murmured Brithos to himself. 'But you are wrong, Aghias, if you think I know what it is.'

*

Two months had passed since that night, two terrible months in which Talos was prostrate with the death of Kritolaos, his mother's wordless grief, his own solemn thoughts of his grandfather's legacy. The days passed, and sometimes the nights, in dark musings. The responsibility that Kritolaos had invested in him was great; he could tell from the changed way in which the mountain people treated him.

Day after day they came and he felt in them a strange hope, a faith of sorts surging up about him. The men of Taygetus now spoke to him as one of their own: they made him understand their suffering, their impotent rage, their fear. But what did they expect from him? How much did they really know about what Kritolaos had revealed to him?

Besides, thoughts of what had happened down on the plain still haunted him: he had challenged the young Spartans. He could not delude himself into believing that the story had finished there. He feared for his mother, for Pelias, for Antinea; he had seen her, fleetingly, one night at the farmhouse on the road to Amyclae. Talos longed for those days he had spent as a simple shepherd without worries or fears, those long winter nights passed listening to the magnificent stories of Kritolaos, those times when only the seasons – passing slowly and regularly one into another – marked the changes in his serene life. Times which seemed impossibly remote to him now.

One day, at dusk, a peasant from the plains arrived at their cottage. Pelias had sent him. He had come to warn Talos to keep on his guard; strange activity had been noticed at the edge of the forest, and that night the moon would be covered by clouds.

Talos thanked his informer but he didn't give much weight to the matter; Pelias often worried over nothing. Normal manoeuvres of some division in training, or regular military drills could have alarmed him. Talos was wrong.

They arrived at the clearing in the middle of the night: four of them, wrapped in dark cloaks, armed only with javelins and daggers, their faces covered by Corinthian helmets.

Talos was rudely awakened by Krios' furious barking. He hurriedly drew aside the window covering, just in time to hear a desperate yelping and then a final gasp for breath.

A pale ray of the moon pierced the thick clouds for a moment and Talos could make out four shadows at the edge of the courtyard. Near the sheep pen, a huge Molossian hound was ripping the lifeless body of little Krios to pieces. Talos ran to the inside room and found his mother near the hearth, dishevelled and paralysed with terror, trying to light a lamp. In that moment, the door was unhinged by a savage kick, and four men with their faces covered broke into the cottage, pointing their javelins at his chest.

Talos knew that his time had come. 'Don't hurt her!' he said, shielding his mother. 'I'll go with you.'

They dragged him outside, wrenching him away from the weeping woman who clung to his waist. Two of them held his arms while another struck him ferociously with the shaft of his javelin on his knees, his chest, his stomach.

The fourth opened the pen, and the frightened sheep ran forth, bleating wildly.

'Look!' he shouted with a voice that echoed ominously in the bronze helmet. And to the waiting dog: 'Now, Melas!'

The black monster rushed into the fold like a fury. He massacred the terrified animals, tore his teeth through the ram's hocks, devoured the lambs with his frightful jaws. When the earth was covered with their corpses, the man called back the beast whose mouth was foaming with blood.

'Here, Melas! That's enough. Let's go!' He gestured to one of his companions whose javelin shaft struck Talos' sternum with such violence that the boy collapsed to the ground without a whimper.

His mother's shrieks kept him conscious for a few more moments. He felt the weight of a boot pressed against his chest, and heard a voice: 'Let's hope this is enough for him. If he survives. Let's get out of here, Brithos.'

Talos saw the Molossian above him, he felt its steaming breath, but then his eyes veiled over red and his mind sank slowly into a frozen silence.

An excruciating pain in his abdomen shocked Talos awake, and he opened his eyes to the darkness of night. He felt two strong arms lift him and gently deposit him on his pallet. By the oil lamp's pale light, he made out a large bearded face leaning over him: the Herculean shepherd who had greeted him when he left Kritolaos' deathbed two months earlier. Talos tried to say something, but could only force out a low lament.

'I am Karas,' said the bearded giant. 'I came too late this time, but it won't happen again. From now on, I will always be ready to protect you. No harm must befall you, not ever again.'

He uncovered the boy's distended, painful stomach.

'They tried to burst you open like a wineskin. Those damned rabid dogs. But their day will come . . .'

Talos turned his eyes to his mother who sat crushed in a corner, her hands in her lap, her eyes red and swollen.

'They shut her up inside,' murmured Karas, 'so she wouldn't be in their way. She thought you were dead when I brought you in here. She's coming back to her senses now.'

Karas clenched his callused fists as if seeking a target for them, grinding teeth as white as wolves' fangs. He turned towards the woman. 'Prepare him something that will make him sleep. That's all he needs now. He'll make it through, don't worry.'

The next day, Talos was awakened by the sunlight that entered from the half-open window shade. His mother entered with a steaming potion in a wooden bowl.

'Drink this, son,' she said, 'before the pain in your

stomach awakens again.' She watched him lovingly as he drank.

'Where is Karas?' he asked, drying his mouth.

'He'll be here in a moment,' answered the woman, lowering her moist eyes. 'He's in the sheep pen, gathering up the carrion of our slaughtered animals.'

In that moment Karas entered with a butcher's knife, a bloody apron tied at his waist.

'I've skinned the dead animals. There are at least a dozen, others will die soon from their wounds. But don't fear, Talos, I'll pass the word to the other shepherds of the mountain, and your flock will be replenished. You won't have to suffer hunger because of the work of our masters.'

'No, I don't want that,' protested Talos.

'But this time misfortune has struck you harder than others. It is only right that we help each other in times of adversity. This is our law, you know that. But tell me, how did they kill those poor animals? Many of them seem to be half devoured.'

'A dog, an enormous hound with huge jaws, as black as night,' answered Talos.

'Ah, the Laconian Molossian. A terrible beast; they say that three of them can slaughter a lion.'

Talos shivered, and the memory of Krios' desperate howl rang in his ears.

'My dog,' he fixed the man with a questioning gaze, 'is dead, isn't he?'

'Yes,' answered the shepherd. 'His throat was ripped open.'

Little Krios, companion of childish games, would never come with him again to pasture, nor would he greet him wagging his tail in the evenings. Talos felt a knot close his throat.

'Bury him next to Kritolaos, please,' he said to Karas, and hid his head between his hands.

6

PERIALLA

TALOS, SHUT UP INDOORS for long days recuperating from the Spartan attack, often fell to thinking about his situation, about the violent changes that had swept through his life in so short a time. With Kritolaos dead, the boy had inherited his moral authority over the people of Taygetus. And maybe not over them alone, as Karas, who had become Talos' inseparable companion, had hinted to him.

Many things puzzled him. He knew very little about Karas: only that he had come from Messenia with his flock and had settled in a cabin near the high spring. He dwelled long and hard on the *krypteia* raid on his family; the men who took part in it had to have been the same ones that he had fought on the plain, defending Antinea. He was sure that he had heard one of them call out Brithos' name. He had no doubts that Brithos was his greatest enemy, and yet for some reason the Spartan youth didn't consider him dangerous enough to have him killed; he could have eliminated him a thousand times over, if he had wanted to, whatever Karas said.

Talos tried to make sense of the confusion in his mind . . . so many different impressions, contrasting emotions. Something had stopped Brithos' hand, down there in the plain, the same something that had prevented him from letting Talos be massacred by his companions, or by that bloody beast that he'd brought with him that night. As much as Talos reflected, though, he could not understand why he had been spared. It was true that the Spartiates instinctively admired anyone who showed valour, but that was no explanation for the fact that he, a Helot rebel who dared to defend a woman and attack a Spartan, had been allowed to live.

Something still attracted him to the city of the Spartiates; the same thing that had tempted him into the plain as a young boy. From time to time, the image of the warrior with the dragon appeared in his mind. He knew, now, beyond the shadow of doubt, that the warrior was the father of his mortal enemy.

What warmed Talos' heart when he felt most alone was his love for Antinea. He would dream of her coming to visit him, even while realizing that it would endanger her life.

Certain things, however, had become clear to him: he could not run away. He had a task to accomplish for his people, and he had made a promise to Kritolaos on his deathbed. He couldn't bear the thought of leaving Antinea, either, and he realized that it was a thousand times better to risk death by remaining than to flee to some distant place, pursued and hunted like an animal, with no one to talk to, to lean on, to confide his fears in.

And then Antinea did come to him, early one morning, and silently entered his room. 'Talos, my poor Talos,' she said, embracing him tightly. A wave of heat rose to his head, and his heart began beating wildly. He held her close, and then, released her. 'You shouldn't have come,' he lied. 'You know that the forest is full of dangers, and so is the plain.'

'No, you needn't worry. No one has threatened me, and I've come with my father. We heard about what happened, and wanted to come to help you. I'll stay here with you and take out the flock myself until you're completely better. My father doesn't need me much just now. In a month, when you're stronger again, you can come and help us with the reaping, all right?'

'Oh yes,' answered Talos, embarrassed and moved at the same time, 'of course I'll come.' He faltered as if trying to find the right words to say. 'Antinea,' he went on, 'I'll be waiting impatiently for reaping time . . . so we can be together again.' He watched her for a moment, feeling profoundly touched as her green eyes brightened. He took her hand. 'Antinea . . . Antinea, why are we slaves? Why can't I think of you without being afraid of what will happen to us?'

The girl covered his mouth with her hand. 'Don't talk that way, Talos, you are not a slave for me, nor am I a slave for you. For me you are a great warrior, the most valorous, the most generous of men. You are not a slave, Talos.'

'I know,' answered the boy, squeezing her hand more tightly. 'I do know what you mean, Antinea, but I also know the fear that seizes me. I know the nightmares that wake me up in the middle of the night. My life is marked. And yet I don't know where it will lead, because it's not in my own hands. And if I tie your life to mine, I don't know where it will end, or how . . . now do you understand me?'

'Yes, I do,' answered the girl, lowering her eyes. 'And that's why, sometimes, I wish that we'd never met.'

Antinea raised her tear-filled eyes to his face. 'Talos, I'm only the daughter of Pelias the peasant . . . and I know that our people now look to you as the special one, the successor of Kritolaos—'

Talos sat up in his bed. 'You're right, Antinea, Kritolaos did prepare me to succeed him; he taught me everything he could, and he left me a difficult legacy. But I don't know why, exactly. One day, maybe . . .'

'Yes, Talos, perhaps that day will come. We cannot force the hand of destiny. The gods have something in mind for you, for our people, and one day you will know, when the moment comes. Now, we must go on living,' she gazed at him intensely. 'Now, we must live, and not ask for anything more.'

She leaned over him slowly, caressed his forehead, kissed him softly and lay her blonde head on his chest to listen to the beat of his heart, slow now, and as powerful as the drumbeat of the warriors.

*

Summer and autumn passed, and strangely enough, nothing more happened to disturb their lives. Talos began working again, and every now and then he returned to the high spring with the bow hidden under his cloak.

In the wood's most isolated clearings he resumed his

training, this time under the guidance of Karas, his enigmatic friend. They even went hunting together, and Talos' infallible arrows brought down deer and boars, which were secretly slaughtered and butchered in Karas' cabin. There would be trouble if anyone noticed such a weapon in the hands of a Helot.

Talos realized that his companion had been closer to Kritolaos than he had imagined; his words hinted at the wealth of things he knew, although he never spoke out about them. Under Karas' guidance, Talos learned to fight with deadly precision using his staff. The two of them engaged in exhausting duels and wrestling bouts, so that Talos often returned home with bruised limbs, his bones crushed from the embrace of those brawny arms.

To Antinea and his mother, who worriedly enquired about his scars and contusions, Talos replied that they were the result of games that they invented to while away the long afternoons on the high pastures.

The tremendous adventures of the past year began to fade as if they had taken place long ago, and Talos became accustomed to the idea of a life that could continue warmed by the timid and humble love of his mother, protected by the massive and reassuring presence of Karas, ignited by his passion for Antinea.

And Antinea loved him, so much that she could think of nothing else. Only a few short months ago, down on her father's farm, Talos was only the lame boy that brought his sheep down from the mountain, the moody young man that she would have liked to tease into laughter. And now she saw nothing else but him: if his forehead wrinkled for a moment she felt gripped by sadness; if she saw him smile, her spirit brightened and her face glowed.

She remembered with infinite tenderness how she had loved him that first time, slowly, careful not to hurt him: that unknown, marvellous force that had guided her body, Talos' hands on her hips, the wave of flames that had set her womb and her heart on fire.

She knew that she possessed the most beautiful thing in the world and she was sure that there would be no end to what she was living. When she stayed with her father, she waited anxiously for Talos to come to her and on the appointed day, before dawn, lying on her bed in the dark, she imagined him lacing up his boots and taking his staff and leaving his home beneath the glimmer of the morning stars. He would open the pen and let out the flock and then he would come down the slope, cross the wood and emerge into the light of dawn, his hair wet with dew, accompanied by the great ram with the curved horns.

He would walk over the plain under the olive trees like a young god. And she would go into the courtyard to wash at the spring, sure of hearing the distant bleating of the lambs and then he would appear, smiling, with his deep, honest eyes, full of love for her. And then she ran barefoot to meet him, calling his name out loud, and she clung to his neck, wrapping herself around him, laughing and ruffling his hair in a game that was always new.

Antinea knew that boys find a companion for themselves when it is time and she knew that Talos did not want anyone but her. His fears and his worries didn't really touch her. The time would come when she could sleep beside him every night, prepare his food and the water that he would wash with when he returned from pasture. And she would mend his clothing on winter nights by the glow of the fire and if he should startle awake at night shaken by bad dreams she would dry the sweat from his forehead and caress his hair until he fell asleep again.

With these thoughts Antinea passed the summer and autumn working with Talos in the fields or following him to the high pastures until Boreas made the leaves of the forest fall. Just as nature followed its course, so she was sure that her life would continue next to the young man she loved.

But the gods had other plans in mind.

One evening at the end of the winter, as Talos sat in front of his cottage watching the sun set over the still-barren forest, he saw his destiny pass along the trail that crossed the clearing: a strange old woman, walking bent under a bundle of rags, leaning on a long cane. Her grey hair was gathered in a bun at the back of her neck, circled by a white woollen band from which metallic discs jangled. All at once, the woman noticed Talos and turned off the path, heading towards him. Talos watched her with apprehension, almost fear: her face was haggard and wrinkled, but her body displayed surprising energy in its quick, decisive step.

Talos shivered. He couldn't help but think, in that moment, of all the stories that Kritolaos had told him as a child to get him to go to bed quickly without crying or complaining: about the harpy Kelenos, who wandered in the form of an old woman at night, searching for small children to carry off to her putrid nest on a faraway island.

'What foolishness!' he thought to himself as she drew nearer. And yet he couldn't understand how an old woman could be roaming about these mountains alone as night was falling.

She was in front of him now, and raised her grey eyes to meet his: eyes glittering with an evil light within their dark orbits.

'Shepherd,' she said in a hoarse voice, 'in this land lives a man whose name is Karas and I must see him, now. Where can I find him?'

Talos was startled; the last thing he had expected was to hear that name on the lips of this strange being.

'How do you know his name?' he asked, perplexed.

'Don't ask me anything,' replied the woman with a peremptory tone, 'but answer my question, if you will.'

Talos indicated the trail that she had been following. 'Return to the path,' he told her, 'and follow it in the direction of the mountain. When you find a fork in the road, go to the left. You'll enter the forest. Keep walking until you reach a clearing. There you will see a spring, and near there, a cabin. Knock at the door three times and Karas will open it for you. But are you sure,' he added 'that you want to go there now? It's dark and the forest is dangerous at night. The wolves are ravenous; they often attack our flocks.'

'The wolves do not frighten me,' replied the old woman with a strange smile. She fixed him with her icy eyes. 'You are not afraid either. Are you not a young wolf, yourself?'

She turned and walked back towards the trail without another word. In the darkness, Talos heard the jangling rattles that hung from the long cane that the old woman used to walk. He returned to his own cottage to warm himself at the fire but the shivers that ran along his spine were not only from the cold.

'Who was that with you just now?' his mother asked as she put a bowl of soup in front of him.

'An old woman that I've never seen before around here. She was asking for Karas.'

'Karas? But where is he now?'

'He went to his cabin, up at the high spring.'

'But you shouldn't have told her; Karas certainly doesn't want strangers coming there.'

'Oh, mother, what harm can a poor old woman do? She's strange, all right, but she seemed more crazy than dangerous. Crossing the forest at this hour, alone . . .' Talos began to eat in silence, turning over the scene in his mind. That strange expression rang in his ears: 'Are you not a young wolf, yourself?' That was what Kritolaos had called him before dying, and Karas had greeted him in the same way. He finished eating quickly, put on his cloak and went towards the door.

'Where are you going?' fretted his mother. 'It's very dark, the moon's not even out tonight. You said yourself there was no reason to worry over Karas.'

'I'm not worried about him. But that poor woman may have been torn to pieces by some wolf.'

'She will have reached the house by now. And if she had been attacked, there would be nothing you could do to help her any more.'

'Well then, I want to know who she is, mother, and I'm going to find out now. Don't worry about me if I don't return tonight. I'm armed and I can defend myself. I'll be up there in no time. You go to bed, you must be tired.'

He walked out, quickly disappearing into the shadows. His mother stood at the threshold listening to the sound of his footsteps, until even that sound was swallowed up by the silence of the night.

*

Karas' powerful shape was framed by the door. Behind him, the inside of the cabin was lit up by the ruddy reflections of the flames that flickered in the hearth. He opened his eyes wide in the darkness, as if not believing what he saw before him.

'Perialla!' he exclaimed. 'You, here?'

'Let me in, quickly,' the old woman said, 'I'm nearly numb with the cold.' Karas moved aside, and the old woman brushed past him, grasped one of the stools and sat down to warm her hands over the fire. Karas sat down next to her. 'Are you hungry?' he asked.

'Yes, I'm hungry; I've been walking since dawn and I haven't found anything to eat but a piece of dry bread and a few olives at an inn.'

Karas brought her bread and cheese.

'Have you no wine?' the old woman demanded. 'My throat is very dry.'

Karas took a flask from a shelf and poured some red wine into a wooden mug.

He waited until she had swallowed a few draughts and, having checked that the door was well closed, he sat down again next to her.

'Then, will you tell me what has happened? I can't understand how you can be here, and how you managed to find me,' he said, fixing her with a suspicious gaze.

'How I found you? Oh, Karas,' she answered, 'what can remain hidden to Perialla, the prophetess, the voice of the god of Delphi?' Karas dropped his stare.

'No,' continued the old woman 'you need not worry, no one has followed me, but . . .'

'But?'

'But I think that we will soon have visitors.' Karas leapt up and reached for the heavy club leaning against the wall behind him.

'Calm down,' continued the woman. 'There is no danger, but if my spirit does not deceive me, a young wolf has just put himself on my tracks.'

'What do you mean?'

'Oh, I'm not speaking of an animal. He is a young shepherd I met down in the clearing who told me the way to your cabin.' Perialla wrinkled her grey eyebrows as if trying to remember something. 'I looked at him well,' she continued slowly, pronouncing each word carefully. 'He is wolf-hearted . . . for he fears not to cross the forest at night. I read the suspicion in his eyes. He will come.'

Karas gazed at her, frowning. 'Do you know who he is?'

'No,' said the woman, 'but he is not a shepherd.'

Karas poured her more wine. 'Why have you left the temple?'

'I was forced to,' sighed the woman. 'I lent my mouth to deception and I sold my soul . . . at a high price.' She gulped down the wine all at once, then broke into coarse laughter.

'Do you know why, down there, in the city of the Spartans, King Leotychidas sits on the throne which was rightfully that of Demaratus, who has been living for years in exile?' Karas did not understand. The woman grabbed a lock of his hair in her hooked hands and shook his head. 'I will tell you,' she continued, 'even if your mind is dull: because I, Perialla, the Pythia of Delphi, the voice of Phoebus, sold him.' She laughed again, hysterically.

'I know that Demaratus was deposed, before the Athenian battle at Marathon against the Persians, because it was discovered that he wasn't his father's son.'

'Fool,' hissed the woman, 'it was I who made him a bastard, persuaded by King Cleomenes who hated him and by the gold of Kobon, his Athenian friend.'

Karas listened, wide-eyed. 'Quite a lot of gold; I had never seen so much gold in my whole life . . . and there would have been some for you, too,' she added, shaking her head. 'I've never forgotten Karas the shepherd, who gathered me up exhausted and starving when I escaped from those who had enslaved me.'

'You shouldn't have done it,' murmured Karas, confused.

'Well, I did it, and it seemed that everything would remain hidden . . . nearly four years had passed . . .'

'Kobon,' pondered Karas, 'I remember him. Wasn't he the temple scribe?'

'Yes, your memory serves you well. Kobon was backed by the Athenians, I'm sure. They never pardoned King Demaratus for opposing King Cleomenes, when Cleomenes wanted to punish the Aeginetans who surrendered to the Persians at the time of the battle of Marathon.'

'Then, if I understand you well, the Athenians and Cleomenes plotted together to destroy Demaratus.'

The old woman looked at him with a strange sneer. 'It's possible, Karas, but I don't think that it's very important to either of us anymore. The Council of the Sanctuary has passed judgement: I am cursed. For ever.'

She lifted her head and the metal discs on her band jingled. 'Ousted . . . yes, but they didn't dare put me to death.' Her eyes glittered in the languishing flames of the hearth. 'They are still afraid – of Perialla.'

'You can stay here, if you like,' offered Karas. 'I have the flock—'

'Quiet!' interrupted the woman cupping her ear. 'There's someone outside.' Karas grabbed the club and flung himself out of the door.

'Stop, Karas, it's me!' It was Talos, who had been just about to enter. 'Quick, follow that man,' he said, grasping the arm that brandished the heavy club and pointing to a hooded figure that was running towards the edge of the clearing. They rushed after him in pursuit, and Karas had almost caught up with him, but the hooded man managed to spring into a dense thicket and Karas quickly lost his tracks. Talos arrived, panting.

'Damn this leg! I could have had him, but I tripped.

Just then you burst out of the cabin and nearly smashed my head in with that tree you've got in your hand.'

'I'm sorry, Talos, but in the dark like that . . . Who was it?'

'I don't know; a Spartan, maybe. I was on my way up here because a strange old woman—'

'I know,' Karas interrupted him.

'Well, halfway up the trail, I saw him come out of the forest and so I started to follow him. Unfortunately, I had to stay quite far behind him, because the path is full of dry leaves and twigs and I didn't want to make any noise. The man came as far as the cabin and seemed to be eavesdropping at the window. I crept nearer and nearer until I could jump at him, but in the dark I tripped on a dry branch; he twisted free as I fell to the ground, and got away. What I don't understand is why your dog didn't attack him.'

'That little bastard ran off again tonight. It's mating season; by now he'll be whining around some penned-up bitch on heat.'

They came through the door, still open wide, but Talos stopped at the threshold, perplexed by the vision of the old woman who had spoken to him down at the clearing, sitting calmly next to the fire.

'The young wolf,' she said without turning. 'I knew that he would come.'

'Right,' said Karas. 'But before the wolf there was a Spartan snake, and he was spying on us.'

'I had noticed something,' said the old woman, 'but my mind is foggy these days. I don't see clearly anymore.'

'Come right in, Talos,' said Karas to the young man who stood timidly near the door. 'This woman is not your enemy. She can do great good or great evil, depending how her heart is inclined, but you must not fear her. One day you will know who she really is. She is going to stay with me now, because she has no place to go, and fortune has dealt her a hard blow.'

'Come forward,' said the woman, still not turning to face him.

Talos went to the other side of the hearth and sat down on the floor, on one of the mats. The woman's face, just barely illuminated by the glowing embers, was spectral. Her grey eyes fixed him from beneath nearly closed eyelids.

'There is something terrible in him,' she said suddenly, turning to Karas, 'but I can't understand what it is.'

Talos was startled; how could this woman speak in such a way? Who was she? He had never seen anyone like her.

The old woman closed her eyes, then took something from her sack and threw it on the embers, liberating a thick cloud of dense, aromatic smoke.

'Perialla, no!' exclaimed Karas. The woman didn't even look at him, but leaned forward over the hearth, inhaling the vapours. She grasped the staff that she held by her side, and began shaking it rhythmically, jingling the rattles.

Talos felt drunk, as if a strong wine had gone to his head.

Perialla panted, shaken by tremors. Her limbs stiffened and her forehead beaded with sweat. Suddenly a lament broke forth from her, as if a blade had penetrated her breast:

'Powerful gods!' she shrieked. 'Powerful gods, let

Perialla see!' She collapsed, her head bent forward, gasping. Suddenly she stood up, leaning on her staff, and opened her eyes. They were fixed, staring, glassy. A distant howl, in the wood. The woman started: 'Your sign . . . O Lord of the Wolves, Phoebus, Perialla hears you . . . Perialla sees . . .'

She began to shake the rattles, intoning a strange cant as the two men, in silence, watched her spellbound, unable to move a finger. In the confused sing-song, words began to surface like branches of a tree in a sea of fog, and then the words tied in, one with another:

'The dragon and the wolf first
with merciless hate
wound each other.
Then, when the lion of Sparta
falls pierced, tamed by the javelin
hurled by the long-maned Mede,
He who trembled takes up the sword,
the herd-keeper grips the curved bow,
Together to immortal glory running . . .'

Perialla closed her eyes and fell quiet. Then, again, she began rattling on the staff in her hand. That strange, even sing-song poured out of her mouth, a cant that began sweet and low, then became hard, strident.

The prophetess seemed to be searching for something in her voice. Restless, terrible thoughts flashed through her eyes and crossed her forehead, which wrinkled violently as if racked by painful contractions. Her eyes seemed to stare into a void, and then suddenly came to rest on Talos' face. Words suddenly spilt forth:

'Shining glory like the sun sets.
He turns his back to the people of bronze
when Enosigeus shakes Pelops' land.
He closes his ears to the cry of his blood
when the powerful voice of his heart
calls him to the city of the dead.'

Then, exhausted, she crumbled to the ground with a low moan.

From that day, destiny began to fulfil itself. Perialla disappeared as she had arrived, although the figure of the wandering old prophetess lived on for years in the stories of the mountain shepherds.

The deception uncovered, King Cleomenes was deposed for having procured the exile of Demaratus. Cleomenes left Sparta one day at dusk, wrapped in his cloak, on the back of his black thoroughbred.

He was joined by some of his loyal friends, among them Krathippos, master of Pelias and Talos. The peasant and his daughter were forced to abandon the farm to follow their master to a distant land.

And so one summer evening Talos, alone in the court-yard, watched Antinea go off with her father, riding on the back of an ass. He continued his waving, both hands in the air, until her image dissolved behind a veil of scalding tears.

He felt his heart close up like a wounded hedgehog: never again would any woman seem beautiful or desirable in his eyes.

He returned to his mountain as the city of Sparta paid honour to the new King, Leonidas, son of Anaxandridas of the race of Hercules.

7

THE GREAT KING

DEMARATUS SAT IN THE ANTECHAMBER of the grandiose Hall of Apadana, morosely watching the enamelled door flanked by two enormous soldiers of the Immortal Guard. Behind that door was the throne of the Great King Xerxes, son of Darius the Great, who would soon receive him.

He watched the Carthaginian ambassador leave the room, wrapped in a beautiful purple mantle fringed in gold, followed by two dignitaries with jewel-studded mitres on their heads. They spoke excitedly among themselves in their incomprehensible language, with a decidedly satisfied air. Demaratus looked at his worn boots with a bitter smile, grasped his sword and adjusted his grey wool cloak on his shoulders, draping it as best he could. He took under his arm his crested helmet, the only remaining sign of his past royalty, and stood: the moment had arrived. He opened the door and was met by the chamberlain and the interpreter, a Greek from Halicarnassus.

'O Demaratus, the Great King awaits you,' he announced. The Spartan followed them through a door that two guards were just opening. As he entered the room, he was dazzled by the splendid marbles, the multi-coloured enamel, the gold and precious stones, the carpets. He would never have imagined that so much wealth could exist in a single place. A canopy at the back of the room crowned the throne of Xerxes, his long beard curled, the mitre of gold on his head and the ivory gem-encrusted sceptre in his right hand. Behind him, two servants slowly waved large ostrich-feather fans. A cheetah, lazily licking its fur at the foot of the step, abruptly raised his small head to stare at the small advancing group.

They stopped at the foot of the throne; the Greek interpreter and the chamberlain prostrated themselves, faces to the ground. Demaratus remained standing and greeted the king with a nod of his head. The king shot him an irritated glance as the chamberlain, his face still to the ground barked something at the Greek interpreter who, twisting his head to one side, whispered frantically, 'You must prostrate yourself, now, kneel down and touch the ground with your forehead.' Demaratus, impassive, fixed the Great King with a steady gaze.

'Don't be a fool,' hissed the interpreter as the chamberlain continued to bark insistent orders in his incomprehensible language.

Demaratus regarded him with a sneer, and then turned to the visibly enraged sovereign, still as motionless as a statue in the solemnity of his heavy regal garments. 'I am Demaratus, son of Ariston, King of the Spartans,' he said. 'I come grateful for your benevolence and driven by necessity and misfortune, but not for this shall I prostrate myself at your feet, sire. It is a custom of all Spartans, free men, never to prostrate themselves before anyone.' He silently regarded the King of Kings.

The Greek interpreter, at a sign from the master of ceremonies who stood at the steps, scrambled to his feet along with the chamberlain, and hurriedly translated Demaratus' words, not without a tremor in his voice. It was the first time, in his long career of docile and punctual servitude, that he had had to translate a refusal for his master's ears. A long moment of embarrassment followed. Even the slow, steady movement of the fans ceased for an instant. Xerxes and Demaratus faced each other for endless moments, as the chamberlain, pale as a sheet, felt his bowels melting within his fat, flaccid belly.

The King of Kings spoke. 'O Demaratus, no man would certainly ever be allowed to challenge our majesty as you have done! But it is our will that you know that we consider you King of the Spartans and as a king, close to us. And thus we comprehend that you are king: even under misfortune, you have not bent your head.'

The interpreter and the chamberlain breathed sighs of relief, hardly believing their own ears. Demaratus bowed his head as a sign of gratitude. The Great King continued, 'Tell us, O Demaratus, who are these Spartans, for their name is not known to us.'

Demaratus was startled; it seemed impossible that the Persian monarch could ignore the existence of the most powerful nation of Hellas! He answered, 'O my Lord, the Spartans are the strongest and most valorous of the Greeks. No one can match them in war, and no one can tame them. They have no master above them but the law, in front of which all are equal, even the kings.'

Xerxes arched his right eyebrow. The chamberlain realized, even before hearing the translation, that what this foreigner had said literally astonished the sovereign, who could comprehend Greek well, despite the fact that he used an interpreter for reasons of etiquette and to ensure flawless understanding. Xerxes made a gesture and the master of ceremonies brought a bench with a purple cushion to seat Demaratus. Then he spoke again:

'We do not know these Spartans that you speak of. We would like to believe your words, even if this is difficult for us. We do know, however, the Athenians. They are the most impious of men, and they dared to bring aid to our Ionian subjects when they rebelled. We have decided to punish them so that their ruin shall serve as an example: so that no one, ever again, shall dare to challenge our power.

'All the Greeks of the continent and of the islands must recognize our authority and never think again of rebellion. You know these peoples better than anyone and you can be of great help to us. This is our belief and our desire.'

The king fell silent. The master of ceremonies waited for the interpreter to finish and then nodded to the chamberlain, who invited Demaratus to exit with him. The audience was over, and the Spartan took leave of the sovereign with another nod of his head, turned and walked towards the door accompanied by the two dignitaries.

The corridors rang under the nailed boots of the King of Sparta.

*

In the years that followed, the couriers of the Great King galloped across every province of the immense empire, calling their men to arms. The rajas of far-away India, the satraps of Bactria, Sogdiana, Arakosia, Media, Arabia,

Lydia, Cappadocia and Egypt began to enrol warriors. In the ports of Ionia and Phoenicia, hundreds of vessels were brought into shipyards, while whole forests were cut down in Lebanon and on the Taurus mountains to furnish the necessary wood. Xerxes' strategists were defining the great plan for the invasion of Europe.

The direction of march cut directly through Thrace and Macedon; these kingdoms were promptly forced into submission. The engineers of Ionia drew up a project for a bridge built on boats that would allow the great army to pass the strait of Hellespont and cut across the isthmus of the Chalcidice peninsula. This would spare the fleet the rounding of the promontory of Mount Athos, full of dangerous surface reefs. All of Asia was preparing to spill out onto Greece; a tide of foot soldiers and horsemen would create a new province, obedient and subjugated to the King of Susa. Or leave a desert scattered with smoking ruins.

The news of these preparations reached Greece with the first ships that springtime brought to the ports of Athens, Aegina and Gytheum. Not that such news was heeded at first: in Sparta internal affairs had been occupying the attention of its rulers. The news had spread that King Cleomenes, enraged at having been convicted and driven out of his city, was gathering allies in Arcadia and Messenia and that he was even considering marching against his own country. Alarmed, the ephors decided to call him back in an attempt to restore control, offering to reinstate his royal dignity.

Aristarkhos and his son Brithos went with a few friends to receive the king when he returned one summer afternoon. Cleomenes was transformed by the passage of years and by his long-nurtured rage. He descended from his horse, removing his crested helmet, and looked around him. He could count the few who had remained faithful. So this is how it is to be, he thought. The old lion has returned only to end up in the trap. But perhaps he was too tired to fight back this time. He grasped the extended hand of Aristarkhos, who kissed him on his bristled cheek.

'We all rejoice at your return, sire, and we offer you the force of our arms and the faith of our hearts.'

The king lowered his eyes to the ground, and murmured, 'Great is your valour, Aristarkhos. You do not fear to show yourself friend of he who has been unfortunate, but take care of yourself and your family. These are times of deception and wickedness. Courage and valour seem to be disappearing from this city.'

He turned down the street that led to his house, abandoned for years. As he passed, doors closed as people scurried quickly into their homes. When he reached his abode, he found five ephors awaiting him. The eldest, bowing slightly, handed him the sceptre. 'Greetings to you, O Cleomenes, son of Anaxandridas. We render you the sceptre of your father.'

The king barely acknowledged them. He walked through the door into his house. He took off his dusty royal cloak, tossing it onto a stool, and sat down, dropping his white head between his hands. He heard a footstep behind him but didn't turn, preparing himself for the thrust of a dagger between his shoulders. Instead he heard a voice that was well known to him:

'I render homage to my king and greet my brother.'

'Leonidas, you?'

'Yes, me. Are you surprised, then, to see me?'

'No, I'm not. But I would have preferred to see you a little while ago, together with the friends who received me at my arrival. From your hands I would have wished to receive the sceptre of our forefathers, not from that poisonous snake out there.'

'Cleomenes, you shouldn't have come back. Everyone knows that you convinced the Pythia of Delphi to prophesy against Demaratus. The ephors have called you back out of fear alone. Unless—'

'I know. Unless this is a trap to eliminate me once and for all; I realized that when I arrived. Almost no one came to meet me, besides Aristarkhos and Brithos and a few friends. Not even you. But I understand that. The city was already celebrating you as king and my return means—'

'It doesn't mean what you think at all,' interrupted Leonidas. 'I never aspired to succession; I would have been preceded by my unfortunate brother Dorieus, who now lies in the distant land of Sicily, buried among barbarian peoples. When you left, my soul was sad and I didn't have the courage to speak to you: I feared that you would think what I see you are thinking now.'

Cleomenes listened, absorbed, as he traced odd signs in the ashes of the hearth. He lifted his head, in the dim light, gazing at Leonidas' face with its short copper-coloured beard.

'I am grateful for your words, Leonidas. This is a moment of supreme bitterness for me and destiny announces itself darkly to my eyes. In moments such as these, the word of a friend is the only remedy. Listen to me, though, listen well: for Cleomenes all is finished. I know this now, although before I arrived here I still nurtured a few illusions. Something is being prepared for me, and perhaps this is only right; wasn't I, after all, he who dared profane the holiness of the temple and insult the god of Delphi? If a curse is upon me, I will not try to escape my fate. But you must not see me again. The sceptre of Anaxandridas will soon be back in your hand. And you will no longer have to grasp mine, the impious hand of he whom the gods have banished from their presence.' Leonidas tried to interrupt him.

'No, listen,' continued Cleomenes, 'you must do as I say, and Aristarkhos must do the same. Tell him that I highly regard his friendship and his courage, but he has a son, a valorous warrior, worthy of the glory of his father. I don't want his future to be stained for having helped me, or for having been my friend. Cleomenes must remain alone, from now on, to face his destiny. There are no other roads for me to take.'

He rose to his feet. 'Farewell, Leonidas. You will remember one day that I didn't hesitate to sell my own soul for the good of my city and for all the Greeks. I did not hesitate to sanction a lie, had it only served to eliminate Demaratus. He has defended the friends of the Persians, of the barbarians, and now I know for certain that he has appealed to the Great King himself. But nothing of this matters, now. It has been written that Cleomenes must die, defamed, in his own city.'

Leonidas gazed into the tired eyes of the old warrior: what remained of the terrible destroyer, of the cold, lucid mind capable of conceiving daring battle plans and executing them from one moment to the next? He felt deep pity for that man his father had generated with another woman, and yet whom he had always admired, if not loved as a true brother.

'Perhaps you are right,' he said. 'Few men have the courage to challenge the gods, and you were one of them, Cleomenes. I will do as you say, so that other wounds do not fester on the body of Sparta. Difficult moments await the city. Farewell, O King of ours. I know that you will do nothing that would tarnish your repute as a warrior. In your veins runs the blood of Hercules.' He left the room, stopping for a moment at the door, his back to the blinding light of the street. He then disappeared into the deserted city.

The end of Cleomenes was appalling. It was said that he had begun to drink in the style of the barbarians from the north: great quantities of straight wine, not mixed with water in the Greek fashion. It was said that he was losing his wits – that he had begun to hate everyone, and that he struck with his sceptre anyone he met on the street. The ephors declared that the city could no longer tolerate this shame; he was taken and tied to a stump in one of the city squares. There the king was a helpless target for his enemies' scorn. On his knees, his wrists torn by the chains, his clothing in rags, he implored passers-by for death. One morning, shortly before dawn, he managed to incapacitate the Helot who as a final insult had been ordered to guard him, by stunning him with his chains when he was asleep. He got hold of the man's dagger, and began to slash away at his body: his legs, his thighs, his hips. Some said that they heard him shrieking in the silence of the morning; others claimed that their houses rang with a prolonged, insane, chilling laugh. The Helot, regaining consciousness, saw the king collapse into a pool of blood, never dropping his fiery gaze, grinding his teeth in an atrocious grimace. The king once more turned the dagger against himself and sliced open his abdomen.

Thus died Cleomenes, son of Anaxandridas, besmirching the face of his city with his blood and his own tortured flesh.

*

Talos, hearing that Cleomenes had returned, hoped to see Antinea again, but he was quickly disappointed. He learned that Krathippos, not daring to return so soon to Sparta, had decided to stay at his estate in Messenia, keeping Pelias and his daughter with him. As much as Talos tried, he could learn nothing more, until one day some Messenian shepherds reported that old Pelias was living in near poverty farming a rocky field, and that the girl worked hard all day to lighten her father's load. She wanted Talos to know that she hadn't forgotten him and that her heart would never belong to another man. It was Karas who told him all this; he had heard it from the shepherds. Karas urged him not to despair: one day, perhaps, the two of them would return to their farm on the plain. But in Talos' mind, only pain lay in hoping.

In Krathippos' absence, Talos continued to turn over his harvest every year to the overseer. He went hunting, when he could, with Karas, and he took care of his mother. The tumultuous events of his early youth seemed far away, and every day that passed made him more like the other mountain shepherds. The secret of which he was the only repository lay at the bottom of his soul covered by a kind of oblivion, like a useless object forgotten at the bottom of an abandoned well.

Rumours that the Great King was mustering troops in Asia began to filter as far as the mountain, rippling the Helots' monotonous existence, arousing first curiosity and then worry. They wondered if the war would ever really reach them, if the King of Persia would truly bring his troops across the sea. The women especially were agitated at these rumours, dreading the day their men would have to depart with the Spartan warriors, abandoning their homes, their fields, their flocks. To face only fatigue, hunger, thirst – terrible hardships without any advantage for them, without even hope. For these people, already oppressed by the burden they carried each day, the possibility of war was a nightmare.

In the last war, fought against the Argives by King Cleomenes, the Helots has suffered greatly, and lost many lives, but at least they were close to their own homes. If the Great King really arrived in Hellas, no one could tell where the armies would have to close ranks, or how long the conflict would last. They were not really concerned about who would win. In any case, nothing would change for the wretched Helots: new victors would certainly not consent to the removal of the heavy yoke that they were forced to bear.

Three years passed, and then news arrived that the forces of the Great King, incredibly numerous, were beginning to concentrate near Sardeis, in Lydia, ready to march against Hellas.

Messages from all corners of Greece reached Sparta, and in turn were sent in all directions. Mobilization and state of alarm: harbingers of war. King Leonidas and King Leotychidas departed one autumn morning with their entourage, headed for Corinth. There on the isthmus, near the great temple of Poseidon, they would meet with representatives from a multitude of city states to devise a common plan of defence. The two sovereigns knew the line of thought of the ephors, the elders and the popular assembly: they were to insist that the lines of defence be drawn up right on the isthmus itself, so as to protect the Peloponnese from the invading army. They were also fully aware, however, that the Athenians, the Plataeans and the Phocians would request that the confederate troops close ranks at the Thermopylae pass, in order to defend central Hellas as well.

In the hall of the Corinthian council sat the representatives of the thirty-one Hellenic states that had decided to join forces against the Great King. When the two Kings of Sparta entered, the guards stiffened in salute, presenting their arms. King Leonidas and King Leotychidas took their places at the seats reserved for them. The hall was nearly full, and the Corinthian representative took the floor to open the assembly. He read the treaty that they would all sign, declaring that complete agreement would reign among them for the entire period of the war against the barbarians. He announced the recall of all political exiles and the constitution of a confederate army. The high command was offered to Sparta.

King Leonidas and King Leotychidas would lead the ground troops. Navarch Eurybiades would be supreme commander of the naval armada, although the great majority of the vessels had been supplied by the Athenians. The Corinthian magistrate announced that the Corcyraeans had joined the alliance and that they would also send their fleet. Syracuse, the powerful Sicilian city, had refused. Their tyrant Gelo had demanded the high command of the army, or at least of the fleet, neither of which could be conceded to him. Informers had already been sent to Asia, to Sardeis, to learn precise facts about the enemy army, the actual size of which was frequently questioned. Some, in fact, maintained that the stories that had reached them were utterly absurd.

Until that moment all went well. The mood was certainly not relaxed, but it was clear that a common cause animated all of the delegates: the will to withstand the enemy invasion. Difficulties arose when operational decisions had to be made. King Leotychidas seemed inflexible on one point: the main line of defence had to be on the isthmus, where a triple barrier wall had been under construction for some time already. Even if the rest of Hellas were forced to capitulate, a counter-attack could still be prepared from the Peloponnese. His arguments were based largely on his claim that there was no other position so easily defendable north of the isthmus.

This was not true; the Athenian delegate, Themistocles, son of Neocles, rose to his feet immediately to take the floor in protest. He was doubtless a man different from all the rest. His words were incisive, dry, sometimes cutting. His arguments were cogent. As he spoke, King Leonidas listened with great attention, not missing a word of what was said. He began to realize that the Greeks needed Athenian brilliance just as much as Spartan force.

Themistocles concluded, 'For these reasons, gentlemen, it is imperative that the line of defence be prepared at the Thermopylae. This pass is not only the door to Attica, as I have heard said today in this hall, but the door to all of Hellas; by defending the Thermopylae, we are also defending the Peloponnese. We must take into account,' he added, 'that if Athens were to be overrun by barbarians or if we were forced to surrender . . .' Leonidas shifted position in his seat, and shot a knowing glance at the other king.

'Well,' continued Themistocles, 'if Athens were no longer in the picture, who would defend your coasts from a Persian landing? What good are the fortifications that are being feverishly constructed along the isthmus if there is not a fleet behind them to defend them? The enemy could land an army in any part of Laconia, of Argolis, of Messenia; they could even land contingents at several points and oblige you to split up as they conduct the final attack with the bulk of their forces. As valorous as they are, not even the Spartans,' the orator continued heatedly, turning directly to the two Spartan kings seated in front of him, 'could hope to repel the attack of all of Asia without the aid of a fleet.'

This gave the Kings of Sparta no choice but to promise to send troops to the Thermopylae. They were not able to commit, however, to the intervention of the entire Peloponnesian army. They knew well, in fact, that the ephors and the elders would never consent to send all of the Spartiate warriors outside of the Peloponnese.

When all of the orators had finished speaking, the doors of the great hall were opened and the priests entered for the pledging ceremony. The confederates swore, by the god of Delphi, not to retreat from the war until the last barbarian had ceased to tread Greek ground; they swore to punish all those Greeks who might betray their own blood by aiding the Persians.

The delegates left at dusk, each returning to his own home. King Leonidas and King Leotychidas spent the night in Corinth, to discuss with the city magistrates details concerning coordination of the war operations, troop enlistment and preparation of the battleships that would move alongside the confederate fleet.

After a modest dinner, Leonidas had retired to the house that the city government had put at his disposal, when the guard at the entrance announced that a man had arrived and desired to have a word with him: it was Themistocles, the Athenian admiral.

'Enter,' said the sovereign, inviting him in. 'You are welcome in this house.' The Athenian sat down, arranging the white pallium on his arms. 'What is the reason for your visit?'

'Sire, I am here to acquaint you with the occurrence of some very serious events that could severely damage our cause.'

The king looked at him, alarmed. 'What exactly are you speaking of?'

'I have learned that, beyond a doubt, the nations of the centre and north are preparing to surrender to the Great King, or, in any case, to collaborate with him. That's not all: the oracle of Delphi is on their side. Do you know the response given to delegates of my city who went to consult the oracle?'

'I heard that the prophecy was discouraging, but I don't know the exact content.'

'Discouraging to say the least,' went on the Athenian, stroking his beard. 'The oracle prophesied frightening misfortune for the city, destruction and grief without end, if the Athenians dared to defy the Medes. The delegates were so disheartened that they would not return to the city. They turned back and asked the oracle for another response. It was then that the oracle offered me the way to save the city from despair and panic. The words that the Pythia professed this time were no less terrible, but at the end she added that the city could defend itself by elevating a rampart of wood. An absurdity absolutely without any significance, but to the people of Athens I interpreted it as meaning that our only salvation could be a great fleet of battleships.'

Leonidas looked at him, surprised. 'You are more clever than Odysseus himself,' he said, 'but what you tell me is very alarming indeed; do you really believe that the oracle is not acting in good faith?'

Themistocles fell into a troubled silence; it seemed too obvious to remind Leonidas of how King Cleomenes had convinced the Pythia Perialla to deny the legitimate birth of Demaratus. When King Leonidas lowered his head, visibly confused, he understood that there was no need to mention this.

'I am absolutely certain of it,' responded the Athenian admiral. 'As you know, the nations of the north control the Council of the Sanctuary of Delphi with an absolute majority of votes. There is only one way we can oppose or neutralize this policy. There would be no end to the trouble if we were marked as adversaries of the god, or as heedless of the wisdom of oracles. We must clearly let our allies know that we have nothing against the sanctuary, but emphasize the part of our oath that declares that traitors will be punished and forced to pay a tithe to the temple of Apollo.

'We must come to terms with the Thessalians, the Boeotians, the Perrhaebians and the Enianians, without counting the Macedonians. King Amyntas of Macedonia is on our side, but his position is unsustainable. He could not resist for a single day alone. The Great King could camp his troops in central Greece, and from there attack us unchecked, confident in the submission and the collaboration of the traitors. If only for this reason, it is absolutely necessary that your government be convinced to marshal all available troops at the Thermopylae.'

The King of Sparta, having listened carefully, answered, 'I agree with your words, O Themistocles, and you may be sure that I will do all that is in my power to convince the ephors and the elders, but you know well that my authority has its limits. Rest assured that I will be present at the Thermopylae, in any case.'

'This alone is a great thing, sire,' said Themistocles. 'And I return content to my city knowing that King Leonidas is not only a valorous warrior, but also a wise and generous man. Your word is of great value to me, so much that I wish to exchange promises with you, as two men may exchange hospitable gifts. You may be certain that when King Leonidas has drawn up at the Thermopylae, Themistocles will be at your shoulders, to protect you from the sea, and that I would rather pay with my own life than dishonour this oath. And now,' he said, rising, 'we all have need of rest: may the night be propitious for you, O King Leonidas.'

'And favourable also to you, Athenian guest,' said the king, rising to accompany Themistocles to the door.

At that moment a horse was heard galloping on the cobbled street. Almost immediately, they heard a whinny and low voices outside the door. A knock, and the guard entered.

'Sire, a messenger asks to see you immediately.'

'Let him enter,' said the king. A man covered with dust and obviously exhausted came into the room, offered Leonidas a leather scroll, gave him a military salute and departed. The king opened the scroll and quickly skimmed its contents. Themistocles saw him grow pale.

'Is it serious?'

'The elders have consulted the oracle about the war we are about to undertake, and the response has arrived.' He began to read slowly:

> 'You inhabitants of wide-roaded Sparta,
> Either your great illustrious fortress
> Devastated will be by the Persians, or a king of
> The race of Hercules, if destroyed it is not,
> Dead will you mourn for.'

Themistocles drew closer, and took the king's arm. 'Don't take any heed of this, Leonidas, the oracle is openly in favour of the Persians. Do not give weight to those words.'

Leonidas regarded him with an absorbed expression. 'Perhaps what you say is true, Athenian guest, but the gods, at times, can make the truth heard even from the mouths of evil-doers.'

He opened the door that led to the street. 'At the beginning of spring I will be at the Thermopylae,' he said in a firm voice. The Athenian nodded and, after shaking his hand, departed, pulling his white cloak close. On the street, gusts of cold wind made the dry leaves of the plane trees spin.

8

THE LION OF SPARTA

MEANWHILE, ON THE DISTANT banks of the Hellespont, thousands and thousands of men worked feverishly under the direction of the architects of the Great King, on the bridge that would join Asia to Europe. The enormous task had to be finished before the bad weather started.

Two anchorage cables, each fifteen stadia long – one made of linen by the Phoenicians, the other of papyrus by the Egyptians – were fixed onto the Asiatic coast. Each was towed by two warships to the coast of Europe, where they were inserted into the grooves of two immense pulleys and stretched tight. They were then lifted from the water to the necessary height, using sixty pairs of oxen and twenty pairs of horses.

The ships that would support the base of the bridge, a platform made of bundled sticks covered by compacted soil, were drawn up between the cables. At the end, the engineers and the architects of the Great King admired their work with satisfaction, but their joy was short-lived: when the season changed, an impetuous north wind drove a violent sea-storm against the bridge, and they realized that an error had been committed. The bridge was perpendicular to the direction of the wind and current.

The linen cable, being heavier than the papyrus cable,

was soon soaked with water and this put the whole structure hugely off balance. The bridge anchors were uprooted, and the breakers soon swept away the marvellous construction. The Great King, enraged, ordered that the sea be flogged with many canes and that these words be pronounced as the punishment was performed:

> O bitter waters, the Great King inflicts this
>   punishment upon you
> Because you offended him without having suffered
>   any offence from him,
> And rightly you are not offered sacrifices,
>   O contemptible current, turbid and salty.

The architects were arrested and decapitated so that those who followed them would be more careful about fulfilling their duties. And so they were. The bridge was rebuilt in the spring; the cables of papyrus and linen were made four, and alternated so that the weight was perfectly balanced. The position of the ground anchors was changed so that the bridge was parallel to the direction of the current, and the cables remained permanently stretched tight. The length of the linen which held the anchors on the sea bed was changed to correspond to the force of the north wind and the westerly winds that blew in the spring.

Three hundred and sixty triremes and light warships were moored between the cables. Tree trunks were sawed to the exact measurement and placed on the ships to support the compacted earth. Reed and wicker screens were built into the sides of the bridge as parapets so that the horses would not be frightened by the sea's waves.

When the storks began to appear in the skies of the

Troad and Bithynia the work was finished and the vast army of Xerxes was put into motion.

The Medes, the Kisseans, the Hyrcanians, and the Assyrians crossed over the bridge with their conical helmets and heavy iron-clad clubs, followed by the Scythians with their small hirsute horses from the steppe. The Bactrians came next, their faces burnt from the sun of Paropamisus, and then the Indians with their bamboo spears and tattooed skin. The Parthians and Korasmians crossed with their long scimitars, and so did the Caspians with their heavy goatskin mantles. Next came the curly-haired Ethiopians, dressed in lion- and leopard-skins, armed with long iron-tipped assegais, the Sogdianians from the southern deserts, the Arabs on their dromedaries, wrapped in wide capes, and then still Libyans, Cappadocians, Phrygians, Mysians, Thracians, Mosynoecians, Egyptians, Paphlagonians and Colchians.

They marched past for days and days, until at the very end came the Immortals, the guard of Xerxes. There were ten thousand of them, wearing long fringed tunics, their arms adorned with gold and silver bracelets, long bows and quivers across their backs. They were the cream of the Persian army: extremely tall, valorous and unswervingly faithful to their sovereign to the very end.

From his ebony throne, the Great King watched them march past; not even he himself had realized how many peoples lived within the confines of his vast empire. On the European coast, a crowd of shepherds and farmers who lived in the villages of the area gathered along the beach to watch the spectacle with incredlous eyes.

In the meantime, from the ports of Ionia and Phoenicia

arrived the various squads that were to form the magnificent fleet that would back up and supply provisions for the army on its long march over land. The population of the coast saw the vessels of Tyre, Sidon, Byblos, Aradus, Joppa and Ascalon pass before them, and the long rostrated ships of Halicarnassus, Cnidus, Smyrna, Samos, Chios, Cyprus, and Phocaea, advancing majestically with unfurled sails, the banners and ensigns of the admirals fluttering on the stern yards.

The first news of the crossing arrived quickly at the general headquarters of King Leonidas and King Leotychidas, who immediately put the Peloponnesian army on a state of alert, and began to amass troops near the Corinthian isthmus. Meanwhile, from the ports of Peiraeus, Aegina and Corinth itself arrived the battleships meant to block the passage of the fleet of the Persian king.

From the quarterdeck of the admiral ship, Themistocles contemplated his superb newly formed squad as they weighed anchor amidst a confusion of calls to order and shouted commands. Drum beats provided the rowing tempo for hundred of sailors below deck at the long oars. One by one, the splendid triremes, jewels of Athenian naval art, left port. Low on the surface of the water, long and sleek to take advantage of both wind power and rowing force, their sharp rams were bolted to the keel's master beam so as to break through any bulwark without damaging the ship's forward structure.

Engineers had designed and built formidable machines that would not be easy to defeat or destroy. Crews had been training for the most daring and dangerous manoeuvres since the summer, the oarsmen had skinned their hands and broken their backs with fatigue, but thousands of hands now moved in absolute synchrony, obedient to the commands of their crew-masters.

In Sparta, the ephors and the elders met with the two kings to decide on a plan of action. All agreed that the Spartiate army should not be risked outside of the Peloponnese. Their only concession was a single contingent of Peloponnesians for the Thermopylae: King Leonidas would be allowed to take only three hundred Spartiates with him. As hard as he tried, the sovereign was not able to obtain a single man more. Not even King Leotychidas, close as he was to the ephors and elders, would back him.

And so Leonidas personally chose the three hundred Spartiates who would follow him to the Thermopylae. Among them were almost all of the members of the twelfth *syssitia* of the third battalion: Aghias, Brithos, Kleandridas, Kresilas and the other young warriors accepted the call with enthusiasm, eager to be pitted directly against the enemy. No thought of their likelihood of survival against an army as vast as that of the Great King even crossed their minds.

King Leonidas also wanted Aristarkhos, Brithos' father, with him. Both his valour as a warrior, and his experience and wisdom would prove invaluable. Thus father and son found themselves in the same contingent departing for the north.

The mountain people received the news of imminent enrolment and finally realized that they were no longer dealing with rumours. The war had already begun and they too had to prepare for departure. A herald came one morning to the great clearing and proclaimed that all able-bodied Helots must report for enlistment. And so, even Talos had to say goodbye to his mother and join the others down on the plain.

When they reached the city they would be chosen by the Spartan warriors, one by one, to serve as attendants and porters. Talos was sure that he wouldn't be chosen; his deformity would be sure to make them pass him over: no warrior would want a crippled Helot with him.

The Helots were conducted into the great square of the House of Bronze and arranged in three lines. The Spartan warriors, in formation opposite them, left the ranks one by one in order of seniority to select their own servants and squires. Finally it was the youngest warriors' turn to choose. Talos, petrified, watched Brithos leave the ranks. He crossed the square and began to move down the line until he was directly in front of Talos. Brithos recognized him and fixed him with a mocking expression that made his blood turn to ice. The young Spartan turned to the recruitment officer and said, 'I want this one.'

'But, Brithos,' said the officer, drawing closer, 'are you really sure? Can't you see that he's lame? Leave him for the baggage carriers. Your personal attendant must be both strong and quick.'

'Don't worry,' answered Brithos. 'This one is strong enough, believe me.'

And so Talos was cast once again into the centre of the whirlwind after having lived for years in peace, if not in happiness.

Going towards the camp that had been set up near the city, he thought with consuming melancholy of Antinea: it had been years since he'd seen her, and perhaps now he'd never see her again. And of his mother, who was still hoping to see him return to their home on Mount Taygetus.

He thought of his grandfather Kritolaos in his tomb covered with oak leaves on the edge of the forest, and poor Krios – all over. Torn from his home, his people, his mother, he was completely alone now and practically at the complete mercy of his worst enemy. He tried to summon up his courage and not feel defeated. The most important thing was survival, and certainly his young master would have enough to concern himself with, if what he had heard was true.

And so, the moment of departure came without anything happening in particular. He saw Brithos only a few times: when he went to the *syssitia* to get his equipment, and when he came to camp to give instructions for the journey. Talos was busy applying new leather straps to the inside of his master's shield. Brithos entered, took off his cuirass, put it into a corner, and went to sit on a low stool. 'Is everything ready?' he asked, without looking at Talos.

'Yes, sir, everything is ready. I've changed these leather straps because they were worn out. The weapon has to be worn close to the arm.'

Brithos fixed him with a questioning gaze. 'You know a lot of things for a shepherd who has never come down off the mountain.'

'The elders of my people taught me everything that I needed to know to do this work.'

'The elders of your people must have taught you some other things, too,' continued Brithos, watching him intently. 'You know full well what I'm talking about. I haven't forgotten, even if years have passed since then, and I don't think you have either.'

'No, sir,' responded Talos dryly, continuing his work, 'I haven't forgotten.'

'I see that the lesson we gave you must have erased certain ideas from your mind. It looks that way, at least. But,' he continued, removing his shin-plates, 'there's still something about you that doesn't quite convince me. So, when I saw you in the square alongside the other Helots, I decided to find out what it was.'

'There's nothing to find out, sir,' murmured Talos, without lifting his eyes from his work. 'I'm only a poor shepherd.'

'We'll see,' said Brithos coldly. 'Strange things have been happening up on your mountains over the last few years. Only a month ago, a deer was found near the Eurotas; it had come there to die, struck by a strange type of arrow that we Spartans have never used. I have the impression that you may know something about it.'

'You're wrong, sir, I don't know anything. I've only ever taken care of my flock.'

'What's your name?'

'Talos.'

'And do you know who I am?'

'You are Brithos, son of Aristarkhos, Kleomenid.'

Brithos stood and began to walk back and forth in the tent. Suddenly he stopped, his back to Talos.

'And your girl ... yes, the peasant. What ever happened to her?'

'Pelias and his family followed noble Krathippos to Tegea and then to Messenia, I believe.' Talos stood up and when Brithos turned he found the youth directly before him. Talos' jaw was tight and he fixed him with a firm gaze.

'Return to your work, shepherd, there is still much to prepare. We'll be leaving tomorrow.' He threw his short military cape over his shoulders and walked out.

The next day the army drew up in perfect order: the three hundred Spartiates first, four men by eight for each company, with their Peloponnesian allies behind them. Last came the Helot servants with the carts and baggage.

The king, surrounded by his officers, arrived when it was still dark. The mothers of the new warriors walked behind him. The women would officiate at the traditional ceremony of the consignment of the shield. Dressed in white with their heads veiled, they took their places before the formation of hoplites. The trumpets blared, and each young man stepped out of the ranks, advancing two paces. The trumpets sounded again, and they set the shields with the red lambda that they had received from their fathers on the day of their initiation onto the ground before them.

At a signal from the king, the first woman went up to her own son, picked up the shield and slipped it onto his arm. Firm-voiced, she declaimed the traditional formula: 'Come back with this or upon it,' which meant, 'You shall return with your shield, as a victor. Or, should you fall in battle, you shall be brought back upon your own shield.'

Ismene's turn came. The king had paid her a terrible honour, breaking with the custom of never putting all of the males of a family on the battlefield and thus risking the loss of the family name; Leonidas had chosen both husband and son.

Ismene knelt, picked up the shield, and rose to her feet facing her son. The grey light of dawn outlined the boy's dark profile, making the lines of his face seem harder, and for a moment Ismene recognized the expression of the Kleomenid heroes sculpted in cypress wood. She froze, and her voice trembled as she pronounced the formula. The sun appeared behind the mountains as the last of the women returned to her place, and sinister flashes lit up the dark, still group of warriors as they stood before their mothers. With dry eyes, they watched their sons, knowing that they had given birth to mortals. Pain and grief were eternal prisoners in the darkness of their wombs.

The king put the three-crested helmet on his head and gave the signal for departure. Talos listened to the drum roll and then the sound of their pipes: that strange, measured melody that he had heard as a child when he had stolen down to the plain for the first time. The column left the camp and marched down the road for Tegea, heading north.

At the gate of the city, a great crowd had gathered to bid the departing army farewell. The old men, no longer able to bear arms, watched the young warriors with pride: their splendid bronze armour flashing brilliantly now in the sun, their tunics and crimson cloaks, their round shields with the great painted lambda. The eldest of the ephors came forward, and King Leonidas stopped his horse and dismounted. He took off his helmet, freeing his long red hair, and tossed back his cape.

'We salute you, O Leonidas our king,' said the ephor. 'Sparta wishes your victory and awaits your happy return.' An ovation rose from the crowd. The king responded by bowing his head. Putting his helmet back on, he leapt into his saddle and again gave the signal for departure. The roll of drums and the sound of pipes was soon lost in the dust along the road to the north.

Two weeks after their departure Leonidas closed ranks at the pass of the Thermopylae, and immediately gave orders to repair the old wall of fortification that closed the pass. He ordered a group of seven hundred Phocian hoplites who had joined them at the Thermopylae to guard the vulnerable pass of Anopaea, the only route by which the enemy could flank Leonidas' position. He then arranged for the organization of guard duty and distribution of supplies.

Themistocles learned that the Persian fleet, having doubled the Chalcidice peninsula, was headed south. He went to lie in wait at the Artemision promontory, to protect Leonidas from the direction of the sea, as he had promised. At night, from the stern of the admiral ship, he launched signals with a torch and a mirror to keep Leonidas informed of what was happening. One day, as he was inspecting the fortifications, Leonidas saw one of the men who usually patrolled the road of the pass racing towards him at full speed. The guard leapt off his horse and began, panting, to make his report.

'Sire,' he gasped, 'they're coming. Hundreds of thousands of them. The rivers dry up when they cross, their fires light up the horizon at night; no one has ever seen such a great army!' The king immediately gave a series of terse orders. The detachments took their positions in fighting order behind the wall while others remained in front to better survey the situation. They performed gymnastics as they waited, to warm their muscles for the battle. Suddenly, at the top of a hill appeared a Persian horseman. He was easily distinguished by his wide embroidered trousers and by the mitre that he wore on his head. The young Spartiates did not even honour him with a glance, but continued with their exercises as if nothing had happened. The Persian, having observed the scene, spurred his horse and dashed down the hill at a gallop.

'They'll soon be upon us,' said Aristarkhos to Leonidas.

'I think you're right,' responded the king. 'They have no reason to delay.'

Instead, after about an hour, a squad of horses carrying a banner appeared on the road.

'They're not armed,' observed Aristarkhos. 'It must be an envoy.'

He was right. The horsemen slowed to a pace and advanced gradually behind the banner, stopping at the foot of the wall. An interpreter who spoke Greek came forward: 'This is an embassy from Xerxes, the King of Kings, Lord of the Four Corners of the Earth. We wish to speak with your commander.'

Aristarkhos emerged from behind the wall and approached the interpreter, announcing: 'Our commander Leonidas, son of Anaxandridas, King of the Spartans.' He moved aside, and Leonidas came out into the open. The three red crests of his great helmet swayed in the wind that blew from the sea.

The Persian ambassador, wrapped in a mantle of blue byssus, wore the sabre of the Immortals with its finely chiselled golden hilt at his belt.

He haughtily pronounced a long discourse, nodding his head to signify that he had finished. The interpreter, with his sing-song Ionic accent, translated: 'The King of Kings, Xerxes, our Master and Lord of the Four Corners of the Earth, has sent us to say, "O men of Greece, abandon this path. Do not uselessly challenge our ire. All the peoples and all the nations have already surrendered at the mere sight of our soldiers, more numerous than the grains of sand along the seaside. Our desire is to be merciful; we will not take your lives if you surrender, so give up your arms."' He paused for a moment. 'What must I answer?'

King Leonidas, who had remained immobile, staring directly into the Persian's eyes without so much as a glance towards the Greek interpreter, answered in his hard Laconian dialect. 'Our arms? Come and get them.'

The interpreter paled, then translated the answer for the ambassador. The Persian stared, stunned by such as outright challenge. Then, with an irritated gesture, he nodded to his entourage, turned his horse, and went off in a cloud of dust.

A short time later, prostrated before his king, he repeated the answer given him. Demaratus, who was in the royal pavilion, advanced towards the throne saying, 'I warned you, Lord, that even when all the others had submitted, the Spartans would go on fighting.'

The Great King, livid with anger, immediately convened his generals and ordered them to launch the attack: he wanted the Greeks taken alive and brought in chains into his presence. The camp immediately rang out with shouted instructions, trumpets blared the fall-in, and the immense horde began to make its way to the pass.

King Leonidas brought his troops outside the wall. He himself was in the front line on the right wing, Aristarkhos on the left. At a certain point they heard from far off the chilling roll of drums, confused with the neighing of horses and the din made by the iron-rimmed wheels of the war chariots. The gigantic army appeared at the end of the road.

*

The Spartiate warriors, drawn up on the right, pressed close together to create an impenetrable wall of shields, thick with shining spears. With a blood-curdling cry, the Persians suddenly threw themselves into the attack, spilling out onto the Greek front line. The row was terrible: the Persians were used to battling with light weapons and cavalry. Crowded into such a narrow space, they fell by the hundreds, run through by the heavy shafts of the hoplites who were completely protected by their bronze armour.

The combat became frenzied. The Greeks, abandoning their spears as they became unusable, unsheathed their short swords and began battling hand-to-hand. Leonidas' red crest could still be seen above the dense cloud of dust that had risen, as he led his men onwards in a relentless charge. The three hundred warriors had forced a passage through the enemy lines, trampling the heaps of cadavers on ground made slippery by the blood of the fallen.

The Persian commander, realizing that the Greeks were

about to encircle the centre of his formation, gave the order to retreat. Amidst the cries of the wounded and the neighing of the terror-crazed horses, his men began to move back slowly, so as not to totally break up the ranks. Leonidas abruptly also gave an order to retreat, and his men, throwing their shields baldric-wise on their backs, fled quickly towards the wall.

Seeing this, the Persian general assumed that the exhausted enemy intended to withdraw behind the wall, and he shouted out a new order to attack. Encouraged, his men rushed forward in disorderly pursuit, and the order of their formation was soon broken. It was exactly what Leonidas had hoped for; when his men arrived at the wall, they made a swift turnabout, presenting a new front in compact ranks to the enemy.

The Persians arrived headlong in chaotic waves, and they were promptly cut to pieces. Terrified, they attempted a retreat but the officers at their backs drove them on with whips, shouting their orders in a thousand different languages. In that inferno of dust and blood, the solid wall of warriors led by Leonidas advanced, destroying everything in their path. The trumpets finally sounded the retreat, and the soldiers of the Great King, wounded and depleted, abandoned the pass.

King Leonidas turned to his warriors, pulled off his bloody, dented helmet, and launched a cry of victory. He was joined by his men as the rocky gorges of Mount Oeta resounded with their joy.

Talos had watched the whole scene from behind the wall as his companions ran back and forth grabbing blunted weapons and broken spears to be repaired, and bringing new ones to the warriors on the line of combat. When he saw the men at the front double back at a run, he found himself leaning over the bastions; he would eagerly have taken up any arm at hand and leapt into the heat of the fray. He would never have thought that he could be moved by such an impulse! But as the battle unfolded, Talso felt his blood boiling in his veins and an urgent desire to combat among the warriors. He was shaken by his inexplicable enthusiasm for their desperate resistance. He recognized superhuman valour in their magnificent compact formations as they followed the red crest of their king. And greater yet was his anger at not being a part of the fire that enflamed the combatants brought together in defence of the liberty of many nations.

*

The warriors of Sparta, Trachis and Tegea returned behind the wall, filthy and dripping sweat, wounded, limping. The infantrymen from Mantinea and Orchmenus had beards white with dust, their spears broken and shields rent. Talos saw Brithos with his splendid bronze cuirass decorated in copper, and with him his father Aristarkhos, his face covered by a Corinthian sallet, his great dragoned shield crushed and dented. How he longed to be one of them!

The Helots' supervisor arrived and barked impatient orders to prepare food and water so the combatants could wash and recover their strength. The wounded were brought to a tent where they were bandaged and taken care of. Other Helots went outside the wall to gather the fallen men and prepare for hurried obsequies.

King Leonidas, indefatigable, went round the camp giving instructions and ordering the shifts of guard duty at the wall. As he rested for a moment without having even taken off his armour, a messenger came with a dispatch: the fleet had confronted the enemy and had succeeded in driving them back.

Themistocles had kept his word, keeping vigil over the sea to protect the small army that guarded the pass. There was no word from the mountain pass of Anopaea where the Phocians guarded the only route over land that could lead the enemy around to the back of the Greek contingent. The king sent a dispatch of his own to Sparta asking for reinforcements. He was sure that the pass could be defended if only fresh troops were available. He didn't know that his destiny had already been decided: not for any reason would his government have diverted troops from the Corinthian isthmus.

Xerxes couldn't believe his eyes when he saw his troops returning in such a state. He realized that his army had found no way to deploy its crushing superiority in that narrow alley guarded by a fistful of such courageous men. Demaratus was right: it had been a great error to underestimate the Greeks, and especially the Spartans. Xerxes gave the order to send the best of his troops, the Immortals, to the attack. The camp resounded with cries and laments, and the drums rolled once more. Soon ten thousand Persian warriors, splendidly armed, were lined up in their ranks. They would charge the pass and overwhelm, once and for all, the obstinate resistance of its defenders.

The news arrived quickly at the Greek camp, brought by a sentinel stationed at the entrance to the pass. 'Sire, a second attack is arriving, but these are different: they're marching in silence, in compact ranks. They seem to be a much more disciplined corps.'

Leonidas had a moment of discouragement – how could he ask his weary men to take up the arms that they had just laid down? How many fresh troops could the Persian king draw up against his depleted men? He sounded the fall-in; the men, in silence, re-formed their ranks in front of the wall. Those who had fought in the front line passed to the third and those who had been in the rear guard moved to the front lines. The Persians advanced in cadenced steps, in a close formation.

'They've drawn up in a phalanx,' said Leonidas to Aristarkhos, 'but their spears are shorter than ours. Give orders to minimize the space between one man and the next as much as possible.'

Aristarkhos shouted the order, and with a metallic roar the front of the army closed up: only the heavy ash-wood spears protruded from the bronze wall of shields, forming an impenetrable barrier. The king nodded towards the wall and a group of Helots gave breath to the pipes and rolled the drums. The enemy phalanx continued with measured steps, lifting a cloud of dust from the ground still littered with corpses.

The warriors moved onto open ground. At an order from their king, drawn up to the extreme right, they charged. The two formations collided with a frightful clangour: for a moment the fronts of both armies wavered uncertainly, since neither could push the other back.

The tense wail of the pipes could be heard along with the roll of drums, until King Leonidas, with a roar, charged forward like an enraged animal with his three hundred *eirenes* behind him. He ran a Persian officer through, chopped in two another who was blocking his path, and advanced with unrestrained rage as Aristarkhos protected him from lateral attacks with his huge shield.

Xerxes, who had had his throne placed on a nearby hill to contemplate the victory of his troops, jumped to his feet as he realized what was happening. King Leonidas had spotted him and was trying to break through the Persian formation to get at him. The King of Kings grew pale: that relentless helmet with its three vermilion crests was cutting a swathe through the body of his army. He had nearly succeeded in opening a passage through which the entire Greek army would spill out onto the Great King himself to decapitate the horde of invaders. Appalled, Xerxes gave the order to retreat; the Immortals, decimated, fell rapidly back to the hill, re-formed their phalanx and moved backwards gradually so that the retreat would not be transformed into a rout.

For five long days, there was no further sign of the enemy army and Leonidas began to hope that he would receive reinforcements. Then, one moonless night, his sentinels saw a signal light blinking repeatedly out at sea. A boat moored on the beach a short time later, and the man who got out asked to confer immediately with the king. Leonidas was in his tent at that moment, speaking with Aristarkhos. The messenger entered bowing and said; 'Sire, I must tell you things that are meant only for your ears.'

'Speak freely,' answered the king. 'This man is the most valorous warrior of Sparta and faithful to me.'

'Sire,' continued the messenger, 'my commander Themistocles salutes you and wishes you to know that he continues to keep his word. But now the entire fleet is at risk of being surrounded by the enemy, and we have no choice but to retreat. To this he adds that he has learned that no reinforcements will be sent from Sparta, because the ephors and the elders refuse to divert men from the isthmus. Your valour has been great and your death would be no advantage for the Greeks, so gather your men on the beach and later this night our ships will come to embark them and bring them to safety on the Corinthian isthmus.'

King Leonidas paled, realizing that he had been completely abandoned. Without betraying his emotions he answered calmly, 'You shall refer the following to your commander. "King Leonidas has answered: Greetings, your words are of great comfort to us because the word of a friend is always precious even in extreme moments, but I cannot consent to your invitation. We must not disobey the orders that have been given us. We will fight as long as our strength endures, then we will fall honourably as befits a warrior." Go now, and may the gods be with you.'

The messenger saluted him, baffled by such superhuman resolve, and slipped through the night back to his boat. Hoisted onto the admiral's trireme a short time later, he referred the king's response to his general, who was still awake by the light of a lamp in the quarterdeck.

'Hard-headed Spartan!' burst out Themistocles, bringing his fist down on the table. 'He'll be slaughtered like a bull at the altar. He doesn't want to understand that they've decided to sacrifice him – just so that they can throw his blood in our faces when the time comes for the fleet to defend the isthmus of Corinth.' He dismissed the messenger, remaining alone to measure the limited space of his cabin with nervous pacing. He walked out onto the deck and looked towards land.

On his right he could see the flickering of a thousand fires in the Persian camp, on the left the nearly extinguished bivouacs of the small condemned Greek army. He moved his lips, as if speaking to himself. 'We can't wait any longer,' he said to an officer who had approached to him. 'Give the order to depart.'

From the side rowlocks, the greased oars plunged silently into the waters of the channel of Euripus. Dawn was breaking.

*

Before lying down to rest that night, King Leonidas gave instructions for the following day. He had one of his men, young Kresilas, who was in the throes of a terrible eye infection, taken to the nearby village of Alpeni. As the youth was nearly blind, he certainly would be of no help in a battle. Having dismissed Aristarkhos, Leonidas collapsed onto his cot. After only a few hours' sleep, he was abruptly awakened by a sentinel.

'My Lord, we are lost. We've just received the news that a traitor has conducted the Persian army to the mountain pass of Anopaea. The Phocians on guard there retreated to the top of the hill to attempt resistance, but the enemy didn't even come near them: they've taken the path on the other side of the mountain. They'll be upon us before the sun is high.'

Leonidas left his tent without even taking up his arms; he threw a cape over his shoulders and assembled the troops. 'Warriors of Greece,' he said, 'great and worthy of praise has been your valour, but valour counts little against betrayal. Someone has indicated the path of Anopaea to the enemy and we will soon be encircled. It would be useless for thousands of valorous warriors to die in vain. Your spears will be able to strike down the barbarians in the many battles that will surely follow all over Hellas.

'So, the allies shall now retreat, each group returning to its own city, to exhort their fellow citizens to have courage and to continue to resist the enemy. The Spartiates will remain here to protect your retreat.

'Do not imagine that you are acting in cowardice: you have already demonstrated your valour and no one can accuse you of having shown fear. You are only obeying the orders of your commander.

'Go now, little time remains to you.'

A heavy silence met the king's words. Slowly, in groups, the warriors left the assembly to prepare for departure. Only the Thespians remained, knowing well that their own city would be the first to be destroyed. King Leonidas thanked them, embracing their leader, then returned to his tent and fell exhausted into a chair. Aristarkhos entered soon after.

'Lord,' he said with a firm voice, 'we will combat at your side until the end. Our warriors do not fear death.'

'I thank you,' said the king. 'But now go, we must

prepare for the final hour.' He extracted from a chest a leather scroll of the type that was used to write messages. He then called the guard and gave him an order.

A few moments later, Brithos and his friend Aghias reported to the commander's tent, both armed. They stiffened in salute and then, at a sign from Leonidas, sat down.

The king spoke. 'The pass is lost and we have few hours left to live. It is essential, however, that the elders, the ephors and King Leotychidas receive this message.' He indicated the leather scroll on his bench. 'It is of the utmost importance, and I could only entrust it to two warriors as valorous as you are. You are capable and clever men; you will be able to overcome the dangers of the long journey from here to Sparta. You belong to the *krypteia* and you are the best men for this mission. Remember: the message must be delivered directly into the hands of the ephors in the presence of King Leotychidas.'

Brithos paled. 'But, sire, how can you order us to abandon you in this moment? Please, allow me to speak. Won't Sparta learn in any case that the Thermopylae is lost as soon as our allies reach their homes? We have followed you never to abandon you.' He paused for a long moment. 'Or, perhaps . . . perhaps my father Aristarkhos, blinded by his love for me, has—'

King Leonidas interrupted him, springing to his feet, anger flashing on his face: 'How dare you!' he shouted. 'How dare you make such insinuations on your father's honour? He has no idea that I've called you here. I haven't told him a thing because I knew he would have opposed me. That's enough now, you have received a precise order from your king; carry it out.' He sat down, pulling his cloak over his knees.

Aghias bowed his head, touching his chin to his chest, and saluted his king, turning to depart. He saw with surprise that Brithos had not moved.

'Sire,' Brithos found the strength to say, 'sire, should there be the smallest possibility that you might change your mind, I beg of you, send someone else with Aghias. My father will die with all of you and I want to be at his side in that supreme moment.'

The king's expression softened as he approached the young warrior and laid a hand on his shoulder.

'Do you really think that your king hasn't thought of all this? Brithos, our country can survive only if her sons continue to do what they must do, without letting their personal desires get in the way. Our duty is to stay here and die if the gods so wish it, yours is to live and to bring back this message. Take your Helot with you. Your father has pointed out to me how strong and agile he is despite his lame foot. You'll need him during your journey. Go. Now. If you don't leave now, it will soon be too late.' The two youths saluted their king and left the tent.

A short time later, having ordered Talos to bring two horses and a mule, they were ready to depart. Aristarkhos, intuitively sensing what was happening, hurried from the centre of the camp where he had been giving orders to the Spartan and Thespian troops.

'The king has commanded us to go to Sparta to deliver a message,' said Brithos. 'I could do nothing to dissuade

him. I leave you with death in my heart, father.' Aristarkhos watched his son with bright eyes.

'If the king has given you this order, it means that it
must be done. Don't worry about me, son, this is the
death that every warrior desires for himself.' His voice
had a slight tremor. 'Tell your mother that the heart of
Aristarkhos beat for her with undiminishing ardour until
the last moment.'

He gazed at Talos, who was waiting a short distance
away on his mule. He stared at him with an intense and
desperate pain, like that day down on the plain. Then
Aristarkhos placed the crested helmet on his head and
returned to take his place in the ranks.

The sun was already high in the heavens when King
Leonidas came out of his tent, his copper-coloured hair
carefully gathered at the nape of his neck. He put on his
helmet and accepted spear and shield from his Helot, then
took his place in the front line of the right wing. Aristarkhos was already giving instructions to the various detachments. They would attack immediately in the open to
inflict as much damage as possible on the enemy.

The Persians soon appeared at the entrance to the pass.
King Leonidas signalled and the pipes began to play. The
obsessive and monotonous music spread through the
valley; only the measured step of the Persian army echoed
back.

King Leonidas raised his spear and the small army
marched to its last battle.

When the forces were almost in direct contact, the
Spartiates lowered their spears and charged furiously.

The king, advancing like the furious force of nature itself, massacred all those in his path. The shield with the dragon, a reef of bronze against the invading waves, was raised at his side each time the Persians tried to strike him.

Behind the shield, Aristarkhos towered above the crowd of enemies, delivering cutting blows left and right, creating a void around him.

Each time that the Persians tried to encircle them, the Greeks ran backwards towards the narrow passage and then, turning suddenly, attacked again wildly, as if fuelled by some inexhaustible energy.

From his throne, Xerxes observed the scene, pale and nervous. Demaratus watched as well, his jaw tense, his gaze hopelessly lost. This incredible carousel repeated itself time after time; the Persians could not get the better of the swift and sudden movements of the small army. But slowly the energies of the Spartans began to flag, and their pace slackened as they were nearly buried by the horde. Then an arrow struck Aristarkhos' left arm, and he dropped the shield.

Before another man could move to take his place, a Persian sabre ran through Leonidas' exposed side. The king's face became a mask of pain but his arm continued to sow death as long as he remained on his feet. Debilitated, dripping blood and sweat, Leonidas collapsed, dying, and a cloud of enemies flew upon him to finish him off and to seize his body.

In that moment Aristarkhos, who had wrenched the arrow from his arm, gripped the shield with both hands and flung himself on the mass of Persians, overpowering them and liberating the body of Leonidas. His comrades pressed together to wall off the enemy, and an intense struggle ensued over Leonidas' fallen body. At the same time, a terrible war cry rang out behind the Spartan warriors: the Persian contingent was descending from the pass of Anopaea.

Aristarkhos shouted an order, and the Spartan and Thespian warriors turned back towards a little hill to the left of the pass where they squared off for their last stand.

Waves of Persians attacked from all sides. The Spartiates continued to battle with wild fury to the last: with their shields, their nails, and their teeth after they lost their weapons, until the officers of the Great King called off the infantry so as not to lose more men and sent in the archers.

Exhausted, riddled with wounds, the surviving warriors raised their shields to protect their king in his agony until they fell, one after another, on the blood-soaked ground.

9

HE WHO TREMBLED

BRITHOS AND AGHIAS RODE day and night, pausing only briefly to eat or to sleep, one of them often staying awake on guard. Talos, on his mule, silently followed them at thirty paces.

They encountered scenes of panic everywhere; the terrified inhabitants of central Greece were abandoning their homes and seeking refuge on the mountains, carrying their humble belongings with them. Those who could not move stayed behind, awaiting the worst. On the first day of their journey they passed Orchomenus and Coronea and arrived at Thespiae at dusk. This small city which had lost seven hundred warriors at the Thermopylae was pervaded by the desperate wailing of women and children who had already had news of the deaths of their husbands and fathers.

Old men wandered up and down the dusty streets, bewildered by the unthinkable disaster. Others sat at the doors of the temples, invoking death. One old man, bent over with age and nearly blind, approached the three horsemen at the doors of the city. He lifted his eyes, red and puffy with tears, to Brithos' face. 'Who are you?' he asked with a quavering voice.

'We are Phocians,' responded Brithos without hesitation. 'We have just come from the pass of Anopaea. And you, old man, who are you? What do you want from us?'

'My name is Diadromus. I am the father of Demophilus, the leader of the Thespian warriors who remained to combat under Leonidas. Please, tell me, is it true that no one was saved? That they are all dead?'

'Yes, old man, what you say is true,' answered Brithos. 'They would not abandon their posts ... they died as heroes.'

'But you ...' continued the old man, his voice shaking, 'but you are not Phocians. I recognize the way you speak ... you are Laconians, Spartans!'

Brithos shivered.

'You are Spartans!' gasped the old man. 'Why are you here? You have fled the battle! You have abandoned your comrades!'

Brithos gave a signal to Aghias and Talos and launched his horse into a gallop down the streets of the nearly deserted city. The old man fell to his knees in the dust, sobbing. 'You abandoned them,' he repeated, his eyes full of tears. 'You left them to die ...'

They rode to the pass in silence, in the darkness illuminated only by the crescent moon that was rising between the olive trees. Aghias watched his companion as they proceeded mutely; Brithos' head was sunken into his shoulders. Suddenly, oppressed by his prolonged anguish, Aghias burst out:

'Enough! That's enough, Brithos. The task that was given us is terrible and thankless, but someone had to take it on. Our duty in this moment is much more difficult than that of our comrades who died gloriously next to

King Leonidas. Their names will be sung by the poets, while ours will fall into the shadows, if not into complete dishonour. But could we have refused because of this?'

'Didn't you hear what that old man was saying?' Brithos answered roughly. 'Didn't you hear him, Aghias? He was grieving for his son, who fell with our men, and he took us for cowards who had fled out of fear. And like cowards, here we are hiding, lying—'

'Listen,' began Aghias, 'this message must be tremendously important; it must contain something more than just the news of losing the pass. If King Leonidas entrusted us with such a hateful mission, it must be because he had something really vital to say to the ephors and King Leotychidas. Don't you remember your own words? Our Peloponnesian allies will certainly have brought the news of the defeat at the Thermopylae before we arrive.'

'What you say is true, Aghias,' said Brithos. 'Our allies from Tegea started off before us, and they can reach Sparta in a few hours from their city. But then, why did King Leonidas want to expose us to such dishonour?'

They continued their long ride in silence. From the top of a hill, they saw the waves of the Gulf of Corinth glittering below them and decided to stop for a bit of food and a couple of hours of rest. They were empty and exhausted from the enormous strain of the days before, and both feverish from the wounds that they had received in the battles.

Talos shackled the horses and the mule and lit a fire under a jutting rock. He began to prepare some barley meal. The thought of seeing his mother and his people again did not cheer him; he felt a leaden weight on his heart.

He huddled in a corner to eat a bit of food, then went to sit on a rock overlooking the sea. The moon spread its silver rays on the peaceful mirror of the waters, while a light breeze, redolent with the intense scents of thyme and rosemary, moved the leaves of the almond and olive trees.

Talos turned to look at the two dark figures slumped over the bivouac a short distance away: he felt no hate and no resentment for them. He saw as in a dream the battlefield that they had left such a short time ago. The fallen warriors for whom there would be no funerals. No women would lament over their bodies. He could almost feel their shadows hovering about the small camp.

He thought of the warrior of the dragon, of his shield that must be lying crushed and filthy among heaps of corpses. He thought of the tragedy that would soon sweep away entire populations. In his heart rang the desperate cries of the Thespian women; he saw that old man's eyes, reddened and full of tears. Where had those peaceful nights on Mount Taygetus gone? Kritolaos' fables, Antinea's bright eyes, her fragrant breasts? He felt his heart swell in pain and anger. Destiny had torn him from his people and from those he loved but would not permit him to be a part of this other people that he hated but also deeply admired. The warriors he had seen on the plain as a child. The young Spartiates who bore their flagellation without a moan. And now the incredible valour and formidable spirit of the three hundred warriors at the Thermopylae.

The sound of a footstep behind him distracted him from his thoughts; he turned and saw Brithos' shield glittering in the moonlight. The two youths remained silent for a long while, the Spartan erect, immobile as a statue, the Helot seated on a stone. Brithos was the first to speak.

'Fate is bizarre,' he said in a nearly distracted tone. 'How many times, watching your people, have I thought that it would be better to die then to live such a squalid, monotonous, unemotional existence.' Talos rose to his feet. 'Now I envy you, Helot. You'll return to your mountains alive; that's the only thing that matters to you anyway. But me . . . I'll return to a city eager to condemn me. I've had to leave my father unburied, at the mercy of dogs and barbarians. My friends have been massacred, mutilated, their bodies disgraced. Before me all I can see is darkness, dishonour, perhaps even contempt.'

He stopped, bursting with anger, desperation and shame. Aghias was sleeping wrapped in his ragged red cloak, and Brithos' anguish was so unbearable that he had been forced to speak to a servant. Talos looked at him sadly. 'Are you really so sure that my life is the only thing that matters to me? What do you know about my life, or that of my people? Do you know what it means to serve silently, to wear a yoke like an animal every day, with no hope of ever breaking free? The gods have not made us slaves; men have, men like yourself . . . and like me.

'Tomorrow, or maybe already today, entire peoples – who were prosperous and free – are being made slaves by these unstoppable invaders. Noble men. Proud, courageous men, like your father, like you, perhaps. Certainly, one who is born in chains can't even imagine what freedom is. But he's well acquainted with courage ... a courage that you can't even imagine. The courage to carry a heavier load each day without giving up, the courage to continue to live, for yourself, for your loved ones.'

Brithos saw a young shepherd, encircled by armed men, fighting savagely with only a staff in his hands. He saw a blonde girl shielding him with her own body.

'Now you will get the chance to learn whether you are a man or a slave,' continued Talos cruelly. 'Live, if you can. Live as you have been ordered; survive your infamy, if you will. Even an ass puts up with being whipped without a whimper.' Brithos felt a sudden flame rise to his face. 'Even animals can butt and wound each other to the death—'

'That's enough!' shouted Brithos, putting a hand on his sword. 'Don't tempt my anger.'

'... But only a man is capable of surviving!' Talos continued. 'Of stifling the cry of his heart, of suffocating the pain, the rebellion, the anger, of carrying the shame on his shoulders like a repugnant burden. You are covered with bronze, Brithos, but isn't that skin on your bones? Or has it become like the skin on the drumhead that calls you to battle?

'Have you ever cried, Brithos? Have your eyes ever been filled with tears? Glory has been taken from you, and you are nothing more than a jar full of sand.' He touched a finger to the Spartan's chest. 'What's behind this breastplate, Brithos? Is there anything there?'

Talos paused, clenching his fists until his nails dug into his flesh. 'And now, unsheathe your sword, warrior,' he said coldly, 'and you'll see how much a slave cares about his miserable life.'

Brithos let his head drop and was silent.

*

A black cloud which had risen at dusk from the distant peaks of Mount Helicon hid the moon in the middle of the night. Sudden darkness closed in on the small field, extinguishing the reflections of the sea and the song of the crickets in the grass; only the embers of the bivouac continued to give off a pale halo of light. Aghias, on guard duty at the time, was overcome by fatigue.

A shadow arose from nowhere, sliding furtively among the sparse bushes. Perhaps one of the spirits that the earth shelters in its hollow womb, condemned to wander in the night seeking its lost life; so silent was its step ... The shadow crept next to Brithos, behind Aghias; it hung over them like a ghost. For a moment it seemed to crouch as if searching for something, then to rise and go away ... or disappear.

So it seemed to Talos that he had dreamed. What was certain was that when the moon shone again the three youths had given themselves up to sleep; only Aghias, when a humid breeze began to blow from the sea, shook himself awake, and shivered.

Shortly before dawn the three young men resumed their journey, stopping only for a few moments to water their horses at a brook; they arrived at the sea as day was breaking. When they reached the isthmus, the sun was already high in the sky and they stopped, weary and disheartened, at an abandoned cottage to eat a fistful of olives and a piece of stale bread that Talos took out of his pack.

In a short time they were at the base of the wall that the Peloponnesian troops had raised to block enemy passage. A Spartan officer leaned from the rampart. 'Who are you?' he shouted. 'What are you looking for?'

'I am Brithos, son of Aristarkhos, Spartan,' was his reply. 'We've come from the Thermopylae.' Excited orders could be heard, and immediately a small iron door was opened at the base of the wall.

'Come in, quickly,' said the officer, stepping aside. 'But tell me,' he added immediately, 'how did you manage to save yourselves? The allies that preceded you told us that no one survived.'

'That's right,' said Brithos in a broken voice. 'Our men remained to cover their retreat. We are here because King Leonidas gave us a message for the ephors. Our orders are to deliver it directly into their hands.'

'The king . . . ?' asked the officer.

'He's dead by now,' answered Aghias. 'No one could have survived the battle; the pass of Anopaea was betrayed to the enemy. We left just in time to avoid being trapped. But now, let us by; we have to bring our mission to its conclusion.'

A crowd of soldiers was pressing around the small group.

'Who are they?' one asked.

'They're Spartans, come back from the Thermopylae.'

'From the Thermopylae? But didn't they say that no one was saved?'

'These managed it, somehow.'

'They say they have a message from King Leonidas.'

Brithos spurred his horse, forcing a passage though the crowd of soldiers. In a short time, crossing entrenched fields, they reached the slope that led to the Argolic plain. They cut around Argos – treacherous city, probably already in league with the Persians – and headed towards Mantinea, which they reached as night was falling. They were at the port of Sparta the next day. The city glowed white under the blazing sun. On a tower, a long black pall hung motionless.

They crossed the city at the time of day when the streets were most crowded. The throng opened to let them pass, but regarded them with a mixture of curiosity and mistrust.

Their mounts, shining with sweat, dragged their hooves in the dusty streets, ears low and tails hanging. The two warriors in their saddles wore dented armour, their clothing was ragged and dirty, their limbs were covered with bruises and festering wounds, their heads swung from their shoulders in the heat.

They arrived at the great square of the House of Bronze and crossed to the building where the council of the ephors was meeting with the elders to discuss what had taken place.

The news of the fall of the Thermopylae, in fact, had already arrived, brought by a Tegean horseman at the first light of dawn.

A sentinel introduced Brithos and Aghias into the council chamber. Their entrance was met by a buzz of astonishment. They were not easily recognized: thin, ragged, dirty, eyes red in black sunken orbits; they seemed spectres called up from Hades. Brithos spoke: 'Venerable fathers, our defence of the pass was condemned by treason. A traitor indicated the mountain pass of Anopaea to the enemy and King Leonidas dismissed the allies so as not to sacrifice them uselessly. He remained with our warriors to protect their retreat. We were spared because the king ordered us to bring you this message.'

He handed the leather scroll to a guard who delivered it into the hands of the ephors. 'He ordered that it be read immediately in the presence of the elders, the ephors and King Leotychidas.'

Without opening the scroll, one of the ephors said, 'We have heard of the great valour of our warriors at the Thermopylae. Their blood was spilled for the liberation of all Greece and their city renders them homage with solemn funeral rites. And we honour you also for having fought with all of your might and for having obeyed the commands of your king. The message will be read as soon as King Leotychidas reaches us; he has already been summoned to the assembly. Go now, you have permission to return to your homes without reporting first to your *syssitia*.'

'Our *syssitia* doesn't exist any more, sir,' muttered Brithos in a flat voice. The two warriors then left the hall, leaning against each other, and entered the square which was swarming with people, all watching them. In a corner of the square Talos struggled to hold the nervous horses, tormented by flies.

'They have come from the Underworld,' whispered a

child hiding behind his father's legs, eyes wide open in fear. Brithos and Aghias staggered down the steps of the council building and the crowd split to let them pass.

'It's the son of Aristarkhos!' said a man, leaning forward to examine Brithos' face.

A woman cried out, 'Why were they saved? Why only them?'

The buzzing in the square became louder, the crowd seemed to close in on the two wretched youths. At that moment, all heads turned as one; from the door of the council chamber one of the elders indicated that he wanted to speak. The crowd fell silent.

'Spartans,' proclaimed the elder, 'the two warriors who are passing among you now are valorous men. They have delivered a message to us from King Leonidas and they left the Thermopylae on the king's orders.'

The crowd parted again and the two warriors dragged themselves across the square to the House of Bronze. Next to a stump, the same one that had seen King Cleomenes' bloody end, stood Ismene, deathly pale.

'Mother,' gasped Brithos. His shield slipped off his arm onto the ground, resounding on the pavement. 'Mother . . . with it, you said . . . or upon it.'

He collapsed to his knees, Aghias swaying on his feet behind him like a puppet dangling from a hook. Brithos lifted his face to his mother, wetting his dry and cracked lips with his tongue. 'Mother, he loved you until the last moment.'

Ismene fell to her knees next to him. 'Mother, I didn't want to leave him . . . I didn't want to leave him!' he shouted with a broken voice. He covered his face with his hands, sobbing.

*

One of the ephors signalled to a guard, who left the room closing the heavy iron door behind him. The ephor advanced to the centre of the room. 'Noble elders,' he said, 'King Leonidas and our warriors have died valorously in the defence of Greece, and now the Athenians cannot refuse to draw up the fleet, commanded by our admiral Eurybiades, to defend the Peloponnese. Our duty is to further reinforce the isthmus.

'We will first pay our honours to the fallen men, and try to recover, if possible, their bodies. They will not go unburied! Our Phocian allies will see that this is done. Next, we must provide for the nomination of a regent, since Leonidas' son, young Pleistarchus, is not old enough to take the throne. The council hereby proposes the name of Cleombrotus, brother of the deceased king.

'He will undoubtedly accept the burdensome charge of the regency in this dangerous moment. We've also already uncovered information about the man who guided the army of the Great King to the pass of Anopaea, condemning our contingent at the Thermopylae.'

An old man with a long white beard rose from his seat in the senate. 'King Leonidas would have died anyway; we all know that his fate was decided from the moment that this assembly established that not a single man would be diverted from the defence of the isthmus.' The first orator paled. 'Or perhaps,' continued the old man, undaunted, 'noble elders and ephors, we wish to deny the true reason for which King Leonidas was sent to die at the Thermopylae?

'Someone, honourable fathers, thought that it was the minimum price to be paid to force the Athenians to draw up their fleet in defence of the isthmus. No one opposed the idea, not even myself, but I invite you now to respect the memory of valorous men that we sacrificed willingly and knowingly, but whom we have no right to deride with our hypocrisy.

'The traitor certainly did lead the soldiers of the Great King to our combatants, but if this hadn't happened, the only thing that would have changed is that the agony suffered by King Leonidas and his men would have been prolonged.' The old man returned to his seat, pulling his mantle over his head and isolating himself in scornful silence.

The ephor, after a long embarrassing pause, spoke again: 'Noble Archelaus has spoken, undoubtedly influenced by the emotions of the moment. But we all know that it is our duty to punish the traitor; his name is Ephialtes, son of Eurydemus of Malis. From this moment, no respite will be given him until he has paid the penalty for his foul act.

'And now,' continued the orator, 'it is just that we read the message that King Leonidas, before dying, wished to send us.' He opened the leather scroll and unwound it slowly as silence fell over the hall.

'Why, it's blank!' he murmured, growing pale. 'There's nothing written here at all.'

*

Brithos and Aghias had hoped to be welcomed back into the city, since the reason for their safe return to Sparta had been made public, but the shadow of suspicion only grew. In assembly, the places next to theirs were always left empty, and their old friends no longer spoke to them. Aghias stopped going out by day in order to avoid meeting anyone. He spent his days lying on his bed, staring glassy-eyed at the ceiling beams.

He went out only at night, and wandered at length through deserted streets, in the dark. His mind was giving way, day by day.

The affection of his parents, who had never lost faith in him, did not count for anything. Excluded from the city that he had always served with devotion, oppressed by the shame that his people had cast upon him, he had lost all attachment to life.

One night he returned home drunk and feverish. A hot, suffocating wind was blowing, making the dust whirl on the silent streets of the sleeping city.

He opened the door to his home and a gust of wind put out the fire that burned before the images of the gods. Frightened by this sinister omen, he backed into the street, refusing to enter. He walked towards the house of an old friend who lived nearby to ask him for a lamp to relight the flame in his home, so that his parents, when they awoke, would not find it extinguished.

He knocked repeatedly at the door, and a chained dog began barking. His friend came out, holding a sheet around himself.

'Aghias,' he said, 'what are you doing here at this hour? What do you want?'

'I was just returning home,' responded Aghias, confused, 'and as I was about to enter, the wind put out our flame; please, let me light it with your lamp.'

His friend looked at him with compassion and contempt. 'No, Aghias, I'm sorry but I cannot give you our flame. My brother was at the Thermopylae . . . remember?' He closed the door. The wind increased in intensity, carrying away the insistent barking of the dog. Aghias backed away, staggering, from the threshold. He leaned against the wall that encircled the house and wept, softly, for a long time.

The following morning they found him hanging from one of the ceiling beams in his home, strangled by his own ragged crimson cloak.

The account of the frightful death of Aghias flew through the city and reached Brithos' house. It was his mother who brought him the news:

'Brithos,' she said, 'something horrible has happened. Aghias . . . is dead.'

'Dead?' echoed her son, jerking to face her.

'Yes, son. He hanged himself, in his own home, last night.'

Brithos stood for a moment as if struck by lightning, unable to control the tremor that coursed through his body. He then left the courtyard, headed towards his friend's house. A small group of women dressed in black was in front of the door, lamenting feebly. He entered the dark room; at the centre was his friend's body, arranged on his funeral bed, dressed in the armour that his parents had polished to restore at least a part of its old decorum.

His mother sat dry-eyed, her face veiled, at the dead

boy's head. His father approached Brithos and embraced him. 'Brithos,' he said in a broken voice, 'Brithos, there will be no funeral for your poor friend, nor will he be escorted by his companions in arms. The commander of your battalion told me that no honours are paid to "those who trembled".'

He fell silent, wringing a corner of his cloak through his hands.

'Those who trembled . . .' muttered Brithos, as if out of his mind. 'Those who trembled!' He embraced the devastated old man again. 'Aghias will have his funeral rites,' he said with a firm voice, 'as befits a warrior.'

He left for his own house as four Helots began to prepare the stretcher that would bear the body to the cremation site, where a modest funeral pyre of branches had been prepared.

Under the astonished gaze of his mother, Brithos took from a coffer the parade armour of the Kleomenids, the same that his father had worn on feast days when he appeared at the House of Bronze with King Cleomenes.

He washed carefully, combed and scented his long raven hair, and gathered it at the back of his neck. Onto his legs he fitted the embossed shin-plates, he donned the bronze cuirass adorned with copper and tin ornaments, he tightened the belt from which the heavy Spartan sword hung. On his shoulders he fastened the black cloak with a buckle embellished by a great drop of amber. He slipped on the immense shield of the dragon and took up the spear.

'Son, why are you doing this? Where are you going?' asked Ismene.

'The commander of our battalion has refused an escort for the funeral of Aghias. He said that Sparta pays no honour to one who has trembled. So it is only fitting that a coward be escorted by a coward to his final resting place. I shall be Aghias' honour guard.'

He put the three-crested helmet on his head and started off towards Aghias' house, ignoring the stupor and wonder of the passers-by. He held a vigil over his friend's body all night, on his feet, like a statue of the god of war.

Shortly before dawn, when the city was still deserted, the small procession started down the silent streets: in front, the four Helots with the stretcher, behind them, Aghias' parents with their heads covered, joined by a small group of relatives. Last came Brithos in the superb parade armour that glittered in the pale light of a grey dawn.

They crossed the centre of the city. The tripods in front of the House of Bronze were nearly extinguished, smoking only slightly. They turned towards the southern port. In the great silence, only the distant yelping of dogs could be heard, along with the crowing of a cock, immediately swallowed up by the stagnant and immobile air.

As they entered the countryside on the road that led to Amyclae, Brithos noticed a figure wrapped in a worn grey cloak: it was Talos. He gestured for him to join them.

'You were the only one missing,' he said hoarsely, 'at the funeral of "he-who-trembled".'

Talos joined the end of the small procession that proceeded along the dusty road. He walked for a stretch of road, staring at the meagre stretcher on which the dead man rolled to the unsteady pace of the four bearers. Then, suddenly, Talos took the reed flute from his pack and began to play. The music that rose from the humble instrument – tense, vibrant – startled Brithos, as he continued to advance solemnly in the slow funeral procession; it was the battle hymn of the Thermopylae.

At the chosen site, the corpse was placed on the pyre and the flames soon consumed the limbs desiccated by fasting and folly.

These were the funeral honours rendered to Aghias, son of Antimakhos, warrior of the twelfth *syssitia* of the third battalion, Spartan.

10

THE LONE HOPLITE

THE EVENTS THAT ACCOMPANIED Aghias' death were the final blow for Brithos. In the days that followed he closed up into himself without speaking, refusing even to eat.

One moonless night he left home, having decided to take his own life. He wanted to spare his mother the awful spectacle that Aghias' parents had been forced to witness, so he headed off towards Mount Taygetus. He waited for the dead of night when all were sleeping, crossed the atrium barefoot and went out into the courtyard.

Melas, his hound, ran to him yelping, and Brithos put out a hand to calm him.

'Good boy, be quiet now,' he whispered, patting the dog until he lay down. He stroked his sleek coat, remembering the proud day his father had presented him with Melas. Brithos rose to his feet and walked through the countryside along the path that led to the forest, the same one he had taken so many times with his friends as a boy.

He wandered at length through the wood, panicking at the thought of such a dark death, without honour and without comfort – a death no one had ever prepared him for. He searched for a place where he would never be found, shuddering at the thought of his unburied body, prey to the beasts of the forest.

He thought of his soul, which would drift restlessly at the threshold of the Underworld. He thought of his city; Sparta had demanded the blood of King Leonidas and his father, immolated like victims on the altar. A senseless sacrifice. His city was to blame for the agony of King Cleomenes, for Aghias' harrowing end, and was soon to be stained with his own blood, without even knowing.

He had reached a clearing on top of a hill near an enormous hollow-trunked holm oak surrounded by a thicket of brambles. The moment had come to silence all rumours; to do what had to be done. Brithos drew his dagger and pressed the tip to his heart. With his right hand open, he prepared to deliver the blow with his palm. But at that moment a great hairy fist pounded like a mallet onto his head, knocking him to the ground unconscious.

'By Zeus, Karas, I told you to stun him, not to murder him,' said a voice.

'The fact is,' muttered the giant, 'that these young boys aren't made of the same wood as in my day.'

'What do you mean by that?'

'Just what I said,' answered the voice from the thick of his beard. 'You should have been with us when we fought on the Hellespont against the Thracians. There was a Spartan mercenary who had lost his spear, so do you know what he did? He smashed in the enemy shields with his fist.'

'You never told me that you fought against the Thracians.'

'I've fought against everyone,' grunted Karas, hefting

Brithos' body to his shoulders. 'Let's get going now before day breaks.' They headed towards the high spring, and reached Karas' cabin by dawn.

'Finally!' muttered Karas, letting his burden down onto a goatskin pallet. 'He was starting to weigh on me.'

Talos removed the hooded cloak that completely covered him, and sat down. 'Why don't you get us out something to eat?' he asked. 'This midnight stroll has made me hungry.'

'Right,' said Karas, 'but I don't think I have much; I haven't had much time lately for such matters.' He pulled a crust of bread out of his pack and took a honeycomb from a cupboard.

'You're lucky I have this,' he said, setting the food on a bench. 'I found it yesterday, in the hollow of that oak on the peak that faces Amyclae. Now,' he continued, 'would you like to tell me what you intend to do with that?' he asked, pointing to Brithos, still dead to the world.

'I wanted him to live, that's all.'

'Ah,' grumbled the bearded giant, 'we've all gone crazy around here. If we had let things take their own course, there'd be one less Spartan by this time. But no,' he continued with his mouth full, 'you have me cover half the mountain to follow this fool, I have to lug him on my back like a sack of flour from the big holm oak all the way back here. Talos must have some plan, I think, he wants to get revenge for some reason. Or maybe he wants to ask for a pretty ransom, or hand him over to the Persians as soon as they show up here, but no, no sir, he only wants to save his life!'

'Listen to me, hardhead,' answered Talos, 'there's

something about this man and his family that I still haven't figured out, and so I don't want him to die, understand?'

'Yes, sure I do,' grunted Karas, swallowing a mouthful. 'I won't argue any more.'

'Good, and now we have to make sure he stays asleep; if he wakes up he's likely to go into a frenzy.' Karas lifted his cyclopean fist.

'By Zeus, not like that! You'll end up killing him.'

'Listen, boy, I'm sure you didn't mean for me to take him into my arms and sing him a lullaby; he's too big, and I'm not in the mood.'

'Come on, Karas, this is no time for joking. Give him some kind of drug that will put him out. What was that stuff you had me drink after the *krypteia* raid? Something that made the pain pass and let me sleep.'

'I don't have any more of that,' grumbled the shepherd, taking some powder from a leather sack and mixing it with wine and honey. Talos smiled. Karas made the semi-conscious boy on the pallet take a few sips of the liquid.

'And now, listen well, Karas, because I have another favour to ask you.'

'What now? You want me to bring you King Leotychidas tied up in a sack, or maybe all five of the ephors?'

'No, I want a suit of armour.'

Karas scowled, fixing the boy's eyes. 'You have your armour . . . if you really want it.'

'No, Karas, the time hasn't come yet.'

'But then what armour are you talking about? I don't understand.'

'Karas, don't worry about whether you understand, just do what I'm asking, if you can.'

'It will have to be stolen, if I'm not mistaken.'

'You're not mistaken in the least – well?'

'Oh, I'm not afraid of anything. What kind of armour do you need?'

'Not just any armour: what I want is the armour of noble Aristarkhos. You can find it in a coffer in the house of the Kleomenids.'

Karas gulped. 'The House of the Kleomenids? By Pollux, couldn't you have found another place?'

'I know, I know, Karas, if you don't think you can do it . . .'

'Oh, by all the witches in hell, if you want that stuff I'll get it for you. It's just that it won't be easy to get rid of that damned beast that's always pacing back and forth in the courtyard. I'd rather be face to face with Cerberus than that black monster.'

'You can count on the servant, he's one of us.'

'All right,' said Karas. 'You'll have that armour within three days at the most.'

*

Brithos tried to sit up but a sudden pain in his head nailed him to the bed. He couldn't understand where he was; figures slowly began to take shape as his vision became clearer.

'So, you've finally woken up,' said Talos, seated at the hearth. 'Know how long you've been asleep?'

'You?' asked Brithos astonished. 'Where am I? . . . Who . . .?'

'I'll explain everything, but you must listen. No,' said Talos, watching as Brithos' hand slipped down to his belt, 'no, your dagger has been taken away. You've shown that you don't know how to use it.'

Brithos tried again to sit up, furious as he realized what must have happened, but another sharp pain in his head made him fall back on the goatskin pallet.

'Karas has heavy hands,' said Talos, 'I'm afraid that your head will be hurting for a while. Then we gave you a potion to make you sleep, as well. Now I'll get you something to eat, you need to get your strength back.'

'I won't eat,' answered Brithos tersely. 'I'll find a way to die. My mind is made up; I won't turn back just because you and this Karas have played a trick on me. Do you think I decided to kill myself because I was a bit discouraged? A Spartiate warrior does not lose heart, Helot. I must die because I cannot live without honour. Just as Aghias could not.'

'Stop talking as if you were the great Zeus in person. At this moment you're just a man, like I am. I know what you're thinking, and I also know what the others in your city call you: "He who trembled".'

Brithos fixed him with a look full of hate. 'It's your moment, Helot, isn't it? Well, enjoy it for as long as you can, because if I can't kill myself, I'll kill you with my own hands.'

Talos sneered. 'What a glorious gesture, killing a lame Helot. I know you're not new to this type of game, although you usually surround yourself with lots of company to make sure you won't fail.'

'Damned cripple,' snarled Brithos, 'I should have killed you that day like a dog.'

Talos slipped Brithos' dagger from Karas' pack and

offered it to him. 'If that's what you want, there's still time,' he said.

Brithos gazed at the blade for a moment as if spell-bound, then lowered his head. 'Why did you stop me from killing myself?'

Talos took a breath, putting back the weapon. 'To tell you the truth, I'm not sure myself. Keeping you alive certainly has no advantage for me. Let's say that I do have a reason, but it only concerns me, and for now I can't tell you about it. I can give you a reason for staying alive, if you're interested.'

'If there were one, I would have found it,' answered Brithos with a bitter grimace. 'Do you think it's pleasant to stick a knife between your ribs?'

'Listen to me,' said Talos. 'I don't understand your code of honour very well, but I think that in any case by killing yourself you'd only have fed into their accusation that you selfishly saved yourself from the slaughter at the Thermopylae along with your friend Aghias. And you would have left your mother completely alone, after she had already lost her husband—'

'A Spartan woman is accustomed to living alone,' interrupted Brithos. 'And she's prepared for the idea that her men may die in the defence of their country.'

'Right,' continued Talos, 'but does it seem to you that you were about to die defending your country last night? As for your women: they may not weep and wail as women do in the other cities. They may be brought up to bear up against any disaster through the force of their wills. But do you really think, Brithos, that they don't feel the pain? That's not the point, though. If you are a man, you must find the strength to survive, and you must prove that the atrocity that you've been accused of is unfounded. You must redeem your family name, once one of the most illustrious of the city.'

Brithos remained in thought for a long time, holding his head between his hands, then broke the silence: 'How can I do what you say? There are no witnesses to what happened at the Thermopylae ... Wait, there's Kresilas! Yes, that's right, Kresilas was taken to the village of Alpeni with that eye infection and perhaps—'

'Kresilas is dead,' Talos interrupted him brusquely. 'When he heard that the three hundred Spartiates were surrounded, he had his Helot lead him by the hand onto the battlefield and into the thick of the fighting; nearly blind as he was, the Persians slaughtered him immediately.'

Brithos sat up slowly and brought his right hand to his forehead. 'You know too many things for a Helot.'

'You're wrong, Brithos; it's exactly because I'm a Helot that I know so many things. Your caste can't do without us, and so our people are everywhere: they were at the Thermopylae, they were with Kresilas, they were at the funeral of Aghias.'

'You're crazy,' murmured Brithos. 'You're not saying I can redeem my honour and that of my family by asking your people to pass on the word of how valorous I was!'

Talos smiled. 'No, I'm not that crazy. Let's say that I'm crazy enough to go one step further.'

'What do you mean?'

'That you can redeem your honour in combat; that's the only way for a warrior.'

'That's impossible,' answered Brithos resignedly. 'My

companions would refuse; no one would consent to draw up next to me in battle.'

'That's not what I meant to say,' came back Talos. 'I realize that you can't take your place back in the ranks of your army.'

'Well then?'

'You can do it alone.' Brithos stared at him, bewildered. 'Yes, that's exactly what I mean; if you are truly courageous and if the only way for you to survive is to redeem yourself, then you must combat alone. Listen to me well. Right now you must worry about regaining your strength. Then we'll leave together for the north to fight against the Persians however we can, in any way possible, until your fame convinces your city to change its ideas and call you back.'

'You really are crazy, Helot,' replied Brithos after a few moments of reflection. 'No one has ever attempted such a thing, and besides I'm unarmed.'

'If you haven't the courage to attempt such a desperate endeavour, then I have nothing else to say to you. But remember, only a venture so extreme can redeem such an extreme situation. As for your weapons, you'll have them before the sun has set twice.'

Brithos began to gain interest, despite himself. He argued with Talos and refuted his answers, he made objections. Talos realized that he had saved him from death . . . at least that death.

'I could return home to get my armour,' he said.

'No,' argued Talos. 'No one must see you until the time is right, not even your mother. Think of what I've told you, consider it well.'

At that moment the door opened and Karas walked in.

'Who's that?' asked Brithos.

'The man to whom you owe your life,' answered Talos, smiling, 'and your aching head. His name is Karas.'

'He looks better to me,' complained the giant, sitting near the extinguished fire. 'You see that there was no point in worrying?'

'What news do you bring, Karas?' asked Talos.

'A lot of news. Important, too: the Athenians have routed the Persian fleet near the island of Salamis; the Ionians passed over to their side, and the Great King was forced to retreat. Athens is in the hands of its people again, and they are rebuilding it, but most of the Persian land forces are still in Greece; it seems that they're preparing to spend the winter in Thessaly and relaunch their attack next spring. Your people,' he said turning to Brithos, 'are sending embassies to all of their allies, in an attempt to muster all the available men for the battle that is foreseen for next spring.'

'So,' said Talos to Brithos, 'you've got several months to get ready.'

'Ready for what?' asked Karas.

'You'll know when it's time,' answered Talos. 'Now go, you still have to do what I've asked.' Karas left with his cloak and his pack.

'Well then,' Talos continued, 'what do you think?'

'Perhaps you're right about this,' said Brithos, 'but what did you mean a little while ago when you said something like "we'll leave together for the north"?'

'I meant that I'm coming with you.'

'I don't understand—'

'I have my reasons, but in any case I'll be useful to you. You know that I'm capable of fighting.'

'With your crook? I don't think that you realize . . .'

'Wait,' Talos interrupted him. He moved aside a cow-hide that covered the cabin floor, lifted a wooden trap-door, and extracted a grease-coated sack. Inside was the great horn bow.

'Where did you get such a weapon?' asked Brithos in awe. 'I've never seen anything like it in my whole life.'

'This is another thing that I can't tell you. All you need to know is that I can use it, and use it well. So, you'll be the heavy infantry and I'll be the light infantry: together we'll form an army.'

'Then what I heard was true – that someone on this mountain was armed with a bow and arrows.'

Talos smiled: 'Karas is to blame. He wanted to use this bow one day when we went hunting. He struck a deer without killing it, and the animal escaped with an arrow stuck in it.'

Brithos stared at him. His curiosity to know who this Helot really was had become even keener. How could he possess such a fantastic weapon, worthy of a king? And furthermore, know how to use it so expertly? And the Helot's idea that he take up his arms once again for a solitary war had begun to call his spirit away from the thoughts of death that had dominated it.

'All right, Talos,' he said after a long silence. 'If you can get me my weapons, we'll leave as soon as you wish.'

Talos smiled enigmatically. As Brithos began to nod off, still under the effects of the drug, Talos left to return to his own home.

'We'll see each other tomorrow morning,' he said. 'In the meantime, don't move from here for any reason.'

'Of course not,' said Brithos, feeling that he had returned from the Underworld. The desire for life had begun to flow again in his veins. He lay down on the goatskin pallet and abandoned himself to sleep.

Next morning at the first light of dawn, he awoke. The cabin was deserted. He took in his surroundings, rubbing his eyes, and started: he wasn't alone! A fully armed warrior was standing in a dark corner of the room. He looked again and realized that it was a suit of armour: the armour of his father, with the crested helmet and the great shield of the dragon.

*

In the centre of the village, the heads of each family had been assembled and lined up against a wall by a group of Persian soldiers. An officer surrounded by several servants and accompanied by an interpreter was imparting the requisition orders.

The army of the Great King that had remained in Thessaly needed wheat, now that their defeated fleet could no longer supply them. One of the older men, a peasant with grey hair, implored him. 'Sir, how can we survive if our whole harvest is taken away from us?'

The officer, a Mede with long curly hair, turned to the interpreter. 'Tell him that we're not here to discuss things. Those two wagons must be filled with wheat. If there's anything left for them that's no concern of mine. I'm only worried about bringing the wheat back to the camp, as I was ordered.'

The interpreter translated and added, 'You'd be better off cooperating, peasant, these men have orders to requisition the wheat at any cost. Their army needs provisions, and they won't hesitate to kill you all if you resist.'

'But you, who are a Greek—' beseeched the poor man.

'I'm not a Greek,' interrupted the interpreter, annoyed. 'I'm a subject of the Great King and so are all of you. Everyone in this whole country, who has dared to defy his army, will become his subjects. What must I tell my commander?'

The wretched peasant lowered his head. 'The wheat is underground, beneath the floor of that cabin over there. It has just been threshed.'

'That's good,' twittered the interpreter with his lisp. 'I see you are a wise man. Well then, get moving, you don't expect the soldiers to load the wheat, do you?'

The peasant muttered something to his companions in a low voice, then led them towards the cabin.

'Very good,' said the officer, contentedly stroking his beard greased with nard. 'They seem reasonable enough. They'll have to get used to the idea that they have a master. This spring, we'll have it out with those others, those damned Athenians and those bastard Spartans—'

He never finished: a whistle was heard and an arrow pierced his collarbone. The Mede collapsed, vomiting blood. His soldiers gripped their weapons and glanced around fearfully: nothing, no one.

Suddenly, from behind a hovel, a man armed with an enormous bow sprang into the middle of the village. He swiftly released an arrow, then darted behind a thick oak tree. Another soldier fell to the ground, run through.

'Let's get that bastard!' shouted one of the Persians, advancing with his sabre unsheathed. The others, enraged, followed him, only to abruptly draw up short, incredulous: from behind the tree emerged a fully armed hoplite, gripping a shield emblazoned with an open-jawed dragon. On his helmet three black crests swayed, moved by the warm mountain wind.

From behind the shield appeared the archer who shot another arrow like a lightning bolt, taking immediate cover behind the hoplite. As another of the Persians fell heavily to the ground with his neck run through, the hoplite tossed back his great black cloak and hurled his spear with enormous strength. A Scythian among the group, as agile as a leopard, swiftly dropped to the ground as the spear found its mark in the shield of the comrade behind him, tearing through his corselet of pressed linen and ripping into his stomach. The wounded soldier writhed screaming in the dust already splattered with his blood.

The remaining six lunged at the hoplite all at once, shouting to give themselvels courage. Leaping suddenly from behind his cover, the archer tripped two of the enemy who tumbled forward. Pouncing on the nearest one before he had time to recover, he crushed the man's chest with one of the horns of his bow.

Meanwhile the hoplite sent another to the ground with a great blow of his shield, and ran through the third with his sword. The three survivors, terrified, tried to flee but found themselves surrounded. The villagers, recovered from their shock, began to pelt the soldiers with a thick shower of stones. They were soon beaten to the ground and finished off by the savage blows of the enraged peasants.

'The interpreter!' shouted the archer. 'He must not escape!'

The villagers looked around: from under a large straw basket, a strip of fabric betrayed his hiding place. He was dragged into the centre of the small dusty square, and brought before the two mysterious figures who had appeared so suddenly from nowhere.

Wriggling out of the grasp of the two men who held him, in a fit of unsuspected energy, the interpreter threw himself at the feet of the hoplite, embracing his knees.

'I'm Greek, I'm a Greek like you are!' he gasped with his lisp. 'Sir, spare me, take me from the hands of these animals!'

The stench of that great sweaty body nauseated him, his nostrils being used to delicate oriental perfumes, but his terror of being torn apart by the enraged peasants kept him wrapped around those powerful legs.

The hoplite kicked him sharply, sending him rolling. Pale, dirty, dusty, the wretch closed his eyes and awaited the killing blow.

'Get up,' the commanding voice of the hoplite ordered. 'Are there other groups in the countryside requisitioning wheat?' he asked.

'Will you save my life if I tell you?' asked the interpreter opening his dazed eyes.

'I don't think you're in any position to bargain,' interrupted the archer mockingly.

'Yes, there are. A group of soldiers with an officer will

be at the village of Leucopedion tomorrow. I was supposed to meet them there. I don't know of any others.'

'Very well,' said the archer, smiling. 'You will meet
them as planned!' The interpreter's large protruding eyes
bulged. 'And so will we, naturally. And now,' he said to
the peasants, 'Tie his hands behind his back so we can
take him away. We'll put him to good use.'

'Who are you?' the one who seemed the village leader
asked, drawing closer. 'Tell us your names so that we can
remember you.'

'You'll remember anyway, friend,' said the hoplite,
washing the tip of his spear in a small trough. 'For now
it's better that you not know our names. Get to work
instead: get rid of these corpses, clean all traces of blood
from the earth, burn their wagons and wipe out their
tracks. You can keep the mules if they're not branded. If
any Persians arrive tell them that you haven't seen a soul.
Hide a part of your wheat and keep it in reserve. They
may try again.'

The archer took hold of the interpreter and they
dragged him off in the direction of a hill to the north of
town, as the crowd of peasants watched them from the
village square.

After crossing the hill, they descended into a small
valley sheltered from inquisitive eyes. Tied to an olive
tree was a mule with its head drooping, flicking its tail
every so often to chase away flies. The hoplite took off
his armour and loaded it onto the mule along with his
companion's bow, then covered everything with a heavy
cloth.

'You fought magnificently, Talos,' said the hoplite. 'I never would have thought you could use that weapon so well.'

'This weapon is deadly,' answered the archer, gesturing towards the bundle on the mule's back. 'As old as it is, it's still tremendously powerful.'

'Keep in mind, though, that these men were mediocre combatants: with the Immortals it would have been completely different. My armour is designed for fighting in a compact formation, protected on each side by my comrades' shields.'

'That's why I insisted on coming with you,' said Talos. 'You need an archer to cover you from behind and to scatter the enemy when they attack you in force.'

They retreated behind a large rock and sat in its shade waiting for night to fall.

*

The next day, at dusk, a satisfied Lydian officer was leading a few men from the village of Leucopedion with a good-sized load of wheat and barley, when he heard a cry for help in his own language, in an unmistakable Sardeis accent.

He thought he was dreaming. 'By the Great Mother of the gods, what's a man from Sardeis doing here?' His men, too, had come to a surprised stop although they couldn't tell where the cries were coming from since the path before them passed between two rocky crags and then curved sharply down towards the ford of the Ascreon torrent.

The officer sent a pair of soldiers ahead to see what

was happening, but after passing the gorge the men did not return and no amount of shouting would bring them back. In the meantime, the sun had set and it was getting dark. As the officer was about to give the command to advance in open order towards the gorge, another cry for help was heard coming from the peak of the impending cliff to the left of the pathway: all turned in that direction, gripping their weapons, just as something shot through the air with a sharp whistle and one of the soldiers dropped to the ground with an arrow in his forehead. Before his comrades had recovered from their surprise, another soldier collapsed, struck full in his chest.

'It's an ambush!' shouted the officer. 'Take cover, quick!' and he flung himself at the base of the rock, imitated by his men. 'There can't be many of them,' he panted, 'but we have to flush them out from up there, otherwise we won't be able to pass. You go that way.' He gestured to three of his men. 'And we'll go this way. Whoever they are, we'll trap them between us and make them regret this joke bitterly.'

They proceeded to follow orders when from behind them resounded such a chilling cry that their hair stood on end. The officer reeled around and had only the time to see, on the cliff's peak, a black demon heaving its spear at him before he collapsed, cursing and vomiting blood, run through from side to side.

The apparition barrelled down from the cliff, still howling, and hurled itself at the terrified survivors, helpless against the arrows that continued to rain from above sowing the ground with cadavers. The few surviving soldiers fled into the forest.

That evening the commander of the Persian detachment camped near Trachis noted that two squads and a Greek interpreter had not re-entered. He dispatched groups of horsemen to search for the missing soldiers but they returned late at night without having found a single trace; the men had simply disappeared.

In the last few months of that torrid summer and into the autumn many other strange and inexplicable happenings were reported in the villages spread on the slopes of Mount Oeta and Mount Kallidromos, and along the banks of Lake Copais.

The most incredible of these incidents occurred when a group of Paphlagonian soldiers in the service of the Great King were surprised by a cloudburst and sought shelter in an abandoned temple dedicated to Ares, venerated by the Greeks as the god of war.

The building had been violated and looted months before, but strangely enough the statue of the god was still on its pedestal, intact with its gleaming armour and carrying a great shield with the image of an open-jawed dragon.

One of the barbarians immediately thought that it was a pity to leave those splendid things at the mercy of the first person to come along. He drew closer to the statue with the intention of completing the looting that his comrades-in-arms had evidently left unfinished in the spring, when to his immense surprise he saw the statue turn its head towards him, its eyes shining with a sinister light in the darkness of its helmet.

He had no time to react, or even to cry out: the god Ares smashed his shield into his face with such force that it broke his neck. Then the god gripped his enormous spear and flung it at the others, piercing the throat of one of the Paphlagonians and nailing another to the door-post. At the same time, from the crumbling roof of the building resounded dreadful cries, certainly inhuman, and a deathly rain of arrows felled a number of the soldiers to the ground, lifeless. When the survivors, mad with terror, related the incident to their commander, they were not believed; rather they were punished severely – it is well known that the Paphlagonians drink immoderately and when drunk are capable of any excess.

Certainly many of these tales seemed incredible and exaggerated, but such incidents multiplied instead of sub-siding as is so often the case with unaccountable events. It was thus that among the Phocians and the Locrians, and even among the traitorous Boeotians, and in every village between the summits of Mount Kallidromos, the massif of Helicon and the disease-ridden banks of Lake Copais, news spread of the solitary hoplite who would appear suddenly along with an archer who had a strange, rolling gait. They were as quick as lightning and as relentless as fate itself.

*

'I'm sure that he'll show up,' said Talos to his companion, all bundled up in a dark cloak. It was late autumn and the evening wind threatened rain. The two men stood in the shelter of an ancient olive tree laden with fruit. Thirty paces away was the Plataea and Thespiae crossroad. Not very far from there, at the foot of a little hill that hid the Asopus river bed, was a shrine with an image of Perseph-one carved in olive wood. Talos pointed it out. 'Karas knows it well, it was he who described it to me. This is the first full moon of the autumn, so we can't be wrong. You'll see, he'll be here.' After some time, as it was beginning to get dark, a massive figure appeared on the road from Plataea, perched on an ass that swayed beneath his weight.

'It's him!' exclaimed Talos.

'I think you're right,' agreed Brithos, sharpening his gaze. The rider spurred on his ass, forcing it off the road and urging it towards the shrine next to the crossroad. He tied the animal and sat down on the base of the sacellum. Talos and Brithos exited their hiding place.

'Ah, here you are,' said Karas, getting to his feet. 'I was afraid that I'd have to wait here and get soaked; it's about to rain.'

'Let's go, quickly,' said Talos taking his arm. 'Let's leave here before someone comes by.' They pulled the ass after them, along a path tucked behind the hill, towards the valley of Asopus. They entered an abandoned pen that shepherds must have used some months earlier, before the horde of invaders had passed. Since then there had been no sheep to look after. They took off their cloaks, spread them on the ground, and sat down on them.

'You've turned the whole region inside out, from what I've heard,' began Karas. 'Wherever I stopped I heard tell of the hoplite with the dragon and of the archer who accompanies him. Some even speak of supernatural apparitions. The old men say that the hoplite could be Ajax Oileus, come back to help his people and to combat the nations of Asia like at the time of the Trojan War.'

'What about the archer?' asked Talos with a smile.

'Oh,' continued Karas, 'with that lame foot they've already taken you for the hero Philottetes. Add the fact that they've never seen a bow like yours and you can imagine how you've worked up the people's imagination and their superstitions. Your fame has spread all the way to Sparta, and that's not all. The city has its informers all over this area to study the movements of the Persian troops, and they transmit anything that they hear said. I don't think they mention Ajax and Philottetes, though; the shield of the dragon is too well known down there. It's the archer that's perplexing them. I think that the ephors would be quite happy,' he nodded, turning to Talos, 'to study you close up.'

'My mother?' asked the youth.

'She knows you are alive but she lives each day in the terror that you'll never come back.'

Brithos lowered his head, not daring to ask anything.

'I can't tell you much about your family,' Karas told him. 'I know that your mother mourned you as dead, that I'm sure of. If she's nurturing any hopes or if she's had some news of what's been happening here, I can't say. Your mother doesn't speak with anyone; she leads an extremely secluded life. It's as if she didn't exist.'

Karas fell into silence. They heard, far off, the screeching of the cranes that were beginning to gather along the banks of Lake Copais, preparing for migration.

'Next spring a great confederate army will come up here to face the Persians,' he began again. 'Preparations have already begun.'

'What can you tell me about the other task that we've entrusted you with?' asked Talos.

'I think I'm on the right path,' he answered. 'The man who led the Persians to the pass of Anopaea is named Ephialtes, and the government of Sparta is actively searching for him. It won't be easy to get to him first. The only advantage that we have is that he won't know that we're looking for him.'

'Do you think that he's trying to reach the Persian army?' asked Brithos, roused from his silence.

'No. As far as I've heard, he's wandering somewhere on the gulf coast. He's staying wide of the Peloponnese, but he's probably trying to embark on some ship, or escape to Asia or Italy. Tomorrow I'm meeting a man from Trachis who may be able to tell me more.'

'You know what you must do if you find him,' said Brithos.

'I know,' responded Karas darkly. 'He'll never even realize that he's dying. I hope you know that you're not doing your country any favour.'

'I know, and I really don't care. Only we have the right to punish him, not the city that decided to sacrifice Leonidas and my comrades.'

'Then,' answered Karas, getting to his feet, 'we have nothing more to say to each other. Be careful if you want to make it through to next spring, because they're looking for you everywhere. If you need me you know where to find me.'

He untied the ass and began to walk alongside it, holding it by the halter. A flight of ducks passed through a sky that seemed empty.

'Tomorrow they'll be flying above the banks of the Eurotas,' murmured Brithos, as if talking to himself.

11

KLEIDEMOS

THE TAVERN STANK OF burnt oil and fish. It was packed full of sailors from the port and pilgrims on their way to the sanctuary at Delphi. The lights of the sacred city could be seen sparkling tremulously on the side of the mountain.

Ephialtes entered, his face nearly hidden by a large broad-brimmed hat that he wore low on his brow. He was famished. He leaned for a moment against the plaster reed-grated wall and looked around.

A group of Arcadians sat around a long table, intent on consuming a whole roasted mutton, grabbing handfuls of olives from a common plate with hands dripping oil. At the centre of the large smoky room, some Thesprotian mountaineers, their curly hair full of chaffs, were sweating under their heavy goatskin clothing as they devoured half-cooked sausage and blood pudding. In a corner a drunken peasant interrupted his snoring with an occasional loud burp.

Ephialtes sat down as soon as two sailors from Corinth got up, cursing as they followed their crew-master who had just appeared at the door.

'Food or drink?' asked the host, coming up to him with a jug of wine in his hand.

'Both,' answered Ephialtes without raising his head. 'Set some wine down here, and a piece of lamb.'

'There isn't any lamb.'

'Mutton, then, and some bran bread.'

'You'd better believe it,' said the host, heading towards the hole that served as a kitchen. 'There's nothing left but bran: with all these armies and these fleets to supply, bran is all we've got.' He returned to his customer's table with the mutton and a chunk of bread.

'That will be five obols,' he said extending his greasy hand.

'Take it, you thief,' said Ephialtes, pulling out the coins. The host slipped the money into the pocket on his belly without a word; he was used to such comments. Ephialtes began eating, forcing down the meat between gulps of wine. Every so often he looked towards the door as if expecting someone. He had almost finished when a boy of about sixteen approached his table.

'The commander of the cargo boat *Aella* has sent me to say he accepts your offer. The boat will be loading in about an hour at the small wharf. Tomorrow the ship sets sail for Black Corcyra. The crew-master is waiting for you outside,' he said, and slipped away among a group of Megarian sailors who had just entered and were bawling at the host. Ephialtes got up, threw a pack over his shoulder, and left.

A man was leaning against the wall outside the tavern. He was wearing a long cloak with a wide hood of waxcloth. As soon as he saw Ephialtes coming out he gestured for him to follow and headed towards the port. They walked for a while along the ill-lit curving roads that led to the pier. Ephialtes was the first to break the silence.

'Do you think the crossing will be bad?' he asked his mute companion.

'I don't think so,' answered the other. 'There are pirates in the western sea but the route that we'll follow is safe enough and the commander knows what he's doing.'

'Thank the gods for that,' said Ephialtes. 'Any kind of long journey is always full of dangers, isn't it?' They crossed a small square and turned behind the corner of an old warehouse onto a dark, deserted street.

The man stopped, turned around, and bared his head. 'You won't have to worry about any danger from now on, Ephialtes. You've reached the end of your journey.'

'How do you know my name? Who are you?' stammered the wretch. 'You're Spartan—'

'No,' said the man darkly, tossing his cloak behind his enormous shoulders and reaching towards the traitor with two hands that seemed the paws of a bear.

'But then . . . why . . . ?' gasped Ephialtes, stunned, as those hands closed around his neck like pincers. His face turned blue, his eyes strained in their sockets. He tried to struggle free with a last spurt of energy, then collapsed into the pool of urine that his body had expelled in its last agonized spasm.

Thus died Ephialtes, son of Eurydemus, he who had betrayed Leonidas at the Thermopylae, by the hand of a stranger.

*

It was late spring, and a new regent had been named in Sparta. After the death of Cleombrotus the regency had passed to his son Pausanias, since Leonidas' son was not yet of age. While the second king, Leotychidas, was in Asia with the allied fleet, Pausanias prepared to battle the Great King's army in the new Persian attack against Greece. This would be the decisive encounter: the Spartan government had recruited all the men that it could, including Helots, who were equipped as light infantry.

As soon as the troops were concentrated, the army began its advance, gathering up allies along the way. Warned of what was happening, the Persian general Mardonios, who had been conducting his army back towards Attica, retreated to Boeotia, where he could count on the support of the Thebans.

Having passed the isthmus, Pausanias penetrated into Boeotia, drawing up his troops along the Asopus river. Such an army had never before been seen: men from Athens, Corinth, Megara, Aegina, Troizen, Tegea and Eretria, thousands of hoplites were assembled to drive the Persians out of Greece once and for all, and to avenge their fallen at the Thermopylae and at Salamis.

But on that open terrain, the quick and agile Persian cavalry was at an advantage and the Hellenic army was often reduced to a position of defence. Cut off from their supply stations, Pausanias' army could not maintain communications and risked running out of provisions. The incursions of the Persian cavalry repelled all of their attempts to get water from the river; the Persians had even filled the Gargaphia spring with mud and polluted it so that the men were in danger of remaining without water.

Pausanias sent a detachment of servants and porters to seek provisions, but they never returned; the cavalry of

General Mardonios must have finished them off at the mountain pass of Cithaeron.

Talos learned all of these things from the Helots who were attempting to replenish their water supplies from the Oeroe stream, which was farther from the front and less exposed to the attacks of the Persian cavalry. From the top of a hill, near the village of Creusis, he scanned the Greek campfires on the plain: they were scattered randomly here and there, revealing the laxness and discouragement that had spread among the combatants. Brithos, observing the scene at Talos' side, pounded his fist against his thigh.

'By Ares!' he exclaimed. 'They're setting themselves up for a massacre; either they get out of there, or they attack and get it over with.'

'Neither would be easy,' responded Talos. 'A retreat could be disastrous: Pausanias has practically no cavalry and we're not at the Thermopylae, here. But I think that the critical moment will come tomorrow.' He turned towards his companion who had fallen suddenly silent.

'So this is the critical moment for me, too?' Brithos asked.

'If you hold to your decision, yes; tomorrow your comrades and your king will know what kind of a man they repulsed as a coward.'

Brithos sat down on the dry grass. It was a beautiful night, thousands of fireflies flitted among the stubble and the persistent song of the crickets spread through the hay-scented air.

'What are you thinking about?' asked Talos.

'Of these past months . . . of tomorrow. I'm alive because you stopped me from killing myself and because you gave me a reason to go on. Tomorrow I'll go into battle. If the victory is ours, if I prove myself, I'll go back to my house, to my city.'

'I know what you're trying to say,' interrupted Talos. 'You'll be a Spartan again and I'll be a Helot. Does this sadden you?'

'I don't know,' said Brithos. 'My hands are all sweaty and that's never happened to me, not even at the Thermopylae. I've been waiting for this moment for months, and yet now I wish that it would never come. There are so many things I still need to know, about myself, about you. But our time has run out. If I win my battle, my life and yours will take different roads. Even if I lose it, I still won't know any more than I do now.

'We've fought together, protected each other's life hundreds of times. We've killed to live, or just to survive, just as you said that night on the sea. Yet I still don't know why any of this has happened; why a Helot saved my life, a man who once found the point of my javelin at his throat. I don't know what kept me from killing you that day. I don't know who put that ancient bow in your hands, or why you left your mother and your people . . .'

Talos, who was leaning against a wild olive tree, his back to Brithos, sat down and turned around to face him. He wrinkled his brow as he twisted a stalk of wild oat between his fingers, as if he were trying to recall something. Then he spoke:

'The dragon and the wolf first
with merciless hate
wound each other.

> Then, when the lion of Sparta
> falls pierced, tamed by the javelin
> hurled by the long-maned Mede,
> He who trembled takes up the sword,
> the herd-keeper grips the curved bow,
> Together to immortal glory running.'

The verses, shaken from the depths of his mind, were suddenly clear: the verses of Perialla, the fugitive, the Pythia.

'What are you saying, Talos?' asked Brithos, jolted from his own thoughts.

'It's a prophecy, Brithos, that has become clear to me only now. The dragon of the Kleomenids and the wolf of Taygetus first wound each other with merciless hate and then run together to glory. "He who trembled" and the "herd-keeper" are you and me.'

'Who pronounced those words? When?' insisted Brithos.

'They are the words of a true prophetess. Do you remember the Pythia Perialla?'

'Yes,' murmured Brithos, 'and I remember the atrocious death of King Cleomenes.'

'I met her once, a long time ago, in Karas' cabin, and she foretold my future. These verses have lain buried in my mind. I'd never made sense of them until, just now, I heard them echoing inside me. Something unites our destinies, Brithos: it's what stayed your hand that day on the plain and what urged me to stop you that night in the forest. But I don't know more than this, I can't see. The gods know, Brithos, but rarely can we learn their thoughts.'

'What else did the Pythia tell you?'

'She said other things that I still can't interpret; the moment surely has not yet come. You ask why the great horn bow is in my hands. Well, it was entrusted to me long ago, so that I would preserve it. The same person who gave it to me taught me how to use it, as he taught me to manoeuvre my lame foot and my body, as he educated my heart and my mind. That bow holds the secret of my people. Don't ask me to reveal anything more to you because you are a Spartan, Brithos, and your race has subjugated my people.'

'You are a warrior . . . Talos, you are a warrior, aren't you? A warrior and a leader of your people. Perhaps this is what has united us and yet keeps our destinies separate; even if our spirits will it, we cannot disregard the limits that the gods have assigned us.'

'Not gods, Brithos, men. Look at me, no one is born a slave. Have you ever seen me afraid? Have you ever seen me betray? And yet for years I pastured old Krathippos' flocks, I cultivated his fields, obeying without rebelling, crying in secret from the humiliation and the pain. My Krios was torn to pieces by the fangs of your hound: but which of the two was more courageous? My little mutt, who gave his life to defend the flock, or your bloodthirsty monster? My people, at times, find the children that you Spartans abandon as prey to the beasts of the forest, and they raise them: this takes more courage than you know. Who then, deserves to be a slave? No, Brithos, don't tell me that fate has made us slaves, that the gods have given you power over us.'

Brithos stared at him, and if Talos could have seen the expression in those eyes in the darkness, he would have recognized the gaze of astonished pain of the warrior of the dragon, down there on the plain, that long ago day of his boyhood.

'Talos,' gasped Brithos with strange excitement in his voice. 'Talos, but you—'

'No, Brithos, what you imagine is not true. My father was called Hylas, son of Leobotes, Helot. And my foot was injured by the midwife who pulled me from my mother's womb. This is the truth told to me by Kritolaos, my grandfather, the wisest and most sincere of men, and this is why he whom you Spartans call "the cripple" is known among his people as "Talos the Wolf".'

The two youths sat in silence watching the fires on the plain. The calls of the sentinels reached them from time to time, blending with the song of the crickets. Talos spoke again:

'And so,' he said, 'with the light of the new day our ways will part. Tomorrow I will help you to don your armour, as is befitting for a Helot, but then you will proceed alone, because on that field there will be no glory for my people – only death. Remember, though, that behind that bronze breastplate the heart of Talos will be beating, along with yours.' He fell silent, twisting the oat stalk, because a knot closed his throat and Brithos wept that night for the first time in his life. In silence.

*

Pausanias consulted his officers and allied commanders and realized that it was no longer possible to remain in that position, where his hoplite infantry was unable to withstand the continuous and deadly raids of the Persian cavalry. Their only option was to withdraw to a more protected position that would be more advantageous for an attack.

The king agreed to put a plan of retreat into action. The allies moved first under the cover of night without extinguishing their fires to give the enemy the illusion that they were still camped in the same place. They would try to reach the narrow stretch of land near the temple of Hera at Plataea. The Peloponnesians and the Athenians, who occupied the right part of the formation, were to follow their allies in two parallel columns. But the darkness that protected their manoeuvres also hindered their march, and the King of Sparta soon realized that troop liaison had been lost.

Only the Athenians managed to proceed together at approximately a stadium's distance from Pausanias' Peloponnesian troops, marching along the line of the hills, keeping halfway up the slope so as to protect themselves from possible cavalry attacks.

In fact, they didn't need to wait long for the enemy: as soon as the first rays of the sun illuminated the plain, Mardonios' scouts realized that the Greek camp was deserted. The general immediately ordered the army to march, and launched the cavalry in pursuit of the retreating Greeks. As soon as they came into contact with Pausanias' rear guard, an infernal carousel began. Groups of cavalry hovered around the marching columns, showering clouds of arrows and javelins at them. Many warriors fell, powerless to drive back their attackers whose long-range bows kept them at a safe distance.

The situation was critical. Pausanias was furious with the allies, believing that they had abandoned him. He ordered his troops to form a compact front against the enemy and the two retreating lines managed to unite, but not without heavy losses.

The Spartan and Tegean hoplites, the Athenian infantry, and the heavily armoured Plataeans were in the front lines. The Plataeans, who were fighting with the ruins of their city – devastated by the Persians – at their backs, were animated by a determined desire for revenge. Pausanias gave orders to close the ranks and the word ran quickly from man to man. The reinforced front began to have some effect against the enemy cavalry.

Meanwhile a messenger, travelling at full gallop, had reached the allies already drawn up in front of the temple of Hera. He enjoined them to return immediately to the line of combat, but was answered with a refusal: since their order had been to close ranks at the temple, they would wait there for the others to join them; to move back out into the open would be madness.

Pausanias' army, unable to sustain the retreat, and kept in constant check by the enemy cavalry, continued to hope for reinforcements. All this time the enemy infantry advanced, confident of their numerical superiority and deploying the traitorous Thebans among their ranks.

The messenger returned on horseback, his mount steaming with sweat, and announced that the allies were waiting in formation in front of Plataea, and did not intend to move from there. Pausanias realized they were lost, and discouragement spread like wildfire among the soldiers, worn out by their march and the continuous onslaught of the enemy cavalry.

Mardonios was preparing to deal the final blow, realizing the confused and frightened state of the Greek troops. He advanced on his splendid white horse to give the order to attack: a deadly silence had fallen on the field strewn with dead and wounded soldiers.

In that moment, a cry that seemed to erupt from the mountainside echoed on the hills that surrounded the battlefield:

'ALALALALAI!'

Everyone turned in the direction from which the cry had come, but all they saw were sun-baked rocks. The Greek hoplites, their faces dripping with sweat under helmets made red-hot by the sun's blaze, turned back towards the enemy. The war cry sounded again:

'ALALALALAI!' and on the grey rock appeared a lone hoplite who descended the slope between the two armies at a run, in what seemed to be but a moment; the three-crested helmet was worn proudly and he gripped the shield of the dragon. He raised his spear towards the Greek army and with a voice like thunder he shouted once more:

'ALALALALAI!' Then, turning towards the enemy, he charged.

Talos, looking over the top of the rocky cliff, saw the gesture and shuddered: Brithos was attacking the enemy army alone! He ran down the hill crying, calling out desperately, tumbling crazily forward. He jolted to a stop on his skinned, bleeding feet and began to shoot his arrows furiously at the point where Brithos was rushing in the course of his folly.

It was but a moment, and the miracle occurred: forty thousand spears were lowered threateningly and the immense phalanx, thick with spikes like some horrendous animal, wavered for an instant and then exploded in that cry like a dry crack of thunder:

'ALALALALAI!' and without awaiting orders the infantrymen of Athens and of Plataea, the hoplites of Sparta, of Macistus, of Amyclae, of Tegea hurled themselves at the Persian front like a river in flood bursting its banks.

They collided with the enemy infantry with a rumble that rent the leaden air, and a group of Athenian hoplites immediately attempted to force a passage to the point where the three black crests waved amidst a sea of pikes.

Surrounded by the mass of enemies, Brithos swung his shield and his sword, cutting down anyone who got near him but, overpowered on all sides, his heart exploding in his chest, drenched in sweat and blood, he felt his knees giving way. A last cry burst from his chest with all the force of his youth, as he poured all of his strength into the arm that continued to smite the enemy before him.

Then he collapsed, cut at his heels from behind. He fell on his back holding his shield out still to defend himself, to strike with the last of his energy, until, pierced at his thighs, his loins, his throat, he lay in a lake of his own blood.

But by then the Greek spears were repelling the screaming tide from his mangled limbs, by then Mardonios was being dragged off his superb mount, and by then the Greek avalanche was overwhelming the Mede and Kissean infantry, overrunning the right wing of valorous Sacians and closing in on the centre like a deadly pair of claws.

Talos, scrambling among piles of cadavers, found Brithos still breathing. He worked frenziedly to free him from the fallen enemy corpses, from his own blood-slick shield. He lifted Brithos' head. Blood streamed from a horrible wound beneath his throat and his face was transformed by the pallor of death.

'You wanted to die,' murmured Talos, his voice low and broken. 'You wanted to die on the day of your triumph . . .'

The dying warrior saw a dirty, ruined face, lined with tears. With superhuman effort he lifted a hand and pointed to his bloody chest. 'What is there . . . behind this . . . breastplate . . . Talos, what is there?' and his head fell back, lifeless.

★

The sun was setting over the blood-soaked field of Plataea, on the obscenely mangled corpses, on the dead piled one atop another, and the thick cloud of dust seemed golden against its dying rays. Talos arose and looked around him, as if awakening from a dream. He saw a huge figure, in the distance, advancing on the back of an ass: Karas.

'You've come too late,' he said mournfully. 'It's all over.'

Karas looked at Brithos' body, already laid out as if for his funeral rites. 'He died as he wanted to die, after having redeemed his name. He will never know disease nor decay, he will be young forever . . . and he'll be buried with full honours.'

'No,' said Talos. 'No, not by them. I will prepare his funeral.'

They took the body and brought it to the edge of the field. Talos went to the river for water to wash him, and Karas gathered the wood, collecting broken spears and wreckage from the chariots in the nearby Persian camp. They raised a modest pyre. One beside the other they sat, watching the corpse that rested on top of the pyre covered by the black cloak that Brithos had worn at Aghias' funeral and that he had carried with him all these months.

'I tried to be here in time,' said Karas, 'but my journey was long and fraught with danger.'

'Even if you had been here, you couldn't have changed anything,' said Talos sadly. 'He had decided to die, there is no other explanation. And your mission?'

'Accomplished. Ephialtes is dead: I strangled him with my own hands.'

'Good. And now, my good friend, let us give the last salute to Brithos, son of Aristarkhos, Kleomenid. "He who trembled",' he added with a bitter grimace.

Karas went towards the still-burning Persian camp and returned with a fire-brand. Something abruptly caught his attention and he gestured to Talos. 'Look,' he said.

Talos turned and saw a hooded figure, his shoulders covered by a long grey cloak. The man advanced slowly to the middle of the battlefield and stopped about thirty paces from them.

'I'd say it's the same man who was in front of your cabin that night,' said Talos.

'That hooded grey cloak is commonly used by the

Spartans after gymnastics or after a battle to absorb sweat. Do you want me to go see, anyway?' asked Karas.

'No, it doesn't matter to me. Let him alone.'

He took the brand from Karas' hand and set the funeral pyre alight.

The flames rose vigorously, fed by the evening breeze. They quickly enveloped the body wrapped in the black cloak. Far off, smoke was rising from the great pyres that the Greeks had erected in their camp; they were beginning to burn the bodies of the fallen as they were brought in from the battlefield.

Talos cut a lock of his hair and tossed it into the flames, then threw in his cornel staff as well: the one – so strong and so flexible – that Kritolaos had chosen for him long long ago.

At that moment he felt a hand on his shoulder. He turned, his eyes veiled with tears, and found the hooded figure before him. He uncovered his head: it was the king, Pausanias, and he carried the great shield of the dragon. On its edge, with the point of his dagger he had carved a name: 'Kleidemos Aristarkhou Kleomenid'

'This is your name,' he said. 'Sparta has lost your father and your brother: two great warriors – such a noble family cannot be extinguished. You have lived far from us for a long time. The moment has come for you to return among your people. Look,' he added, and pointed towards the Greek camp: lined up in their ranks, still covered with blood and dust, a long column of soldiers marched to the tune of the pipes and to the roll of drums.

They drew up before the nearly extinguished pyre in silence. An officer unsheathed his sword and gave an order: the soldiers stiffened in salute raising spears that shone in the last rays of the sunset. Three times they launched to the sky that war cry that had given them the courage to win their last battle: the cry of Brithos, 'he who trembled'.

The soldiers withdrew, and the sound of pipes faded away into the distance. Karas gathered the ashes and the bones from the pyre and placed them in the shield, covering it with his cloak. He looked at the red clouds on the horizon, and then turned to Talos and murmured:

> 'Shining glory like the sun sets.
> He turns his back to the people of bronze
> when Enosigeus shakes Pelops' land.
> He closes his ears to the cry of his blood
> when the powerful voice of his heart
> calls him to the city of the dead.'

'Remember these words, Talos, son of Sparta and son of your people, the day that you shall see me again.'

Karas took the ass by the halter and disappeared into the shadows of the night.

PART TWO

That which comes from the gods must be borne with resignation, that which comes from our enemies, with courage.

Thucydides, II, 64, 2

12

THE CROSSROADS

KLEIDEMOS REMAINED THE WHOLE night next to the fire that had devoured the body of his brother Brithos. Found for a moment and lost for ever. He stared stonily at the fiery shadows slipping through the embers, gasping softly like a wounded animal. Behind him stretched the endless field of death that was Plataea; the stench of the blood that saturated the earth rose and was carried by the wind from the banks of the Asopus to the solitary columns of the temple of Hera. Dozens of stray dogs, emaciated by the long famine, roamed howling among the slaughtered bodies, ripping flesh from the stiffened limbs of the warriors of the Great King.

A trumpet from the Greek camp announced the third shift of guard duty as an enormous moon, red as a bloody shield, rose over the heat-scorched brush. Kleidemos raised his eyes to the gigantic disc, staring with wild pain. A terrifying figure was taking shape and substance behind the bleeding moon: Ares, god of war, glittering with metallic scales like a serpent. He wielded a double-bladed axe which he whirled through the air with an evil roar. The corpses suddenly came to life, spilling their guts, faces disfigured; they rose to their feet in the field of blood and marched silently towards the great warrior. He spun his obscene hatchet, renewing the carnage, seeding the plain with yet more mangled limbs, more and more . . . until the night dissolved.

Kleidemos shook himself, looking around with red eyes. His thoughts were awakened by the impending dawn. The din of the massacre that had sounded incessantly in his mind all night began to quieten.

A trumpet sounded fall-in at the Greek camp and a soldier soon appeared to collect Brithos' ashes and consign his weapons. Kleidemos rose to his feet. He slowly put on his brother's armour, took up his shield and his spear and began walking. The buzz of flies vibrated all around him . . . the flies, companions of *Thanatos*. He crossed the field unseeing, as if he were dreaming. A guard's voice startled him.

'Follow me, Kleidemos. Regent Pausanias awaits you in his tent.'

He entered the tent a short while later, passing between two guards who raised the mat hanging at the entrance. As soon as his tired eyes could make out his surroundings, he realized that the king was standing before him. Not very tall, he had grey hair and a short, pointed beard. His manicured hands did not seem those of a warrior and even his clothing had an air of elegance that Kleidemos had never seen in a Spartan. Two silver cups filled with red wine gleamed on a little table.

'Drink,' invited the king, handing him one of the cups. 'Today is a great day for Greece and this Konos wine is delicious. We found abundant quantities of it in Mardonios' tent, and these cups are part of his tableware. These barbarians certainly know how to appreciate the fine things in life!'

Kleidemos refused with a gesture of his hand; he hadn't eaten in so long that his stomach was riddled with cramps. Pausanias set the cup down and drew up a stool. 'Sit down,' he said, 'you must be tired.' The young man dropped onto the seat: his eyes were bloodshot, his face was weary and his hair was plastered with ashes. Pausanias looked at him carefully. 'The same big dark eyes,' he murmured, 'the same thin lips – you are the very portrait of your mother.'

Kleidemos started. 'My mother,' he said, 'has small, grey eyes.'

Pausanias sat in an armchair, twisting the Persian cup in his hands as if trying to find the right words. 'I understand what you mean,' he said. 'We are all strangers for you. Enemies, perhaps. But you must listen nonetheless to what I have to tell you, because your life among the sons of Sparta will be a long one.

'The armour that you wear belonged to your father and to your brother. Your mother has never forgotten you. We could have very well denied the fact that you exist, and let you go back to the mountain Helots to live out your life as a simple shepherd, but we are convinced that you could no longer live that way – you have become a warrior. You fought side by side with your brother Brithos for months. You were with him at the Thermopylae, you returned to Sparta with him, you helped him to regain his honour. And now you are the last survivor of a great family that must not be extinguished.'

Kleidemos raised his eyes from the floor. 'There are many things that I can't understand and many others that I can't yet even imagine. If what you say is true, tell me how I can return to the woman who gave birth to me only to abandon me. And how I can abandon the woman who has no blood ties to me, yet saved me from death, nurtured me and loved me. Tell me how I can leave the humble, unfortunate people who welcomed me as their own – even though I was the son of their enemy – and return to the city which enslaves them? The city that wanted me dead just because I was lame. Do you believe that a man can be born twice? I was torn from the clutches of the Underworld. The man who saved me, Kritolaos, the wisest of all men, gave me my name – Talos – so that I would never forget my misfortune. How can I begin to call myself Kleidemos now? I've never seen my mother, and my father is nothing more than a face, a look, the dragon on the shield of the Kleomenids. And my brother Brithos . . . is no more than ashes now, ashes on the field of Plataea . . .'

Pausanias wiped his sweaty brow. 'Please listen to what I have to say. I have no answer to any of your questions. But don't judge us . . . yet. Many are the mysteries of a man's life, and his destiny is in the hands of the gods. But there is much that I can tell you which you do not know. Sparta is not cruel with her sons. But we must all yield to the law which is greater than any one of us, even we who are kings. The mothers of Sparta know this well – the mothers who must watch their sons march towards death. And your father knew this well. When he carried you up to Mount Taygetus, that night so long ago: a stormy night, an anguished night, gripping you to his chest. The weight of that terrible yet necessary gesture weighed on his heart for all the years he had left to live. The blade which pierced his heart at the Thermopylae was no more sharp nor more cruel than the one that rent his spirit that night. A black veil descended over his eyes, and no one ever saw joy in his face again. He was spared nothing: from the moment he learned that you were still alive, his torment only worsened. That night that Brithos went to the mountainside armed, intent on killing you, his blood turned to ice. And yet he could not say a word. Burning tears that no one ever saw – not even your mother – gnawed away at him year after year in an endless agony. He loved you until the end, grievously. He fell, disdaining his own life, spilling his blood in the burning dust. Suffering . . . for you. This was your father, the great Aristarkhos – the Dragon.'

Kleidemos was looking the king straight in the eye now. He stood stock still, hands frozen on his thighs. Two large tears were the only indication of life on his face of grey stone. Pausanias set down his cup on the table and his hands rose to his face. He fell silent as if listening to the drone of the cicadas, the confused buzz of voices outside the tent. When he spoke again his metallic voice betrayed his emotion.

'And your mother was treated no more kindly by fate . . . or by the malevolence of the gods. Her beauty faded early, destroyed by grief when you were torn from her arms. She lost her husband, the man she had loved with all her soul since her maidenhood. She saw her son Brithos return alive from the Thermopylae after she had already

225

given him up for dead. Only to lose him again, when he disappeared after the suicide of his friend Aghias. And tomorrow she will learn that he was alive, when they deliver the urn containing his ashes. The women of Sparta know well that their sons are born mortals, but their pain is no less for this. You are the only one left to her, although she has never dared hope that you would return.'

Kleidemos dried his eyes. 'There's another woman waiting for me in her little cottage on Mount Taygetus. The woman I have always called mother,' he said in a flat voice.

'I know,' replied the king. 'That woman is very dear to you. You will be able to see her whenever you like. Remember nonetheless that she has been much more fortunate than the unhappy creature that gave birth to you. But this is not all you need to know. I realize that our laws seem merciless to you, but is the world outside any different? We must survive in a world that has no pity for the vanquished. You were witness to the fury of the invaders yesterday. The body of King Leonidas was found decapitated and crucified at the Thermopylae. The same fate would have been mine today had we lost.

'Brithos' sacrifice saved the lives of thousands of his comrades, young men like yourself whose mothers would have had to mourn for the rest of their days. You'll tell me that he was unjustly disgraced by those same comrades just one year ago, that they pushed him to the verge of suicide. But he vindicated himself and his name will be celebrated for centuries – a name that you inherited with his last breath of life. Brithos now wanders in the reign of shadows and his spirit will find no peace until you have accepted the legacy of sacrifice and honour carved on the Kleomenid shield. You have a great crossroads before you: one road leads to a quiet life, tranquil, but insignificant; the other will lead you to a difficult, turbulent existence, but offers you the heritage of a race of heroes. Only you can choose. No one can assist you. The gods have led you here, to where you are now. Your destiny is marked and I don't believe that you will turn back.'

Pausanias fell silent. He then touched his sword to the shield hanging from the tent post. Several women came in, bringing water with them. They undressed the young man and washed him, as others prepared a bed. Kleidemos let them massage his aching limbs and accepted a cup of warm broth. Then he lay down and fell into a deep sleep.

The king took a last long look at the boy and smiled to himself. He called one of the guards. 'No one shall enter this tent or disturb the sleep of this man until I have returned,' he ordered. 'If he should awaken on his own, let him go where he likes. But follow him, without being seen, and keep me informed of his whereabouts.'

The guard took up his post. Shortly thereafter the king exited the tent, fully armed. He leapt on his horse and galloped towards the Persian camp, followed by a group from the royal guard. His troops had been garrisoning the camp since the night before. The allied army commanders awaited him in the tent of the former Persian general.

'Friends!' exclaimed King Pausanias, raising a cup. 'My friends, let us drink to Zeus our King and Hercules our Leader! They have granted us victory over the barbarians. I salute the concord of all Greeks that has made this day so great and so memorable!'

A chorus of acclamations greeted his words, as the servants passed to fill the quickly emptied cups. But Pausanias had not finished. 'My fellow officers,' he began again, 'allow me to say that these barbarians are truly mad! They already possess all these marvellous things, and yet they have suffered such great pains and taken on such a long journey to fight over our wretched black broth!'

The guests laughed in appreciation and gave start to the banquet which lasted all that night. But that was the day that Pausanias was struck by the splendour of Persian riches and luxury and began to be dissatisfied with the frugality of Sparta.

13

HOMECOMING

THE CLOUDS PASSED SLOWLY across the sky, urged on by a light breeze. They sailed over the disc of the sun, hiding it as it sank towards the horizon and cast long shadows on the plain. Kleidemos saw the peak of Mount Taygetus burst into golden flame. He'd been away for so long. He could almost hear the dogs barking, the bleating of the sheep as they entered their fold on the high pasture. He thought of the tomb of Kritolaos, the wisest of men, covered with oak leaves. He saw himself as a child again, sitting on the banks of the Eurotas with his flock, little Krios happily wagging his tail. And the woman whom he had always thought his mother; he imagined her sitting at the threshold of her little cottage on the mountain, sad and alone, spinning wool with her callused fingers, staring at the horizon with her tiny, grey, hope-filled eyes.

The path that led up the mountain was just a few steps away when Kleidemos stopped, leaning on his spear. A horseman raced by at a gallop, raising a cloud of dust and disappearing as suddenly as he had come.

The wind was still, but big black clouds had now piled into an enormous mass in the middle of the sky. They seemed to throb slowly, a living thing. Kleidemos was gazing up at them when a lightning bolt flickered for an instant in the belly of the gigantic mass, which seemed to shudder. Then, as he watched, the cloud mass broke free of its form, stretching, twisting, writhing, to form a shape there in the sky. A clear, unmistakable shape: the shape of a dragon.

Kleidemos heard the voice of Kritolaos in his mind, echoing words pronounced one distant night: 'The gods send signs to men, sometimes . . .'

He turned, leaving the trail that led up the mountain behind him, his heart swollen with sadness. He continued on down the dusty road as if pushed by some invisible force, until he found himself standing in front of the home of the Kleomenids, guarded by majestic oaks. The faint light of a lamp which filtered from under a window was the only sign of life in the big, austere house.

Kleidemos stopped, expecting to hear Melas barking, but no sound disturbed the utter silence. He started towards the centre of the courtyard but pulled back instantly, horrified: the hound lay on the family altar, his throat cut. His white fangs were bared in a horrible grimace. The animal had been sacrificed to the shade of Brithos, and his fierce soul was now roaming the paths of Hades in search of his master.

Kleidemos walked to the doorway, from which a black veil hung. He laid his hand there and the heavy door opened, creaking. He saw the great atrium, faintly illuminated. Sitting on a stool at its centre was a woman dressed in black, her hands clasped in her lap. She looked up at him with blazing eyes, while her still body seemed stiffened by death itself. Kleidemos froze on the threshold as if turned to stone by this apparition. He couldn't take a step. The woman got to her feet, swaying, and moved towards him. She stretched out pale hands. 'I've been waiting so long,' she said in a whisper. 'My son, it's taken you so long to come back to me . . .'

Kleidemos regarded her in silence.

'I know,' she said, 'you don't know how to answer, but you recognize me, don't you?' Her arms dropped to her sides.

'I'm your mother. Ismene, bride of Aristarkhos, mother of Brithos . . .'

She turned her bewildered eyes to the sacred images of the Kleomenid heroes, blinded by dark strips of cloth. 'Dead . . . they're all dead. And you were dead, too, Kleidemos.' The boy trembled as Ismene lifted her hand to touch his face. 'But you've come back to your home, now,' she said, pointing at the open door. 'Twenty-two years . . . twenty-two years have passed since I saw you for the last time at that very threshold, in your father's arms.'

'My father?' murmured Kleidemos vacantly. 'My father abandoned me to the wolves.'

Ismene fell to her knees. 'No, no! No, my son, your father entrusted you . . . to the pity of the gods. He sacrificed all of the lambs of his flock so that the gods would take pity. His anguish had no rest, his torture no end. He had to choke back his tears. And when the pain was too much for him, he fled from this house, wrapped in his cloak. He fled to the wood . . . to the mountain . . .'

Kleidemos looked towards the wall, where he saw a grey wool cape with a hood hanging from a nail. He shuddered. In his mind's eye he could see that hooded man . . . up at the high spring, on a windy afternoon: his father! Ismene's broken voice brought him to his senses. 'He offered his own life to the shades of his ancestors so that you might be spared. Oh son . . . my son . . . none of us can ever disobey the laws of the city, and none of us knows any other way. Only this everlasting pain. Incessant pain, awaiting only death. And everlasting tears.'

Ismene moaned, hiding her face in her hands. Her curved back shook and her soft crying cut him like a blade in the deep silence of the house, moved him like a lullaby. Kleidemos felt a hot wave encompass his heart, melting away the numbness that had overcome him. He bent over her, took off her veil and laid his hand on her grey head, caressing her hair softly. Ismene raised her red eyes to his face.

'Mother,' he said with a tired smile, 'mother, I'm back.'

Ismene grasped his arms, pulling herself laboriously to her feet. She gave him a long look of incredulous love.

'Mother . . . it's me. I'm back.'

Ismene clutched him to herself, whispering incomprehensible words into his ear. Kleidemos held her close and he could feel his mother's heart beating against his chest, stronger and wilder, like that of a sparrow that a boy squeezes too tightly in his hand. Her heart beat fast and then suddenly weakened until it stopped beating entirely. Ismene collapsed, lifeless, in her son's arms.

Kleidemos looked at her without believing. He lifted her and held her to his chest, walking towards the threshold. Legs planted wide, he raised her still body to the sky. A dull lament escaped him, a confused whimper which became shrill and harsh until it exploded into a cry which rose, full of horror and despair, up to the cold distant stars. He howled like an animal being ripped apart by a pack of ferocious wolves and his howl flew over the fields, over the city rooftops, to the banks of the Eurotas, reverberating on the harsh slopes of Mount Taygetus. It dashed against the rocks and was lost in a thousand echoes, over the sea.

14

LAHGAL

KING PAUSANIAS UNROLLED a map onto the table. He
weighed down the edges and raised his eyes towards
Kleidemos, who was sitting opposite him. 'Come closer,'
he said. 'I have to show you something.' The youth stood
and leaned over the table. 'Look,' said the king, pointing
at a jagged line on the right of the map. 'This is Asia – the
land of the rising sun. Or rather, this is the coast of Asia
that faces our country. It then extends to the east for tens
of thousands of stadia, all the way to the river Ocean. But
no one has ever been there, except for the men of the
Great King, and we know very little about those distant
lands. What you see here,' he continued, indicating little
red circles along the coastline, 'are the Asian cities inhabited by the Greeks: Aeolians, Ionians and Dorians. Each
one of them is larger, more populous and richer than
Sparta. Our victories at Plataea and Mycale have liberated
them from the dominion of the barbarians for now, but
we cannot rule out another invasion. The Great King has
never contacted us or admitted his defeat in any way: do
you realize what that means?'

'That the war isn't over, and that hostilities could start
up again at any moment.'

'That's right. Don't forget that the Great King is still

demanding that all of Hellas recognize his sovereignty. He has understood that he cannot dominate the Asian Greeks without controlling those of us on the continent. When he makes another move, it will be to bring his army back to this land. So we must absolutely establish outposts in Asia to keep a watchful eye on the movements of his armies. The barbarians are best fought in Asia, not at the doors to our own homes. The ephors and the elders have decided that I should depart with a squad of Peloponnesians to occupy the island of Cyprus. Afterwards, I am to install a garrison at Byzantium, the city that controls the Hellespont strait. This is it, here.' He pointed his finger at the map. 'This narrow waterway separates Asia from Europe.'

Kleidemos could not understand how it was possible to draw the land and sea on a piece of sheepskin, and how such a drawing could help one to journey towards one place or return to one's point of departure. 'Tell me,' he asked timidly, 'is Mount Taygetus shown in this drawing?'

'Certainly,' replied the king, smiling. 'Look, your mountain is right here, and this is Sparta, our city.'

'But are there other lands past the borders of this drawing?'

'Yes, very many: towards the north and towards the south, towards the east and towards the setting sun. They are all surrounded by the river Ocean, whose waters cannot be navigated by any ship built by man. And no one knows what is beyond the river Ocean.'

'Have the ephors and elders decided on the moment of departure?'

'The ships will set sail with the new moon, and I want

you with me when we leave. I will command the allied fleet which will take possession of the island of Cyprus. It is a very beautiful land and we must gain control of it; the Persian fleet must no longer have any base in our sea. Why do I think you should accompany me? Because you must forget the events of your past and begin a new life. You'll see new lands, beautiful cities, things you've never even dreamed of. Your servants will take care of your home while you are away.'

'My home?' murmured Kleidemos. 'I no longer know where my home is. I no longer know anything. At night I dream of my past life and when I wake I don't recognize anything around me.'

Pausanias rolled up the map again and put it away. He approached Kleidemos. 'I understand how you feel. Few men have had a destiny like yours, and even fewer have had to deal with trials so difficult. But now the first part of your life has ended. You can take the time that remains to you in your own hands and build a new life – with the help of the gods, and of the men who know your strength and your resolve. Life does not hand out only suffering and misfortunes; joy and pleasure can yet be yours. The gods have tested your heart sufficiently; they have certainly reserved a great future for you, and I believe in you as well, Kleidemos, son of Aristarkhos.'

*

The allied squad, equipped with almost two hundred warships, sailed into the waters of Cyprus one morning at the beginning of the summer. Kleidemos had never seen anything like it. Gone were the stomach cramps and the nausea that had gripped him on their journey from Gytheum to Cythera. The wind filled the sails of the great vessels drawn up in a column, their bronze rostra slicing into the sea, which foamed up around the brightly coloured figureheads.

A blue standard flew on Pausanias' flagship as he began his approach. The oars dipped into the sea and the fleet started to press portside along the southern coast of the island. The head squad moored in the early afternoon, under a splendid sun, without encountering any resistance; the Great King's forces had already withdrawn. The Phoenician ships from Tyre and Sidon had returned to their own ports, apparently biding their time. Pausanias took quarter in a beautiful house in the city of Salamis, attended to by a number of servants.

Kleidemos spent his time at the training grounds and gymnasiums of the city, learning combat technique from his instructors. Wearing hoplite armour took some practice; its weight seemed suffocating. One day, as he was drying off after a bath, a boy with a mass of black curls approached him. 'Are you Spartan, sir?' he asked curiously.

'Yes, I am. And who are you?'

'My name is Lahgal. I'm Syrian. My master owns this bathhouse and he bought me at the market of Ugarit. That's a beautiful city: have you ever been there?'

'No,' answered Kleidemos, smiling, 'I haven't. It's the first time I've ever left my homeland, and my first voyage by sea.'

'Do you mean to say that you don't even know this island?'

'No, I don't; I've never been outside Salamis.'

'But then you haven't seen anything, sir! This island is marvellous. The best oil is produced here, and the most inebriating wine. Pomegranates grow here, and the sweet dates that grow on the palms will be ripe at the end of the summer. The goddess of love, whom you Greeks call Aphrodite, was born in these waters. We Syrians call her Astarte.'

'I see that you've come to love this land. Don't you miss your home?'

'Oh no, sir,' said the boy, shrugging, 'I was brought here when I was very small. I must not have cost much, but my master made a good deal. I run errands for him and clean the baths. I make sure that the girls do not rob from him when they go to market, or prostitute themselves behind his back to put the money in their own pockets. He gives me a lot of freedom. I can come and go as I please after I've done my work.'

'Well,' continued Kleidemos, amused, 'would you like to show me this island that you say is so beautiful? Do you think your master would allow you to take me around?'

'To tell you the truth, sir,' said the boy, a bit perplexed, 'my master says he doesn't do good business with you Spartans. No one wants your ugly iron coins. The Athenians are much better; they pay with pretty silver coins with an owl on them. They drink much more and like to have fun with both the boys and the girls. But I like you even if you are Spartan. If my master doesn't need me, I'll be waiting for you here, in front of the door, tomorrow morning when the cock crows. Do you have a horse?'

'No, Lahgal, I'm sorry. But maybe I can take one of the

porters' asses; I don't think they need them now that we're stationed here.'

'All right,' said the boy. 'I would have preferred a horse, but an ass will do. Goodbye!'

The following morning as the sun was rising they were already travelling down the coastal road that led to the city of Paphos, where the temple of Aphrodite stood. The road wound through the hillside studded with olive trees and little white houses, descending every now and then towards the sea. The air was redolent with pine resin and salt water, and the green fields were dotted with white and yellow flowers graced with fluttering butterflies, now that the sun was drying the dew from their wings.

Kleidemos felt light-hearted, riding along on his ass with his young friend sitting in front of him.

'You haven't told me your name,' observed Lahgal.

'It will seem strange to you,' replied Kleidemos smiling, 'but it's not easy for me to answer that question.'

'You're teasing me,' objected the boy. 'Even little children can say their names.'

'Well, Lahgal,' explained Kleidemos, 'the fact is that I have two names because I have two families, yet I have no father and the mother who remains to me is not my real mother, who died ... a couple of months ago in my home, which I had never seen. Or rather, which I lived in for several months when I could neither understand nor remember.' Lahgal turned around to look at him, utterly confused.

'You think I'm mad, don't you?' he asked with a smile. 'And yet everything I've told you is absolutely true.' Lahgal's expression went from bewilderment to something deeper, more intense. He turned forward to face the dusty road.

'Perhaps . . .' he said after a brief silence, 'perhaps you're different . . . different from the other men who live on this earth.'

'No, my young friend, I'm not. I'm a person just like you, for whom the gods have reserved a strange destiny. If you like I'll tell you my story.' Lahgal nodded. 'Well, long ago, before you were even born, a child was born in a noble home of Sparta. His parents called him Kleidemos. But they soon realized that he was lame, and the father carried him away one night and abandoned him on the mountainside. This was the law of Sparta: no male child who was deformed, and so could not become a warrior, was allowed to live. But this child was found by an old shepherd, a Helot who brought his master's flock to pasture on the slopes of Mount Taygetus. He saved the child and his daughter raised him as her own. He named the boy Talos, and that's what the Helots called him.

'The child grew and learned to wrestle and to use a bow and arrow. He called the woman who raised him "mother" and the old shepherd, "grandfather". He also learned to force his crippled foot to support the weight of his body and to move with dexterity.

'This boy had a brother, a little older than him, raised to be a Spartan warrior. One day they met, and they fought without ever knowing that they were brothers. Talos was nearly killed—'

'Why did you fight your brother?' interrupted Lahgal. 'You are Talos, aren't you?'

'Because my brother and his companions had attacked

a girl who was my friend, the daughter of a peasant who lived on the plain. From that day on, he hated me. One day he came to finish me off, or so I thought. He let his ferocious hound slaughter all my sheep, and my own little dog. But it didn't end there ... War broke out, you see, between the cities of Greece and the Great King of Persia.

'We Helots were brought to the city to be chosen as the warriors' attendants, and my brother chose me. I accompanied him to the Thermopylae, and I saw my father there as well – the father who had abandoned me as a child. I did not know who he was, but he knew ... I think. I remember the way he looked at me; there seemed to be infinite pain burning within him, held in check by the power of his will. My father was a great warrior, the cousin of King Cleomenes and King Leonidas. He perished with the other warriors of Sparta, butchered all on the rocks of the pass.'

Kleidemos fell silent and only the scuttling of the ass's hooves could be heard on the stony path. A farmer who was scything the grass in a nearby field raised his head to wipe away the sweat and waved at them with his wide-brimmed hat. Some storks who had been poking around for insects in the cut grass took flight, disappearing behind a hill.

'I've heard tell of the three hundred heroes of the Thermopylae.' Lahgal said suddenly. 'I heard a funeral lament that was written for them by a great poet who lives on the island.'

'Did the dirge mention that two of those warriors were saved?'

'No, I thought they all died.'

'That's not what happened. Two of them were spared, and I accompanied them to Sparta on orders from the king. One of them was my brother Brithos. They had a message to deliver to the elders, but no one was ever to know what it said. It was rumoured that they had lied or sought to escape, and no one in their city would have anything to do with them. They were branded as cowards and traitors. One of them hanged himself in his own home. The other, my brother, tried to kill himself one night on the mountain, but I'd been watching him, and managed to stop him. I brought him back to my mountain cabin and convinced him to vindicate himself by fighting a solitary war against the Persians.

'I arranged to have the armour of our father taken from his home and Brithos wore it that autumn, winter and spring, fighting in Phocis, Locris and Boeotia. I was with him, fighting at his side. We hid in the wood, sleeping in mountain caves. By day we would take Persian detachments by surprise, attack isolated groups requisitioning food and forage. My brother was a fury: he killed more than two hundred Persian officers and soldiers, while I covered him with my bow and arrow.'

The sun was high and the day was hot. The road led down to a little clearing where a shimmering plane tree stood. The ass trotted towards the shade, attracted by the cool green grass. Kleidemos let him go and, as he grazed, sat in the shadow of the huge tree with Lahgal. The waves of the nearby sea lapped the beach, wetting a myriad of brightly coloured pebbles that glittered like gems in the sunshine.

'You never knew you were brothers?' asked Lahgal, his back still turned to Kleidemos.

'No,' he replied, watching the swirling sea. 'Only Brithos' eyes looked like mine. He was the image of our father. Taller than me and more muscular; wearing that heavy armour had made him very powerful. When he stripped to wash himself in the river he looked like Hercules. I resemble my mother.'

'Didn't that give it away?' asked Lahgal, surprised.

'No, it didn't, because I looked like a servant and he looked like a nobleman. Servitude accustoms you to keeping your head down. It takes the light out of your eyes, it makes you similar to the animals you spend your time with—' He stopped; Lahgal had turned around and was looking at him sadly. Kleidemos shifted to face him as well, as though he had felt the weight of his stare. 'Did I say something that has made you feel bad? I have . . . I can see that.'

The boy lowered his head, wiping his eyes with his sleeve.

'You mustn't feel sorry for me, Lahgal,' continued Kleidemos. 'I was happy as a servant, there with my grandfather on the mountain, with my dog, my lambs and now . . . I have lost my family, my people. I wear the shield and the armour of the Kleomenids, one of the most noble families of Sparta, but I no longer know who I am. I regret leaving, but I can't turn back, and I see nothing before me. Brithos died at Plataea: he redeemed his honour but he lost his life. It was King Pausanias – the man who has occupied this island – who gave me my brother's weapons and told me my real name: Kleidemos. I went back to the house where I was born and there I met the woman who gave birth to me: my mother Ismene. If I live to be a thousand, I shall never forget that night. My heart was as hard as a stone at the thought that she had had the courage to abandon her son to the wolves of the mountain. I was relishing the idea of torturing her, of making her suffer – the proud bride of Aristarkhos. But the creature I found before me was shattered, her face furrowed by tears. Her mind . . . vacillating at the threshold of madness.

'When I held her to me and promised that I'd never leave her again, her heart couldn't bear it. She died in my arms.'

Lahgal got to his feet and held out his hand to Kleidemos, who got up as well. They walked in silence along the seashore, the water at their ankles, listening to the sound of the waves. Lahgal bent down to collect a beautifully coloured shell and handed it to Kleidemos. 'This is for you. It will bring you luck.'

'Thank you, Lahgal. It's lovely,' he said, accepting the gift.

'Oh, it's nothing, but it will remind you of me when you go away, Two-Names.'

Kleidemos tightened his fist around the shell. 'Two-Names? Did you call me Two-Names?'

'Doesn't that seem like a nice name?'

'Very nice. And very . . . appropriate.'

Lahgal smiled and winked. 'I'm hungry, Two-Names, aren't you?'

'I could eat an ox with his horns!'

'Well, run then! Let's see who gets back to the ass first!' challenged the boy as he raced through the water, raising iridescent splashes.

★

The sea seemed to be on fire when the bay of the port of Paphos appeared; the sun was low over the water and its golden glow reflected onto the houses of the city. Towering palms swayed above the roof tops, revealing clusters of yellow flowers among the serrated leaves. Scarlet pomegranate blossoms peeked through shiny dark green foliage in the gardens. The surrounding hills were covered with olive trees, sparkling silver amidst the black tips of the cypresses. Kleidemos stopped the ass to enjoy the spectacle. 'I've never seen anything so beautiful, Lahgal, in all of my life. Is that the city of Paphos?'

'No,' replied the boy, 'that is just the port. The city is behind those hills to our right. It is very ancient, and was built around its temple. I've never been able to enter the temple, though, because I'm a child . . . or perhaps because I'm a slave. I don't know. They say that there are marvellous things inside. Let's go, the road is still long.'

'We won't reach it before nightfall,' observed Kleidemos. 'There won't be anything to see.'

'You're wrong about that!' said Lahgal, winking. 'The temple remains open until late at night for pilgrims who want to make a sacrifice to Aphrodite. They say that the goddess watches them as they make their sacrifice, and if she likes one of them . . .'

'Just what does this sacrifice consist of, Lahgal?' asked Kleidemos, intrigued.

'Come on!' exclaimed Lahgal, turning around to look at his companion. 'Then it's true what they say about you Spartans – that you are thick, and a little slow up here,' he said, knocking against his head.

'What do you mean?' insisted Kleidemos.

Lahgal pressed his heels into the ass's flank. 'All right, so I have to explain everything. You see, there are many beautiful maidens who live inside the temple: they are the servants of the goddess. The pilgrims enter, make an offering to the temple and then choose one of the girls and then they . . . make sacrifice to the goddess of love. Now do you understand?'

'I do,' admitted Kleidemos, cracking an embarrassed smile. 'I understand. But what does the goddess have to do with all this? To me it seems like a ploy to fatten up the temple priests through some thick-headed dolt like me.'

'Don't say such a thing!' interrupted Lahgal. 'You must be mad! If the goddess hears you, she will strike you down!'

'That's enough, Lahgal, no more teasing. The gods cannot afflict me more than they already have. Nothing can frighten me after what I've lived through.'

Lahgal twisted around and took Kleidemos' hand tightly between his own. 'Beware, Two-Names. The goddess truly exists, and she reveals herself in this temple. Many people have seen her take on a number of shapes, or so they say. But anyone who has seen her remains so profoundly impressed that his heart and mind are never the same. They say that a Persian satrap to whom the goddess appeared was struck speechless, and never spoke another word.'

It was getting dark, and there was no one around. The road wound upwards through a forest of holm oaks which rustled in the light sea breeze. The birds nestling among the branches filled the wood with their twittering. Lahgal, tired of the long journey, shivered and pulled his cape tight around his thin shoulders. The last ray of sunlight sunk into the distant sea, which became leaden.

'I have to urinate,' he said suddenly, breaking the heavy silence.

'Right now? Can't you wait until we can see the city, at least?'

'I said I have to urinate!'

'All right, all right, don't get upset,' Kleidemos pulled on the ass's halter and he stopped. He got down while the boy, slipping down the packsaddle, was already at the side of the road. He was back in a moment.

'That was it?' asked Kleidemos.

'That was it.'

'Well, get back on, it's late.'

'My bottom hurts and I'd rather walk. You're comfortable there on the saddle, but I've been sitting on a bunch of bones. I've had enough.'

'All right. Let's walk.'

A thin crescent moon appeared over the tops of the trees, shedding a pale glow on the dusty white road. They walked for a while in silence.

'Two-Names, don't you want to go to the temple any more?'

'No, I'd like to go, really. After what you told me, it would be foolish not to go. Who knows, maybe the goddess has something to tell me.'

'You're not afraid, Two-Names?'

'Yes,' replied Kleidemos, 'I am a little afraid. The gods can tell us things we'd rather not know.'

The city began to appear behind a curve in the road: it stood on a hill, ashen in the moonlight.

'Lahgal,' Kleidemos began again, 'do you know what the statue of the goddess looks like?'

'I've heard it described. But I've never seen it, as I was saying. It doesn't have features; it doesn't have a face and a body, like the statues of the other gods.'

'What does it look like, then?'

'Well, they say it is a double spiral that tapers at the top and comes to a point.'

'That's very strange. I've never heard of anything like that.'

'They say it is the symbol of life, or the shape of life itself.'

'But life has different shapes: in men, in animals, in plants, in the gods themselves. Don't you agree?'

'This is what we see. But I have the feeling that life is a single thing. When it's there, men move, they talk, they think, they love and they hate. Animals graze and chase each other over the fields. Trees and bushes grow and flourish. When it's gone, bodies dry out and decay. Trees wither.'

'And the gods?' asked Kleidemos, astonished by the words of the boy who trotted along at his side, trying to measure his steps with Kleidemos' rolling gait.

'The gods cannot be alive if they can't die. Or perhaps they are life itself. Anyway, the artists who make them look like us are wrong. That's why the goddess you'll see is a double spiral. She has the shape of life.'

Kleidemos stopped in his tracks and turned to Lahgal. 'Who taught you these things? I've never heard a child talk like this.'

'No one. I've listened in on the pilgrims who remain at the temple. They speak an old dialect from this island that you would never understand. No one pays attention to a child. A slave-child to boot. They talk as if only their dogs or horses were around, but I listen because I want to learn everything I can. And some day ... perhaps I'll be free and be able to come and go as I like, and visit distant lands.'

The first houses of Paphos were just a stone's throw away. Lahgal headed straight towards a sorry-looking city gate, seemingly in disuse, but the road soon led to the high part of the city and the temple lights glittered before them. They stopped at a spring.

'Wash yourself,' said Lahgal. 'You smell sweaty.'

'Listen, Lahgal, you surely don't imagine that—'

'I'm not imagining anything, you fool. You are going to wash before going into the temple, aren't you?'

Kleidemos took off his chiton and washed himself at the spring. Lahgal then brought him to the entrance of the temple. It was not very tall, built of blocks of grey stone with a portico in front. Its wooden columns supported a lintel which was decorated with brightly painted panels. Kleidemos stopped to look at them.

'You'll see them better in the light of day,' protested

Lahgal. 'Go inside now,' he said, pushing him towards the entrance. 'I'll wait for you out here.'

Kleidemos approached the threshold: a reddish glow filtered from the half-open doors. He entered a large hall, divided by two rows of wooden columns, each of which supported a three-flamed oil lamp. The air was permeated with a sharp, inebriating odour coming from a bronze brazier at the end of the hall, in front of the image of the goddess. The large bronze sculpture stood as Lahgal had described it on a pedestal. The flickering light of the lamps cast rippling reflections into the spirals, sudden flashes which seemed to animate the statue with a sinuous upward movement.

Deep silence surrounded the idol; Kleidemos could hear the soft crackling of the incense on the brazier coals. He sat down on an oxhide there on the floor; his limbs felt sluggish, sleepy somehow. He couldn't take his eyes off the statue, as the double spiral seemed slowly to take on a life of its own, rotating upwards, its coils sparkling with a bloody light. The movement seemed to become imperceptibly faster and Kleidemos blinked to chase away the illusion. It had to be an illusion . . . or was it the effect of that strange fragrance that pervaded the air? He was so tired, and hungry, as if he hadn't eaten all day – yes, that must be it; he was seeing things.

In fact, the image was now motionless on its pedestal, but to its right . . . to its left? . . . a woman appeared. He rose to his knees as she stood before him, and her crimson dress slipped off her golden limbs . . . slipped to the floor, where it seemed a scarlet rose, withering at her feet. Her legs, like those of a magnificent deer, bore rings of silver, shining ... the same reflections in the image of the goddess and on her thighs of bronze. And the fragrance ... it was stronger, and different, scented with almonds, bitter somehow. But why couldn't he see her face? Long flaming hair covered her face, fell over her breasts. She came closer ... closer ... lifted her head – a soft music caressed his ears, the indefinable melody of distant flutes – and she showed her face. O most powerful gods ... most powerful gods! It was the face of Antinea.

He reached out his arms. 'O goddess, lady of this place, don't let this be a cruel dream,' he whispered. 'O my far-away love ... why was our season so short? ... Antinea – her face dissolving behind a veil of tears, that night, with the dying sun, never to return – Antinea!' he gasped. 'Antinea ...'

He lay back in a wave of fragrant hair, set ablaze in an ardent embrace that seemed never ending. The light of the lamps trembled and faded, the last sparks scattering in the gloom that enveloped the sanctuary. The idol of bronze, perfectly still now, cold and dark, reflected only the pale rays of the moon.

*

Dawn began to lighten the great hypostyle hall of the temple. A man wrapped in a dark cloak entered through a door behind the image of the goddess and walked to where Kleidemos was still in a deep sleep. He turned to the woman lying next to him.

'Well? Did he talk?'

The girl covered herself and got up. 'No, nothing of any interest,' she said softly. 'The fumes from the sacred brazier had totally inebriated him. But he kept calling me by a certain name—'

'What name? It could be important.'

'Antinea, I think. He was so passionate, his eyes were full of tears. I felt terribly sorry for him,' she said, looking over at the youth. Kleidemos stirred but did not open his eyes. 'You could have spared me this one,' she added, whispering.

'Don't complain,' said the man. 'You'll be paid enough to make you forget the inconvenience. But are you sure he said nothing else – not even in his sleep?'

'No, nothing. I stayed awake all night, so I wouldn't miss a word, just as you ordered. But what makes this young man so special? He's no Persian satrap or Sicilian tyrant.'

'Don't ask me because I don't know myself. I don't even know who is behind all this. It must be very important, nonetheless; perhaps he is from a powerful family on the continent. Are you absolutely sure he said nothing in his sleep?'

'Nothing that means anything. If there's a secret in his mind it's hidden so deeply that not even the abandon of sleep and love can liberate it. I can tell you that he loves this woman called Antinea with immense passion. He must have lost her just when he loved her most, beyond any imagining. And so the wound never closed. He saw Antinea in me, his lost love. That's all that I can say. But his love was so intense that it frightened me. He might have destroyed me had the illusion been broken.'

'I don't think so. The illusions that are aroused in this place sacred to the goddess always spring from some source. His soul must be split: another force, another will, lives within him. Like another person.'

'Then why didn't you allow the great priestess herself to intervene? She would have been able to see all the way into his soul and to understand.'

'The great priestess was watching him as he entered the temple. The shadow of a wolf was behind him, flashing an evil light from his red eyes and baring his fangs when she tried to delve into his mind.'

The young girl wrinkled her brow and pulled her cloak close around her naked body. She turned away and walked towards the end of the room, followed by the man. They disappeared through the little door which had remained open. Kleidemos opened his eyes and looked up. The light of morning was pouring through the opening in the ceiling. White doves cooed and pecked on the roof cornice, sparrows fluttered into the luminous space, chirping finches announced the rising sun. Kleidemos struggled to get up, bringing his hands to his temples. He crossed the large room and went outside under the portico. Lahgal was there at the bottom of the stairs on his feet, with the ass.

Kleidemos approached him with a surly look. 'You little snake!' he accused him, dealing him a sharp slap. 'You had it all planned, didn't you?'

He leapt onto the ass and spurred it into a trot down the city streets to the western gate, which led to the port. After a while, he slowed the animal to a walk, his thoughts absorbed in what he had heard in the temple. He heard shouting behind him.

'Two-Names! Two-Names, stop! Stop, please!' It was

Lahgal, running fast, crying and shouting all at once. Kleidemos did not turn. The boy rushed up, panting.

'Two-Names, I don't know what you think, but I didn't want you to get hurt. My master told me to take you to the temple – what could I do?' Kleidemos did not answer. 'Listen to me, Two-Names, what happened in the temple? Did they hurt you?'

'I told you the true story of my life and you tricked me, instead. I don't want to see you again. Get out of here!'

Lahgal tugged at his chiton. 'You are a free man, Two-Names, and you can say whatever you like. I'm a slave and if I don't do what I'm told they beat me to a pulp, leave me without eating, won't let me drink.' He ran ahead of the ass and stopped in the middle of the road, his back turned to Kleidemos. He pulled up his robe, baring his thin, scar-crossed back.

'Look at me, Two-Names!' he shouted, crying. 'You're lying if you say that you were a slave and you can't understand what Lahgal did.'

Kleidemos got off the ass and approached the boy.

'I do understand, Lahgal. I know what you're trying to tell me. Forgive me for hitting you.' He put a hand on the boy's bony shoulder.

'Do you mean that I can come with you? You're not angry any more?'

'No, I'm not.' The boy dried his tears and covered himself up. They walked silently down the road, holding hands. The sun was rising from behind the hills that sloped down to the sea, casting long shadows over the golden dust on the streets. The sky was filled with swallows.

*

The horseman was granted an immediate audience with King Pausanias, who was still awake in his room by the light of a large six-branched candelabrum.

'May the gods preserve your health, sire,' said the man. 'I have come to report on the outcome of the mission that was entrusted to me.'

'Sit down,' answered the king, 'and speak.'

'Well, sire, everything went according to plan. Young Kleidemos suspected nothing, and entered the temple of his own volition. He spent the entire night there. Unfortunately, however, he revealed nothing of that which you wanted to know. In his drug-induced rapture, he believed that the girl who appeared to him in the temple was a woman that he must have once loved and lost.'

'Did he call her by name?' asked the king.

'Antinea. He called her Antinea. The girl had no way of really impersonating this woman, because she learned nothing more than her name. The young man seemed to remain in control of a certain part of his consciousness, and she dared not push him further in the fear of unleashing a drastic reaction. The great priestess herself examined him as he entered, and was afraid.'

'Antinea . . .' murmured the king, bringing his hand to his forehead. 'She must be a girl from the mountain . . . And he said nothing else that could reveal his state of mind?'

'No, sir. Only words . . . of love,' replied the man with a touch of embarrassment.

'I understand. All right, you may go. You will receive the sum we agreed upon from my treasurer.'

The man left, bowing, and the king was left alone to ponder the matter. 'So the young Kleomenid seems to have no secrets, aside from private, personal matters. Thoughts of love are certainly comprehensible in a young man his age! It's better this way, all things told – better for what I have in mind for him.' He would have time, more than enough time, to convince the young man to join him. Kleidemos had no experience of the world he would be living in, after all, and he didn't have a single friend on the face of the earth.

15

ASIA

PAUSANIAS' ARMY, PROVISIONED BY the fleet cruising on the Thracian Chersonesus, moved from Byzantium to occupy all the territories north and east of the Sacred Mountain, up to the fields of Salmydessus. For more than three years of campaigns, Kleidemos always acted under the direct orders of the king, even after the Athenians and their allies had assumed command of the naval forces. Day after day, war hardened the young man's heart, and the iron discipline of the Spartans turned him into a lucid, implacable destroyer. But was this not the will of the gods? An invincible destiny had pushed him to the point of no return and the life he led had banished any innocence or generosity from his heart. The units that he commanded now, the hundreds of men who moved at his orders, had become a monstrous power in his hands. Like an inexorable machine, his battalion swept away any effort at defence and squashed any resistance. But the same fire that devoured the villages, the camps and the houses of the wretches who dared to challenge Sparta was burning up Kleidemos' tormented soul as well.

In the evening, he sat under his standard watching the prisoners file by in chains, his whole life reduced to the knowledge that power could – with a single gesture –

exterminate countless men, grant them hope or administer anguish, torture and death.

His men called him 'the Cripple', but without mockery, without derision. That word expressed all the fear that men feel towards someone who has been stricken by the gods, but not broken. Strange stories circulated about him; after all, no one had ever seen him train in the gymnasiums of Sparta or bathe in the Eurotas river like the rest of them. What were his limbs, that not even the wolves of Taygetus had dared to sink their fangs into them? He was so quick on his feet, his legs were untiring, grey as iron, soiled with blood and sweat. And his hand, always numbly clenching the hilt of his sword. His eyes were so cold. Who was Kleidemos, really?

The dragon displayed on his shield meant that he was of Kleomenid stock, but he seemed more a son of the grey cliffs of the great mountain . . . or had he been raised by the wolves, its denizens? No one had ever seen him weep, or laugh. Only the soldiers guarding his tent had heard him shout and cry out in his sleep. The women who were brought to him left his tent in tears, stunned, as if they had lain with a monster. The primitive, barbarian lands where he had battled for so long, sowing destruction, had made his soul hard as stone.

He was ready in the eyes of the king. Ready to move on his own in the immensity that was Asia. Pausanias needed a man who would enforce his will as victor over the Great King, and implement his plan. A plan that would change the destiny of Sparta, as well as the destiny of all Greeks and barbarians.

There was only one man in the world who could carry

it out: Kleidemos. And Pausanias knew how to tie the youth to him indissolubly.

He had plunged Kleidemos for four years into the hell of a horrifying war, turning him into a death machine. It was time to bring him back to life; to offer him the chance to become human again, to feel those emotions which must still be alive at the bottom of his heart. That was all it would take. He'd have him forever.

★

One cold dawn at the end of the winter, Kleidemos was sitting wrapped in his cloak under a solitary oak tree which raised its bare branches towards the grey sky of Thrace. All around him, the damp, deserted countryside sounded with cocks' crows, although he could see no farmhouses for as far as his gaze would carry.

He had death on his mind. He had believed that he would fulfil his destiny by resuming his rightful place in the house of the Kleomenids, taking on the legacy of his father Aristarkhos and his brother Brithos. But he had found no glory in what he did: killing, plundering, fornicating – this was the life that Sparta offered him. He had never seen nobility, nor greatness, nor strength of mind in any of those who surrounded him. Perhaps the age of heroes had finished at the Thermopylae with King Leonidas. His life no longer had any meaning.

Turn back? Where? He thought of the woman he had believed to be his mother for so many years . . . he thought of Antinea . . . he wanted to die. Immediately.

A damp cold wind blew from the north, lashing at the few dry leaves left on the oak tree. He watched the iron sky blacken, gazed at the putrid countryside around him, the grey, muddy trail. An infinite anguish invaded his soul. He felt profoundly alone in that desolate land: he wished he had a friend with him, someone who could help him die. He drew his sword, slowly, and thought of Kritolaos, the wisest of men. He thought of Antinea's warm breasts, her deep eyes . . . so many hopes, so many dreams, at the high pasture, on the mountain, on those autumn evenings when the wind rustled the red leaves of the beech trees and the swallows flew off into the distance . . . *But was the earth shaking? or was it some distant noise?* . . . He knelt, pointing the weapon against his chest . . . *But there was something on the horizon, a black spot, moving – and why had the cocks stopped crowing?* – He was terrified of the realm of the shadows from which no one returns; he saw *Thanatos'* grinning skull . . . *A gallop, that's what the sound was* . . . Thanatos Thanatos Thanatos . . . Suddenly, a bolt of lightning twisted free, viper-fast, from the horizon, followed by a clap of thunder. He lifted his sweat-beaded forehead: a horseman. A horseman was drawing closer, spurring on his mount furiously.

Like a rotting wineskin that suddenly spills its contents, the sky released a downpour of rain, but the horseman kept urging his animal on, belly to the ground. He was waving a hand, shouting, 'Two-Names!' He yanked short the bridle, practically downing his horse, and leapt to the ground. Kleidemos had let his sword fall into the mud.

'Two-Names! I've found you . . . I've found you!' he shouted, embracing him hard under the rain.

Kleidemos raised his dripping face. 'Lahgal, it's you . . .

I can't believe it! Where have you come from? How did you find me, why are you here?'

'I'll tell you everything. Listen, I have important news for you; we need to talk. That's why I was headed towards your camp. But what are you doing here, at this early hour? And so far away from camp?'

Kleidemos took a deep breath. 'Nothing. I couldn't sleep, and I thought I'd take a walk.'

Lahgal stared at him. 'You are lying, Two-Names. Your eyes are full of despair . . . and fear. I don't even know how I recognized you. You've changed.' Kleidemos lowered his gaze. His sword glittered, clean now, under the pouring rain.

'Pick that up,' said Lahgal, 'and put it back in its sheath. I really don't know how I recognized you . . . from so far off, in the rain. Get on behind me, we'll go to camp together.'

They started off at a lope down the muddy path. Neither said a word as they rode, until Lahgal broke the silence. 'I can't say why, but I feel as though I reached you just in time. I feel like I've prevented something terrible from happening. Am I right, Two-Names?' Kleidemos didn't answer. 'Well?' Lahgal insisted.

'You're right, Lahgal . . . Thank you for coming.'

Lahgal turned around. 'Nice welcome for a friend you haven't seen in such a long time!' he teased, smiling. 'And here I was expecting to be greeted by a fully drawn-up phalanx, with you sparkling in your parade armour!'

'Just wait until we get to camp, and you'll see that I'll give you a fine welcome. Right here and now I'm afraid

I don't have much to hand.' They looked around them and burst out laughing. The rain was abating and a few pale rays pierced the clouds on the horizon. Then the light of the rising sun flooded the earth, enflaming the scattered puddles and covering the sparse bushes in silvery pearls. It saturated the great solitary oak, marking out the figure of a despairing giant, arms bowed, dripping with moss. Kleidemos recalled the day in which Lahgal, just a boy then, sat in front of him as he did now. On the bony back of an ass riding on the hills of Paphos. He was a young man now, in the prime of his years.

'Who sent you here, Lahgal?' he asked abruptly.

Lahgal looked at the Spartan camp which was coming into view at the foot of a low hill past a curve in the trail. He said, without turning, 'Pausanias – the king.' And he spurred the horse into a gallop.

*

'The last time I saw you, you were a child. How old are you now, Lahgal?'

'Sixteen, more or less,' replied the youth.

'From a slave in a public bath to the courier of the King of Sparta in just four years . . . not bad,' observed Kleidemos. 'How did you manage it?'

Lahgal smiled. 'You are asking me this question, Two-Names? Weren't you just an unknown Helot shepherd a few years back? You who command a Spartan army and sow terror among the fierce Thracians? The destiny of men is in the hands of the gods . . . But let's speak of other things. I've been in the personal service of Pausanias for two years, and I can tell you that he has followed your every move with great attention. Not a single one of your endeavours has escaped him. He greatly admires your strength and your intelligence, and he needs you by his side for a very important secret mission.'

'What do you know about this?'

'The king does not confide so much in me! But I can tell you that when you've accomplished the mission, you'll be free to return to Sparta and to be reunited with the woman you call mother.'

Kleidemos was startled. 'Are you sure of this? It's not just another trick? What do you know about my mother?'

'She's alive and enjoys good health, although she is distressed by your absence. She still lives in the mountain cottage. She's visited by a man at times, a giant of a man, with a beard.'

Kleidemos was shaken. 'Karas!' he thought, trying hard not to betray any emotion.

'Do you know who he is?' asked Lahgal, watching him closely.

'I may have seen him once or twice, a big man with a beard. I think he's one of the mountain shepherds. But tell me more about my mother, please!'

'I don't know anything besides what I've already told you. But you will be allowed to take her into your service – in the house of the Kleomenids.'

Kleidemos grabbed the young man's hand. 'Are these truly the words of the king?'

'They are,' replied Lahgal. 'You can believe me. I haven't come all this way to tell you lies.' He fell silent, looking deep into Kleidemos' eyes. The glacial light shining there had suddenly caught fire. 'What must I tell my king?'

'I accept,' he said without hesitation. 'I'll do whatever he wants. Leave immediately, and tell the king—'

'Leave immediately? Is this the hospitality you promised me?' said Lahgal, laughing. 'I shouldn't have hurried!'

'You're right, I'm behaving terribly but there's something you must understand: nothing is more terrible than solitude, and these have been the loneliest days of my life. But you haven't told me, how did all this come to be? How did you enter into the service of the king?'

'Pausanias bought me from my master when the fleet left Cyprus. I've always served him as best I could. I learned your dialect and I mastered the language of the Persians. I realized that there was no one the king could trust; he was spied on by his own allies, his own government. So he needed someone who would be absolutely faithful to him. This was my fortune. Little by little, the king assigned me increasingly important tasks, and now he trusts me with even the most sensitive missions. Like coming here to talk to you.'

'When will I be relieved of duty here?'

'Immediately, if you like. You can return to Byzantium with me. Your deputy commander will take over until the king sends another officer to conduct the next campaign.'

'Byzantium . . . I can't believe that I'll be able to leave this life, return to Sparta—'

'Wait, the mission you'll have to carry out will be neither easy nor brief, I believe.'

'It doesn't matter. Anything will be better than continuing this massacre, than spending another year in these desolate lands. Let's leave right away, Lahgal. Tomorrow.'

'As you wish,' replied the young man. He took a leather scroll from his cloak. 'These are the instructions for your deputy: you'll have to read them on the *skythale*.'

'Fine,' agreed Kleidemos. 'I'll have him called immediately.' He gave orders to the guard posted at the entrance to the tent, who returned shortly thereafter with the taxiarch of the first battalion. The officer saluted him and, at a gesture from his commander, removed his helmet and sat down on a stool. Kleidemos removed the *skythale* from its case. It was a smooth boxwood stick marked with two parallel spiralling lines, the guides where the leather scroll was applied in the prescribed way so as to become legible. Kleidemos fastened the scroll to the stud at the top and then carefully turned the stick until the leather strip was rolled onto it, following the guide. He attached the bottom end to another stud at the opposite side of the stick. The message, which had been written horizontally on a similar stick of the same length and thickness, was apparent now:

Pausanias, King of the Spartans, to Kleidemos, son of Aristarkhos, commander of our army in Thrace: hail!

We commend your great valour, worthy of the name you bear, and thank you for the service you have rendered to your country in the many battles you have won over the barbarians. Your presence is now required elsewhere. You shall turn over command of your troops to your deputy Deuxhippos, and join me in Byzantium as soon as possible.

Kleidemos handed it over to his deputy, who read it as well, noting the seal of Pausanias at the end.

'When will you leave, commander?' asked Deuxhippos.

'Tomorrow at dawn. Prepare to take command.' The officer got to his feet. 'I know I'm leaving my men in good hands,' added Kleidemos, reaching out his right hand.

'Thank you, commander,' gripping his hand in some surprise. 'I shall attempt to show myself worthy of this honour.' He put on his helmet and left.

'You'll sleep in my tent,' Kleidemos said to Lahgal. 'I don't have a pavilion for guests – I haven't had many visitors.'

Lahgal stripped to lie down, tired after his long journey. He had a man's body, but his burnished skin glowed with the delicate beauty of an oriental. Kleidemos noticed that he had shaved his thighs and pubes, as if to soften the full exuberance of his virility. After Lahgal had fallen asleep, he still sat watching the coals in the brazier that burned in the centre of the tent. He stretched out his hands to warm them and his gaze fell on the studded armlet that Philippides, the champion of Olympia, had given him that long-ago day. Dangling from it was the coloured shell that Lahgal had given him as a child, on the beach in Cyprus. He ripped it off and tossed it onto the ground, smashing it under his heel.

*

'Tell me now, Kleidemos: you who were born twice, you of two names, who are you really? Can you tell me whether you are a son of Sparta or of the people who brought you up on Mount Taygetus?'

King Pausanias was waiting for an answer, but Kleidemos was silent and confused.

'You cannot answer me, can you? Your heart is still with those who raised you. But at the same time you cannot suffocate the call of your true race, the blood of Aristarkhos the Dragon. And this is why I know that you will understand and support my plan. Sparta can no longer hope to survive by governing in the same way as when she was founded by the descendants of Hercules. The number of equals is decreasing year after year. One day, not long hence, our army will no longer have enough warriors to fend off any enemy attack. The Helots themselves, constantly growing in number, could pose a threat. For this reason, Sparta must change, and all the inhabitants of Laconia must become her citizens, eliminating all distinctions.'

'But that's impossible,' protested Kleidemos coldly. 'The Helots hate you.'

'And they will as long as this state of affairs lasts. But if we give them the status and dignity of free men, the right to possess land and weapons, the chasm that now divides them from the equals will cease to exist. Slowly, perhaps, but it will be bridged. In many other Greek states, this happened a hundred years ago. Look at Athens: she is building an empire on the sea and prospering in her riches. My plan can – must – be accomplished,' exclaimed the king, 'but for this to happen, the custodians of our institutions must be eliminated. Destroyed, if necessary.'

Kleidemos was shocked by Pausanias' words, even as he continued in a calmer tone. 'I am practically alone in this endeavour, and I do not have the power to bring it to fulfilment. I need a powerful ally – the most powerful.' He seemed absorbed in his thoughts for a moment, then stared straight at Kleidemos, eyes flashing: 'The King of Kings!'

The young man shuddered. 'My father and my brother died in the attempt to rid Greece of the Persians, and I shall not betray their memory,' he said, and got up to leave.

'Sit down!' ordered the King with a peremptory tone. 'Your father and your brother, as well as Leonidas and all his men at the Thermopylae, were sacrificed in vain, betrayed by the blind obtuseness of the ephors and the elders of Sparta. They are the ones truly responsible for the deaths of your family. The inhumane laws they rule by forced your father to abandon you on Mount Taygetus. But now one age has drawn to an end and another is about to begin: Sparta must change, or she will die, dragging the Helots with her in her plunge towards ruin. This is why I need you. I know the Helots will listen to you and follow you.

'The time has come for me to reveal something to you. I know about the bow that you used at Plataea, I've seen the mark carved into it: the wolf's head of the King of Messenia. The man who you thought was your grandfather, old Kritolaos, must certainly have told you about him. There isn't much I don't know, Kleidemos – I commanded the *krypteia* for ten years. When your brother Brithos went up the mountain that night with his

Molossian hound, I knew what was happening. And I also know about the Spartan warrior who roamed the mountain for years, wrapped in a grey cape, his head covered with a hood . . .'

'My father,' admitted Kleidemos, trembling.

'Yes, your father. Listen to me, you bear one of the most illustrious names of Sparta, and at the same time you are the heir of Kritolaos, the leader of the Helots. One day you will return among them and convince them to support my plan. I'll get rid of the ephors and the elders, and even of King Leotychidas if necessary – with the help of the King of Persia.

'Xerxes is prepared to back me with impressive means, certain that I will one day become his faithful satrap in a Greece reduced to a province of his immense empire. This shall never come to be; I defeated his army at Plataea and I shall defeat him once again. But right now I need his money.

'You should know that I have powerful friends in other cities of Greece, including Athens. Now I must return to Sparta, because the ephors have begun to suspect something, and I must ensure them of my loyalty. But you will bring my message to the King of Persia. You will deliver it to the custodian of the imperial palace at Kelainai in Phrygia and remain there until you receive his answer. And then you will return to Byzantium. I would calculate that to be at the beginning of the autumn. And I shall be here once again, in my place.'

Kleidemos was absorbed in thought. What he had heard was nearly unbelievable, but he was struck by the realization that what Pausanias wanted to achieve was right. In such a world he would be able to set free the people he had lived with since birth without spilling blood, and without denying the Kleomenid name.

'I will leave as soon as you wish,' he said suddenly. Pausanias walked him to the door. He laid a hand on his shoulder.

'There's something about you that I'd still like to know,' he said. 'Who is Antinea?'

'Antinea . . .' murmured Kleidemos, lowering his head. 'Antinea was someone that Talos knew.'

And he fled into the starry night.

*

Kleidemos beheld wealthy Cyzicus, straddling two seas, populous Adramyttium and Pergamum, and then Ephesus, its port teeming with ships. He journeyed up the majestic Meander to Hieropolis, with its hot springs. He saw Sardeis, vast and rich, and the tumbledown temple of the Great Mother of the gods, incinerated by the Athenians during the Ionian revolt.

Lahgal accompanied him, acting as his interpreter with the barbarians who escorted them across certain tracts so they would not fall prey to the thieves who infested the interior. Asia was immense, and lovely: mild hills sloped into verdant plains, covered with purple thistle flowers and the red poppies whose juice brought oblivion to men's troubled souls. When the sun descended towards the horizon, the heavens flamed with scarlet clouds, edged in a deep violet that melted into the intense blue of the sky. Endless flocks headed off then towards their pens, raising dense clouds of dust that could be seen from a distance.

The fleece of the lambs and sheep shone like gold, and their bleating faded off into the silent plain when the last shaft of sunlight went out with a flash. And then the firmament, so incredibly clear, would teem with millions of sparkling stars, while the monotonous chant of the crickets rose from the earth, joined by the howling of dogs from isolated houses. The smell of Asia was intense and penetrating: the fragrance of the yellow broom, so strong it was inebriating, and the dry, bitter scent of absinthe. Only the sharp odour of wild sage recalled his boyhood on the mountain. At night, they would see silent groups of men, their faces veiled, riding on monstrous animals with faces like sheep and two huge humps on their backs. Distasteful beasts that let out a rude moan when they knelt to allow their masters to mount them.

As time passed and the sun carved an ever-wider arch into the sky, the terrain itself changed. Yellow and ochre, swathed with deep green wherever a stream or river meandered in wide turns across the sunny plain. The heat became nearly unbearable, and in the evening a furious wind would pick up, creating dozens of whirlwinds that danced over the parched earth. These columns of dust twisted and turned, darting here and there, then vanished like spectres amidst the crumbling rocks.

But nightfall did not extinguish that scorching wind. The incessant hissing went on for hours, tumbling dried amaranth bushes over the arid grass like gigantic spiders. When it finally abated the vast high plain filled with rustles, crackles, murmurs. The eyes of the jackals sometimes glittered in the dark, and their mournful calls rose from the rocks to the red moon as it ascended slowly between the solitary peaks. Its pale rays lit the misshapen wild fig bushes and the fleshy foliage of the carob trees.

Off in the distance, here and there, they could make out the black shapes of volcanoes that had been dormant for centuries. Typhon, the father of the winds, was said to live deep in their bellies: from his horrendous mouth escaped the fiery breath that withered the grass and flowers and enfeebled travellers' tired limbs.

One day, as he was approaching his destination, Kleidemos saw something that he would never forget: a colossal plane tree towering in the middle of the dusty plain, so enormous that he had never seen one like it in his whole life. Its smooth white trunk immediately branched off into four limbs, each of which was as thick as a fully-grown tree. He drew closer, to admire it and to rest in its shade. His astonishment increased when he saw an armed man standing under that immense tree. Kleidemos knew those weapons and decorations well: it was one of the Immortals, the personal guard of the Great King!

He wore an embroidered overgarment, open at the sides, with a pair of trousers made of precious fabric gathered at the ankle and woven with a rose pattern in silver thread. His curly black beard, framing an olive-toned countenance, met with his thick, carefully combed and scented locks. Golden rings hung from his ears and a colourful leather quiver swung from his shoulder. His bow was finished in silver and a spear sparkled in his right hand.

'Greetings,' said Kleidemos, as Lahgal translated his words. 'I am Kleidemos of Sparta and I have stopped to rest in the shade of this tree. Are you on a journey as well, noble sir? I see none of your servants or companions.'

The warrior smiled, showing white teeth under his corvine moustache. 'No,' he replied in his language. 'I am not on a journey. I am here by the orders of my king, Xerxes, the King of Kings, light of Ariah, favoured son of Ahura Mazda. Returning from Yauna and crossing this arid land he found shelter in the shadow of this tree, whose size and beauty enchanted him. He decreed that an Immortal from his guard would always watch over this tree, so that no harm could ever come to it.'

Kleidemos was astonished, as Lahgal translated the words of the Persian soldier. 'Do you mean to say that a man from the king's guard remains here permanently to protect a tree?'

'That is right,' replied Lahgal. They lingered for a while, drinking from the spring which flowed next to the plane tree. The Immortal was seated on his stool, gazing off towards the horizon. Then they resumed their journey. After walking for nearly an hour, they looked back: the tree looked even bigger, while the warrior could barely be seen in the quivering air. But the tip of his spear, struck by the sun, flashed silver.

16

THE SECRET

LAHGAL FELL ILL. The climate on the high plain had sapped all of his resources. When their supplies had run out and they could find no more wheat, the rancid mutton they were forced to eat turned his stomach causing him to vomit violently. Kleidemos stopped in several villages to allow him to rest and wait until his fever passed and the cramps in his stomach eased off. It was in one of these villages that he learned from its chieftain himself that the worst risk came not from eating, but from drinking; on the plateau, the waters were prevented from flowing down towards the sea by the huge mountains in their way. And so they stagnated or seeped very slowly underground, becoming saturated with noxious humours. The damage done could be so great as to bring about death. 'It is the stomach that suffers,' the chief assured Kleidemos. 'It becomes so ruined that it can keep down no food at all; even a simple piece of fruit will cause overwhelming sickness.'

'Is there a remedy?' Kleidemos asked the chief in Phrygian, which he spoke a little after two months of travelling through so many villages. The man took out an earthenware jug and poured some murky liquid into a cup. It was an infusion of the poppy that produced oblivion.

'This calms the cramping of the stomach and the spasms in the gut,' he said. 'In this way, your friend will be able to eat a little food; his body will slowly become stronger and fight off the sickness.'

The potion was very bitter, but it was aromatized with wild mint and the savory which abounded in the surrounding fields; in fact, the Phrygian name for the village meant 'place of savory'. Kleidemos trusted the chieftain's word; he remembered seeing a river – a month before, in a place called Kolossai – that abruptly disappeared underground, as if swallowed up by the earth. The inhabitants claimed the water fell in a cascade two stadia long, and that on many a winter's night they could hear the waters churning in underground caves.

Lahgal felt better within a week; his fever broke and was gone and he could manage to keep down the flat wheat bread they roasted on stones. Given his condition and his surroundings, he had stopped dedicating himself to his grooming: his hair had grown to shoulder length and his tanned face was framed by a thick beard. His razor, strigil and tweezers were long forgotten at the bottom of a saddlebag.

'Now you look like a man,' Kleidemos said to him one day as he was bathing in the river. Lahgal shrugged.

'You Spartans are boors. You don't appreciate beauty or gentleness. You have no art of your own, nor poetry. Only military songs to beat time as you march.'

'I see you know a lot about Sparta, and Spartans,' said Kleidemos, with a touch of irony.

'Of course I do,' replied Lahgal. 'I've been living with them for years.'

'You mean that you live with . . . King Pausanias.'

'Yes, and so?'

'Are you his lover?' he asked bluntly.

Lahgal began to tremble and his eyes were fixed to the ground.

'Is that what you want to know about me, Two-Names? Does our Kleomenid hero really want to plunge his hands in the shit? To poke around in the misery of a Syrian slave? Well, if that's what you want and you'd like to have a little fun listening to obscene stories, Lahgal can satisfy your curiosity. Oh yes, Two-Names, Lahgal has lots of stories to tell: besides the scars that I showed you on my back, I have worse, and much more intimate scars.' He raised his black eyes, burning with rage and shame. 'When you met me in Cyprus, my master was already prostituting me. I even had orders to let you have your share, if you liked me—'

'That's enough!' shouted Kleidemos. 'I don't want to know—'

'Oh yes, you do want to know and you shall, by the gods! You asked me something very specific, Two-Names, just a moment ago, or have you forgotten already? And so now let me tell you . . .

'My good looks became my curse. How I envied those who were deformed! I was forced to submit to sordid, repugnant beings and to undergo abominations, choking on my vomit and disgust.

'Yes, Two-Names, I have become the lover of the king. But did I have a choice? Have I ever had a choice? All I could do was try to avoid the worst. Pausanias has never mistreated me, not once, and he has promised that he will set me free.' Kleidemos couldn't say another word; Lahgal continued in a lower tone of voice. 'When you left Cyprus I hoped ardently to see you again one day. You were the only person who had ever shown me sincere affection, and when I saw you drenched and desperate under that tree in Thrace, I realized that I had saved you from taking your own life. My joy at seeing you again was immense.'

'As was mine,' said Kleidemos.

'Well, at first it seemed that way to me, too. But then you either imagined or found out, and you were repulsed. I've felt your scorn for months, even though you try to hide it. And the shell that I gave you that day on the beach is no longer on your armlet – you had it when I first saw you in Thrace.'

'Lahgal . . . I didn't want to hurt you,' said Kleidemos. 'I can't judge you for what your destiny has forced you to endure, perhaps against your own will. I've been living as a soldier for four years and I have seen so much blood and so many massacres that I can hardly believe that a man loving a woman or loving another man makes the world any worse than it already is.

'Maybe the real reason that I asked you that question is because there is a terrible doubt that seizes me when I'm trying to sleep at night. I'm alone in the world, Lahgal, and I have no one to confide in. All those I've loved are dead, or so far away I feel as though I've lost them forever. Your reappearance and the words of the king reawakened hope in me; I felt alive again. But what I fear is that perhaps not everything I've been told is true.

'I don't know whether the king is sincere about his plans or is merely using me to satisfy his own ambitions.

There were a lot of rumours going around the camp in Thrace about him. They say he is a hard, cruel man, consumed by his insatiable thirst for power. That his soul has been corrupted by his desire for wealth and luxury . . . and that he is a slave to his passions.

'I'm sure you can understand how I feel, and yet, in all these months of travelling together, you've never said a word. I'm sure you can read the doubt in my face, and yet if you know things that I don't know, you haven't revealed a thing. And so I imagined that your bond with Pausanias must be stronger than anything else; that the little Lahgal who gave me coloured shells on a beach in Cyprus was a person I'd have to forget.'

'You've changed too,' said Lahgal. 'Your eyes are vacant and troubled and your voice is often harsh and cutting. I've felt like I've been travelling with a stranger this whole time. How could I speak to you as a friend? I thought you despised me. When we left, it seemed that you were happy to carry out this mission and to support Pausanias' plan; how could I imagine you had any doubts? And I know that . . . there's a secret you're keeping from me.' Kleidemos looked at him with a puzzled expression. 'Pausanias gave you a message that you can read on your *skythale*,' Lahgal insisted.

'You can know anything you want about me, Lahgal. When I told you the story of my life you were only a boy. But what is written in that message regards neither you nor me. It concerns the destiny of many men, entire populations, perhaps. I can't—'

'But have you read that message?' interrupted Lahgal.

'No, not yet. I have orders to read it only after my mission has been accomplished.'

'And you haven't even thought about reading it before then?'

'I gave the king my word, and I have but one word, Lahgal. But tell me, why do you want to know what's written in the message?'

'Two-Names,' Lahgal wrung his hands as if searching for words. 'Two-Names . . . I'm afraid.'

'I don't understand. We're not in any danger here.'

'I'm afraid of dying.'

Kleidemos looked at him in suprise. 'Why would you? You've been ill, but it was nothing serious. It's easy to fall ill when you're travelling in foreign countries – the food, the water—'

'That's not what I mean. King Pausanias has already sent other messages to the Great King, but those who carried them . . . never returned.'

'I don't understand.'

'I know only what I've said, Two-Names, nothing more. I know for certain that the bearers of those messages never returned. You don't understand why I'm afraid? That message might be an order for you to kill me. If not, why would the king have ordered you not to read it until you had completed the mission?'

'Listen to me. When I brought you the king's message in Thrace, I realized that the mere thought of returning to Sparta, of reuniting with the woman who raised you, of seeing the people you love, was enough to make you want to live, to fight again. I think . . . I'm afraid . . . that you would do anything to have what was promised you. I don't know what the king told you in the meeting you had with him alone. Important things, certainly. I know that he thinks very highly of you. And the life of a Syrian servant is certainly nothing with respect to all this. And that's why I'm afraid, Two-Names.

'In two days we will reach Kelainai where you will deliver your message, and then you will read Pausanias' orders. I beg of you, if that order is to kill me, please do not open my throat with your sword; let me take my own life. I know of a potion that produces a sweet stupor which lets you pass without suffering from life to the endless night . . .'

Two big tears fell from Lahgal's dark eyes. He fell still, not daring to look his companion in the face. Kleidemos fell silent as well. Shaken, he thought of everything that had happened: of the huge hopes that Pausanias' words had awakened in him; of the horror of the act that might be looming before him. But maybe Lahgal was wrong. Perhaps the men he was talking about had disappeared for other reasons; they may have lost their way, or been ambushed on the long journey home. But his knapsack held the roll of leather with the king's orders, and the *skythale*, his walking stick, held the key to reading them. He no longer carried the cornel crook which Kritolaos had chosen for him; he had burned it on Brithos' pyre at Plataea. It had been destroyed, as had his boyhood life, on that blood-soaked field. He was startled by Lahgal's trembling voice.

'You've read many a death order on **your** *skythale*

before, Two-Names, for thousands of men. You are a Spartan warrior and you must surely follow your destiny. The gods have spared your life many times. When you were a child, you were saved from the fangs of the wolves, and as a man, from thousands of Thracian arrows. Your soldiers have never been able to understand how you can challenge death with such impunity on the battlefield. You, the lame warrior, you who were destined to have two names and two lives, you who escaped the death that you yourself were about to administer with your own sword. It's the truth, Two-Names. There must be a great destiny awaiting you, perhaps a terrible one. You cannot escape it.

'That day that I saw you under that tree in Thrace you'd touched bottom. I could see the distress in your eyes, yet your face was stony, resolute. What could the life of a mere servant mean, sold before he could ever hold it for a moment in his own hands. A body prostituted for five obols—'

'That's enough, Lahgal!' shouted Kleidemos, his head in his hands.

But the voice continued, without a tremor now. A voice deep and dark, a voice of pure pain: 'You've reached the point where you can't turn back. Read that message now, as if I were not here, and if I must die let me die. I will accompany you today and tomorrow as your faithful servant, but the morning after that there will be no awakening for me. You'll never even notice. There's just one thing I ask of you. Don't leave my body to the jackals. Bury me as if I had been a free man, a friend, whom you

281

loved. Do not let my shade wander in despair along the icy banks of the Acheron, which they say is the fate of those who go unburied—'

Kleidemos placed a hand on his head: 'You will not die by my hand, Lahgal. Nor shall you be forced to kill yourself.' He took the sealed roll from his knapsack and wrapped it around the *skythale* to make it legible. It said:

> The servant I sent with you has completed his task.
> Now you know the return route, a road you will take
> alone because there shall be no witness to your journey
> in the interior. You will destroy this message as well.

'You were right to be afraid, Lahgal,' he said, tossing the roll into the river. 'The king orders me to kill you.'

*

The walls of Kelainai stood out against the blue sky. On the top of each tower sat a stork's nest. The huge birds soared slowly over the city, gliding with unmoving wings spread wide, buoyed by the wind of the high plain. The silver ribbon of the Meander descended behind a hill; the river's source was said to be in a dark cave within the city, once inhabited by nymphs and satyrs, surrounded by a forest of poplars filled with singing birds.

'We have arrived,' said Kleidemos to Lahgal. 'The envoy of the Great King, Satrap Artabazus, will meet us in the city.'

'Look, the summer residence of the Great King, above the fortifications. The satrap lives there,' observed Lahgal. They approached the southern gate, guarded by two

Phrygian archers. Kleidemos handed Lahgal a sealed wooden tablet, which he delivered to one of the archers.

He told the man, in his language, 'Bring this to Satrap Artabazus, and tell him that noble Kleidemos of Sparta, son of Aristarkhos, Kleomenid, waits to be received.' The archer had him repeat the long, difficult name twice so he was sure of remembering it exactly, and went off.

'Tell me about this city and these lands,' Kleidemos asked Lahgal, as they sat on a stone bench along the city wall, stretching their tired limbs, still sluggish from the damp night's ride.

'I don't know much,' said Lahgal. 'I've been told that this is the last Phrygian city to the east. Behind those mountains,' he added, pointing to a bluish chain that crossed the plateau at about two days' journey from where they were, 'begins Lycaonia, a dangerous, unstable region, roamed by fierce marauders that not even the Great King's soldiers can keep at bay. After six days, you reach the foot of Mount Taurus, an impassable range that can only be crossed through a gorge so narrow that a pair of yoked oxen cannot pass. From the mountain you can reach the sea in three days, crossing a region called Cilicia. To the east Cilicia is delimited by another very tall range of mountains that the inhabitants of that place call Saman. Beyond them extends Syria, the land where I was born.

'As for this city, I only know that the Meander river flows through marvellous gardens filled with every kind of plant and wild animal. The Persians call these gardens "pairidaeza" in their language, and you Greeks "paradeisos": paradise. The Great King hunts there with his noblemen when he is in his summer residence. There is another river that flows through the city as well, smaller than the Meander, called Marsuas by the inhabitants. I believe you Greeks call it Marsyas; do you remember the legend? The satyr Marsyas was said to have challenged Apollo to a musical contest along its banks. Defeated, he was flayed alive, and his skin was hung in the cave at the river's source. It's still there – we can see it if you like, although I imagine it's just the skin of some goat sacrificed long ago to one of the local divinities.'

'I like hearing these stories,' said Kleidemos. 'They remind me of the ones my grandfather Kritolaos used to tell me when I was a child. I think it was he who told me of the satyr Marsyas. I never would have imagined that one day I would see the place where the story originated.' Kleidemos let his gaze range over the plain which stretched as far as the eye could see. The Meander glittered under the sun which had climbed high over the horizon. Just then the archer ran up, saying, 'Our lord, Satrap Artabazus, awaits you. I shall take you to the palace.'

Kleidemos and Lahgal followed him through the city as its streets were filling up with people: men and women dressed in an odd fashion, who regarded the foreigners with curiosity. Children began to follow them, pulling at their robes and trying to sell them the odds and ends they carried in their straw baskets. The archer chased them away, shouting and flailing his bow at them. They swarmed off, shrieking, in all directions, only to stream back towards the little group that was making its way towards the centre of the city. The acropolis appeared: a hill surrounded by walls, green with poplars that thickened at the banks of what must have been the Marsyas river. The children ran laughing and shouting towards its gravelly shore. Throwing off their clothing, bags and baskets, they dived naked into the water, splashing one another. The three men climbed the staircase that led to the palace, and soon entered its atrium. Kleidemos was brought to a room where he was bathed and dressed, and finally conducted into the presence of Artabazus. The satrap was seated on a pile of cushions. He rose to greet his visitor.

'Hail, O Spartan guest,' he said in Greek. 'You are most welcome in this home. I hope that noble Pausanias is in good health.'

'He was when I left him at Byzantium about two months ago,' replied Kleidemos, bowing. 'He should be in Sparta by now.'

'Sparta!' exclaimed the satrap with a surprised and vexed expression. 'I thought he had not moved from Byzantium. But sit down, please, you must be tired.' He indicated a puffy woollen pillow placed on a blue carpet. Kleidemos found it a little difficult to sit in such an uncomfortable position, pulling his Persian garments between his legs.

'The king has had news of growing mistrust in Sparta and did not want to fuel rumours that could have become dangerous. He is sure that no one has the slightest proof against him and that envy is at the root of it all. I would say that his style of living in Byzantium, which certainly breaks with Spartan conventions, has given the ephors and the elders – always fearful that the kings' power will become too consolidated – the excuse to call him back and find some pretext against him. The king however assures you that his freedom will not be curtailed, and that he will soon be back in Byzantium. I will bring your words, or the words of the Great King, to him there upon my return.'

Artabazus stroked his grey moustache pensively, then spoke again. 'You shall give him this message from the Great King: "Hail, Pausanias. The proof of friendship that you send has profoundly moved us. You have liberated persons very close to our heart who had fallen prisoner under your soldiers. We are henceforth willing to consider you our ally and to provide you with everything you may need, whether this be money or another form of assistance. As far as your request for betrothal with one of our daughters, we are pleased to give our consent and await news from you on your movements in the future. Your answers may hereafter be communicated to our satrap in Dascylium, in the province of Caria, whom your messengers can reach easily from Byzantium."'

Kleidemos replied, 'His words have been written in my mind, and will be relayed as you have pronounced them.'

'Very good,' said the satrap. 'But please tell me now, what actions does King Pausanias plan to take?'

'He must first remove any distrust from the minds of the ephors and the elders,' answered Kleidemos. 'They regard him with suspicion, despite the great prestige he enjoys for his victory at Plataea.'

Kleidemos noticed a slight but perceptible expression of disappointment on Artabazus' face, and he realized that perhaps he should have started with something else. He continued nonetheless. 'He is also commander of the Army of the Straits and of the Peloponnesian fleet, and the guardian of King Pleistarchus, Leonidas' son, who as you well know is still a child. In any normal situation, the ephors and the elders usually manage to set one king against another, provoking a rivalry that effectively allows them to exercise and reinforce their power. But Pausanias is practically alone, and concentrates enormous strength in his hands: this is the reason for which he arouses their misgiving and apprehension. It's evident that the ephors and the elders are looking for some pretext by which to control him, nothing more ... I believe. In any case, Pausanias seems very sure of himself. And you must remember that he can count on the support of the assembly of equals: our warriors greatly admire his intelligence and his military valour. Traditionally, they feel much closer to the king that guides them in battle than to the ephors and the elders.'

Artabazus was pacing the room, back and forth. He stopped at its centre to offer his point of view. 'It is thus in our interests to act while we can count on an ally at the height of his power. If Pausanias were charged with some offence or relieved of his command of the army, all of our plans would have to change. As you know, the situation in Athens is in great disarray at the moment.' Kleidemos, completely unaware of what the satrap was referring to, nodded in assent. 'Themistocles, the Athenian commander who defeated our fleet at Salamis, has been expelled from his city and is in exile.' Kleidemos found it difficult to hide his surprise. 'He could also become our ally one day, if for no other reason than to take revenge on his thankless homeland. You can tell your king now to be ready to act at a moment's notice, because the time

could be very near. You were able to take your time
arriving here because you knew that Pausanias would
not be back in Byzantium before the end of the summer,
but you will have to rush on your return journey. You
must be waiting for the king in Byzantium, to give him
this message as soon as he returns. Make contact with
the satrap at Dascylium immediately, but ensure that this
journey remains a complete secret. I know you have a
servant with you; we cannot risk him talking and ruining
everything. I will provide you with another servant. Do
you prefer a young woman this time, or a good-looking
boy?' asked the satrap solicitously.

'Oh, no, sir,' replied Kleidemos promptly. 'Too much
of a luxury for me, and besides, it might attract the
attention and the envy of my comrades. I'd rather not be
too conspicuous. I will eliminate the servant myself as
soon as we are near the coast. I've already been instructed
to do so.'

'As you wish,' nodded the satrap. 'Now let me offer
my hospitality, so you may have several days to restore
your strength before your long journey back.'

Kleidemos accepted, curious to see how those the
Greeks called 'barbarians' really lived.

The palace was much more beautiful than any he had
ever seen in Greece or Asia. Lahgal was taken to the
slaves' quarters, but Kleidemos was given a large, spacious
room in the upper quarters of the palace, open both to
the east and to the west, refreshed by evening breezes.

He dined towards dusk with Artabazus and found the
food delicious: all sorts of roasted game flavoured with

savoury herbs. He was most surprised by a huge bird that the cooks brought to the table garnished with all the long, iridescent feathers of its tail, each of which had a big green-blue eye at the tip. Noticing his guest's amazement, the satrap had a live specimen brought in a cage so he could see the bird in its natural state. It was a gorgeous animal, so brilliant in colour that Kleidemos was speechless. The plumage on its neck and breast was intensely blue, and its tail was nearly two cubits long. But its call was the most ungracious sound one could ever imagine. He was told that the bird came from distant India, the last eastern province of the Great King, beyond which extended the endless Ocean.

He was shown yet another bird, smaller but with an even more brightly hued plumage: red, purple, black and white. They explained that it was hunted in the land of the Phasians, a northern tribe that took their name from the River Phasis that originated in the Caucasus and flowed into the Pontus. After the game, sweets and fruits were served: pomegranates, figs and a sort of rosy apple covered with fuzz, deliciously juicy and thirst-quenching. It was very sweet and had a hard pit at its centre. Kleidemos nearly broke his tooth biting into it, to the great hilarity of his fellow diners. These fruits were grown only in the palace garden, and the trees had been brought directly from far-off Persia, so they were called 'Persian apples'.

After dinner, a eunuch accompanied Kleidemos to his room, which was decorated with enamel flowers and trees with gaily coloured birds and wild animals. But it was the bed that surprised him most: it was so big that four people could have slept in it, and was supported by gilded bronze legs in the shape of winged human figures.

On the bed lay a dark-skinned girl who was very beautiful, her body gracefully veiled by a Milesian slip. The eunuch said in his broken Greek that he hoped she would be satisfactory; she came from the northern Mosynoecian tribe, famous for disregarding any constraints. In fact, their men and women coupled in the open air, without a care as to who might see them; with a few obscene gestures, he tried to let Kleidemos know the delights that were in store for him. He added that other girls were also available if he preferred: Bithynians, Cappadocians, Lycians, even Egyptians – all experts in the rites of Aphrodite.

Kleidemos thanked him, assuring him that she would be quite all right and that he would let him know if he wanted a different one on the morrow. The eunuch left with a naughty grin, wishing him a restful night and closing the scented cedar door behind him. Kleidemos looked at the girl, who was examining him from head to toe with great curiosity. He walked over to one of the balconies to look outside. The view was enchanting: the city beneath him was still red with the last light of dusk. The immense upland plain to the south was dotted with what seemed dusty clouds, close to the ground. They quivered with golden reflections before fading off into the shadows. They were flocks of sheep, their shepherds guiding them into the Kelainai valley, in flight from the rapidly descending darkness.

Kleidemos could almost hear their bleating, or perhaps

he was just imagining it, as he saw himself leaning on his crook among his sheep and lambs, followed by the big ram, the leader of the flock. As he did once, so long ago . . . how long ago he couldn't even say. Then the valley darkened all at once and the black shadow invaded the plateau, lapping at the foot of the mountains which were still topped by a sky as blue and weightless as a byssus veil. At that moment, opposite the setting sun rose the moon, white and luminous as though it had long left the waves of the Ocean from which it was said to emerge.

Kleidemos felt a light touch on his shoulder and turned to look at the girl who stood nude before him, illuminated by the moonlight. He let her lead him by the hand to bed, he let her undress him and caress him. She would look at him, smiling and whispering little phrases that he couldn't understand, but her voice was so sweet, her hands so soft and smooth that he could barely feel her touch. And while she kissed him with lips as moist and cool as violet petals, her firm breasts against his chest, he thought that the bodies of the gods must be like hers. Never touched by fatigue or withered by pain. He thought of Antinea, the only woman he had ever loved in all his life. Her hands would have become callused from years of hard work and her skin would be burnt by the sun, but her eyes perhaps . . . her eyes perhaps shone still, so green, like the fields of Taygetus.

17

THE HOUSE OF BRONZE

KLEIDEMOS AND LAHGAL LEFT Kelainai with Satrap Artabazus' answer for King Pausanias and travelled without
interruption for about a month. They came within view
of Sardeis by the end of the summer. They had left when
the wheat in the fields was still green; now the farmers
had already threshed it and were winnowing: tossing it
into the air with blades so that the wind could separate
the chaff from the grains. Near one of the farms, Kleidemos tied his horse to a fence post and gestured for Lahgal
to follow him into a poplar wood.

'Lahgal,' he said, 'it's time for us to part. Someone may
recognize you in Sardeis. I will tell Pausanias that I have
carried out his orders, but you must disappear forever.'

'And so I shall, Two-Names,' answered the young man.
'Thank you for saving my life. I'll never forget it.'

'Where will you go?' asked Kleidemos.

'I don't know. It's not easy for a runaway slave to find
a safe haven. Maybe south, to Patara; I should be able to
find a ship sailing west. They say that Sicily is a rich and
beautiful land. The money that you've given me will pay
for my passage.'

'That seems like a good decision. No one will look for
you there, but you'll have to find a new name.'

'Yes, just like you. I've never told you that I'd already been given a Greek name by Pausanias, because he couldn't pronounce Lahgal. Haven't you ever heard me called by another name?'

'Perhaps, once or twice, but I can't remember it now . . .'

'Argheilos. He called me Argheilos, but I don't like it. I'll find another.'

The two men were silent for a while.

'This moment is very bitter for me,' said Kleidemos. 'Regaining a friend only to lose him forever is very sad.'

'Don't say that, Two-Names. Would you ever have imagined when you left Cyprus that one day you would find that little boy, who had turned into a man, on a lonely grey morning in Thrace at the foot of a solitary oak tree? Who knows, Two-Names – A man's destiny is on Zeus' knee; perhaps one day we'll meet again.'

'Perhaps,' murmured Kleidemos.

'Farewell, then,' said Lahgal, with a slight tremor in his voice.

'Won't you embrace an old friend before abandoning him forever?'

Lahgal held him tight. 'May the gods protect you, Two-Names. Your life has been hard, as has mine,' he said without letting go. 'What's to come can't help but be better.'

'May the gods grant it,' said Kleidemos, separating from his friend. 'Go now.'

Lahgal jumped onto his ass, dug in his heels and rode off across the green plain. He would vanish in the golden clouds of chaff the farmers were pitching into the air, then reappear as they cleared. Kleidemos watched him until the wind picked up, whirling the sparkling straw dust. He untied his horse, preparing to continue on his journey. As he hoisted himself onto the saddle, he heard a far-off sound, carried by the wind. He turned: beyond the dust, on the top of a hillside lit up by the sun, he could just make out a small black figure, waving its arms. He heard, just for an instant, distinctly, 'Two-Names!' Then the wind changed direction and the figure was hidden by a cloud of dust that rose to cover the sides of the hill.

*

Pausanias urged his mount up the steep climb, headed towards the ruins known as the 'tomb of Menelaus'. Close now, he pulled on the reins, slowing the horse to a lope. He turned around to scan the road that he'd taken from Sparta: no one had followed him. The king dismounted and tied the bridle to a tree. He walked towards the ruins, invaded by brambles and the stumps of wild fig trees. The sun was setting in the distance behind the Taygetus range. He entered the crumbling walls, sword in hand, proceeding cautiously. A time-eroded pillar hid the structure's main room – what must have been the funeral chamber – from sight, while the collapsed ceiling let in a wide stretch of sky. He leaned forward soundlessly, and saw ephor Episthenes sitting on a square stone. He stepped out into the open then, and returned his sword to its sheath. 'Hail, Episthenes. Have you been waiting long?'

'No, not too long. I left the city yesterday morning, saying that I was going to my farm, which as you know is quite nearby. If you were not followed, no one will learn of this encounter.'

The king sat on a tree stump. 'Don't worry; no one followed me. Well, what have you to tell me?'

'The council of ephors found no cause to incriminate you.'

'What about the *krypteia*?' asked Pausanias uneasily.

'The *krypteia* can fabricate proof where none exists, as well you know. You are fortunate that justice still has the upper hand in the city.'

'So I'm free to resume my command at Byzantium. The season most propitious for navigation is coming to an end; I'll have to leave as soon as possible.'

The ephor's forehead wrinkled. 'Beware, Pausanias: this is not over yet. Despite the fact that nothing emerged against you, keep in mind that the ephors and the elders are wary of you, and sooner or later will succeed in toppling you.'

'But the assembly—'

'You know better than I do that the assembly does not have decisional power. It wouldn't be the first time that the elders acted contrary to the opinion expressed by the assembly of equals.'

'What do you think will happen?' asked Pausanias, with a note of apprehension.

'Nothing for the time being, but I'm very worried nonetheless. The ephors won't need to strike out directly at you with a trial or dismissal. They can have you destroyed without compromising themselves in the least.'

'Who would dare—'

'Listen to me,' the ephor interrupted him brusquely. 'You have been away for a long time and you are unaware of many things that have happened in your absence.

Themistocles has been ostracized – the city aristocrats succeeded in stirring up the people of Athens against him, and he was driven into exile. The enormous prestige of his victory at Salamis was not enough to save him, and you can easily draw the conclusion that the glory of Plataea won't serve you any better. The Persian invasion is long over, and people forget so quickly. The democrats in Athens are very weak; the man of the moment is Cimon.'

'The son of Miltiades?'

'That's right, his father was the victor of the battle of Marathon. Cimon is intelligent, able, with old-fashioned ideas; he's very popular here as well. As far as I can see, there's an air of agreement, which should culminate in a pact between the aristocratic party in Athens, with Cimon at its head, and the government of Sparta. If a treaty of this kind were made, I doubt that there would be any room for you.'

'I don't understand,' protested Pausanias. 'I've never met Cimon, but I know that he regards me highly. His politics are anti-Persian – why would he want to take sides against the victor of Plataea?'

'It's very simple, although it may seem complicated to you,' explained the ephor. Pausanias could not hide his irritation.

'Running an army and wielding a spear are not the same thing as dealing with politics,' continued Episthenes, calmly. 'Listen to what I have to say; all I want to do is help you. It's clear that Cimon doesn't have anything against you personally, and he considers you a great commander, but if what he wants is an alliance with

Sparta, and the government of Sparta is against Pausanias, then Cimon will be against Pausanias as well. When Themistocles was in power, our relations with Athens deteriorated to such an extent that war seemed imminent. Now that Themistocles is out of the way, Cimon is ready to contract an alliance with Sparta against the Persians. It's really none of our concern if the patriotic goal of combating the barbarians coincides with the much more practical goal of silencing the democrats in Athens. The fact is that relations between the two greatest powers of Greece stand to be stabilized. Illustrious men and eminent leaders have been sacrificed for much less.'

Pausanias let his hands go in his lap, greatly discouraged. 'Tell me, at least, what is the true reason for which the ephors and the elders want me out of the way?' he said, raising his head.

'There are many reasons, Pausanias, and unfortunately, all valid: since King Pleistarchus is but a child, you are actually the true king. By occupying Byzantium you control the straits, and thus the commerce of wheat from the Pontus in Greece is entirely in your hands. You have great influence over the equals who fought in your army and the majority of the assembly supports you. Moreover, many rumours have been circulating about the way you behave as an oriental king in Byzantium, dressing in Persian gowns and dealing with barbarian commanders without consulting your government. It is said that you have great sympathy for the Athenian democrats, and direct contact with Themistocles – although this has not been proven. Some have found fault in the personal interest you've taken in that young Talos—'

'His name is Kleidemos, son of Aristarkhos, Kleomenid!' burst out Pausanias vexedly.

'As you like,' said Episthenes with an air of condescension. 'The fact is that that man is now a high officer of the Spartan army, although we do not know what relations he has maintained with the Helots.'

'What relations are you talking about? He fought in Thrace for four years, spending no more than a couple of weeks in all at Byzantium. Kleidemos did battle like a hero at Plataea and he is one of my best officers.'

'I understand. But you know that any relations between Spartiates and Helots that are not exactly . . . traditional, are seen with much suspicion.'

'Kleidemos is not a Helot.'

'No one can say that. He lived with them for twenty years, and he practically never knew his true parents. You have been warned; you now know the danger you are in.'

'Thank you, Episthenes, I won't forget this,' said the king, getting to his feet. 'I must go now. I don't want my absence from the city to be noticed. Farewell.'

'Farewell,' replied the ephor. 'And stay on your guard.'

Pausanias walked out, glancing around carefully. He waited until a farmer with a load of hay disappeared behind a curve in the road, then leapt into his saddle and galloped off across the countryside.

*

Kleidemos reached Byzantium shortly before Pausanias arrived aboard a warship. He was received immediately by the king, who greeted him warmly.

'I'm very glad to see you,' said Pausanias, embracing him.

'As am I,' replied Kleidemos, returning the embrace.

'How was your journey? Did you encounter any difficulties?'

'No, the journey went well and I was able to carry out my mission.'

'Completely?' asked the king, looking away.

'Completely,' replied Kleidemos coldly.

'Do not judge me too harshly,' said the king. 'The servant I sent with you was very dear to me, but I had no choice. I had to send someone I could trust completely, and yet I could not allow him to survive. The stakes are so high that no risks can be taken.' The king stopped for a moment, and then asked with a touch of embarrassment, 'Did he understand he was going to die?'

'No,' answered Kleidemos, 'he didn't realize a thing.'

'Better that way. I was fond of him.'

'I understand,' replied Kleidemos, his tone indicating that the matter was closed.

'Tell me, then,' continued Pausanias, 'what did Artabazus say?'

'The Great King greatly appreciated the favour you did him by liberating the persons you know of, and considers this gesture proof of your sincerity. He is also willing to satisfy your . . . request for his daughter's hand.'

'Fine, fine,' said the king, pretending indifference. 'Is that all?'

'No, there's more. I spoke at length with Artabazus and I've come to understand the Persian point of view on this matter. They feel that the time to act has come. They realize that you are at the peak of your power right now, but don't know for how long this situation may last. They know that Admiral Themistocles has been exiled from Athens, and I had the impression that they would be glad to welcome him among them. From now on, you will report to the satrap of Dascylium.'

'*We* will report to him,' said the king. 'Am I right, Kleidemos?'

'Certainly, sire,' answered Kleidemos.

'You don't seem entirely convinced of what you say, but perhaps you – like the Great King – require proof of my friendship. I can give you that proof. Since my plan relies extensively on you, it is only fair that you have every certainty and assurance. In Sparta I saw someone who is very close to you.'

Kleidemos started. 'Who? Tell me, please!'

'A bearded giant.'

'Karas!'

'Yes, exactly.'

'How did you find him?' Kleidemos trembled, shaken by emotion.

'It was not very difficult,' replied the king. 'I let a mountain Helot know that I had news of Talos and that I wanted to talk to a trusted friend. Six weeks passed, and I thought that nothing would come of it. Then one night, returning home, I heard a voice behind me, saying "Talos' friend is here." I resisted the temptation to turn around, and replied, "Follow me at four paces." I knew that someone might be following me, and I didn't want to arouse suspicion. Without turning around or slowing my pace, I managed to give him a time and a place to meet. Then I heard his footsteps moving off. I met him a few days later in a run-down hut on my property. Our conversation was long and difficult; he is an extremely diffident man. He wanted me to give him some proof that you were alive and that you trusted me. I did so, and told him that you would soon be back to put our plan into action.'

'But how did you know you could trust him?' asked Kleidemos.

'That man was with you at Plataea,' replied Pausanias calmly, 'and I know that he calls on the woman you consider your mother in her house on Mount Taygetus. When I mentioned him the last time we saw each other, you couldn't hide your emotion. That man is very important to you, isn't he?'

'Yes, he is,' admitted Kleidemos.

'Won't you tell me who he is, in reality?'

'I don't know myself who he really is,' replied Kleidemos. 'He appeared when my grandfather Kritolaos died. When I met him, I realized by his words that he had come to help me and protect me, and that I could trust him. He knew the secret of the great bow.'

'The bow with the head of the Wolf of Messenia.'

'Yes, but not only. There's more to it than that, more than even I can understand. But tell me, what did Karas say?'

'That he was ready to join us, but that he would not make a move until you had come back yourself to confirm my every word.'

'He didn't say anything else?'

'No. When we'd finished, he got up and vanished. I didn't see him again.'

As the king was speaking, Kleidemos was reminded of his past. His mother's eyes, so full of sadness, Karas' bullish head, his deep voice. He realized how badly he wanted to go back.

'When can I go?' he asked the king, his eyes betraying his longing.

'You must be patient,' answered the king, putting a hand on his shoulder. 'I know how you feel, and I understand how much you want to return, but there are other important things to be done first. You must take my answer for the Great King to the satrap at Dascylium immediately. When we have the Persians' gold, I'll enlist an army and equip a fleet: that's how we'll return to Sparta. We will rouse the Helots, and the equals will all be on my side as well; I led them at Plataea.'

Kleidemos lowered his head. 'As you wish. When shall I leave?'

'Immediately. We have very little time. You'll leave before the moon appears in the sky.'

Kleidemos departed, but that was not the only mission he carried out to Dascylium; he returned several times during the winter, always exercising great caution. At the start of the following spring, however, Pausanias' worst fears were realized: the Athenian fleet at Cimon's command showed up at the mouth of the Bosporus, and the admiral ordered him to abandon the city. The order was countersigned by the Spartan authorities. Pausanias attempted at first to resist, but knew that he could not hold up for long alone against a naval blockade of the city. Nor did he feel he could fully trust the mercenaries he had signed up using Persian gold. He left Byzantium and marched to the Troad, stopping at a place not far from Dascylium where Kleidemos met up with him.

His position was already in serious jeopardy and even the Persians treated him with detachment. The only option he had left to him was to attempt to carry out his plan in Sparta. The time had come for Kleidemos to leave Asia and return to Laconia, the official reason being that he did not intend to remain under the orders of a commander who had been repudiated by his own government, and that he wished to report directly to the ephors and elders.

'Farewell, Kleidemos,' said the king, grasping his hand, 'all of our hopes are placed in you now. Do not lose heart: I will return, and you will see that all is not lost.'

'Farewell, my king,' responded Kleidemos. 'When you return I will be waiting for you at the house of the Kleomenids. There we will meet again, if the gods so will it.' He mounted his horse and rode off in the direction of Cyzicus.

Pausanias walked back towards his headquarters, leading his horse by its halter. It was a beautiful day. A fresh breeze was blowing, and huge white clouds sailed by in the clearest of skies.

'*When the wind blows from land to sea, a good day it is to sail for the Greeks.* At least that's how the proverb goes,' the King of Sparta thought to himself as he turned to look at the Aegean Sea shining in the distance like a mirror dropped by the hand of a goddess. Then a cloud covered the sun and the king slowly made his way down the road.

*

Kleidemos disembarked at Gytheum, had his horse brought ashore and started off towards Sparta.

It was early morning and he was counting on coming within sight of the city before sunset, so as to report to the ephors with the story he and Pausanias had agreed. He soon reached the right bank of the Eurotas and followed it along its course all day. In the early afternoon, approaching the city of Pharis, he saw the Taygetus mountains. He contemplated the view at length, exploring the peaks, the gorges and the forests with eager eyes until he managed to locate the exact spot where he hoped that the woman he had never stopped calling mother was waiting for him.

He ate a piece of bread from his knapsack with a chunk of cheese and drank the river water. He then readied himself to enter Sparta.

He put on his cuirass and his greaves. He removed the great shield with the dragon from a leather sack and hung it from his saddle. He then slipped on the helmet with its three crimson crests and rode into the city. A guard who saw him from an observation tower was shocked: the warrior who advanced solemnly on his proud Nisaean steed, encased in flashing armour, seemed the great Aristarkhos himself, back from the Underworld. Only when the horseman drew closer did he realize who he actually must be. He watched him closely until he entered among the houses and disappeared in the maze of streets.

Kleidemos headed towards the square where the Council House stood and asked one of the guards to announce him. 'Say that Kleidemos, son of Aristarkhos, Kleomenid, commander of the fourth battalion of Thrace, requests to be received.'

He was soon brought before ephor Episthenes who came towards him smiling. 'It is an honour for me to welcome to his homeland the son of great Aristarkhos, the noble Kleidemos, whose endeavours in Thrace have not gone unnoticed. The venerable fathers of the council of elders will be glad to receive you as soon as possible and to hear your full report on the events that have occurred in Byzantium . . . And on the situation of King Pausanias, whose conduct has recently been quite worrisome for us. I will let you know personally when they are ready to hear you. You will now be accompanied to your battalion quarters where you can take refreshment and rest. I will arrange for you to take possession of your house, which has been abandoned for years. An old servant has remained to look after the property; he will tell you everything you want to know about your estate and the Helots who are farming your land.'

'I thank you, sir, and I will await your call,' said Kleidemos. He offered a military salute and followed the guard who took him to his *syssitia*.

He crossed the city on foot, holding the horse's reins. He passed through the districts known as Pitane and Cynosura and reached the acropolis. He turned to look at the facade of the temple of Athena, the House of Bronze, and he saw himself as a boy again, cloaked in Pelias' cape, watching Brithos being lashed. How full of hate his heart had been! He could still hear the crack of the whip, as if no time had passed at all. He walked on through the city streets, wrapped in his thoughts, and the guard's voice startled him. 'We're here, commander. If you'd like to give me your horse, I'll take him to your home so he can be groomed.'

Kleidemos removed the shield from the saddle, took its leather case and his knapsack and entered the quarters which had been assigned to him. The long, bare room contained thirty-two beds, at the heads of which were the same number of chests. Leaning against the walls were racks for holding spears and swords, with a row of hangers for helmets and armour. In that vast space, so sad and unadorned, the shining weapons seemed more like ornaments than instruments of death.

A Helot helped him off with his armour and placed the few items he carried with him into a chest. He told him that a meal would soon be distributed in the adjoining room. Kleidemos lay down on the little bed that the Helot had indicated as his. He felt restless, troubled . . . he wanted to take his horse from the Kleomenid house and race up the mountain, reach the clearing, find his cottage and shout, 'Mother!' so loud that everyone would hear him – even Kritolaos, buried at the edge of the forest. He wanted to go to the high spring, to Karas' cabin, to feel his bones crack in the giant's powerful embrace. O powerful gods, would Karas still be there waiting for him? Would they still go hunting together, taking up the King's bow once again? Karas . . . Karas would know where he could find Antinea. He wanted to go straight to her. 'I'm mad!' he thought, tapping his forehead. 'Mad! What do I expect from her? She's surely become the wife of some shepherd or farmer and I won't even recognize her. Her body, worn out by hard labour and pregnancy. Or her soul, exasperated and disappointed by an endless wait, then tamed and hardened by years of servitude.'

But he still had to see her. Perhaps something from their life together had remained, a part of her soul that could never, never leave the high pastures of Mount Taygetus. He had to find Karas; Karas would take him to her.

A chorus of shouts interrupted his thoughts and thirty nude youths burst into the big room, laughing and joking, the members of the *syssitia* he'd been assigned to. As soon as the first of them noticed the new arrival, they stopped dead in their tracks. Shouting to be heard over the general confusion, one young man ordered his companions to draw up. 'Fall in, men! You have the commander of the Thracian battalion before you. Can't you see his shield? He is the son of the great Aristarkhos! Do you hear me, men?'

He turned to Kleidemos, who had risen to his feet. 'Commander, I am Aincias, son of Onesikritos, commander of the *syssitia*. Welcome, sir, and forgive me if I have not ordered a military salute. Since we're all naked, as you can see, it is prohibited by regulations. In just a moment, my men will be dressed in full armour, and you may review us in the courtyard if you so wish.'

'Thank you,' replied Kleidemos, with a gesture of his hand, 'but I'm sure you are tired and hungry. Fall out, and prepare yourselves for dinner. I'll meet you in the mess.'

The meal was served just after sunset and Kleidemos

took part, although he didn't feel like company. His conduct had to be in line with what was expected; he did not want to attract undue attention. Kleidemos was convinced that Pausanias' plan was already seriously jeopardized, but in any case, it was best to continue as they had agreed. If the plan became feasible, all the better. If Pausanias, as he suspected, had his hands tied upon his return to Sparta, Kleidemos would certainly not want to stir up the Helots, to push them into a futile massacre.

It was important to establish a good relationship with the warriors. The men from the battalion in Thrace had nearly all returned, and would have spread his fame as an irreproachable commander and tireless fighter. During the meal, he realized that a phrase he had pronounced on the field in Thrace two years ago had made the rounds of all the barracks in the city. An officer had come from Byzantium to inspect the troops, and he'd made an ironic comment regarding Kleidemos' lame foot. He had replied, 'I'm here to fight, not to take to my heels.'

Hundreds of stories about him had been bruited about, and the men were curious to hear more. The youngest wanted to hear about the Battle of the Thermopylae – he was the last living Spartan to have witnessed it. Others wanted to know whether it was true that Pausanias had taken to living like the Persians, and that he was putting together a personal army and would return to Sparta. But what interested them the most, and which none of them dared to voice openly, was his incredible past: surviving the wolves of Mount Taygetus, finding his brother Brithos and fighting by his side at Plataea, and reclaiming his place among the equals. He who had begun life crippled and disinherited.

Kleidemos chose to ignore the hinted questions that emerged during the conversation, letting them know that he had had a painful life, but that he did not consider himself better than or different from the others for this reason. This increased the esteem of these men who were accustomed to seeing their kings share their frugal meals and sleep on the same rough pallets, kings who took first place only in times of danger and hardship. And so the conversation turned back to Pausanias. 'What I cannot understand, commander,' said one of the soldiers whose name was Boiskos, 'is how the victor of Plataea can be scheming with the Persians. It makes me think that someone wants to destroy his reputation and his fame in order to remove him from power. What do you think?'

Kleidemos reflected on this, weighing his answer carefully. 'My friend, no one has ever demonstrated that this rumour is founded in fact. But for someone to wilfully create such a rumour . . . well, that seems just as incredible to me. I must say personally that Pausanias has always helped me and shown me his esteem, and I am grateful for this.'

'You've abandoned him, though. You must have a reason.'

'When I heard that the ephors and elders had revoked his command, I realized that my duty as a citizen could not be reconciled with my personal feelings of gratitude, and so I returned.'

'What does the king intend doing now?' asked another.

'I don't know,' responded Kleidemos. 'I imagine he will return, if for no other reason than to defend himself, to explain his actions.'

*

Kleidemos could never have imagined that in the dungeons of the Council House the same question was being asked in a much more threatening tone by an officer of the *krypteia*. The man expected to answer had been tortured, chained, and was covered with blood and bruises: Karas.

'We know that you met Pausanias in secret. The king of Sparta cannot have encountered a miserable slave without a very specific purpose in mind!'

'I tell you that the king brought me news of a man whom we call Talos and you call Kleidemos,' answered Karas, his voice exhausted.

'Hidden away, in a broken-down hut, removed from any prying eyes?' persisted the officer with a sneer, lashing cruelly with a whip. Karas moaned in pain, clenching his teeth. 'Take pity on me,' he said, as soon as he could talk again. 'I've done nothing wrong. A servant of the king came to my cabin to tell me that Pausanias wanted to talk to me, that he had news of Talos. I don't know why he wanted to meet me in that place; maybe he was embarrassed to meet a man of such miserable conditions in a public place, or in his home. He said only that Talos had asked him to look for me so that I could take word of him to the woman who raised him.'

'And you expect me to believe that that's all you said

to each other? What did Pausanias ask you?' shouted the officer. 'Talk, you sorry wretch, or you'll never leave here alive!'

Karas raised his sweat-soaked forehead. 'Sir,' he said, panting, 'you know that I had never seen your king before that day. Why would I stand to be tortured for him? I would say anything to persuade you to let me free.'

The officer sent a quizzical look to ephor Mnesikles who was listening to the interrogation; he came out of the dark corner where he had been concealed. 'He has a point,' he said in a tone that made Karas shiver. 'Why should he put up with pain and risk his life for a Spartan king he barely knows and certainly does not love? We do know, however,' he added, taking the whip from the officer's hand and approaching the prisoner himself, 'that your friend Talos has enjoyed Pausanias' full trust for all these years. And you would do anything to protect him, wouldn't you?'

Karas lifted his chained hand to wipe his brow and to gain a little time. He wouldn't fall into their trap, betray himself. 'I don't know what I should be protecting him from,' he said, 'but why would I, even if I did? Talos no longer exists for the mountain people. The man you call Kleidemos is no one for us, and I hope I never see him again. But the woman who raised him like a mother would have given her life to know he was alive and well. That's why I accepted to see the king.'

'You're lying!' screamed the ephor, hitting his nose with the handle of the whip. Blood spurted from his tortured flesh, spilling into the mouth and over the chest of the chained giant. Karas' face had become a shapeless mask, eyes swollen shut and lips split open. His breath came out as a painful wheeze.

'Sir,' he found the strength to say, 'I can't tell you what I don't know. But if you can let me know what you want to hear . . . I'll say anything, to save my life.' His head rolled onto his chest. The ephor stepped away to consult with the *krypteia* officer.

'He's very strong,' he said. 'We haven't been able to wrench a single word from him. Maybe he really doesn't know anything. He has just offered to back us up in an indictment of Pausanias . . .'

'I'm not sure about that,' replied the officer. 'He may be familiar with our laws, and know that the testimony of a servant cannot be used against any of the equals, let alone a king. He may have just been trying to mislead us, knowing that we can't accept such an offer.'

'How do you think we should proceed?' asked the ephor.

'Continue with the torture. Perhaps we haven't worn down his resistance yet. In the end, we'll have to kill him, regardless of whether he talks or not. He hates us more than he fears us right now, and that makes him dangerous. Remember that last night he split the yoke he was tied to with his bare hands and when the guard got there he was already forcing the bars on the gate . . .'

The ephor glanced over at Karas, who seemed to have fainted. 'I don't agree. There are men who won't be broken by torture, and he seems that kind to me. If we kill him, we'll never know what he's hiding from us. Push him as far as you can; the pain must be annihilating. You must terrify him.' He looked over at an iron which was glowing red-hot in the brazier. 'You know what I mean.' The officer nodded. 'If he manages to resist, let him go, but have him followed. Don't lose him, and be sure to let me know if he tries to contact Kleidemos, or even meets with that woman up on the mountain. You have Helots working for you; it won't be difficult for them. If what we suspect is true, he'll betray himself sooner or later. I'm going now, you don't need me any longer. You will report to me tomorrow.' He pulled his hood over his head and left.

The officer approached the prisoner and brought him to his senses by throwing a bucket of cold water over his head. He walked towards the brazier. Karas' vision was still foggy. As it cleared, terror exploded within him, ripping open his soul: a scorching iron, burning with white light, loomed just a palm's breadth from his face. He could feel the heat.

'Now you'll talk,' said the officer calmly, grabbing him by the hair.

Karas tensed his muscles in a futile and desperate attempt to get away, but paralysing cramps racked his body, already pushed beyond every human limit. He sat very still, calling up all his reserves of energy, like a wounded boar facing a pack of dogs, bloody and weary, backed up against a tree trunk waiting for the hunter's spear to tear through his throat.

'Talk!' said the officer, pushing the poker even closer. Karas blew blood out of his nose. 'I know . . . nothing,' he roared, his mouth foaming. The officer gripped him tighter and plunged the burning iron into his left eye.

Karas' scream exploded in the dungeons and charged through the walls of the Council House, a long, atrocious bellow that filled the square, startling the two hoplites leaning drowsily against their spears.

Not long thereafter the *krypteia* officer left the Council House and, without returning the guards' salute, crossed the deserted square and walked off into the night. He had done his job conscientiously, following the orders he had received. And he was convinced that that poor devil down in the dungeons knew nothing, nothing at all. A wretched shepherd could not be so obstinate or so strong. He had made him believe that he would have blinded both eyes, and yet he hadn't said a word. He had seen unfathomable terror in the man's single, swollen eye before he had collapsed, senseless. He had unchained him before leaving, and left open the door to an underground passage that came up outside the city. His men had been ordered to wait there and follow him. The ephor Mnesikles was right. If that man was still alive – and didn't have the good sense to flee as far away as he could – and if he had actually plotted with Pausanias, he would be devoured by hate and his hate would give him away. Everything would become clear eventually. He was glad to finally return to his quarters and rest after such a tiring day.

Karas began to regain consciousness, roused by the cold wind that was blowing in from the open door. The immense pain in his left socket reminded him of the cruel mutilation he had suffered. The utter night around him made him believe for a moment that he was completely blind. He burst into tears; it was all over, he only hoped that death would come quickly now. But the shadows began to clear and he realized that he could make out the edges of the objects around him. He saw the chains hanging from the wall: he had been freed! He blundered to his feet and looked around, noticing the open door. He walked down the murky passage at length, stumbling, recoiling at the contact with the horrid creatures that lived in those dark recesses. A gust of fresh air hit his face at last, and from the mouth of the tunnel he could see the stars of Orion, shimmering in the opalescent sky. Dawn was not far off. He crept out and made his way across the deserted fields until he reached the banks of the Eurotas.

He knelt and washed out the bloody socket, gasping at the stabbing pain caused by the cold water. The moon was beginning to pale when the wounded cyclops rose to his feet, panting with agony and rage, and raised his fists against the city glowing whitely in the false light of dawn. He walked towards Taygetus. The great mountain was still enveloped in darkness. It welcomed him and hid him within its impenetrable forests.

*

Pausanias no longer had any justification for remaining in the Troad and thus convinced himself that his only option was to return to Sparta, where the ephors surely still had no evidence against him. But what the ephors had sought in vain to learn from Karas was about to be offered to them by a person they didn't even know existed.

They had imagined that Pausanias would attempt to put himself in contact with Karas through the Helots working in the king's home. They'd already wooed these servants over to their side with a mix of promises and threats. They were also keeping Kleidemos under constant surveillance.

Pausanias was well aware of the situation and felt like a lion in a cage. Shunned by all, he could contact none of the people he thought he could count on. Nor could he risk meeting Kleidemos, whom he knew was surrounded by *krypteia* spies. He resigned himself to submitting to the ephors and elders, biding his time until the situation was favourable again.

One morning before dawn, ephor Mnesikles heard a knock at his door. He opened it and found a young dark-skinned foreigner with a hood hiding most of his face. He asked to speak with him.

'My name is Argheilos,' he said. 'I was in the service of King Pausanias at Byzantium. I have things to tell you that you will find very interesting.'

'Come in,' invited the ephor, closing the door immediately behind him. The young man sat down and took off his hooded cloak. He was definitely a foreigner, Asian perhaps.

'Your name is Greek,' he observed. 'But you seem a foreigner to me.'

'I am,' replied the young man. 'My true name is Lahgal, and I am Syrian. I served King Pausanias faithfully for years, but now I am here to denounce him. I am no spy, trust my words, but a man who seeks revenge for a monstrous injustice. In exchange for my loyalty, the king attempted to have me murdered, so that his scheming with the Great King would go unknown.'

'What you say is extremely serious,' said the ephor. 'Do you realize that you are accusing a Spartan king of betrayal? Careful: if you cannot prove your accusations, you risk your life.'

'I can prove what I've said, whenever you like,' replied Lahgal.

'Then the truth must come to light as soon as possible. Tell me what you know: you will not regret having helped us to put a stop to such infamous betrayal.'

Lahgal told everything that he had seen and surmised during the years he lived with Pausanias. He told of the journey to Kelainai as well, portraying Kleidemos in a way that absolved him of blame.

'You know Kleidemos, Kleomenid, very well, then,' observed the ephor. 'We are aware that Pausanias esteemed him greatly and entrusted him with important missions.'

'I do know him,' said Lahgal. 'I brought him the king's instructions personally when he was commanding the Thracian battalion. I can assure you that he knew nothing of Pausanias' betrayal. The king had ordered him to go with me to Kelainai to study the location of Persian garrisons in the interior, on the pretext of supposedly preparing a military expedition which would chase the Persians beyond the Halys river. Only I knew the mission's true purpose: to report to Satrap Artabazus that Pausanias was ready to march against Sparta, and that he needed money and men. Kleidemos was given a message that I was a spy; when his mission was completed and he didn't need me any longer as an interpreter, he was to kill me. I managed to read the message unknown to him while he was sleeping and I escaped.'

'Well,' the ephor said, 'what you must know is that as

a foreigner you may not testify against one of the caste of the equals, nor against a king. Pausanias is both, although his regency is about to draw to a close: Prince Pleistarchus is about to reach puberty. Pausanias must be persuaded to unfold his plans in the presence of Spartan citizens who can testify against him.

'This is my plan: first you must let Pausanias know that you are here and want to meet with him. I'm sure he will agree to it. There is an old abandoned building on the Taenarum promontory; it is there you will go. You must get him to talk so that several witnesses who are hiding behind a false wall can hear him. We'll worry about the rest. Now go. It is not opportune for you to be seen here. Try to remain hidden and not to attract undue attention. You will be rewarded for this service, but as you know the equals cannot handle money. I cannot pay you now, but I will find a way. Do you prefer Athenian or Euboean silver . . . or coins from Cyzicus?'

'I'm not doing this for a reward,' replied Lahgal. 'I won't take your money.' He stood up, covered his face and walked out.

Three days later Pausanias found a message in his house, although none of his servants could say how it had got there. What the message said filled him with dread: Lahgal was alive! Kleidemos had lied to him or worse, betrayed him. He thought of fleeing, but realized that it would be like admitting his guilt. And who would provide a haven for a fugitive stripped of all power? It was better to face the situation. If it was truly Lahgal who had written the message, and certain phrases left no doubt in his mind, perhaps he could convince him to keep quiet.

Or at least find out who else knew. He decided to meet him at the appointed place. He knew it well: an old observation tower in ruins nearly at the tip of the promontory. A barren, desolate, wind-swept place.

He entered through a ramshackle door and heard a voice he recognized very well ringing out in the gloom. 'They say that no one ever comes back from the Underworld, don't they Pausanias? And yet here I am. Come in, come in, don't just stand there.'

'Listen—' began the king.

'No. You listen,' interrupted the young man, emerging from the shadows, 'I'm stronger than you are now.' Pausanias' hand fell, perhaps inadvertently, to the hilt of his sword.

'You fool!' said Lahgal. 'Do you think I am so imprudent that I have taken no precautions if you should try to kill me a second time?'

Pausanias let his arm drop and lowered his head. 'I'm listening,' he said resignedly.

'I've asked you to come here so I can know for what offence you condemned me to death. If having served you loyally, irreproachably, having cured you when you were ill, followed you like your own shadow, endured your lust—'

'I thought you loved me,' Pausanias said plaintively.

Lahgal laughed scornfully. 'Have you fallen so low? Come now, you know there can be no love between one who commands and one who serves – only violence: inflicted and suffered. So don't think you can try to play with my feelings for you; they never even existed. I pledged my complete dedication in exchange for the promise of my freedom. An honest exchange, man to man.'

'I was sincere when I promised to free you, and I would have done so.'

'Of course,' snarled Lahgal. 'Exactly what you thought you had accomplished: freeing me from every worry while ridding yourself of me forever!'

'Don't make jest of me,' interrupted the king with sadness in his voice. 'And please listen, I can explain . . . if you promise you will reflect on my words and not let yourself be dominated by rancour and anger. If you called me here, you must be willing to listen to me.'

'Talk, then,' replied the young man coldly.

'I will. But first I want to know why Kleidemos deceived me.'

'Your spirit must be truly vile,' said Lahgal, 'if you see betrayal where none exists. Kleidemos carried out your orders faithfully, all of them . . . except one. I read your scroll while he was sleeping and I fled. Not because I feared that he would really murder me; Kleidemos is a good man. But because I didn't want to make him struggle with his conscience. That's not what I came here to talk about, Pausanias; I want to hear other things from you.'

Pausanias was greatly relieved by his answer. All was not lost; he could still manage to convince Lahgal. He began again, not knowing that in that very moment, he was pronouncing his own death sentence. 'I did not want you dead, Lahgal, I swear it. The Persians forced me to accept this condition. I couldn't withhold my assent at that point; they would have become suspicious and all my plans would have gone up in smoke. I couldn't risk them considering me an enemy. The lives of thousands of people were at stake. But you must believe me, it was against my will, and with unspeakable bitterness, that I forced myself to write that order.

'Perhaps you were merely putting up with me all those years we lived together, Lahgal, thinking only of obtaining your freedom. But I loved you, and you cannot deny the sincerity of my affection. Tell me, my young friend, did I ever hurt you? Didn't I help you in every way I could? Didn't I make you part of my life, my plans, my dreams? You certainly deluded me by letting me believe that you loved me as well.'

Lahgal looked at that broken man, practically at the mercy of his enemies now. The hero of Plataea! The Panhellenic leader, reduced to a shadow of his former self. The tone of his words seemed sincere and Lahgal felt moved by pity, but the desire for revenge had pushed him so far that he could no longer turn back. It was all over now. And so he replied using words of guile and Pausanias left, sorry for ever having ordered his death.

The king returned to Sparta towards evening, wondering how he could get in touch with Kleidemos. Absorbed in his thoughts, at first he didn't notice the five ephors in front of the Amyclae Gate, surrounded by about twenty armed men. As he drew closer, he realized they were waiting for him. Ephor Episthenes, who stood behind the others, made a gesture and Pausanias realized that this was the end. He spurred on his horse in an attempt to escape, but the spear hurled by one of the warriors hit the animal in its side. The horse fell heavily to the ground with its rider, and Pausanias rolled in the dust. He swiftly got to his feet and began to run, his pursuers close on his heels. He was near the acropolis; he looked around, bewildered, for someone who would offer him shelter. All the glances he met were hostile or indifferent, and the doors were bolted against him. He sought refuge in the House of Bronze: no one would dare profane that holy place. He closed himself in, panting, and went to crouch in a corner.

The ephors, powerless to enter and arrest him, had all the doors walled up and removed the roof. And there the king remained, for days and days, parched with thirst under the flaming rays of the sun and tormented by hunger. His enemies watched with indifferent eyes, perched on the bare beams of the roof, awaiting his death. His shouting and cursing could be heard long into the night. Then nothing.

The ephors realized that the holy place would be profaned nonetheless if he died there, so they decided to open the doors and carry him out while he was still alive. They dragged him into the outer courtyard. Trembling with fever, his glassy eyes rolled around horror-filled in hollow sockets.

Thrown into the dust, Pausanias tried to raise his fleshless arm to curse them all, but his strength abandoned him and he fell on his back, gasping his last breath.

Such was the agony and death of he who had vanquished the army of the Great King at Plataea.

18

THE SACRILEGE

THE ASSEMBLED EPHORS AND elders decided at first that the corpse of Pausanias would be thrown into the Keadas torrent, as was customary for traitors, but ephor Episthenes, who had secretly remained the king's friend, argued that although Pausanias had disobeyed the orders of the city and was guilty of plotting with the enemy, outside of Sparta he still enjoyed great fame among the Hellenes as the man who had liberated Greece from the barbarians. His death was punishment enough, and his mortal remains must be conceded the dignity of a proper burial. The ephor's proposal seemed a wise one, and so Pausanias was buried with his arms at the very place where he had breathed his last.

But the spectre of Pausanias continued to disturb many a night in Sparta nonetheless. Some insisted that his terrifying screams could still be heard in the House of Bronze late at night, and others claimed that just after dusk on the seventh day of every month, a hollow metallic noise could be heard coming from his tomb, as though he were striking its walls with his weapons. It was decided that the oracle in Delphi must be consulted, and the following response was given:

A body was stolen
from the goddess of the House of Bronze.
To placate the ire of the deity
two bodies must be rendered in exchange.

Long was the discussion in the Council House to interpret this response. Some suggested sacrificing a couple of Helots; others argued that death must not be added to death, and that amends must be made in another form. In the end they decided to build two statues to be dedicated to the temple, and so the ephors and the elders imagined that they could appease the anger of the gods with two lifeless effigies forged by human hands.

No one spoke any longer of these events, and their echo was extinguished because the mind of man is prone to forgetting, but it was written that the blood of the king would bring a curse upon the city.

Lahgal vanished as he had appeared and nothing more was ever known about him. Kleidemos, unaware of the whole plot, prepared for the worst when he learned that Pausanias had been confined within the House of Bronze, but no one ever came looking for him, nor was he ever asked anything. His only encounter with the ephors remained his account of his conduct in Thrace, which was confirmed by the men of the fourth battalion who had since returned. The great prestige of his name protected him from humiliating inquisitions, and his word as a warrior was sufficient for the authorities. Nonetheless, the ephors had him watched, looking out for any sign of collusion or guilt. His close relationship with Pausanias and his time among the Helots perpetuated the suspicion and diffidence of the city, regardless of the irreproachable conduct of the son of Aristarkhos.

The death of the king destroyed any residual hope in Kleidemos that the plan which Pausanias had proposed in Byzantium might be realized. It was no more than a dream, that had once given purpose to his life but had quickly dissipated, leaving a hollow place in his soul. It made him keenly aware that he could not escape his life: if he had managed to survive yet again, despite the mortal danger he had been in when Pausanias' plans were discovered, he really must have a destiny to fulfil. He had no choice but to live his life as it was, while waiting for the situation to mature.

He did not hide his desire to return to the woman who had raised him on Mount Taygetus, and when he took possession of the house of the Kleomenids, his wish was granted. The ephors imagined that this would make it even easier for them to trace any suspicious contacts.

And so, at the beginning of the winter, Kleidemos was given permission to leave the *syssitia* where he had lived for months in complete compliance with the rigid military standards of communal life, and to take charge of his own home and possessions.

He left the barracks one morning as the sun was rising, followed by a Helot from his father's house who had loaded up his belongings and armour onto the back of an ass. He left through the eastern gate, walking slowly and taking in his surroundings: he could just make out the Kleomenid house about ten stadia away, still enveloped in the shadows of the night. Contradictory sentiments possessed his heart: he would soon see the place where he was born, the house in which for a moment he had known Ismene, the woman who had brought him into the world. And he would soon be bringing there the woman who had raised him and given him the love that his true mother had denied him.

He felt uncertain, torn: would the people he had spent his youth with still remember him? Would he ever return among them? Kritolaos had once made him their leader, and the great bow still secretly waited to be taken up once again by Talos the Wolf. In a dark underground chamber, the armour of King Aristodemus and his cursed sword still hoped to see the light, but when would that day ever dawn?

The house of the Kleomenids was just a stone's throw away now. The house of the Dragon. The home of Aristarkhos, his father. There, down on the plain, was where he'd first seen him, and he had never forgotten the sorrow deep in the warrior's eyes as he saw the boy's lame foot.

Perialla, running from her own destiny . . . what had she said?

> The dragon and the wolf first
> with merciless hate
> wound each other.

That starry night on the hills of Plataea, those words on Brithos' lips . . . the Kleomenid Dragon and the Wolf of Taygetus. But Aristarkhos was dead, Brithos was dead. Where was the dragon now if not deep within himself, in the heart of Kleidemos, Kleomenid, there together with the Wolf of Messenia? There the two beasts attacked each other, feeding on their endless fury, no truce, no peace . . . for how much longer? Why had the gods reserved so perverse a fate for the little lame boy?

He realized that the Helot had drawn up in front of the gate of the house. The courtyard was invaded by weeds, the enclosure wall was cracked and crumbling, the bones of Melas gleamed white on the family altar. No one had set foot here for years.

'Do you know where my mother Ismene is buried?' he asked the Helot.

'Yes, noble sir,' replied the servant. 'Down there, among those cypress trees.' He pointed at a rough-hewn stone sarcophagus in the field surrounding the house.

'Wait here for me,' he said to the Helot, and walked towards the tomb of his mother. The sun rose just then, flooding the valley with its light. The house emerged from the darkness and the cypresses swayed in the early morning breeze. Kleidemos remained at length beside the tomb, his head bowed. He suddenly realized that there was an inscription on her burial stone, half hidden by the thick coat of moss that had grown there. He took out his sword and scraped away the moss; the inscription read:

ISMENE DAUGHTER OF EUTIDEMUS
BRIDE OF ARISTARKHOS THE DRAGON
UNHAPPY MOTHER
OF TWO VALOROUS SONS

THE GODS BEGRUDGED HER
THE PRECIOUS GIFT
OF THE LION OF SPARTA

Kleidemos called out to the Helot, who tied the ass and hurried promptly over.

'Who dictated that inscription?' he asked in a quiet voice, indicating the sculpted stone.

The Helot stopped to consider the writing, then said, 'Sir, I have been assigned to your service, because for many years I farmed the land of your father Aristarkhos, may he be honoured. The elders called upon me to build this tomb, along with several companions. I can't read those written symbols, but if I remember well, only the first four lines were carved into the stone. I'm certain of it. If you don't believe me, you can question my fellow workers or consult the archives of the Council, where there must be a copy of this inscription, since it was carved at public expense.'

'Are you absolutely sure of what you're saying?' urged Kleidemos.

'I've told you the truth, sir. But you can verify it yourself without going to too much trouble.'

'I thank you,' he replied. 'Go on ahead to the house; take my baggage with you. I'll soon join you.' As the servant was leaving, Kleidemos observed the inscription closely: it was obvious that the last three lines had been added. The hand was different and the first four lines were well centred on the slab, while the others continued so low that they nearly touched the bottom edge of the stone. There was no need to question the other workers. But who could have added those words? And what was the gift they referred to? There seemed to be a message there, perhaps an important one. He had to discover for whom those words were intended, and what their significance was.

The Helot was in the stable, arranging food and shelter for the ass. He walked towards the house. The oak door creaked open with difficulty on its rusted hinges. The interior was the picture of desolation: the ceiling of the atrium was draped with spider webs and a thick layer of dust lay everywhere. Large rats scurried away in haste at Kleidemos' approach. In their niches, the Kleomenid heroes too were coated with dust and cobwebs. He moved into the other rooms, and saw what must have been his parents' bed chamber. All that was left of the great bed was the frame of solid oak; the mattress and covers had been shredded by the mice for their nests. He heard the sound of footsteps in the atrium: the servant had come to ask for instructions.

'I want this house to be cleaned and restored to its former dignity; I'd like to live here,' Kleidemos told him. 'When everything is in order, I'll call the woman who raised me on the mountain as a son of your people. What is your name?' he asked the elderly servant.

'Alesos, sir.'

'Do you know of whom I'm speaking?'

'I do, sir. You're speaking of the daughter of Kritolaos. Your story is well known in this city.'

'I see that it is,' replied Kleidemos. 'I'll sleep here in the atrium tonight.'

He worked all day alongside Alesos and the other servants he had called in from the fields. As dusk was falling, a fire was burning at the centre of the atrium and the votive lamps were lit. Kleidemos felt as though he had returned to his ancient home. He sat next to the hearth with the old servant who had accompanied him.

'How old are you?' asked Kleidemos.

'Over seventy, sir.'

'How long have you been serving in this house?'

'Since my birth – like my father before me and his father before him.'

'You lived many years with Aristarkhos, the master of this home, then?'

'Yes, sir. And while I was vigorous and my limbs strong I followed him to war as his personal attendant.'

'Tell me about him. What kind of man was he?'

'He was a great warrior, but not only; valiant warriors are common in this land. He was a just man, and generous, and he could rely on us always.' He got up to add wood to the fire, then sat down again and spoke in a low voice. 'Our people do not love the Spartans, sir.'

'I know, Alesos, I lived with your people.'

'They are shells of iron and bronze; they have no soul.'

'You are courageous to speak thus with the commander of the fourth battalion of the equals.'

'But your father was a real man, and none of us ever suffered beatings or humiliations at his hand.'

'And what do you think of me?'

'Do you really want to know my thoughts?'

'Yes, I do, speak freely.'

'The voice of your blood cannot be silenced, and it was written that you would return to where you had come from. Only you know the secrets of your soul, but I believe that the heritage of Kritolaos has not been lost either. Embers smoulder long under the ash, and stupid men believe them extinguished, but when the wind starts to blow again, the flame is reawakened.'

Kleidemos lowered his gaze. 'I don't know what you are talking about, old man.'

'Sir, among your servants there are some who, due to unfortunate necessity or fear, have become the eyes and ears of the powerful lords who oppress our people. Beware them; I will reveal their names to you. As for me, I knew Kritolaos well and held him in great esteem, as I loved your father Aristarkhos. You are a tree with your roots in two different fields, but I have cultivated both fields with love. I can give you proof of this, if you want. You have taken possession of the house you were born in and honour the memory of your father, so illustrious and so unfortunate. Rightly so. But the road you must walk is perhaps still hidden even to you, and only the gods can reveal it.'

Kleidemos got to his feet and poked at the fire. 'The gods know the road we must take,' he said, staring at the flames dancing brightly in the hearth. 'Tomorrow you will go up the mountain and you will bring the woman who was my mother for twenty years back to me. You will tell her that I've never stopped thinking about her, and that only destiny kept me away . . . that I am awaiting her with the love of a son.'

'At dawn I will have already departed,' said the servant, getting up, 'and so with your permission I will retire now.'

'Yes, go ahead,' said Kleidemos. 'And may the gods grant you a restful night.'

'The same to you, sir,' replied the old man, opening the door to leave.

'Will she come?' asked Kleidemos without turning, as if he were talking to himself.

'She will come,' replied the servant, closing the heavy oak door behind him.

*

He saw her far off, riding on the ass that Alesos was leading by the halter, and he recognized her immediately. He threw down the scythe that he had been using to cut the weeds in the courtyard and started running as fast as he could, even though his lame foot pained him greatly with the turn of the seasons. But no pain could have stopped him at that moment. He lifted her off the packsaddle and held her in his arms, unable to say a single word. Alesos led the ass into the stable.

'Mother!' he gasped finally. 'Mother, how long has it been? Your hair . . . is all white.'

He caressed her head and face, then pulled her to him in a close embrace. Her hot tears wet his face and then came her voice, trembling. 'Son, the gods are good if they have conceded me this day. Ever since you left, every evening before I closed the door I looked towards the trail that comes from the plains, hoping to see you come up the mountain.'

'Oh, mother!' replied Kleidemos. 'It had to be you, old and tired as you are, to come looking for me.' He put his arm around her shoulders and walked with her towards the house. They went in, and in the solitude of that great silent place they poured out all the feelings that they had kept so long locked up in their hearts, and their weeping was sweet as they looked upon one another without saying a word.

Kleidemos realized that his mother's lips no longer pronounced the name 'Talos' that he had expected to hear from her. She called him 'son' and her soul was filled with that word, more precious to her than life itself. But the name 'Talos' stayed inside her like a memory that she guarded jealously as if she was waiting for events to take their course. Kleidemos had so many things to ask her, and at the same time he didn't dare: what had happened to Antinea and what news had she of Karas? He had been gone for so long, without being able to send them word of himself. How could the memory of Talos have remained alive in those he loved?

It was his mother who spoke first, before he could ask anything. 'Do you have a woman?'

'I have had many in the years I was away, but I never loved any of them, and so I am alone.'

'You are nearly thirty, my son. You know that when an equal reaches this age, it is customary to choose a wife.'

'Mother, I've never stopped loving Antinea. How could I ever choose another woman?'

'Listen to me: Antinea is one of our people and you know well that—'

'Where is she? Mother, tell me where she is. I have to know!'

'Why? You could only make her your concubine, certainly not your wife. The city will not allow the Kleomenid name to be extinguished. Don't you understand that this is why the house of your fathers was returned to you? If you don't make your own choice, the elders will exercise their prerogative and select a virgin from a noble family who will be brought to your home so she may become your wife. You'll be able to see her first, if you like, as she exercises in the *palaestra* with her thighs bared—'

'It's not possible!' cried out Kleidemos, frowning. 'No one can force me—'

'It's true, no one can force you to marry. But they will put her in your bed nonetheless so you may deposit the seed of the Kleomenids in her womb. Oh, son, you have been away so long! I realize now that you are not even aware of all the customs of this city.

'Sparta has always been obsessed with the fear that the number of equals will diminish. There are Spartiates who do not know their fathers, although they see them every day. Men incapable of begetting sons have their wives impregnated by famous warriors to ensure strong, robust progeny for themselves, in the same way as we give a mare to the most vigorous stallion, in order to improve the breed of our horses. The city cannot allow the number of equals to drop, nor can it permit a family of equals to die out, especially at times when there are few births. This is why you cannot think of reuniting with Antinea.'

Kleidemos fell silent, his heart crushed. His life was cursed; but while once he had been ready to put an end to it, that day in Thrace, he was now determined not to bow his head in the face of adversity, even though his problems seemed insuperable.

'Mother,' he said then, 'I want you to tell me what you

know of Antinea, even if what you tell me may hurt me. I will know how to act when it is time.'

'What I know of Antinea was told me by Karas. She lives with her father Pelias in Messenia at about three days' journey from here. Pelias is old and weak, and Antinea is his only support. Their master Krathippos died three years ago, and his son fell in battle during the war in Asia. The proceeds from his farm now go to the city, but it is not impossible that they will be called back and assigned to the service of another family here. I can also tell you, since you want to know, that Antinea has never forgotten you and has not united with another man. The love she had for her father has held her back as well. If she had married she would have had to abandon old Pelias to care for the farm alone, something he would never have been able to manage. Had that happened, he would have certainly been dismissed and died in utter poverty.'

'Karas – Mother, tell me about him. Where is he now, when did you see him last?'

'Karas has been my support over all these years, even though he would disappear for months at a time. But this never created difficulties for me: the people of the mountain always remember Kritolaos and I've never gone wanting. Unfortunately, I have heard nothing from Karas for over three months and no one knows where he has gone. I've asked the shepherds and the farmers who come up from the plains, but no one has been able to tell me anything. At first I was not worried, because I know that he has left his cabin up at the high spring before, but as time goes on, I have become anxious; when he went away for so long a time he would always send word.'

'Did he know that I had returned?' asked Kleidemos, suddenly troubled.

'He did know. It was he who told me. He said that I would embrace you again soon; he said that he would turn the whole city upside down to find you!'

'I'm sure of that!' exclaimed Kleidemos, smiling despite himself. 'But if it's true that he was looking for me, that doesn't explain why he has disappeared. Mother, there are so many thoughts crowding my mind; I need time to reflect on them. Ever since I was a boy, I've felt surrounded by mysterious happenings and events. Since that night that Kritolaos took me out into the forest – you know about that, don't you mother?' The woman nodded, keeping her eyes low. 'Strangely enough, Kritolaos never spoke to me clearly; he never told me exactly what he wanted me to do. And when he died, Karas appeared. He has been my guide, as Kritolaos was. More than once, he has shown me the way, but he has never told me where that way leads; where exactly I am headed.

'I can tell you, mother, that I don't know who he is in reality. What I know for certain is that Kritolaos must have called him before he died – he knows the secret of the cursed sword, and he knows where the weapons of King Aristodemus are. The time has come when I must decide my fate: Karas will come back, and then I will know. All the questions that I've been asking myself for years, trying to remember looks, words, gestures ... all of this must have an answer. And you, mother? Are you hiding something from me, as well?'

'Oh no, my son, I've always told you everything, and even now I've told you all I know. Among our people, the men decide, never the women; they take charge of matters that involve the common good. But I'm sure that one day Karas will be back, and that day all of us will know what we must do.'

'Mother,' said Kleidemos, 'I left the mountain ten years ago to find my way, but fate unfortunately has prevented me from succeeding in my quest. I have learned other things, though. Many things that were unknown to me are now clear: those who abandoned me as a child loved me, although the laws of the city never permitted them to show it. My brother Brithos was, in his soul, a sincere and generous man, and he loved me too. I met Pausanias, one of the most illustrious men of Hellas, and I learned what his dream was: I thought that he would make it possible for me to save my Spartan blood while I delivered the people of Kritolaos from their long servitude.

'I am lost now because I am alone. I don't know who I can trust among the equals of Sparta and I'm not sure that I can trust the Helots who surround me either. I've been told that some of them have been compelled or convinced to spy against me for the ephors and elders. Mother, now that you are here, tell me who, among the people of the mountain, is against me and who is with me.'

'It is arduous to answer what you have asked of me, my son,' replied the woman, 'perhaps because there are those who love Talos the Wolf but hate Kleidemos the Dragon.'

Kleidemos stood and stared at her, his gaze unwavering. 'I am what I am, mother! The gods have given me two births and two mothers and two names. They have made me son of two mortal enemies, but I will weep no longer, nor bow my head.' His eyes glittered even as he scowled, and his voice was firm and resolute. 'And the gods will have to show me the way! As far as men are concerned: those who know me understand that I am incapable of duplicity and betrayal. They know that I have suffered like a dog, and that I am unafraid of death. I only need to know, if you can tell me, who I must beware and who I can speak with without the fear of being betrayed. I have a servant in this house; his name is Alesos—'

'I know him well, you can trust him completely without fear. It was he who warned us to be on guard when the *krypteia* visited us that terrible night. And Karas would never have been able to bring Brithos his father's armour without Alesos' help. He is one of the elders of our people, and they listen to his word.'

'He told me that he served my father Aristarkhos faithfully and that he was devotedly attached to my Spartan family.'

'You can believe him. He is a wise man, and he loves courage and truth wherever he finds them. Perhaps he can understand you better than anyone else, because he knew both Kritolaos and Aristarkhos.'

'What about you, mother? Can you understand me?'

'The gods willed that I should bear no children,' she replied, raising her white head, 'but you are my son . . . you are my son . . .' Her grey eyes filled with tears.

The short winter's day was already drawing to a close

and the shadow of the mountain descended on the house of the Kleomenids like a giant's paw. It stretched out over the plain, over the cottages, over the icy waters of the Eurotas. It crept among the white houses of Sparta, the invincible, until it swallowed up the acropolis and the proud walls of the House of Bronze.

*

The *krypteia* officer inspected his squad in the moonlight: fifty men on horseback, lightly armed for quick, decisive action. All the Helot chiefs, representing the people of the mountain and the people of the plains, were meeting at an abandoned mill near the Taenarum promontory. He expected to find among them the man he had tortured and deprived of an eye in the underground chambers of the Council House. Their orders were to exterminate the whole lot; they were said to be preparing a revolt. Not one of them would survive, so that the Helots would finally realize that there was no hope of breaking free. Their bondage was destined to last forever.

Giving the signal, he set out at a gallop along the dark streets of Cynosura, followed by the squad of horsemen, and led them to the road for Amyclae. It was nearly midnight when he stopped his men at the foot of the hill on which the abandoned mill stood. The operation was proceeding smoothly; the moon was hidden from sight and his men had succeeded in stealing up in the darkness. They would be able to encircle the building without being seen. But when he gave the signal to dismount, a dog began to bark, then another, until the whole area echoed with furious barking. The Helots had their sheepdogs with them and they were sounding the alarm. The horses balked, pawing the ground and whinnying, and their riders, taken by surprise, could do little to hold them in check.

'Let them go!' shouted the officer. 'We'll round them up later. Forward, now, don't let them get away!'

In the meantime the Helots, forewarned, had fled the building in the opposite direction, seeking refuge in the darkness, but the place they had chosen was deserted and barren, a windswept rocky clearing on the sea. Just a short distance away, at the very tip of the promontory, rose the temple of Poseidon Enosigeus; the god of the sea was called upon to protect mariners as they rounded Cape Taenarum, crowned by sharp cliffs. The fugitives rushed to seek haven in the sacred enclosure, but escape was futile: the *krypteia* agents entered and swiftly surrounded the landing in front of the sanctuary colonnade.

The Helots backed towards the altar and there they remained, like supplicants, putting their lives under the protection of the god. The Spartans hesitated and turned towards their officer but he drew his sword and ordered them to charge. The warriors lunged at the unarmed victims and slaughtered them. Their swords descended implacably, sinking without mercy into that tangle of bodies, cleaving their bones, rending their naked chests. Their blood streamed and drenched the sacred stone of the altar. The temple colonnade rang with desperate cries and curses which mixed with the frenzied barking of the dogs and the whinnying of the horses as they ran terrified through the night.

The officer had entered the temple and came out with two lit torches, to illuminate the landing. The scene before him was so atrocious that, although he was inured to the sight of blood, he felt his stomach heave. In the darkness, his men had struck not with the precision of warriors, but with the brutality of butchers.

He turned away from the bloodbath and ordered his men to withdraw. The temple esplanade was plunged back into silence. The two torches, abandoned on the ground, sputtered and gave off a tremulous glow.

A black shape appeared then in the bloody halo. The dying flames lit a bearded face, jaw tight, bullish brow deeply creased. Beneath his forehead a single eye stared, casting sinister flashes like a smouldering ember.

That night on the mountain the wolves howled and howled and the people of Taygetus were puzzled, because it was not yet mating season. But the old men were awakened by that mournful choir and felt their hearts turn to ice. They knew that a calamity had befallen their people and they wept bitter tears in the darkness.

19

ANTINEA

ALESOS RETURNED, DEVASTATED, to warn his master of the massacre perpetrated by the Spartans at Taenarum but couldn't find him: Kleidemos had left before dawn, headed for Messenia. The bay horse, the one he'd brought with him from Asia, was missing from the stable. By that time, Kleidemos had passed Sellasia, crossed the northern spurs of Mount Taygetus and was on his way down the mountain's western side to take the road to the village of Thouria.

He rode the whole day, descending from the saddle now and then to stretch his legs and warm up a little by walking. The sky was overcast and the wind pushed huge grey clouds towards the Gulf of Messenia. The landscape before him was fractured into many small valleys separated by hilly crests sometimes covered with forest, sometimes barren, with rocky outcrops. Every now and then he would run into a shepherd whom he could ask about the road and exchange a few words with. Their dialect was very similar to the one spoken by the Helots on Mount Taygetus.

He sat in the shelter of a rock to eat a piece of bread with some dried figs while his horse grazed on a little yellowed grass, then started off again in a westerly direction. Towards evening the sky grew dark, threatening rain, and he began to look for a refuge for the night. At the centre of a clearing, near a little stream, he saw a modest wooden cabin with a fence, certainly the abode of a Helot shepherd. He turned the horse in that direction. As he approached, a dog started to bark. He dismounted and waited at the edge of the courtyard, certain that someone would come out. Smoke spiralled from the chimney, a sign that its occupants had just returned from their daily labour. The door opened and an elderly but robust man appeared, dressed in a long grey woollen chiton, peering intently into the night.

Kleidemos moved forward, saying, 'Greetings, my friend. My name is Kleidemos. I'm a stranger and nightfall has surprised me here. I fear it may rain. I need lodging for myself and a shelter with some hay for my horse.'

'You're right,' said the man. 'It will certainly rain, or perhaps even snow tonight. Come in, stranger.' Kleidemos held out his hand and noticed the man's eyes falling to his spear.

'Where are you from?' asked the man, preceding him into the house.

'Megara. I'm directed towards Thouria, to buy some wool.'

The man had him sit down. 'I don't have much to offer you,' he said, 'but if you would like to share my dinner, I would be pleased.'

'I will gladly have dinner with you,' replied Kleidemos. 'But I have something in my knapsack as well,' he said, taking out some bread, olives and cheese and putting them on the table.

'Fine,' said the man. 'Make yourself comfortable and warm yourself by the fire. I'll go to take care of your horse; he must be tired and hungry as well.'

Kleidemos looked around: the cabin was very humble; the only furnishings were a table and a couple of stools. Some tools stood in the corner: a hoe, a rake and a sack with some barley. On a wooden plate on the table were some roots seasoned with vinegar and a little salt, a couple of eggs and a clay jar filled with water. His host must be very poor. He could hear him bustling about in the hayloft for a while, then the door opened again and he came in, rubbing his hands.

'I was right,' he said. 'It's starting to snow. I'd best add some wood to the fire.' He took a bundle of twigs and threw them into the hearth. A big crackling fire began to spread a little warmth in the room. There was no lamp; this shepherd obviously couldn't afford to burn oil, if he didn't even use a little to season his food.

They began to eat; Kleidemos took some roots, to honour the man's hospitality, and offered the food he had, which the man seemed to appreciate greatly.

'May I know your name?' asked Kleidemos.

'I'm Basias,' replied the man. 'Please forgive me for not speaking up myself. You see, no one ever comes this way, and I'm not accustomed to receiving guests.'

'Aren't you afraid, living here all alone?' asked Kleidemos.

'Of what? There's nothing for thieves to take. The flock belongs to my master, who is Spartan, and no one dares steal from the Spartans. Tell me about yourself: you have a horse and a spear; you must be a rich man.'

'Does it seem strange to you that a merchant travels armed with a spear? Well, let me tell you that my spear and my horse bought me my daily bread for a long time. I fought for years as a mercenary in Asia until one day I injured my leg falling from the saddle and I decided to retire and earn my living running a small business.'

'Isn't it too early in the season,' asked Basias, 'to be buying wool? The sheep won't be sheared for a couple of months, maybe even three if the weather stays so bad.'

'That's true,' replied Kleidemos, 'but I thought that by arriving early I could ensure myself a better price. There's also a man I need to see . . . a farmer by the name of Pelias. Do you know him at all?'

The man raised his face from his plate, eyeing his guest with a certain surprise. 'Pelias? I do know a Helot peasant who lives about one day's journey from here.'

'One day's journey?' repeated Kleidemos. 'That could be him. If the bad weather continues perhaps I could ask him to lodge me tomorrow night . . . I can pay.'

'Yes,' nodded Basias, fingering his beard and gathering the crumbs from the table, 'I think you'd do well. You'll find his farm on this same road tomorrow, after dusk I would say. Your horse won't be able to cover much ground in the snow. If you don't lose your way, you should arrive a couple of hours after sunset. Tell him that Basias the shepherd sends you, and that you have been my guest: he will be happy to accommodate you. But give him something if you can – he's very poor.'

'Does he live alone like you do?'

'No, he has a daughter living with him, if I remember well. But he has fallen upon very hard times . . . do help him if you can.' He put more wood on the fire, then went out again to fetch some straw for his guest to lie on.

'I have nothing else,' he said, spreading the straw around on the floor. 'You'll have to put up with this poor bed.'

'Don't worry about me,' said Kleidemos. 'I was a soldier and have often slept on the bare ground. This straw is nice and dry, I'll sleep very well here. But where will you go?'

'In the shed, with the sheep.'

'Oh no, I won't take your place. I'll sleep in the shed.'

'No, it's not that; there's room for both of us here. I'd rather sleep in the shed because I'm afraid the wolves will be out tonight.'

'If that's how it is,' nodded Kleidemos. 'But wake me if you do hear the wolves; with my spear I can come to your aid.'

'Thank you, my guest,' said Basias. 'I will certainly do so. May you have a restful night.'

'And a good night to you, as well,' replied Kleidemos. He accompanied Basias to the door and saw that the snow had covered everything and was still falling in big flakes. Its faint glow delimited the courtyard and the wooden shed with its straw roof where the animals were sheltered. Basias walked to the shed, leaving deep footprints in the snowy mantle. He opened the door, was greeted by lowing and bleating and closed it right behind him.

Kleidemos stayed outside to watch the snow falling. It reminded him of those long winters in Thrace, the infinite sadness of that solitude, the long marches through the snow, wearing an icy shell of armour. Raids in sleeping villages, women's screams, fire, mud, blood . . . Now the snow fell softly, blanketing the world in a white veil that seemed like a sign of peace; it seemed to be falling inside him as well, soothing the deep wounds, extinguishing the cries, the panic, the fear . . . all white . . .

All he could hear from the shed was low bleating: surely the little lambs huddled against their mother's fleece were dreaming of flowered fields. The great ram with his curved horns lifted his steaming nostrils in the stable, searching for the acrid odour of their predator: the wolf.

Kleidemos pulled his cloak tightly around him and was about to go back in when the soft sound of breaking twigs made him turn on the threshold. He scanned the darkness before him: nothing, he must have imagined it. But all at once two yellow eyes blinked and a huge wolf moved forward, a male with a silvery coat. He thought of putting his hand to his spear but did nothing as he looked deep into those glittering eyes. The beast came closer, stopping just a few steps away. He lifted his snout as if to sniff him and dropped his tail to the snow, then turned and disappeared in a whirl of white flakes. But the dog had not barked, nor had the animals in the shed shown signs of fright . . .

Kleidemos closed the door behind him. He lay down next to the fire, watching the flames flicker blue amidst the embers slightly veiled by ash. He added another couple of pieces of wood and stretched out, pulling his cloak over him. The warmth began to spread through his tired limbs and his eyes closed. As sleep was about to take him, he heard a prolonged howl and then another, longer and more distant. But the dog was still sleeping outside, curled up under the overhanging roof, and the lambs slept huddled into their mother's fleece and the great ram of the curved horns . . . slept.

*

He was awakened by a chill in the middle of the night: the fire had gone out and the wind was whistling through the numerous fissures in the walls. He blew on the embers and added twigs until the flame was revived. As he was about to fall asleep again, he heard the shed door squeak and the dog whimpering softly, as if someone he recognized had arrived. He opened the door a crack and saw a couple of men wrapped in dark cloaks entering the shed. He stole out of the cabin without making a sound and approached the wall facing the house. Through the split wooden beams he could see inside the shed, dimly lit by a smoky torch.

One of the two men began to speak. 'Basias, we bring you bad news: the chiefs of our people, who had gathered at the old mill at Cape Taenarum, were surrounded by the *krypteia* last night and massacred. They had sought asylum in the enclosure of the temple of Poseidon but the Spartans, from what we have heard, showed no respect for the sacred place, and killed them on the very altar as they clung to it. Revolt has become impossible; we thought it best to warn you, so you can spread the word. We can take no more risks; we must wait for the times to change and for a more favourable situation.'

Basias lowered his head as if stunned by a heavy blow. 'Was no one saved?' he asked after a long silence.

'No one,' responded the other. 'Our people have been given permission to bury the bodies.'

'Not even . . . the Keeper?'

'No, his body was not among the others. Perhaps he managed to escape, or perhaps the others were all dead already by the time he arrived.'

'The Spartans may have concealed his body. Has no one seen him since then?'

'Not as far as we know. But why would they have taken his corpse? They'd have no reason to. No, he must be alive. Hidden away somewhere. Someone betrayed us, and he probably trusts no one anymore. But you can be certain that he will come back and then he will tell us when we will have the day of our revenge . . . the day of our freedom.'

The three of them fell silent and Kleidemos, overwhelmed by what he had heard and trembling in anger and indignation, did not even feel the cold. The clouds had parted and the stars now twinkled in the clear night sky.

'There's someone in your house,' said one of the visitors suddenly. 'We saw smoke coming from the chimney and the glimmer of flames in the hearth.'

'I know,' responded Basias. 'He is a wayfarer who asked for my hospitality. He told me he was a merchant from Megara, once a mercenary in Asia, but he made a strange impression on me; he seemed more Laconian than Megarian.'

'Be careful, *krypteia* spies are everywhere. The Spartans have become very suspicious and are set on ridding themselves of any of us who seem to have rebellion on our minds.'

'By the gods!' exclaimed Basias. 'If that is the case I'll strangle him with my own hands! I certainly won't be held back by the law of hospitality, just as the Spartans weren't dissuaded by the sacred enclosure of Poseidon.'

'No, Basias. Whoever that man is, you must not raise your hand against him. Let the Spartans stain themselves with sacrilege and provoke the ire of the gods. If he were a spy from the *krypteia*, he wouldn't make it easy for you to kill him, and if you did, the revenge of Sparta would only sow more grief on our land. Farewell, Basias, and may the gods protect you.' The man stood and wrapped himself in his cloak. Kleidemos backed into the house, wiping out his tracks with the edge of his *chlamys*, and closed the door behind him, just in time.

The two men silently walked through the snow of the courtyard and started back along the road leading east. The light went out in the shed, and Kleidemos lay down, devastated and unable to sleep. He could still hear the words of those men; he imagined the carnage, the screams, the bloodied altar. Another thought allowed him no rest: who was the one Basias called the 'Keeper'? Not even Kritolaos had ever pronounced that word, nor had he ever spoken about a similar figure. But deep down in his soul, Kleidemos thought that this must be the key to the mystery.

He tossed back and forth on the straw, finding no peace, until the thought of Antinea took him, and the image of her face appeared clearly before his eyes. Sleep overcame him, dissolving the pain in his heart and the weariness in his limbs.

The wind had carried away all the clouds and the seven stars of the Great Bear glittered low over the hills of Messenia.

*

It was not difficult for Kleidemos to stay on track, because although the path was covered with snow, it ran down the centre of a valley and the only way to stray from the trail was to climb up the rocky hills at its sides. He made much better time than he had expected. At a certain point, the valley swerved towards the sea, and there was much less snow on the path than there had been higher up. And so he arrived at the farm where he hoped to find Pelias just after sunset, famished and tired.

He left the path and drove his horse up the ridge until he could look down on the little farm surrounded by pens for the animals. To the east was an olive grove and a vineyard with perhaps a hundred or so trees, although he could not be sure because it was becoming hard to see. He looked towards the cottage and saw the chimney smoking ... finally, he had arrived. In a little while he would go down and knock on the door, and his heart would tell him the words to say. His heart, which he already felt hammering in his chest.

He would enter with the evening wind. With past years weighing heavily on his shoulders, with his soul tormented by doubt. He would enter like a wolf, pushed on by the chill and by his hunger. He stroked the neck of his horse who was blowing clouds of white steam from his frosty nostrils. The ground was becoming hard again with nightfall and the cold was numbing. He touched the bay's sides with his heels and the animal started down towards the clearing. A dog tied on a rope began to bark loudly. As Kleidemos approached the middle of the courtyard the door opened and a figure stood out in the doorway . . . Antinea. Black against the red glow of the hearth, a figure with neither face nor eyes. She was holding a shawl to her breast and raising her head as if straining to see through the darkness. And she saw the horse and its rider, still as a statue on the back of his frost-covered bay.

The dog had stopped barking and the place fell into deep silence. The woman shivered at the sight of the dark horseman gripping his spear, and she dared not say a word. Kleidemos heard a low, rather sharp voice calling, 'Antinea?' A word immediately swallowed up like lightning in a black cloud. He took a step forward as he heard the quavering voice inside the cottage insisting, 'Is there someone there?'

She sharpened her gaze to try to make out the features of the stranger's face, and his voice said 'Antinea,' piercing her heart and buckling her knees. He had descended from his horse now and was walking towards her, entering into the faint beam that came from the open door.

'I'm cold!' called the voice from inside. She stared at him, trembling like a leaf: a bristly face, framed by a black beard, eyes shining under a furrowed brow. He had wrinkles around his eyes and a bitter crease, like a scar, at the corners of his mouth, but his eyes . . . his eyes shone behind a veil of tears as they had that day long ago on the plain when he had watched her go and waved with his arms raised high against the dying sun.

She could neither speak nor move as he drew closer and said 'Antinea' in his deep, resonant voice. And when the flame of the hearth lit him up she dropped her hands from her breast and raised them to his face. And only when she touched him did the tears start flowing from her eyes. 'It's you,' she said, caressing him, touching his eyes and his forehead and his neck. 'You've come back . . . you've come back to me.' Her voice trembled even harder as she continued to whisper, 'You've come back!' And she burst into tears, beside herself.

He saw that she was about to collapse and he embraced her, covering her with his ample cloak, standing there in the snow, weeping in silence. The winds of the night ruffled his hair and froze the tears on his cheeks, and he felt nothing but the heartbeat of Antinea and that heartbeat reawakened in him a life he had thought lost forever. When he finally released her and lifted her face, he saw that the years had left no mark in those fervid eyes . . . time had stood still. It was the same look that he had never forgotten, the look that a goddess had stolen to seduce him one hot night in distant Cyprus, the light that he had forever sought in the eyes of the women of Asia and of Thrace. Clear as spring water, the light of springtime remembered, as warm as the sun itself . . .

He wrapped his arm around her waist and led her through the still-open door. An old man wrapped in a blanket sat next to the fire. He lifted his white head and turned to stone at the sight before him. He thought that his weak eyes were deceiving him and only when he heard his daughter's voice saying, 'He's back,' did he raise his knotty hands and murmur, 'Immortal gods! O immortal gods, thank you for having consoled your old servant.' The door swung closed behind them and Kleidemos forgot to tie his horse, but the steed found shelter under the roofing of the fold. The timid bleating of the lambs did not disturb the proud animal, used to the whistle of arrows and the blaring of the battle horn. He knew that the next day his master would reappear, holding the shining spear, to stroke his blond mane.

*

For hours Kleidemos told Pelias and Antinea of the events he had lived through in all the years he'd been away. When he saw the old man was nodding off, he picked him up in his arms and laid him on the bed in his room; the old man was so frail it felt like carrying a child, and as he covered him up, Kleidemos thought of how Antinea had lived, taking care of a sick old man and working in the fields. Softly he closed the door to the little room and went back to the fire. Antinea was adding wood, and had snuffed out the lamp.

'Did you think I'd come back one day?' he asked her.

'No. I wanted you, badly, but I never let myself think about it. My life was hard enough as it was. Karas would come to visit every year, usually at harvest time, and would help me with the heaviest work. We would talk about you; of when we were all together, back on the mountain.'

'Did you know that I had come back to Sparta?'

'No. I haven't seen Karas for nearly a year.'

'I returned at the end of the summer and I'm living in the house of the Kleomenids.'

'You are . . . Spartan, now.'

'I'm me, Antinea, and I've come back for you.'

Antinea stood without taking her eyes off him and unfastened the ties of her dress. She let it slip to the ground and then removed the band that swathed her hips.

'They say that the women of Asia have bodies as smooth as marble and are scented with the essence of flowers,' she said, lowering her head, but he was already embracing her. He lay her back on the oxhide in front of the hearth and kissed her with infinite tenderness, trembling, like the first time he'd known he loved her. And only when his soul was full and his loins were weary did he abandon himself to sleep, laying his head on her bosom. Antinea stayed awake at length, watching him and touching his hair. She could not get enough of the sight of him, his face burnt by the sun and frost of long summers and freezing winters. Suffering and grief had carved deep furrows. His face was different from how she had imagined him for so long, and yet the same as the boy's she had first loved. Was it truly time for her to come alive again, or was this just a flash of light that would illuminate her existence for a mere moment before it disappeared, plunging her back into sorrow? He would certainly leave again . . . but would he ever come back? She could not know the will of the gods who governed the fate of men, but she knew that she had desired this moment more than anything else in the world, and she could not tire of looking at him.

Often over the years the night had seemed anguished

and interminable and she had awaited the light of day to free her from its dark ghosts. Now she wished the night would never end, because she already had the sun in her arms: she could feel its warmth and its light.

She thought of how he had possessed her, depositing his seed in her womb and she was full of fear: hadn't he thought that if a son were born to him it would have to bear the same curse he did: son of Sparta and son of slaves? Or had he forgotten everything, overwhelmed by the same indomitable force that had gripped her? Spring would soon come with its tepid winds, and the bitter wormwood would grow again; eating its leaves provoked acute spasms of the womb and would dry the life that had taken root there . . . no, she would not do that.

Her father, old Pelias, would not live much longer; she had no idea of what destiny had reserved for her future, but she would not chew the bitter wormwood . . . She looked again at his face, his forehead, his hands, and she hoped with all her soul that she would never be deprived of them again. She thought of the fields on Mount Taygetus which would flower again with the coming spring. The lambs would return to the high pasture and the wheat would ripple blond in the breeze. She didn't know that sleep had overcome her and that she was dreaming, stretched out on an oxhide.

20

ENOSIGEUS

'DON'T RETURN BY THE same road,' said Pelias. 'The snow will be much deeper at the pass by now and you might not be able to get across. Go east until you find a river called Pamisus; travel up the valley until you reach a fork. There go right, towards Gathaei; you should reach Belemina in about two days' time. Then head towards Karistos, which is in the Eurotas valley. Turn south, and in another day you will have reached Sparta. We will await your news anxiously and will try to let you have word of us. May the gods accompany you and assist you. You do not know the consolation that you have given us.'

'I'll send one of my men for the spring labours,' said Kleidemos, putting on his cloak. 'Use the money I've left you for anything you need. I'll see what has happened in Sparta during my absence and try to find a way to have you return. Perhaps the ephors will allow me to house you on my land. If I pay the price requested by the treasury they will undoubtedly agree to it. When we are together again, everything will change – you'll see. Perhaps we can be happy again, or at least take comfort in each other after these long years spent apart.'

He held them in a long embrace, then mounted his horse and spurred him into a gallop, later slowing to a walk. The sun was appearing between the clouds when he arrived at the banks of the Pamisus, a fast-flowing torrent with muddy waters. He journeyed up its shore until midday, crossing two small farming villages, and reached the fork in the river in the early afternoon. He ate a little, taking shelter against a wall enclosing an olive grove and then began riding again along the right tributary of the Pamisus. Dusk was approaching when he noticed a bleak mountain which dominated a stretch of hills covered with sparse lentiscus and juniper bushes. He could see some buildings on the top and hoped he might find a haven for the night. He turned off the road onto a dirt path, and he soon found himself at the foot of the mountain. The place was strangely deserted and desolate, without a village or even a house in sight. As he ascended, the structures he had glimpsed at the top of the mountain began to take shape; he could make out the ruins of a great wall, decrepit flaking towers rising here and there from the dismantled bastions. This could be none other than the dead city of the Helots!

He reined in his horse as if taken by fright and was about to turn back, when his curiosity overcame his fear and he decided to continue up. The dying sun still cast a slight glow at the mountain's peak. The circle of walls must be incredibly ancient; he could tell by the huge, barely squared-off boulders that formed their base. When he finally made it to the top, it was pitch black. He entered the city, passing through one of the gates, of which only the jambs remained: the architrave lay on the ground, broken in two. He moved forward amidst the ruins and strangely felt no fear, despite the terrifying tales he'd often heard told as a boy about this cursed and sacred place. Under those stones, in some dank underground chamber, slept King Aristodemus: he who had once gripped the great horn bow.

He returned to the wall and tried to find a niche where he could shelter for the night along with his horse. He would have liked to light a fire as the Thracians had taught him, by rubbing together two very dry pieces of wood, but he could find nothing but a few damp twigs. 'This is how superstitions are born,' he thought to himself. 'If I had managed to light a fire, who knows what story a shepherd down at the bottom of the valley would invent, seeing a flickering light amidst the ruins of the dead city!'

He took his blanket from the horse and covered himself as best he could. The moon was rising and he could see the stretch of ruins well; it must have once been a large, thriving city. It had surely been abandoned since time immemorial and no one had ever dared to rebuild it after its destruction. He thought of Kritolaos, of Karas, of all those who had always hoped for the liberation of the mountain people. The massacre at Cape Taenarum filled him with despair. What an answer to such great hopes! The only true possibility of a great change had died along with Pausanias; the king's plan would have had a chance, had he managed to overthrow the city institutions with the backing of the equals, and perhaps with the outside support of the Athenians. But now it was completely doomed; Themistocles had been exiled and the conservative Athenian government was friendly with the ephors who exercised strong influence over King Pleistarchus, the son of Leonidas, and his young colleague Archidamus.

Both were valorous but had no experience, and would have great trouble freeing themselves from the grip of the elders and ephors. And yet the memory of how the city of Ithome had fallen had kept alive the pride of the Helots and the hope of Kritolaos.

Kleidemos curled under the blanket to sleep, but other thoughts began to throng into his mind. Distant words, phrases that echoed within him, faded images that seemed to come to life. That tremendous dream he'd had as a boy when he fell asleep clutching the bow of the King to his chest. The oracle of the Pythia Perialla; Karas' reminder of her revelation as they stood on the battlefield of Plataea with his exhortation: 'Remember these words, Talos, son of Sparta and son of your people, the day that you shall see me again.' And that day couldn't be so far off now. The words of Kritolaos as he lay dying: 'A man blind in one eye will come to you; he can remove the curse from the sword of the King.' What could he have meant by that?

And the inscription on Ismene's tomb . . . who had added those lines? What message did they convey? What was that precious gift? Perhaps the life of Brithos, that King Leonidas, the Lion of Sparta, had wanted to save? But the king had died in combat at the Thermopylae. There were no survivors among the Spartans. No one, save Brithos and Aghias, returned alive from the Thermopylae . . . Who could have known the will of the king?

Weariness began to weigh on Kleidemos' eyelids, and he abandoned himself to sleep within the walls of Ithome, the dead city. He seemed to see – or maybe he was just dreaming – a small camp fire . . . Brithos asleep . . . Aghias nodding off, a shadow approaching . . . bending over Brithos as if to take something from him, then slinking off. O most powerful gods! The message of the king! The message of the king had been stolen!

He started to a sitting position. Everything seemed suddenly clear: the gift of King Leonidas that Ismene's funerary inscription alluded to must have been the life of Brithos (and perhaps his own as well?). The king had wanted to save Brithos' life. He had given him a companion, Aghias, as his escort, a Helot (just what had the king truly known about that Helot, Talos the cripple?), and a message. A message to be delivered to the ephors and elders. Just what had that message said? No one had ever told him. When they were fighting together in Phocis and Boeotia, Brithos himself had admitted that the message had always remained shrouded in mystery. And Brithos had always wondered why the rumour had spread that he and Aghias had intrigued to save their own lives, abandoning their comrades at the Thermopylae. Why hadn't the ephors ever done anything to deny those rumours? It was even said that the scroll was blank, but this made no sense at all: King Leonidas would have had no reason to send an empty message to Sparta.

Unless the scroll had been stolen and replaced . . . that night, near their campfire. Whoever inscribed those last lines on Ismene's tomb seemed to be aware of the last will of King Leonidas, surely set down in the true message that Brithos and Aghias were carrying to Sparta. And now, his testament – hinted at in the words carved into the tomb of his mother – cried out to the last of the Kleomenids . . . or to Talos the Wolf. But who could have seen that message and carved those words into the stone? One of the elders? An ephor? It all seemed impossible.

All at once he no longer felt sure that he had seen someone stealing close to Brithos that night; perhaps he had just dreamt it. Could he no longer distinguish dream from reality?

He hoped that the night might still bring him a little rest, and he stopped racking his brains; he would have to wait until he returned to Sparta to seek an answer. The ground he was lying on was dry and the big woollen blanket kept him warm. He drowsed again. The wind had eased and the place was immersed in deep silence. A sudden beating of wings: the birds of prey were rising from the ruins in search of food, soaring through the darkness.

The neighing of his horse woke him abruptly shortly before dawn: the animal was nervous, as if something had spooked him. He was pawing the ground with his hooves and blowing hard out of his nostrils. As Kleidemos was getting up to calm him, he reared and attempted to break free, clearly terrified. Kleidemos looked all around but saw nothing. He approached the horse, calling out to him and slackening the reins he had tied to a bush. He tried to pet his muzzle but the bay showed no signs of calming down; if anything, he was increasingly upset. Kleidemos picked up his blanket while holding tight to the reins, and dragged the horse away from the walls.

At that moment he heard a dull rumble, a suffocated roar coming from under the ground. He was afraid: all the stories he'd heard about that place as a little boy suddenly seemed credible, and he was sorry he had ever set foot there. As he tried to pull his horse down the hill, he heard another roar and he felt the earth tremble. A light shock at first, then a strong, prolonged tremor that made him sway. A much harder shock made him fall to the ground with his horse, who nearly crushed him. As he rolled down the muddy path he heard the crash of the ruins; raising his head, he saw huge boulders tumbling to the ground from the top of the walls and the towers. The earth trembled again, shaking beneath him, and more stones gave way, raising great billows of dust; the gods were destroying what was left of Ithome while huge leaden clouds, swollen with rain, gathered above.

A bolt of lightning darted among the livid cloudbanks, illuminating the mountain with a blinding light, chased by a thunderous roar. More bolts swiftly followed, flattening the ghostly shadows of the bulwarks and bastions onto the ground. Peal upon peal of thunder cracked with such a din that it seemed that the earth would split open and swallow up the city.

Kleidemos stood petrified, contemplating the scene, certain that the undermined walls would tumble down on him and bury him. Just for a moment; then he turned and ran down the slope as fast as he could, stumbling and falling again and again, filthy with mud, elbows and knees bleeding. He finally reached the base of the mountain and called his horse. The steed raced over with his reins tangled between his legs and Kleidemos jumped into the saddle, spurring him on furiously. The animal galloped forward, whipping the air with his tail, blowing huge clouds of steam from his dilated nostrils, his pupils widening with every bolt of lightning that flashed on the road.

His horseman continued to urge him along the narrow trail at a mad pace as the rain began to fall. Gusts of wind swept over the deserted road and the rain turned into a downpour, but Kleidemos continued to drive him on as if out of his mind until he heard the horse's breath coming in short pants and he began to pull in the reins to slow him down.

Leaving the storm behind him, he slowed the drenched, sweaty animal to a walk. He crossed a village, and then another; everywhere he witnessed scenes of terrified people digging with their hands through the ruins of their homes or chasing after the animals who had mown down their pens and were frantically running through the fields.

In the late afternoon, exhausted and starving, he reached Gathaei and then, towards evening, Belemina, both devastated by the earthquake. He realized that as he neared Laconia the effects of the earthquake worsened. The wooden houses were still standing, but the stone structures had crumbled under the force of the shocks. Everywhere weeping women and bewildered men wandered among the debris or dug through the rubble. Children screamed in despair, calling parents who were perhaps buried forever in the wreckage of their homes. Kleidemos slept a few hours in a hayloft, crushed by fatigue and anguish, and then set off again in the direction of Makistos, stopping every now and then to let his horse rest. He was fearful of what might have happened to his house, to his mother. It was clear that the earthquake had struck most of the Peloponnese and he couldn't even be sure that Pelias and Antinea's home had not been destroyed. Macistus appeared to be devastated as well and he saw hundreds of corpses lined up along the roads, more being added constantly as the survivors succeeded in opening a passage between the demolished houses.

He stopped a couple of horsemen who were arriving at full gallop from the southern road. 'Where are you from?' he shouted at them.

'From Tegea. Who are you?'

'I am Kleidemos, son of Aristarkhos, Spartan. What news is there of my city?'

'All bad,' replied one of the men, shaking his head. 'Most of the houses have collapsed or are precarious. There have been thousands of deaths. All able-bodied men have been asked to help in the rescue efforts and ensure order in the city. Many of the elders are dead, as are several of the ephors. Confusion is rampant.'

'The kings?'

'King Archidamus is alive; one of my comrades saw him near the acropolis, where he has set up headquarters. I know nothing of King Pleistarchus.'

'Where are you directed now?'

'North to seek help, in Arcadia, even in Achaea if necessary. But we've found naught but death and ruin. We met two royal guards headed towards Sicyon and Corinth in search of aid. Amyclae has been levelled to the ground; Gytheum is almost completely destroyed. Make haste if you have any of your family at Sparta, because the city is devastated.' They galloped off towards the north while Kleidemos spurred his mount in the opposite direction.

Along the road he encountered columns of refugees with carts and pack animals. Groups of horsemen raced by, covered with mud, whipping their horses and shouting in the attempt to make their way among that homeless multitude. He left Sellasia behind him, ravaged by the disaster, and reached the banks of the Eurotas, in full flood; in just a few hours he would be in Sparta, if his horse could only endure the strain. The generous animal devoured the road, his belly to the ground, stretching his head rhythmically forward and arching his powerful neck. Kleidemos had to slow him down every so often so that his heart would not burst.

The marks of destruction lay all around him, terrible and dramatic; the closer he got to the city, the more he saw villages reduced to piles of debris, without a single wall in sight. Entire populations must have been exterminated, if the shocks that he had felt at Ithome were but the distant reverberation of the frightful tremor that had shaken all of Laconia and flattened city after city to the ground, surprising most of their inhabitants in their sleep.

He gradually began to note groups of hoplites in full battle gear guarding crossroads and patrolling the countryside, sinking into the ploughed, rain-soaked fields. What on earth could be happening? As he proceeded, the patrols were increasingly frequent and included young boys and even wounded men with makeshift bandages, nonetheless carrying the shield with the red lambda. Kleidemos did not stop to ask for explanations, worried as he was about his mother's safety.

He finally came within sight of the Kleomenid home as night fell. All he could make out was a dark mass in the countryside and he could not tell whether the house was still standing or had been reduced to a shapeless heap of ruins. As he reached the entrance to the courtyard he breathed a sigh of relief: there were cracks here and there, and the roof had partially caved in, but on the whole, the robust stone structure with its jointed corners had held, while the stables and the peasants' dwellings had all crumbled. There was no light inside, however, and he could hear no sound. He pushed the door open, shoving aside the rubble that was partially blocking the entrance. Some embers still glowed faintly in the hearth; he managed to rekindle the fire and lit a torch.

Many of the ceiling beams had been jarred out of place and several hung down. He called his mother and then Alesos, repeatedly, but there was no answer. He ran from one room to another but found no one. The house was completely empty, although a fire had certainly been lit here the night before, and he could see no traces of blood anywhere. The bed in his mother's room was full of debris and dust, but it seemed that no one had slept there. He returned to the great atrium and sat near the fire, seized by anguish: what had happened during his absence? It seemed that his mother had abandoned the house; or had she been dragged off by force while he was away? He couldn't believe that she would have gone without leaving a message. He was so exhausted that he didn't have the strength to start searching for her in the dark countryside or, worse yet, in the devastated city.

He went out to take care of his horse: the poor animal, drenched in sweat and weakened by the strain, had to be protected from the cold, gusty night. He dried him off as best he could with a little hay he found by groping around the ruins of the stable. He put a blanket on his back and took him to shelter, throwing a little forage in front of him and then finally re-entering the house. Oblivious to the danger that further shocks might send the whole ceiling crashing down upon him, he dragged his bed close to the fire and dropped onto it like a dead man.

The muffled cries and suffocated screams of the tormented city arrived from a distance. Sparta, the invincible.

On the distant surf-beaten Taenarum promontory, the temple of Poseidon had collapsed onto its foundations. The statue of the god, whom mariners called Enosigeus – 'he who shakes the earth' – had fallen from its pedestal and tumbled to the foot of the altar, still stained with the Helots' blood.

Kleidemos rose before the sun, awakened by the lowing of the starving oxen who had survived the earthquake and were huddled near the crumbled stables, looking for food. He sat for a few moments, trying to organize his confused thoughts. He was distressed about his mother's disappearance, but hoped that she and Alesos had sought refuge on the mountainside, where the Helots' wooden cottages would have better resisted the earthquake.

He thought bitterly of the night spent amidst the ruins of Ithome: he had been struck by the idea that he might uncover the truth behind the deaths of his brother and Aghias, rejected by Sparta, one driven to suicide, the other killed seeking to redeem his honour. At the very moment when the truth seemed close at hand, the city had been destroyed by the earthquake. What sense now in attempting to discover the true contents of Leonidas' message? Sparta had decreed the death of his father Aristarkhos, and of his brother Brithos. Sparta was responsible for the end of Ismene, her life cut short by a pain no human being could withstand. Those words remained on her tomb, engraved by an unknown hand but meant, perhaps, for him. Perhaps. A fleeting clue, leading him towards a truth that had little significance any more. Sparta was paying for its inhuman harshness, paying for its horrible sacrilege at Taenarum. The gods were wiping them off the face of the earth.

The time had come to make a decision. He got up to look for some food to calm his hunger cramps; after having eaten a piece of stale bread found in a cupboard, he walked out into the courtyard. The wind had risen, drying the ground a little and carrying away the clouds. He looked in the direction of Sparta and noted numerous clusters of soldiers patrolling around the razed houses. Something strange was certainly going on; he could hear trumpet blasts, see warriors rushing in every direction, a man on horseback caracoling back and forth and waving his right arm as if giving orders. He wore a crested helmet; it may have been one of the kings – Pleistarchus, perhaps, or Archidamus. What could be happening?

He turned his gaze to the mountain and understood: hundreds and hundreds of men were descending from Mount Taygetus, emerging from the forests and the brush, disappearing and then re-emerging further down the valley. They were armed with spears, swords, sticks. They had nearly reached the olive grove extending from the lower slopes of the mountain to the city.

The wrath of the gods had not yet been appeased: the Helots were attacking Sparta!

21

THE WORD OF THE KING

THE MULTITUDE OF HELOTS soon reached the plain. When they were a short distance from the city, they all stopped, as if an unseen commander had halted the disorganized rush. The first ones formed a line, and those behind them followed suit, until they had produced a passably regular front, much longer than the scanty line of warriors that Sparta had managed to send into battle. Kleidemos left his courtyard and walked through the fields until he reached a wreck of a house from which he could watch what was happening.

An awesome shout rent the air and the Helots lunged into an attack. The Spartans slowly drew back towards the ruins of their city so as to keep their flanks covered, then tightened into a compact front, lowering their spears. The two formations clashed: the Helot lines soon tangled in the fury of their assault, as though none of them could refrain from the massacre of their enemies, hated and feared for centuries. But the Spartans fought for their very lives, knowing that if they succumbed that day, it could mean the end for their city. Their wives raped and killed, their children run through. All those that the earthquake had spared: annihilated.

Kleidemos felt like rushing home to take up arms and

throw himself into the thick of the battle: this was the day that Kritolaos had dreamed of for him and for his people. But how could he don the armour of Aristarkhos and Brithos to deal a death blow to the city for which they had given their lives? He was immobilized, trembling and angry, in his hiding place and could do nothing but watch the fray wide-eyed, his heart violently unsettled. His heart was the true battlefield; there the two peoples fought with savage fury. Death, blood, screams sowed horror and agony. He could no longer watch and he slowly crumpled to his knees, leaning his head against the wall, racked by painful spasms, weeping inconsolably.

But the battle before the crumbling houses of Sparta was becoming more and more violent. The Helots fought on without respite, rotating as the combatants in the front lines were wounded or debilitated. The wall of shields before them was already dripping blood, and seemed unyielding; thick with spears, the front line of the hated enemy was not giving way. King Archidamus himself had drawn up at the centre of the line and was battling with great valour. The hoplites alongside him fought prodigiously so as not to dishonour themselves in the eyes of their king. Reinforcements arrived and were deployed at the sides where the risk of being encircled was greatest. With them came the pipers, whose music rose amidst the broken houses above the shouts of the combatants, and wafted through the fields – the voice of one mortally wounded who refuses to die. In the end the Helots began to retreat into the forest, taking their injured and their dead with them.

The Spartans did not follow, satisfied with having

repulsed them. They laid down their arms, assisted their wounded and gathered up their dead. The king stationed groups of sentries all around the city, took the fittest men with him and went to the aid of those still trapped among the ruins. For the entire day he could be seen in the midst of all that debris, untiring, his clothing torn, wherever his help was needed. As evening fell, many of the survivors had already found shelter in the field tents that he had had raised in many parts of the city, wherever there was an open clearing. The women had lit fires and were cooking what food they could to reinvigorate their weary, hungry companions. Military surgeons worked ceaselessly by the light of torches and lamps, stitching wounds, setting fractured limbs, cauterizing with red-hot irons to prevent infection from spreading or to stop the flow of blood.

King Pleistarchus, in the meantime, was galloping north towards Corinth, accompanied by a group of guards. From there he would be able to organize rescue efforts and establish contact with the Athenians. Cimon would certainly not refuse his help, and might even agree to send the fleet with stores of wheat to feed his people. The son of Leonidas felt that he could appeal to the son of Miltiades, the winner of Marathon, for the aid he so desperately needed.

When the Helots had withdrawn, Kleidemos had collapsed to the ground unconscious and there he remained for many hours in a dazed state until the chill of the night brought him to his senses. His stomach was cramping with hunger pangs and he decided to go back to his house. He managed to light a fire and to bake himself a little unleavened bread in the ashes, and then fell back onto his bed, completely done in.

In the middle of the night he was still sleeping deeply when he thought he heard a knock at the door. He forced himself awake; yes, someone was there. He leapt up and drew his sword, took a torch and opened the door but saw no one.

'Who goes there?' he demanded, scanning the darkness.

He walked down the steps of the threshold to look into the courtyard, lifting his torch high to spread a little light. He cast his eye to the right, towards the stable and then to the left, illuminating the outer wall of the house. It was then that he saw a man, standing motionless, wrapped in a cloak that covered half of his face, wearing a black patch over his left eye. He started, taken completely by surprise, and thrust out his sword.

'Who are you?'

The man brought his right hand to the edge of the cloak and uncovered a scarred face: Karas!

Kleidemos dropped the sword and stood looking at him, speechless.

'Is that how you greet a friend you haven't seen for years?' asked Karas, approaching him.

'I . . .' babbled Kleidemos, 'I couldn't believe . . . I never expected. O powerful gods . . . Karas . . . it's you! But your eye!' *One day a man will come to you, blind in one eye . . .* 'What happened to your eye?'

Karas tossed the cloak back off his shoulders and opened his arms.

'Oh, my friend, my dear, old friend . . .' Kleidemos said,

clasping him tight. 'I was afraid I'd never see you again . . .
He can remove the curse of the sword of the King . . .'

They entered the atrium and sat by the hearth, where
Kleidemos rekindled the dying fire.

'By Pollux . . . your face!' he said, staring at Karas' black
bandage, the deep gouges. 'Who did this to you?'

'The *krypteia*. I had agreed to meet Pausanias when he
returned from Asia, and the ephors wanted to know what
we'd said to each other. They tortured me, would have
killed me, but I never talked. They were finally convinced
that I knew nothing and let me go, probably with the
intent of sowing their spies all over the mountain to
follow my every movement. I've had to stay hidden for a
long time, but the time has come to make them pay, once
and for all.'

'I've just come from Messenia,' said Kleidemos. 'I saw
Antinea and Pelias.'

'I know. I brought your mother back up to the
mountain.'

'I've heard that the Helots attacked the city today.'

'True, but they were driven back. They would not
listen and moved too soon, putting everything at risk.
There were terrible losses – many died and a great number
were wounded. They need someone to guide them . . .'
Karas lifted his forehead and his eye flashed in the reflection of the flames. 'The time has come for you to choose
your road, Talos. The gods have manifested their will.'
He spoke with emphasis:

> 'He turns his back to the people of bronze
> when Enosigeus shakes Pelops' land.'

'The gods have devastated this land with an earthquake . . . this is the sign.'

Kleidemos closed his eyes. There was no doubt about the indentity of the one-eyed man Kritolaos had spoken of on his deathbed – it was Karas: Karas who was back here, with him, after so many years. And now, it seemed like just a few days since he'd left him. He saw him on the field of Plataea, in the glimmering dusk, murmuring the words of the Pythia Perialla, and adding, '*Remember these words, Talos, son of Sparta and son of your people, the day that you shall see me again.*'

'You are right, Karas,' he said. 'The gods have sent me the sign that I'd been waiting for, for years, and yet I still feel uncertain. Divided. I lied to you just now; it's not true that I've just come from Messenia. I arrived yesterday. Today I saw the Helots descend from the mountain.' Karas stared, suddenly scowling. 'But I couldn't move. I wanted to run, to take up my arms, but I just stood there, watching, trembling, tearing out my hair. I did nothing. I could not take up the sword of my father and my brother and use it against the city for which they gave their lives. And there's something else I have to tell you: my mother, Ismene, is buried just a short distance from this house. There's an inscription on the tomb which seems like a message; it says: "*Ismene, daughter of Eutidemos, bride of Aristarkhos the Dragon, unhappy mother of two valorous sons. The gods begrudged her the precious gift of the Lion of Sparta.*" I'm certain that the last phrase was added on later, and I've been trying to find out who did it and why.

'Karas, if I'm to make the greatest decision of my life, if it is true that the gods have sent me a sign with this earthquake, if I must take up arms once again and face my destiny without hesitation, I don't want to leave any unsolved mysteries behind me. Everything must be clear, so I will not feel remorse or regrets. No man can walk his path with confidence unless his soul is serene. I know what you want from me and I know that if Kritolaos were still alive he would want the same thing. It will seem strange indeed to you that I'm searching for the significance of an inscription carved on a tomb while the Helots are rising up to redeem their liberty – an entire people putting their very existence at stake.'

'No, I do not find it strange,' replied Karas, with an enigmatic expression. 'Continue.'

'You know that I escorted my brother Brithos and his friend Aghias from the Thermopylae to Sparta, as commanded by Leonidas. They were to bring a message to the ephors and the elders, but no one ever discovered what it said. I have even heard that the scroll was blank, that not a word was written on it. You know well how Aghias ended up and what would have happened to Brithos had I not stopped him. And Brithos met his death nonetheless at Plataea, waging solitary war against the Persians single handed.'

He had got up and was pacing up and down the atrium, then went to the door and looked towards Sparta. Few lamps were lit and their glow was faint, but campfires blazed all around the city: Sparta's warriors were on alert. He closed the door and returned to the hearth.

'I'm convinced that whoever added those words to Ismene's tomb knew the true content of Leonidas' message. What else could the Lion of Sparta's gift refer to?

Leonidas wanted to save Brithos . . . and perhaps me, as well. Leonidas must have known. My father had always been close to him, and to King Cleomenes before him.' A distant roar was heard, like thunder, and it shook the house already damaged by the earthquake. Karas looked at the ceiling beams without moving.

'I think I can help you,' he said. 'And if what I believe is true, you will be able to guide the Helots against Sparta, without remorse.'

'What do you mean?'

'Think about it,' continued Karas. 'If it is true that the scroll was blank, as I too have heard, it's clear that the original message was replaced with another.' Kleidemos shuddered, thinking of that night on the gulf, of the shadow slipping furtively into their camp, bending over Brithos and then vanishing. 'And if that is the case, only the *krypteia* could have managed such a trick. And the *krypteia* must have reported to the ephors. Now, one of them, Episthenes, was a friend to King Pausanias, and was privy to his plans. It may have been him; he may have carved that phrase on your mother's tomb so you would see it and seek the truth. The earthquake has sown many victims among the Spartans, and if Episthenes has died, he has certainly carried the secret to his tomb. But if he's alive . . . you know where he lives. I will accompany you.'

'No, it's too dangerous. I'll go alone. This very night.' He opened the door and looked up at the sky. 'There are still a couple of hours of darkness before the dawn,' he said. 'They will suffice.'

'I wish this weren't necessary, my boy,' said Karas, getting up and following him to the threshold.

377

'As do I. But I cannot act otherwise. The thought has been tormenting me for days, since my return road brought me to . . . the ruins of Ithome.'

'You've been to the dead city? Why?'

'I don't know. I saw it standing before me, suddenly, as the sun was setting and I knew I had to enter those walls. Go now, Karas, and stay on your guard.'

'Be on your guard as well. And when you find your answer, you know where to look for me.'

'At the cabin near the high spring.'

'No,' replied Karas. 'You will find me at the entrance to the underground chamber, near the clearing of the holm oaks. The time has come for the sword of King Aristodemus to be taken from under the earth. His people shall be delivered.' He wrapped himself in his cloak and left, as Kleidemos followed him with his eyes. A few steps, and he was nothing more than one of the many shadows in the night.

*

Kleidemos took the grey hooded cape from the wall and went out beyond the courtyard in the direction of the city. He reached the Eurotas and descended into its gravelly banks so as to escape the notice of the guards patrolling the countryside around Sparta. He approached the House of Bronze, slipping among the crumbling houses of the Mesoa district, still wrapped in darkness. The city seemed deserted; the aftershocks had scattered any survivors far from the precarious structures. Certain areas of the city were dimly lit, here and there, by fires that had been kept burning in the public squares and the *agora*. Kleidemos slunk along the walls trying to get his bearings as best he could. The pitch darkness protected him but also made it very difficult to recognize the sites around him. He would often find his path blocked by rubble and be forced to turn back and search for another way through.

All at once, he made out a little shrine with an image of Artemis and he realized that the entrance to the Council House square was just a couple of blocks away. As he had feared, the square was being guarded by a group of soldiers sitting on the ground around a fire. Kleidemos stayed flush to the portico wall which stretched along the building's south side; slipping from one column to another, he succeeded in avoiding the illuminated area without bring seen. He soon found himself in front of the house of ephor Episthenes; it was half in ruins. He drew up to the shattered door and placed his ear against it but heard nothing. He plucked up his courage and entered. Most of the roof had fallen in and the floor was full of beams and debris, but part of the ceiling had been propped up to make the house inhabitable and a lamp burned before an image of Hermes – Episthenes must have survived the quake and was perhaps still living there. Footsteps sounded in the road – the hobnailed boots of hoplite soldiers: two of them, maybe three.

He slipped into a corner, hoping that they would continue past the door but they stopped right at the threshold. He heard the men exchanging a few words, after which they resumed their marching; they must be a patrol squad. He leaned forward to make sure they'd passed, and saw a man with an oil lamp in hand entering the atrium and closing the door behind him. When he turned and the lamp light illuminated his face, he recognized him: it was Episthenes, dressed in a ragged chiton. His fatigue was evident in his face. He took a stool and sat down, setting his lamp on the floor.

Kleidemos came out into the open and announced himself. 'Hail, O Episthenes. May the gods protect you.' The man was startled, and raised his lamp to the intruder's face.

'By Hercules, the son of Aristarkhos! We'd given you up for dead.'

'The gods have spared me, as you see, but I have run terrible risks. Forgive mè if I have entered your house in secret, but the reasons which have impelled me to make such an unusual visit are pressing, and serious.'

Episthenes lowered his reddened eyes. 'I was hoping you would come to visit me one day,' he said, 'but events have prostrated us, and we can no longer speak with serenity.'

'There's a phrase,' said Kleidemos, 'carved on the tomb of my mother. I think you can explain it to me.'

'You have a quick mind, as I thought, but I'm afraid that what I have to tell you no longer has much meaning. I had those words carved in the name of justice, hoping that when you returned home you would wonder about their meaning and seek out the truth. I was too old and too tired to do any more than that. But now . . . nothing is important any more. The city has been struck by the wrath of the gods in punishment for our terrible deeds.'

'I do not know to what you are alluding, Episthenes. You know the secrets of this city. But you cannot imagine how important it is for me to know the truth about myself and my family. And I must learn the truth now, before the dawn of this day breaks.'

The ephor stood with difficulty, and drew very close. 'You knew Pausanias' plans, didn't you?' Kleidemos remained silent. 'You can speak freely, no one is listening to us and the man you see before you tried to save the king from death – unsuccessfully, as you know.'

'It is as you say.'

'And you would have helped him to achieve them?'

'I would have, yes. But why are you asking me this? Pausanias is dead and my hopes with him. The only thing which has kept me tied to this city is the memory of my parents and my brother Brithos. I want to know if there is any reason why I should remain bound to Sparta.

'Episthenes, I served this city for ten years, I killed people I did not even know for her. My parents were forced to abide by her cruel laws and to abandon me. My mother died of grief; my father and my brother died in combat. I need to know what mystery lies beneath this whole horrible story. I know that custom has it that all the men of a given family are never sent into combat together: why was this law broken for my father and my brother Brithos . . . and for me as well? Because I'm sure that you knew who Talos the cripple really was.'

'You are right. But if I tell you what I know, I fear that your only desire will be revenge.'

'You are mistaken, noble Episthenes. At this point, I feel pity for this city that the gods have cursed. I need to know, because I am tired of living in uncertainty and anguish. It is time for me to find my own road, once and for all.' He neared the swinging door, looking through the cracks. 'Dawn is not far off.'

'That's true,' replied the ephor. 'Sit down and listen.'

He offered Kleidemos a stool and both men sat down.

'For many years in this city, the kings and the ephors and elders have been at odds, and the battle for control has been merciless. It was the ephors who provoked the death of King Cleomenes, poisoning his foods with a drug that made him slowly go mad, day by day. Your father Aristarkhos and your brother Brithos were very close to the king and many believed that they may have suspected something. And so when Leonidas was sent to the Thermopylae, my colleagues arranged for both of them to leave with the king, naming Aristarkhos his aide-de-camp and making your brother one of the royal guard. It seemed an extraordinary honour rendered on the family; in truth, everyone knew that those men would never come back. The king must have realized all this, and before the last battle he sent a message to Sparta, through the two sons of Aristarkhos, adding another warrior to make sure they arrived.'

'Do you mean that Leonidas knew that I was the brother of Brithos?'

'We all knew. As you were returning across Thespaie, a *krypteia* spy noticed you, and he saw the scroll with the royal seal at Brithos' neck. He imagined that it must have contained something important . . . something that perhaps should not reach the public domain. That man followed you on your entire journey and when you had set up camp at the gulf and had all fallen asleep, he saw his chance and stole the king's message.'

'But then what did Brithos deliver to the ephors?'

'A different scroll. A blank one. The spy, who today is an officer of the *krypteia*, falsified the royal seal but did not dare compose another message, because he did not know what to write, and he could not forge the king's signature.'

Kleidemos punched his knee in anger. 'By Hercules! I saw the whole thing, but I was so overcome by weariness and fatigue that I thought I had dreamt it all ... if only I had realized ...'

'It was I who opened the scroll in front of the assembled elders and I was shocked to see that it was blank. I did not know the truth then, nor did any of those present at the assembly. And so the rumour spread that Brithos and Aghias had plotted to escape death at the pass of the Thermopylae. It is even possible that this rumour was started by those who knew the truth and wanted Brithos out of the way, fearful that one day he might discover what had happened. And so Aghias hanged himself and your brother disappeared. We all thought he was dead, until news spread that in Phocis and Boeotia a warrior bearing the shield of the dragon was fighting against the Persians. *Krypteia* spies were dispatched everywhere to discover who this warrior really was. When Brithos appeared at Plataea and died in battle my colleagues were greatly relieved. Brithos could be celebrated as a hero and no one would ever probe into the story of the king's message—'

'But I was still in the picture,' interrupted Kleidemos. 'I was at the Thermopylae and I had returned with Brithos, accompanying him in all his exploits in Phocis and Boeotia.'

'Pausanias took you away with him at my suggestion and so you remained safe and under surveillance for years. When Pausanias was killed . . .' the ephor's voice quavered and he pulled his cloak tight around his shoulders as if shaken by a sudden chill, 'the ephors tried in every way possible to uncover whether you were involved in his plans, but your conduct was very prudent. They captured a Helot shepherd, a giant of a man with incredible strength, because they knew he was your friend and that he had met with Pausanias. They turned him over to the *krypteia* and he was brutally tortured. But he evidently never said a word because they let him go, planning perhaps to follow him and trace him back to you. But he must have been very prudent, as well. Perhaps he realized that his cabin was being watched, because he has never been seen since, not even yesterday, when the Helots attacked the city. No one has seen him.'

'I've seen him,' said Kleidemos. 'It was he who told me to come here, convinced that you might be able to answer my questions.' The ephor fell silent and Kleidemos could hear a cock crowing: it would soon be dawn.

'His intuition was correct,' admitted Episthenes. 'I saw the message of King Leonidas and I copied it before it was destroyed. I never had the courage to tell you of its contents, so I had those words carved on your mother's tomb. If the blood of great Aristarkhos flows through your veins, I knew that one day you would seek out the truth, wherever it was hidden.'

He stood and pointed at the statue of Hermes in its niche on the wall behind Kleidemos. 'It's there,' he said. 'Inside the statue.'

Kleidemos lifted the figurine, his hands shaking. He turned it over and extracted a leather scroll.

'Go now,' said the ephor. 'Flee; the sun is rising. May the gods accompany you.' Kleidemos hid the scroll in the folds of his cloak and walked to the door. The road appeared to be deserted.

'May the gods protect you, noble Episthenes,' he said, turning back, 'for they have cursed this city.'

He pulled his cape tight and raised the hood as he walked swiftly down the road. He skirted the Council House square and penetrated into a maze of dark narrow little lanes in the Mesoa quarter until he had reached the Eurotas valley. He ran at breakneck speed alongside the river, sheltered by the bank, until he was close enough to his own home. A thick fog had risen, so that he was able to walk in the open without fear of being seen. He could see the tops of the cypress trees surrounding Ismene's tomb in the distance, waving over the white blanket of fog, and he was able to direct himself with a sure step to the Kleomenid house. He entered, checked that the place was empty, and then closed the door behind him. The sun, just over the horizon, spread its faint milky light into the room. Kleidemos pulled out the leather scroll and unwound it with shaking hands. The words of King Leonidas appeared before his eyes, the words that the king had wanted to send his city in the anguish of his final hour, words that had remained secret for thirteen long years:

> Leonidas, son of Anaxandridas, king of the Spartans, Panhellenic leader, hails King Leotychidas, the honourable ephors and venerable elders.
>
> When you read these words I will be no longer among the living, nor shall the valorous sons of Sparta here with me, who have met the dreadful force of the barbarians head-on. It is only right that he who pays with his own blood make his voice heard. I have desired, in this my final act, to save from destruction a great family of valorous men, and to prevent them from being unjustly sacrificed. These men are Brithos and Kleidemos, sons of Aristarkhos, Kleomenid – the first would be destined to die here, in violation of the laws of his city, while the other lives as a servant, having escaped the death that the laws of his city had prescribed for him. They are the living image of the condition of Sparta: among these very rocks, the Helots will spill their blood as surely as the warriors. These two sons of Sparta come from the same stock, and it is my desire that a new order be founded so that the two races who live on this same land and who equally give their blood for her, may live in peace in the future under the same laws. I ask you that the memory of my brother Cleomenes, your king, be redeemed, as he was pushed into the darkness of folly and death by no divine hand, I believe, but by human will. If all this does not come about in the city for which I am about to give my life, the gods will one day curse her, for all

of those who have suffered her injustice and abuse without reason, if it is true that the deities send truthful premonitions to those who are about to die.

Kleidemos let the scroll fall to the ground and went into his parents' bed chamber. He opened the great cypress coffer, took out the armour and the shields of the Kleomenids, and dragged them to the tomb of Ismene. On the stone slab he placed the storied cuirass, the splendidly embossed shin plates, the helmet with the three black crests and the shield of the dragon. He knelt and leaned his head on the icy stone. Then, one last time, he touched the shield he had slept in as an infant and which had held the bones of his brother. One last time. And he took off at a run towards Mount Taygetus, vanishing in the fog.

A bellow erupted then from the bowels of the mountain and the earth shuddered and shook, down to the abyss of the Underworld. The powerful walls of the Kleomenid house swayed, the cornerstones broke asunder and the ancient home collapsed from its very foundations with an immense roar.

22

ITHOME

KLEIDEMOS PASSED THE CLEARING of the great holm oak, entered the bush and reached the base of the mound. Karas was sitting there, enveloped in his cape near a little fire of twigs. He sat as still as a boulder.

'I've been waiting for you,' he said, getting to his feet. 'Come, let's go in.'

Kleidemos moved aside the stones that blocked the entrance to the mound, on which a soft blanket of moss and ferns had grown. No one had touched those stones since he had visited that place with Kritolaos, that rainy night long ago.

Karas picked up a stick wrapped in tow and lit it in the campfire; he entered the cave first, followed by Kleidemos. He hung the torch on the wall of the inner chamber, and opened the great chest. The fantastic armour glittered in the dim light and Kleidemos stood staring without blinking. Karas took out the cuirass with its three large connected plates, then the bronze shield decorated with a wolf's head in sparkling electrum and the helmet crowned with wolf fangs. As he stretched his hand out towards the sword, Kleidemos was shaken by a sudden tremor. Karas detached the torch from the wall and brought it close to the blade. The grease which had covered it caught fire and the sword became a flaming torch itself. When the brief flame had extinguished itself, the tempered blade was a dazzling blue.

Karas lowered his head and recited in a low voice, 'He will be strong and innocent, and moved by such a strong love for his people that he will sacrifice the voice of his own blood.'

'I heard these words from Kritolaos,' said Kleidemos.

'They are the words of an ancient prophecy which has come true in this moment. You, who sacrifice your Spartan blood for the love of your people, you are the last Wolf of Messenia, Talos, son of Sparta and son of your people ... The moment has come for you to grasp the sword of Aristodemus, king of the Messenians, heir of Nestor, shepherd of peoples. The ancient curse ... shall be undone.' Karas' eye shone under his powerful brow, perhaps with tears. But his voice was firm. He pressed the tip of the sword against the chest of Kleidemos, who did not move. Blood spurted out, and Karas lifted the sword high with both hands. The red drop trickled slowly along the central groove until it touched the amber hilt. Karas then plunged the sword into the ground and knelt before it, his sweat-beaded brow against the hilt. With a quivering voice, he pronounced words which Kleidemos could not understand, and yet which burned into his mind, one after another.

Karas raised his face towards Kleidemos, who seemed to have turned to stone. He said, 'Take it, now.'

Kleidemos stretched his hand out to the amber hilt. He gripped it, pulled it from the ground, and held it to his chest. Karas stood. 'Kritolaos was the last Keeper of the

Sword. I am the Keeper of the Word – words passed down for one hundred and eighty-four years. Now you possess the Sword and you know the Word. You are the Wolf.'

*

All the able-bodied men of the mountain had gathered in the big clearing at the high spring. They had been waiting, armed and drawn up into tribes. They watched the forest as if waiting. One of them suddenly pointed towards a thicket of oak trees. 'Here they come!'

Karas' imposing figure was first, the spear in his right hand, a leather shield in his left. Behind him was a warrior, armed to the teeth, his head covered by a helmet crowned with wolf fangs and a huge horn bow over his shoulder. From the belt which crossed his chest hung the amber-hilted sword. At the sight of him, the elders fell to their knees, raising their hands in the air while Karas lifted his spear and shouted, 'The Wolf has returned. Render him honour!' The men tightened their ranks and began to beat sword on shield. A powerful, confused roar arose, becoming ever stronger and more rhythmical, an incredible din that echoed over all the surrounding mountain peaks.

An old man with a long white beard advanced with an unsteady step until he stood before the warrior. He raised tear-filled eyes and said in a broken voice, 'We have been waiting for so long, my lord, for this day. May the gods be with you and give you the strength to guide this people.' He took his hand and kissed it.

Kleidemos removed his helmet and held up his hand in

a request for silence. 'People of the mountain!' he shouted. 'Listen! Many signs from the gods, and the fulfilment of many presages have convinced me to don this armour and to take up the sword of Aristodemus. I have been away for a long time, so that I could learn the truth about my life and about the world that surrounds us. I have suffered greatly and undergone much pain, because the gods have reserved a difficult fate for me. But now my Spartan roots have dried up and my road is marked out before me. I will lead you, men, with the help of Karas, the Keeper of the Word, whom my grandfather Kritolaos singled out as my companion so many years ago.

'I witnessed your battle, two days ago on the plain, and I've seen what Sparta has in store for you. You are no longer accustomed to fighting; you've never fought against such perfectly equipped and trained troops. Believe me, there are still many able warriors in the city, led by two young and courageous kings. And I know for certain that the city is seeking aid and reinforcements from its allies, including the Athenians, the lords of the seas.

'What I believe we must do is return to the original land of our people, Messenia, and reoccupy Ithome!' Murmurs ran through the lines of warriors. 'The Spartans will be long occupied with rebuilding their devastated city and reorganizing their forces. We'll have all the time we need to reach Ithome and raise its walls. Ithome's location is excellent; its position will make it easy to defend the city without having to face the Peloponnesian phalanx on open ground. We will repair the wells and cisterns and fortify the bastions. The herds of cows and sheep that you have always put to pasture for your masters will sustain us. Call your families, your women and children, and have them make preparations. Tomorrow we begin our march.'

A shout was raised from one thousand mouths, all the warriors lifting their spears. Karas began immediately to assign duties. He had sentries posted on all the paths and at all the points of surveillance. He divided the sound men into groups and chose the best as their commanders. He had them gather all the pack animals and all the available carts with the oxen to pull them, ordering each family to bring their own household goods to the big clearing, so they could load them up along with their provisions.

Kleidemos spent the night in the cottage of Kritolaos, with the woman who had been his mother for so many years. The animal pens were still there and everything was in perfect order inside, as though it had never been abandoned. There was Kritolaos' stool, where he would sit on long winter nights and tell his marvellous stories as he wove baskets with thin twigs of broom. And there was the bed where he had slept as a child, dreaming half awake and half asleep in the early morning as he listened to the song of the skylarks fluttering up from the bushes towards the disc of the sun, or to the twittering of the courting blackbirds.

In just two days he would be rejoined with Antinea and remain with her forever. He fell asleep, done in by long days of emotion and fatigue. Next to him waited the armour of the kings of Messenia, created long ago by an inspired craftsman in a splendid palace. The armour that had lain buried for entire generations in the mountain cavern. Not far away, Kritolaos slept at the edge of the oak wood under a simple mound. A pious hand had planted a young flowering ash alongside him; its buds were already swelling under the soft tepid sea breeze.

*

The long march began at dawn, when the sentries reported from their guard posts that the entire area was clear. Kleidemos arranged the armed men five abreast in two columns, one at the head of the group and the other at the back. In the middle were the carts, the pack animals, the women, the old people and the children, with their belongings. Groups of scouts on horseback covered their advance and others, riding at a distance, closed off the long train of men and animals, ready to give the alarm if they were attacked from behind.

But there were no surprises during the entire journey, which lasted for five days. The people of the mountain arrived within sight of the ruins of Ithome on the afternoon of the fifth day. Kleidemos had them set up camp at the base of the hill where they could draw water. A nearby forest offered an abundance of wood. Builders and carpenters immediately assembled their tools and in just a few days shelters were up. All of the able-bodied men and many women worked in shifts inside the city to repair the walls and close the breaches; they built roofs as well, and cleared away the debris from the streets. Even the youngest children did what they could to help.

Antinea and old Pelias had joined the migrating column when it passed over their land; Karas had them climb onto a cart and told them about everything that had happened. Kleidemos, at the head of the column, greeted her with a wave and a long look but did not abandon his position. There would be time to be with her and talk with her. The most important thing now was to lead all these people to safety before the Spartans decided to attack.

Strangely, the Spartans did not show up for a full three months. When the first small group of enemy scouts on horseback was spotted by the sentries at the entrance to the valley, Ithome had returned to life and was home to all the people of Mount Taygetus. There were three thousand eight hundred of them, of which eight hundred were able to bear arms.

Kleidemos trained them thoroughly in all the combat techniques he had learned in his years of serving Sparta. One night, as he was inspecting the walls along with Karas, he stopped on a tower to look out over the moonlit valley.

'What are you thinking of?' asked Karas.

'Of when we'll see the Spartan army heading in.'

'Perhaps we won't,' answered Karas. 'Perhaps they'll leave us in peace.'

'No,' said Kleidemos, shaking his head. 'You and I both know that they cannot tolerate an independent – and hostile – city at just five days' march from their gates. I only hope that the ephors consider the possibility of a truce. We could recognize their formal sovereignty over this land in exchange for peace. We know nothing of what has been happening in the valley of the Eurotas, but I'm not nurturing false illusions.'

'This city cannot die,' said Karas after a long silence. 'I've already heard the old men telling the children the story of the great march from Mount Taygetus, the story of Talos the Wolf. It will be sung as part of our history, like the endeavours of the ancient kings.'

'I know what you're saying,' replied Kleidemos. 'I chose with your help to bring our people here because I thought it was the only possible path to safety and freedom. But now I'm afraid.'

'The Messenians have already accepted us; there's no hostility on their part, none at all. The elders of the nearby towns and villages have told us that they consider us their kinsmen, descendants of the same fathers.'

'It's true. And this may become a great advantage for us should the Spartans attack, although I don't think they will go so far as to take up arms for us. But it's useless trying to predict the future. We must prepare for the worst. If destiny should prove favourable, all the better for us. Just watching this city rise from the dead has been marvellous. Kritolaos' dream! If only he could see this.'

'Kritolaos was the Keeper of the Sword,' said Karas. 'His spirit will always be with his people.'

'All this seems impossible. It's as if I were dreaming sometimes. Finding you again, Antinea, my mother . . . and this people, ready to fight after such a long wait.'

'We've always been ready to fight,' said Karas. 'When the Greeks won at Plataea, that very night many of our men sacked great riches from the Persian camp and kept them ably hidden. They were used to buy weapons for our warriors. Arms with which they will defend their liberty, should it cost them their lives. These people will never go back to being slaves. Remember that: never. They'd rather die. All of them.'

That night Kleidemos lay next to Antinea and held her tightly.

'My father is dying,' said Antinea. 'Serenely. He feels that life is abandoning him, but he regrets nothing. You have shown him the city of his ancestors, you have fulfilled his lifelong dream.'

Kleidemos held her even tighter. 'Antinea,' he said. 'Oh, Antinea, I would like this dream to be never ending. But I'm afraid of what awaits us. Sparta is implacable.'

'It doesn't matter what awaits us if we're slaves. Nor does living a long life. All of us are ready to fight and we are all happy that we've followed you here. My father is dying but in my womb a child is growing. This is a sign of life that continues, not life that ends.'

Kleidemos sought out her eyes in the darkness and he felt a knot tighten his throat. 'A child,' he whispered. 'A child will be born in the dead city . . .' He kissed her and caressed her smooth belly.

*

The first Spartan troops arrived at the beginning of the summer, but the contingent was quite small at first. The ephors had decided to keep an eye on the city of the Helots in order to prevent others who had remained in Laconia from joining up with the rebels. More time passed before the Spartans attempted to force entry into the valley, which had been fortified with a rampart. The people of Ithome had planted crops and wanted to harvest them before the winter came, and so the ramparts were kept under close surveillance day and night to prevent the enemy from passing. When the wheat had begun to turn golden, the Spartans sent a legation demanding the surrender of the city and the return of the Helots to Mount Taygetus. They were willing to forego any revenge or punishment as long as each one of them returned to their work on the fields and pastures.

Karas responded from high on the rampart. 'These people have long suffered as slaves. Many of our men died in battle, serving your warriors, but their blood was held of no account and reviled. And so we left Laconia to return to our ancient homeland and we rebuilt this city. There is not one of us who hasn't suffered injustice or beatings or torture at your hands, but it is not our desire to exact revenge. We only wish to live freely and in peace. If you leave this land, you will have nothing to fear from us, but for nothing in the world will we accept to take your yoke back onto our shoulders. We would rather risk our lives defending our freedom, and we will never surrender. Never.'

'Beware, Helots!' shouted the Spartan. 'Our ancestors destroyed this city once and we will do so again!'

'Out of here!' ordered Karas, furious.

The Spartan looked up derisively. 'A one-eyed man and a cripple,' he sneered, turning to the men accompanying him. 'Fine leaders this ragged crew has chosen for themselves!' But he had no time to say another word. Karas lifted up an enormous boulder, raised it above his head and hurled it with a roar. The Spartan realized the giant's might too late and his bronze shield was lifted in vain. The boulder flattened him to the ground, crushing his chest and spraying his guts through the openings on his cuirass. The others, stunned, laid down their spears. They gathered the corpse onto a shield and crept off in silence.

The scouts that Karas sent off over the surrounding hills to estimate the strength of the enemy troops reported back that their number seemed quite small. In fact, the ephors had not dared strip Sparta of defences, fearful that the Arcadians and Messenians would rise up against them. They had requested aid from the Athenians and hoped that a large contingent would be sent from Attica, trusting mainly in the support of Cimon, who led the aristocratic party and had championed a strong alliance between the two most powerful forces in Greece. At that point they would unleash the decisive attack and annihilate the Helots entrenched behind the walls of Ithome. But by the time Cimon had overcome with great difficulty the strong opposition of the democrats, thanks solely to his personal prestige, and the assembly of Athens had agreed to send five battalions of hoplites to Messenia, the summer was ending. No one could hope to conquer the city before the rainy season. The bad weather would make it difficult, if not completely impossible, to maintain a siege.

Antinea gave birth to a boy at the beginning of the autumn. He was given the name Aristodemus, in accordance with the wishes of the elders. He was strong and healthy, with dark hair like his father's and green eyes like his mother's. When the midwife brought him to Kleidemos in a basket, his soul was deeply moved. He took the child in his arms and held him to his chest, covering him with his cape. He prayed, from the bottom of his heart: 'O gods, you who live eternally and have power over life and death, you who reserved such a bitter fate for me, taking me – so small and defenceless – from my father's arms . . . if it was written that my suffering was necessary to atone for some ancient misdeed, I beg of you, be satisfied now with the harsh punishment inflicted on an innocent person and spare this child, whom I have generated with immense love.'

So prayed Kleidemos, his soul full of hope and of anguish.

*

The arrival of the Athenian troops did little to advance operations and the Spartan officers soon realized that many of their allies were of the democratic persuasion and were loath to fight against the Helot rebels in order to reduce them to slavery. It was even rumoured that several of the Athenian commanders had made contact with the Messenians in the surrounding countryside. The Messenians were actually Spartan subjects and were tied to the city by a rigid pact of alliance, but they admired the courage of the defenders of Ithome nonetheless.

Suspicious and embarrassed, the ephors dismissed the Athenian contingent in the end, claiming that their aid was no longer needed. The Athenian army returned to Attica, but Sparta's gesture raised such intense indignation in the assembly that Cimon, who was held responsible for the stinging rebuke, was violently attacked by his adversaries, who demanded his dismissal and exile. The proposal was put to a vote and the valorous commander, winner of many battles on land and at sea, was forced to abandon his city. The democrats reclaimed power and the already difficult relations between Sparta and Athens became even colder.

In the meantime the ephors and elders, having repaired most of the earthquake damage and regained control of the situation in Laconia, decided to take the city of Ithome by storm. It was time; many Messenians had joined the rebels and there was a real danger that the entire region might be lost to them.

The following spring an army of five thousand hoplites surrounded the city and laid siege. When the hot winds from the south had completely dried the earth King Archidamus gave orders for the final attack. It was a hazy day at the beginning of the summer and the king had divided his troops into four large battalions, preceded by Cretan archers and light infantry whose mission was to batter the bastions with any type of projectile, while the line infantry scaled the walls. The warriors began their march at daybreak, converging at the base of the mountain below Ithome.

Kleidemos and Karas, armed from head to toe, positioned all the able men on the walls, while the women and children brought stones and sand which were loaded onto shields to heat them under the blazing sun. Antinea would not leave Kleidemos' side, passing him the arrows for his great horn bow.

When King Archidamus had the trumpets sounded, his warriors began climbing the slopes of the mountain in a silent march, compact, shoulder to shoulder. His archers were the first to reach the walls, and began to shoot clouds of arrows at the bastions, where the defenders were trying to protect themselves with their shields. When the hoplites, slower and weighed down by their armour, drew close to the walls, their archers and slingers parted ranks to let them through without ever interrupting their attack. A strong wind had come up, raising clouds of dust on the sides of the mountain and the Spartan warriors pushed on through that fog, heads low, their armour and crests whitened. Horrible spectres, harbingers of death.

Kleidemos drew his sword to give the signal from the bastions on high. His archers took aim at the enemy with a zeal born of desperation. Many of the light infantrymen supporting the Spartan troops fell, but the descending arrows accomplished little, shattering against the shields of the hoplites, who continued to advance in the dust. The sun was high now, and their armour gleamed through the haze. The various divisions had reached the top of the mountain and they locked together, enclosing Ithome in their grip.

From the tops of the towers, they seemed a swarm of monstrous insects in metallic shells. The defenders began to hurl down stones and overturn their shields full of burning sand which poured down on their assailants, sinking in between the plates of their cuirasses and causing them to back off, tormented by burns. But others came forward to replace them, while the light infantrymen approached with tens of ladders, covered by the dense rain of Cretan arrows. Kleidemos realized that responding with arrow fire had become useless, since the enemy were now sheltered by the protruding bastions. He abandoned his horn bow and turned back towards Antinea to ask for a spear.

At that moment an arrow shot by a Cretan archer

descended from above in a long fall and struck Antinea, who collapsed with a cry. Kleidemos dropped his shield and took her into his arms, but in the meantime hundreds of Spartan hoplites had reached the top of the ladders and were clambering over the bastions from every direction. The defenders were at a loss to contain them. Karas, just a short distance away, was assaulted by a group of light infantry who had surmounted the bastion. He ran one of them through with his sword; the invader fell headlong over the parapet with the iron blade stuck in his body. Unarmed now, Karas grabbed another of his aggressors, lifted him up bodily and threw him against his comrades who were still climbing up, pitching them into a ruinous fall.

The giant turned and saw Kleidemos on top of the eastern tower. He was holding Antinea, her breast stained with blood, and he was being attacked by a group of Spartans with their swords bared. Karas was horrified at the sight: It was as if King Aristodemus had returned from the dead, his sacrificed daughter between his arms, ready to be swallowed up into Hades. He filled his huge chest and roared, overriding the din of the battle and the cries of the wounded. He shouted 'Save the king!' as he lunged forwards, pulling a spear from the grip of a cadaver that lay on the sentry walk. Kleidemos reacted, laying Antinea gently on the ground. He spun around, drawing his sword: he was completely surrounded. Overcoming every obstacle, Karas arrived just in time to break up the enemy circle. One of them turned against him, but Karas thrust out his spear. It penetrated the warrior's shield and cuirass and pierced his breast; the giant lifted him up on its tip and threw him at the others, who backed off, terrified. Kleidemos flanked him, whirling his sword, and the assailants were flung back over the parapet.

At that sight, the Helot combatants took heart and regained control of the bastion, driving off the enemy and pushing away the ladders, engulfing those beneath in a hail of stones and darts, hurling beams torn from the parapet. Kleidemos picked up Antinea then and brought her to safety inside a shelter where the women were caring for the wounded.

The Spartans sent a delegation asking for a truce so they could recover their dead. It was granted, and the litter bearers ascended slowly beneath the walls of Ithome to collect their fallen men, recomposing as best they could their mangled, stone-crushed limbs. King Archidamus, standing at the entrance to his camp, watched the sad procession of bearers returning with the corpses of his hoplites. He looked at them, one by one, his jaw tight and his fists clenched. When they had all passed, he raised his gaze towards the city. The setting sun stained the mountain slopes red, dark red, like the blood of his warriors.

23

THE WOLF

ANTINEA FOUGHT OFF DEATH at length. After the arrow had been removed from her shoulder, she was devoured by a raging fever. Kleidemos would spend long hours at her bedside every night when he returned from the walls, stroking her burning brow and imploring the gods to save her. The baby was cared for by a wet nurse, a woman whose own child had been stillborn and who had enough milk to nourish Antinea's son. The elders of the city had raised a modest sanctuary over the ruins of the ancient temple of Zeus Ithometa, where they offered supplications to the god for the health of their chief and the salvation of his bride.

In the end, their pleas were heeded and Antinea slowly recovered but her life was filled with anguish whenever she saw Kleidemos donning his armour and taking up his sword. Rain and cold came with the winter, and a little peace as military operations relented. The Spartans restricted their efforts to maintaining a small contingent in the valley, making it possible for the people of Ithome to take in supplies. They would leave at night, a few at a time, with their pack animals, loading them up with wheat in the nearby towns of the Messenians.

In the villages they could also glean news on what was

happening in the surrounding area and the rest of the Peloponnese. And so Kleidemos realized that Sparta was in serious difficulty with its neighbouring states, especially with the Argives, who had always been hostile, and the Arcadians, who could not tolerate their hegemony. For this reason, he hoped to be able to prolong Ithome's resistance.

As spring drew near and his son had begun to walk and babble his first words, Kleidemos considered what might happen if Sparta decided to concentrate all its forces on an attack of Ithome. When rumour reached the council that the ephors and elders had decided to put an end to the stalemate in Messenia once and for all, they urged Kleidemos to take little Aristodemus and Antinea to safety.

Kleidemos asked Karas to take his wife, his son and his ageing mother far away from Ithome, to some safe place in Arcadia or Argolis where he could reach them or from where they could be called back once he had won freedom for his people and himself. Karas thought it best to carry out the mission before the spring campaign, and so Kleidemos one night told Antinea about his intentions.

'Listen to me,' he said. 'I've learned that Sparta has decided to terminate this war, which can mean only one thing, in their minds: destroying Ithome and annihilating or enslaving our people. I've come to a decision. I want you out of harm's way, along with our child and my mother. Karas is ready to take you to a secret place in Arcadia where you will be safe with a family of good people he knows well. I will stay here to defend the city. If we manage to hold out, or to defeat the Spartans, we will finally have earned our freedom. And then you'll come back to me, or I'll come to get you.' Antinea burst into tears. 'Is this the luck you're wishing me? You're crying as if I were already dead.'

Antinea turned towards him and held him tightly. 'Please don't send me away! I beg of you, do not send me away. I will die of anguish without you, without knowing what's happening to you. I'm sure I won't be able to bear it!'

'You will,' replied Kleidemos firmly, gently breaking off her embrace. 'Think of our son: he needs you.'

Antinea was inconsolable. 'You'll never survive! The Spartans won't stop until they've razed the city to the ground. I want to die here with you, with my son, if the gods will it, with my people.'

'No, Antinea, you don't know what you're saying. Now, I've made a decision and you must abide by it. You will depart the first night of the new moon, with Karas. I'm having you leave to protect you from a serious risk, but the situation is not hopeless. The next Spartan campaign will be led by King Pleistarchus. He is the son of Leonidas. I will ask to meet with him, to talk – perhaps we can avoid a fruitless massacre. Not even Sparta can put its warriors' lives recklessly at risk. Many of them died in the earthquake, and many more have fallen in this war.'

Antinea said nothing but she was consumed by unrelenting sadness. She lay her head on Kleidemos' chest and listened to the beating of his heart.

'Fate kept us apart for many years,' he began again. 'When I saw you going off on your ass that day so long ago, I wept bitterly because I was sure I would never see you again. And yet I found you, after laying my life on the line hundreds of times in distant lands. We must continue to hope, Antinea, hope to see each other again. Sometimes the gods allow us no comfort, but there's a force deep down inside of us that won't let hope die. It's the force that brought me back to you from the lands of far-off Asia, from the solitude of savage Thrace. I will always be with you, Antinea, and with our little one, but don't let me be the only one believing and hoping. If you are certain of seeing me again, we will be reunited one day, free to live in serenity until we have grown old and have seen our children's children growing up strong around us like young olive trees. At the height of the storm we forget that the sun exists and we fear that darkness will dominate the world. But the sun continues to shine above the black clouds and sooner or later its rays force their way through, bringing us light and life.'

Antinea was still, embracing him tightly. She tried to open her heart to his words and to hold back the burning tears that rose into her eyes.

The first night of the new moon, Karas had the two women and the little boy climb onto a cart so he could take them far away from Ithome. Kleidemos watched them going off, holding his arms high above his head like he had that long-ago day on the plain. He felt solace that they were going to a safe place, shielded from danger. And yet he felt death in his heart at separating from those he loved better than life itself. The people of Ithome watched him, standing at the northern gate of the city, so full of sadness and of hope. They too wanted the son of Talos the Wolf to be saved. And they knew that a chief, in the supreme moment, must be alone.

The siege began that spring. It was led at the beginning by two high commanders and four battalion commanders. King Pleistarchus would arrive later, after the celebration of Artemis Orthia; he would be presiding over the feast, along with King Archidamus. In Sparta the ephors had sought at length to discover who was commanding the Helots; when the first accounts arrived from Messenia of a mysterious warrior wearing a suit of armour, the likes of which had never been seen before, they attempted to track him down but were unsuccessful. The man was reported to be lame, and some named Kleidemos, the son of Aristarkhos, but he had been missing since the time of the earthquake and was presumed dead. No certain evidence was ever found, and although ephor Episthenes sensed the truth, he said nothing. None of the Spartan warriors had ever seen his features, because Kleidemos always fought wearing the helmet that covered most of his face.

Karas carried out his mission successfully. He did not return immediately to Ithome, but stopped in Arcadia to gather news. When he finally came back, just in time before the siege closed in on the city, he related all he had learned to Kleidemos. The Athenians had been deeply impressed by the Helots' strenuous resistance and they were pressuring Sparta to free them once and for all. No one knew what the Spartans thought of this proposal. When King Pleistarchus finally arrived at the camp, Kleidemos tried to arrange an encounter, but to no avail. One day he saw the king passing on horseback down the trail that led up from the valley, inspecting the fortifications of the besieged city. He wrote a brief message and tied it to an arrow. Pointing his horn bow towards the sky, he calculated the trajectory, and let fly. The dart shot off with a whistle, followed its long course and stuck into the ground just a few steps from the king's horse.

Pleistarchus dismounted and hurriedly picked up the arrow, scanning the message. He looked up towards the city: the bastions were completely empty, but on the very top of one of the towers he saw an immobile warrior covered in gleaming armour who seemed to be looking at him. The king returned his stare, then gestured for his escort to leave. He weighed his spear in his hand and then hurled it with great strength; it stuck into the trunk of a dried olive tree that stood halfway between where he stood and the city walls. The warrior vanished from the tower and shortly thereafter one of the city gates opened. He reappeared on the edge of the mountain, planted his spear into the ground, and advanced slowly on foot towards the olive tree. Under the eyes of his bodyguards, the king walked towards the tree as well. The warrior raised his hand in salute and the king scrutinized him for some time without speaking. He was disturbed at the sight of that strange armour, and his gaze sought to penetrate behind the visor crowned with wolf fangs. The eyes blinking in the narrow slot of the gilded bronze sallet were certainly not those of a slave, son and grandson of slaves.

Kleidemos found himself, for the first time, face to face with the king. He had seen him a few times in Sparta, but always at a distance. He was an attractive young man, just a little over twenty, muscular and dark-skinned, his long wavy hair touching the edge of his cuirass. His shield bore a carved sparrowhawk, symbol of the Agiads, the dynasty of his father, great Leonidas.

'Who are you?' demanded the king.

'Is my name important?' came the reply.

'No, it is not. But your shield bears the wolf's head of the King of Messenia—'

'The man standing before you wears the armour of Aristodemus and thus has authority over the people of Ithome.'

Pleistarchus seemed surprised. 'What do you want from me?' he asked.

'I know that you are the valorous, worthy son of a great father. For this reason, I believe that you respect the courage of this people, who have resisted for three years in their battle for liberty. This war has lasted too long; too much blood has been spilt in vain. Allow these people to live in peace on the land of their ancestors. If you withdraw your warriors, you will have nothing to fear from us. We are ready to vow to a pact of peace that we will never recede from.'

'I have no power to offer you a peace pact, even if I desired to do so,' said Pleistarchus. 'If you want to save these people, persuade them to return to the fields they have abandoned. If you truly have authority over them, convince them and I give you my word as king that they will not be harmed.'

'That is not possible. They would rather die. If they were afraid of death, they would have surrendered long ago.'

'Than I have nothing more to say to you. Prepare to

die in combat.' He yanked the spear from the olive tree and turned to rejoin his men.

'Wait, if you hold your father's memory dear!' shouted Kleidemos. At those words, the king spun around.

'Listen to me,' said Kleidemos. 'Because what I am about to tell you may seem incredible, but I swear on the gods of Hades that it is the truth.'

'Speak!' said the king.

'This war would have been avoided, had it been for your father. Before he died at the Thermopylae, he sent a message to the ephors and the elders asking them to recognize the dignity of the Helots and grant their liberty, as he had seen them die in battle alongside the equals. To recognize them as sons of the same land – a land where he wanted the two peoples to live together in peace. The message also demanded restoration of the good name of King Cleomenes, your uncle, whom the ephors had poisoned slowly, driving him to madness and death.' Pleistarchus removed his crested helmet; his face was drawn. 'But the message, which was to be brought to Sparta on the king's orders by Brithos, son of Aristarkhos, Kleomenid, and Aghias, son of Antimakhos, was stolen by the *krypteia* and replaced with a blank scroll. And so the two warriors carrying it to Sparta were disgraced and preferred death to dishonour.'

'How can I believe you?' said the king.

'I was at the Thermopylae. I returned with Brithos and Aghias and I saw the message stolen,' replied Kleidemos, removing his helmet. 'For I am Kleidemos, brother of Brithos, son of Aristarkhos. The Helots call me Talos the Wolf.'

'And I should believe the words of a traitor?' Pleistarchus said harshly.

'I am no traitor. When I learned who I really was, I
decided to serve the city whose laws had condemned me
to be abandoned as a child to the beasts of the forest. I –
whom Sparta had destined either to die or to live as a
servant – fought in the front line at Plataea. I commanded
a battalion of equals for four years, and I have been
holding your army in check for three years. Do you know
when I chose to return to the people who saved my life
and raised me? When I learned that the government of
Sparta had deliberately tried to exterminate my family by
plotting to send father and sons together into a military
expedition that they knew had no hope of succeeding.
When I learned that Sparta had betrayed the last will of a
great king, valorous and wise: your father, Leonidas. And
when I learned that Sparta had massacred men, Helots,
seeking asylum in a sacred place—'

'Stop! I won't listen to you!' interrupted Pleistarchus.

'You can walk away, if you like,' Kleidemos persevered,
'but the truth will pursue you. It will give you no peace.
Try to forget my words, and give the order to attack
Ithome, but if one day you want to understand the futility
of all this slaughter, read the message carved into the
tomb of my mother, Ismene, who died of a broken heart
between my arms. Dig among the ruins of the house of
the Kleomenids and in an iron casket next to the altar,
you will find the true words of the king, your father!'

Pleistarchus stood for a few moments as if stunned.
Then he put his helmet back on and walked slowly
towards his horse. Kleidemos returned to his city; on its

bastions a multitude of warriors, of women, of old men with eyes full of anguish, watched him ascend wearily, bent over, as if the splendid bronze of his armour had turned to lead.

*

King Pleistarchus slept fitfully, starting awake and pondering the words he had heard. Many in Sparta had interpreted the earthquake as a sign of the gods' wrath at the sacrilege of Cape Taenarum. The terrible story of the Kleomenids, the atrocious death of Pausanias for which the oracle of Delphi had demanded reparation ... the city's elders had long been tormented by these events. And now Sparta, the invincible, unable to put down the rebellion of a handful of servants: was this another sign from the gods?

And his father's message? Was it truly possible that two valiant warriors had brought a blank message from the Thermopylae? It made no sense. Was the real message indeed buried under the ruins of the Kleomenid house? Those people behind the walls of Ithome ... they would soon be without food, and yet they were ready to continue their fight.

He could not imagine that at that very moment two priests from the House of Bronze were returning from Delphi, where they had been sent by the assembly of elders to query the god about the war that Sparta was conducting against Ithome. Nor could Kleidemos imagine it; having gathered the chiefs of his people, he was planning a desperate sortie, perhaps the only way his people could avoid the long agony of starvation: a night-time attack on the Spartan lines. Perhaps, if the gods assisted them, victory could still be theirs.

At the same time the priests, having returned to Sparta, related the verdict of the god of Delphi to the elders and the ephors:

> 'Free the supplicants
> of Zeus Ithometa'

There could be no doubt about the meaning of this prophecy, and the elders bowed their heads in deference to their gods. The Athenians had already declared their willingness to provide a homeland for the Helots of Ithome, and the ephors dispatched a messenger to Attica to make the necessary arrangements. In a day they would have their answer.

When the messenger departed at the first light of dawn, the crescent moon was paling over Mount Taygetus. It was the last quarter before the new moon: that night Kleidemos would launch the attack. His men were greatly proven by their hunger; their only hope lay in the darkness and the aid of the gods.

When the moment came, he assembled them in the centre of the city and divided them into two columns. One, which he was to lead personally, would sow confusion in the enemy camp. The other, stronger and more numerous, was led by Karas: their task was to break out in a compact formation towards the rampart and provide cover for the fleeing population. If the attack met with success, the two contingents would take turns in fighting off the enemy at the rear guard, until the column of refugees had reached Arcadia. The last of the booty carried off from the battlefield of Plataea fifteen years earlier would serve to buy food during their journey.

'If we manage to reach the sea,' concluded Kleidemos, 'perhaps we can take ships and establish a new homeland beyond the sea, where no one will ever reduce us to slavery again. Karas has told me that in the land of Sicily stands a great city founded by Messenians who fled there many many years ago. Perhaps they will take us in when they learn that we are their brothers and have suffered their same fate.' He looked at his men in the torchlight; their faces were tired, hollowed out by fatigue and hunger. Could they manage to beat the most powerful army of all Greece? Their souls were ready, but could their limbs withstand that final, immense effort?

He got to his feet, donning his helmet and taking up his sword. He was a fearful sight in that shining armour.

'We are fighting for our lives and our liberty,' he said. 'They will not stop us. Now put out your torches and follow me.' He headed towards the gate and the warriors lined up in silence behind him, passing between two silent wings of old men, of women, of young boys.

The mountain was completely enveloped in darkness; a few sparse clouds obscured the dim light of the stars. They descended along the trail that led to the valley until they were nearly at the first Spartan outposts. Kleidemos, hiding behind a rock, could see a couple of sentries sitting next to a campfire. He was reminded of the tactics of the Thracians when he was commanding the fourth battalion of equals: they would light huge fires, so as to illuminate a wide tract of land, but their sentries would hang back in the shadows so as not to be seen. He beckoned to a group of archers and pointed out their target. 'They must fall without a cry!' he said, and gave the signal. The archers let fly all at once and the two sentries collapsed, pierced through by a swarm of arrows.

'Now,' he said, 'we can get right up to the camp without anyone sounding the alarm. When I give the signal, attack with everything you've got: cut the tent ropes so that they fall in on the men sleeping inside and yell at the top of your lungs; they must think that there are thousands of us. Set fire to everything you can, free the horses, destroy their provisions, but don't ever isolate yourselves; stay in groups, company by company. When you have crossed the camp and destroyed it, head towards the rampart at the bottom of the valley, as we've established. The archers will remain behind in the dark and strike by the light of the fires. May the gods assist you.'

He raised his arm and gave the signal: his men opened into a fan formation and ran forwards shouting. They were upon the outposts in no time. They lunged at the guards, overwhelming them, while the Spartan warriors, jolted awake in the dead of night, were scrambling to take up their weapons and head outside, where they met with the raiders, who were everywhere by then. In the darkness, hand-to-hand combat rose to a furious pitch and in the reddish light of the flames the scene was frightening to behold. Shouts, excited orders, curses, the whinnying of horses and tangles of bloodied bodies all about. But Kleidemos' men soon found themselves on open ground, and they realized that the bulk of the camp was about a hundred feet over. King Pleistarchus must have changed the set-up in the last hours, fearing just such a sortie. These were only the light infantry.

When the Helots began to run across the clearing, the trumpets had already sounded the alarm and Pleistarchus' hoplites were forming their ranks. Attacking under such conditions in the open field would have been sheer madness, and Kleidemos ordered all his men to run directly to the rampart, in the hope that Karas would have already occupied it. The battle resumed, while the Helots tried to make an orderly retreat. The archers managed to hold off Pleistarchus' phalanx momentarily as they were forced to advance slowly over the uneven ground so as not to break rank.

At dawn, the Spartan army was lined up before the rampart where all of the Helots who had been able to reach the position had regrouped. Behind them, the entire population of Ithome, defended by a handful of armed men, was walking westwards. Pleistarchus advanced on his horse, ready to command the attack that would wipe out the enemy. There would be no surprises now; they were utterly exhausted and no longer protected by the walls of their city. He raised his spear as the rays of the sun tried to pierce the clouds, but before he could lower it, a horseman burst into the space between the phalanx and the rampart.

'O King,' he said, jumping to the ground in front of Pleistarchus. 'My King, a message from the ephors and the elders.'

'I'll read it later,' replied the king, raising his spear once again.

'No!' insisted the messenger, holding out a scroll. 'You must read it immediately.'

Pleistarchus took off his helmet as the two armies faced off in silence, and read:

The ephors and the elders of Sparta, to King Pleistarchus, son of Leonidas, hail!

The calamities suffered in our city, and our fear of the wrath of the gods, have impelled us to ask for a response from the oracle of Delphi. These were the oracle's words:

'Free the suppliants
of Zeus Ithometa'

Accordingly, O King, allow the inhabitants of the city to go free, and put an end to this war. This is the will of the gods. The Athenians have offered them a place to live, if they wish to follow the delegates from this city who accompany the bearer of this message. May your valour, and your faith in the laws of our land, be honoured.

The king raised his astonished eyes to find two Athenian officers before him who had just caught up with the messenger.

'O King,' said one of the two, 'for quite some time we have been demanding that the ephors and the elders end this war which has brought nothing but blood and disaster; when they asked us to take these people in, we willingly agreed. Allow us then to lead them out of this land and accept the greetings and the regards of the Athenians who still honour the memory of your father.'

'If it has been decided thus, then thus shall it be done,' replied the king. He called an officer. 'Give the order to retreat. We will be going back to Laconia this very day.'

The Spartan soldiers were stunned at the orders of the king, and began to wheel and return to their camp under the incredulous eyes of the Helots, who could not fathom what was happening. The two Athenians spurred on their horses and rode up to the rampart.

'Men of Ithome!' shouted the officer who had spoken to the king. 'Your city is lost, but the god of Delphi has willed that a new homeland be given you. Thanks to the piety of your sovereigns, Archidamus, son of Zeuxidamus, and Pleistarchus, son of Leonidas, and to the generosity of the Athenians who have sent us to guide you there, men of Ithome, you are free!' A confused murmur rose little by little as those closest to the Athenians repeated what they had heard to the others.

'You are free!' cried out the Athenian officer again. The murmur grew then until it exploded into an unrestrainable shout. The Helots embraced each other like men gone mad. Some fell to their knees, arms raised towards the sky and eyes filled with tears, others ran among the ranks screaming, still others had already taken off to bring the news to the refugees marching under the protection of Karas' men.

When their enthusiasm finally calmed, they formed a long column behind the Athenian officers on horseback, heading down the road that led to the sea. At midday they had caught up with Karas' group, already weakened by their long march but filled with joy at the incredible news that the fast-riding couriers had already brought them.

When the head of the column reached the banks of the Pamisus, Karas gave orders to set up camp. He reported immediately to the Athenian officers. 'I thank you,' he said, drying his sweaty brow and holding out his hand, 'in the name of this unhappy people who have been snatched from the jaws of death when hope no longer existed. Our leader will have told you what happened last night.'

The two officers looked at each other in surprise. 'We have not met your leader, although we have heard tell of him and would be pleased to speak with him.'

Karas scowled, realizing that he had not seen Kleidemos since he had first launched the attack. He excused himself hurriedly and ran through the camp, asking all those he met if they had seen him, but he was soon convinced that Kleidemos was not among them. The warriors who had taken up position on the rampart assumed that he had reached the advance guard, while the advance guard was sure that he had remained behind. Karas assembled all the chiefs and gave them orders to follow the Athenians; he would go back and search for Kleidemos on the battle-ground. He found a horse and raced towards the trail they had just left, as the sun began to wane. He arrived at the foot of Ithome at dusk and jumped to the ground, allowing his horse to roam free.

The deserted field was sown with corpses: the Spartans had already left, taking their fallen with them. He began to search feverishly for his friend, overturning the bodies one by one, scrutinizing their disfigured faces. He was nowhere to be found. Out of his mind with grief, Karas climbed the slopes of the mountain as the sun still cast out a little bloody light. The silence was tomb-like, broken every so often by the screams of the crows who hungrily encircled their repast. On high, the open gates on Ithome's black walls stared down at him like the eyes of a skull.

Karas paused to catch his breath on the mountainside, half dead with exertion. He looked down into the shadowy valley: it was completely deserted. He brought his hands to the side of his mouth and started to call with all the breath he had in him, but only distant echoes answered. He sank to the ground, his heart filled with despair. All energy had abandoned him and, as he thought sadly that he should return to the others, he noticed a faint flickering on his right, just tens of feet away. He rose to his feet to see better. They were eyes, shining in the night, the yellow eyes of a big grey wolf. The animal moved towards him, lifting his snout as if to sniff him, and then let out a long howl. He went off along the ridge of the mountain, stopping and turning around now and then.

Karas took heart and followed him until the animal stopped at the great parched olive tree which seemed a creature in pain, claws raised beseechingly towards the sky. There the wolf vanished behind a rock. Karas ran towards the tree, causing masses of pebbles to roll and rattle onto the rocks below.

When he reached the tree, he was overcome by astonishment. There, on its gnarled roots, lay Kleidemos' magnificent armour, shining and bloodied: the storied cuirass, the horn bow, the great shield, the amber-hilted sword and the helmet crowned with wolf fangs.

The giant fell to his knees weeping hot tears. He planted his fists in the dust and remained in that position, unmoving, until he heard the wolf's howl echoing through the valley. He shook himself, collected the armour piece by piece and began to descend the slope. He reached the valley and the banks of the little stream where the people of Ithome had first drawn water upon their arrival from Laconia. In its limpid waters, he washed the cuirass, the sword and the shield. He called his horse and loaded the armour onto its back, covering it with his cloak. He began walking east, towards Mount Taygetus, to bring it whence it had come.

One day, when his people needed him, Talos the Wolf would wear it again.

Author's Note

Spartan society – as described by the authors of the fifth century BC – is the most archaic, contradictory construct imaginable. They had not one but two kings, a fact that has been explained in a variety of ways, although a completely convincing hypothesis has never emerged. These two kings in theory held the maximum authority; in fact they were subject to the control of an executive body of five ephors ('inspectors'). Any king who happened to have a strong personality tended to generate institutional conflict, both with his fellow king and with the other authorities, with consequences that were often devastating.

Male citizens who enjoyed full rights – the so-called 'equals' or 'Spartiates' – belonged to a closed number of families. They met in a general assembly called the 'Apella', which had a purely advisory function. They spent all their time on a single pastime: combat training. Raised from boyhood outside the family home in groups of 'dining companions' in their *syssitiai*, they were also expected to undergo survival training in the wood, without any type of support or aid. These bands of adolescents behaved like packs of predators; they were allowed to steal, and even to kill or terrorize the Helots, who were considered an inferior class. Their raids were called *krypteiai*, and they may have been guided or inspired by the political authorities, with the aim of maintaining constant pressure on the Helots, who periodically tried to regain their freedom through insurrections which were almost always drowned in blood.

Although Spartan society was completely militarized, their politics were generally pacifist, because war had become a luxury they could ill afford. If a family of equals was extinguished, it could not be replaced. In addition, since each family was assigned a limited (and equal) lot of land, births were strictly controlled so estates would remain intact. In the long run, this suicidal demographic policy led to the extinction of the 'Spartiates', their ranks continually reduced as well by combat losses and the growing number of marriages between close relations. When in 198 AD Roman emperor Septimius Severus asked the Spartiates to follow him in the war against the Parthians (obviously for propagandist purposes), he found a few haggard weaklings before him. The Spartan obsession with preserving their numbers is already well documented in the myth of the *Partheniae* – when the Messenian Wars (seventh century BC) kept the warriors away from home for years, the ephors realized that this would eventually mean a long period of time in the future without new conscripts. A group of warriors was promptly sent back to Sparta with the mission of coupling with all virgins of child-bearing age.

And yet Sparta, which is often considered the dark side of Greek civilization, had certain fascinating and surprising aspects: for example, women had a dignity and freedom unimaginable in democratic Athens. They could possess and bequeath property, and girls competed bare-legged in the gymnasiums like the boys of the same age. The Athenians considered this a scandal, and called them 'thigh-barers'. What is more, Plutarch has handed down a series of 'maxims of Spartan women', which suggests a storehouse of traditional female wisdom, practically unheard of in any other ancient Mediterranean civilization. When the legation of Aristagoras of Miletus arrived at the home of King Cleomenes I, they found him on all fours giving his little daughter Gorgò a 'pony ride'. Noting his visitors' surprise, he told them, 'This isn't the best way to receive foreign guests, but if you are fathers, you'll understand.' This anecdote clearly illustrates the fact that the Spartans must have loved their daughters at least as much as their sons.

Actual slavery didn't exist (although the Helots had no political rights, they could not be bought or sold), nor did luxury; all excess was frowned upon. The Spartans saw themselves as a proud, austere race, and it is probable that the life of an 'equal' was no less harsh or difficult than that of a Helot servant. In battle, their only alternative to winning was to die, and losing one's shield was considered an intolerable disgrace. They were so confident of their strength that they did not wall in their city (the term 'city gates' in the novel is purely symbolic), declaring that the chests of their soldiers provided the best defence.

I've attempted to set my story in this archaic and in many ways primitive society, which is nonetheless admirable for its spirit of sacrifice, its ideals and its honesty. I've respected the original sources as closely as possible, seeking even in the language to reproduce the mentality and manner of living. I was inspired by the story of two survivors of the terrible battle of the 'three hundred' Spartans at the Thermopylae: Pantites and Aristodemus, (Herodotus, VII, 230–2), whom I have called Aghias and Brithos in this novel, maintaining a certain liberty in telling their story, while the figure of the protagonist, Talos/Kleidemos, is wholly imaginary. Everything that surrounds him is based on fact, however: the Persian Wars (based on accounts by Herodotus, but also Diodorus, Thucydides and other minor authors), the habits and customs, the political institutions, the religion and rituals, the folklore and the popular traditions of a world so distant in time and yet so close, in this age when world conflicts are being re-proposed in such dramatic terms.

PARTICULAR NOTES

The term 'slave' is used in the novel, when referring to the Helots, in the generic sense of 'servant'. As we've mentioned, slavery per se was not practised by the Spartans.

The term 'regent,' with reference to Pausanias, is often substituted by the term 'king,' since his function was the same and was perceived as such by the people. The chronology of King Leotichidas' succession is deliberately vague, since it has never been definitively established.

The chronological span of this story extends more or less from 505–504 BC to shortly after 464 BC, the year of the earthquake and the revolt of the Helots in Sparta.

The two episodes of suicide in the novel are based on several dramatic pages by Herodotus. The shameful epitaph given to the survivors of the Thermopylae, ò *trésas* ('he who trembled') is authentic as well (Herodotus, VII, 231), as is the macabre suicide ritual of King Cleomenes I (Herodotus, VI,

75), which reflects a mysterious rite whose meaning escapes us, reminiscent in a way of Japanese hara-kiri (although obviously not connected in any way). It may not be going too far to speculate that suicide was perhaps the only option left to a Spartiate who had lost his honour.

The custom of 'exposing' disabled children on Mount Taygetus is documented by historical sources, although it is not clear for how long this went on. Parents forced to comply with this practice must surely have suffered. In any case, inbreeding may have led to an increase in the number of children born with physical defects over the years.

Pausanias' project of giving freedom and full rights as citizens to the Helots is documented in the sources (Thucydides I, 132,4), and it might have been a possible solution to the fundamental problem which led to Sparta's ruin, that is, the rigid division between its castes and the impossibility of injecting new blood.

In the final analysis, the distortions of Spartan society originate from taking a basic principle – aberrant from a modern point of view – to an extreme: that is, that the state is more important than any of its citizens, although its original interpretation may simply have been the sacrifice of the individual for the greater good of the survival of the community. Behaviour that still today is termed 'heroism'.

V.M.M.

THE LAST LEGION

**A new historical epic from the bestselling author
of *Spartan* and the Alexander Trilogy**

The Roman Empire lies in ruins. Barbarians have executed
the Imperial family and exiled the young Emperor, Romulus Augustas.

But not all the Romans are dead. From the dust of
the battlefield, a band of seemingly immortal legionaries
rise up, intent on restoring the Roman Empire. They are
the Last Legion, and a new myth, destined to span the
centuries, is waiting to be born . . .

The Last Legion is a bewitching novel of bravery, love,
myth and magic. Brilliant, captivating and utterly convincing. Valerio Massimo Manfredi has written an epic which
will hold you spell-bound until the very last page.

1

Dertona, fieldcamp of the Nova Invicta Legion,
Anno Domini 476, 1229 years after the foundation of Rome

THE LIGHT PIERCED through the clouds covering the valley, and the cypresses straightened up suddenly like guards, alert on the ridge of the hills. A shadow bending over a bundle of twigs appeared at the edge of a stubble field and vanished at once, as if in a dream. A cock's crow rose from a distant farmhouse, announcing another grey, leaden day, only to be swallowed up instantly by the fog. Nothing penetrated the mist, save the voices of the men.

'Blasted cold.'

'It's this damp that gets into your bones.'

'It's the fog. I've never seen such thick fog in all my life.'

'Nor have I. And not a sign of our rations.'

'Perhaps there's nothing left to eat.'

'Not even a little wine to warm us up.'

'And we haven't been paid for three months.'

'I can't take it any longer, I've had it with this whole thing. A new emperor practically every year, barbarians controlling all the main posts, and now, to top it all off: a snotty-nosed kid on the throne of the Caesars! A thirteen-year-old brat who hasn't even got the strength to hold up the sceptre is supposed to be running the world – the West, at least. No, this is it for me, I'm getting out. As soon as I can I'm leaving the army and going my own way. I'll find myself a little island where I can put goats out to pasture and make cheese. I don't know about the rest of you, but my mind is made up.'

A light breeze opened a breach in the mist and revealed a group of soldiers huddled around a brazier. They were waiting to go off the last shift of guard duty. Rufius Vatrenus, a Spaniard from Saguntum and a veteran of many battles, commander of the guard corps, turned to his comrade, the only one who hadn't yet said a word or sounded a complaint: 'What do you say, Aurelius, are you with me?'

Aurelius poked the tip of his sword into the brazier, rekindling a flame that crackled into life and set a swirl of sparks dancing in the milky mist.

'I've always served Rome. What else could I do?'

A long silence fell. The men looked at each other, gripped by a feeling of dismay and restless unease.

'He'll never hang up his sword,' said Antoninus, a senior officer. 'He's always been in the army. He doesn't even remember what he used to do before he joined up. He simply doesn't remember ever being anywhere else. Isn't that true, Aurelius?'

He got no answer, but the reflection of the nearly burnt-out embers revealed Aurelius's melancholy look.

'He's thinking of what's ahead,' observed Vatrenus. 'The situation is out of control again. If the reports I've heard can be believed, Odoacer's troops have rebelled and attacked Ticinum, where the emperor's father Orestes had taken refuge. They say that he's heading for Placentia, and that he's counting on us to knock some sense into these barbarians and buttress the tottering throne of his young Romulus Augustus. You know, I'm not sure we can do it this time. If you want to know what I think, I really doubt it. There's three times as many of them as of us and—'

'Wait – did you all hear that?' asked one of the soldiers, the one closest to the palisade.

'It's coming from the field,' replied Vatrenus, his gaze searching the semi-deserted camp, its frost-covered tents. 'It's the end of the night shift; it must be the daytime picket coming on duty.'

'No!' said Aurelius. 'It's coming from outside. Sounds like—'

'Horsemen,' nodded Canidius, a legionary from Arelate.

'Barbarians,' concluded Antoninus. 'I don't like it.'

The horsemen appeared all at once out of the fog along the narrow white road that led from the hills to the camp. Imposing, on their massive Sarmatian steeds covered with metallic scales, they wore studded iron helmets, conical in shape and bristling with crests. Long swords hung at their sides, and their blond or reddish locks fluttered in the misty air. Their black cloaks were worn over trousers made of the same coarse, dark wool. The fog and the distance made them look like demons out of hell.

Aurelius leaned over the paling to observe the band drawing closer and closer. The horses plodded through the puddles that had formed on the road after the rain of the night before had melted the snow, raising muddy splashes. 'They're Heruli and Skyrians from the Imperial Army, Odoacer's men probably. Looks bad to me. What are they doing here at this hour, and why weren't we notified? I'm going to report to the commander.'

He clambered down the stairs and ran across the camp towards the praetorium. The camp commander, Manilius Claudianus, a veteran nearly sixty years old who had fought as a young man with Aetius against Attila, was already on his feet, and as Aurelius entered his tent he was hooking his scabbard to his belt.

'General, a squad of Herulian and Skyrian auxiliary troops are approaching. No one said anything about them coming, and I don't like it.'

'Neither do I,' answered the officer in a worried tone. 'Deploy the guard and open the gates. Let's hear what they want.'

Aurelius ran to the palisade and instructed Vatrenus to have the archers take position. He then went down to the guard post, drew up the available forces, had the praetorian gate opened and walked out with the commander. In the meantime, Vatrenus woke the troops with a whispered alarm, one man to the next, almost in silence and without sounding the trumpets.

The commander was completely armed and wore his helmet, a manifest sign that he considered this a war zone. His guard flanked him on both sides. One man towered head and shoulders above all the rest: Cornelius Batiatus was a gigantic Ethiopian, black as coal, who never abandoned the general's side. He carried an oval shield built to measure by an armourer to cover his huge body. A Roman sword hung from his left shoulder, while a barbarian double-edged axe hung from the right.

The band of barbarians on horseback were just paces away by now, and the man at their head raised his arm as a signal to stop. He had a thick head of red hair which fell at the sides in two long braids. His shoulders were covered by a cloak trimmed with fox fur and his helmet was decorated by a crown of tiny silver skulls. His demeanour denoted his importance. He turned to Commander Claudianus without getting off his horse, speaking in a rough, guttural Latin:

'Noble Odoacer, head of the Imperial Army, orders you to deliver your charge over to me. As of today, I shall assume command of this legion.' He threw a roll of parchment tied with a leather cord at his feet, adding: 'Your certificate of discharge and retirement orders.'

Aurelius stooped to pick it up but the commander stopped him with a peremptory gesture. Claudianus was from an ancient aristocratic family proud of their direct descent from a hero of the Republican Age, and the barbarian's gesture stung him as an intolerable insult. He replied without losing his composure: 'I don't know who you are and I'm not interested in finding out. I take orders only from noble Flavius Orestes, the supreme commander of the Imperial Army.'

The barbarian turned towards his men and shouted: 'Arrest him!' They spurred on their horses and surged forwards with their swords unsheathed: it was evident that they had been ordered to kill them all. The guards retaliated in kind, as a unit of archers simultaneously appeared at the bastions of the camp, their arrows already nocked to the bowstrings. They let fly, at Vatrenus's order, with deadly precision. Nearly all of the horsemen in the front line were hit, as were many of their horses. Wounded or lamed, they pulled their riders down with them in calamitous falls.

This did not stop the others, however, who jumped to the ground so they wouldn't be so easy to hit and rushed headlong at Claudianus's guards. Batiatus hurled himself into the fray, charging like a bull and delivering blows of unstoppable power. Many of the barbarians had never seen a black man, and they backed up, terrorized at the sight of him. The Ethiopian giant sheared off their swords and smashed their shields, chopping off their heads and their arms, whirling his axe and yelling: 'Behold the Black Man! I hate you freckled pigs!' In the fury of his assault, however, he had come too far forward and Commander Claudianus's left flank was left unguarded. Aurelius had just rid himself of an adversary when he saw, out of the corner of his eye, an enemy warrior lunging at the general, but his shield arrived too late to stop the barbarian's pike from sinking into Claudianus's shoulder. Aurelius shouted: 'The commander! The commander is wounded!'

Meanwhile the gates to the camp had been thrown open and the heavy line infantry was charging forward full force, in complete battle gear. The barbarians were driven off, and the few survivors leapt on to their horses and fled with their chief.

*

Shortly thereafter, on the other side of the hills, they reported to their commander, a Skyrian named Mledo who regarded them with scorn and contempt. They looked pitiful: weapons dented, clothing ripped, filthy with blood and slime. Their chief muttered, head low: 'They . . . refused. They said no.'

Mledo spat on the ground, then called his attendant and ordered him to sound the falling-in. The deep bellow of the horns rent the cloak of fog that still covered the countryside like a shroud.

*

Commander Claudianus was eased gently on to the plank bed in the infirmary and a surgeon prepared to remove the pike still stuck in his shoulder. The shaft had been sawn off to contain the damage caused by its swaying back and forth, but the tip had penetrated just below the collar bone and there was the risk of its perforating the lung as well. An assistant brought an iron to a red heat over coals, readying it for cauterizing the wound.

Trumpet blasts and cries sounded a new alarm from the bastions. Aurelius left the infirmary and ran up the stairs until he found himself beside Vatrenus who was staring at the horizon. The entire line of the hills was black with warriors.

'Great gods,' murmured Aurelius, 'there are thousands of them.'

'Go back to the commander and tell him what's happening. I can't see that we've got much choice here, but tell him we're awaiting his orders.'

Aurelius reached the infirmary just as the surgeon was wrenching the tip of the pike from the shoulder of their wounded leader, and he saw the noble patrician's face twist in a grimace of pain. Aurelius moved closer: 'General, the barbarians are attacking. There are thousands and thousands of them, and they are completely encircling our camp. What are your orders?'

Blood spurted copiously from the wound on to the hands and face of the surgeon and his assistants who were doing their utmost to staunch it while another approached with the red hot iron. The surgeon plunged it into the hole and Commander Claudianus moaned, gritting his teeth so as not to cry out. The acrid odour of burnt flesh saturated the little room and a dense smoke arose from the scorching iron which continued to sizzle in the wound.

Aurelius said again, 'General . . .'

Claudianus stretched out his free hand towards Aurelius: 'Listen . . . Odoacer wants to exterminate us, because we represent an insurmountable obstacle for him. The Nova Invicta is a relict from the past but we still frighten them. All Romans, from Italy and the provinces; he knows we'll never obey him. That's why he wants us all dead. Go at once to Orestes, he must be told what's happening here. Tell him that we're surrounded . . . that we desperately need his help . . .'

'Send someone else,' answered Aurelius, 'I beg of you. I want to stay. All my friends are here.'

'No. You must obey my orders. Only you can succeed. We still have control over the bridge on the Olubria; it will certainly be their first objective in cutting us off from Placentia. Go, now, before the circle closes in, hie to it and never stop. Orestes is at his villa outside the city with the emperor. We'll manage to hold out here.'

Aurelius lowered his head: 'I'll be back. Fight them off

for as long as you can.' He turned. Behind him, Batiatus stared mutely at his commander, wounded and deathly pale, stretched out on the planks soaked with his blood. Aurelius didn't have the courage to say a word. He ran out and reached Vatrenus on the sentry walk: 'He has ordered me to go and seek reinforcements: I'll be back as soon as I can. Hold them off; I know we can do it!' Vatrenus nodded without speaking. There was no hope in his gaze, just the determination to die like a soldier.

Aurelius couldn't bring himself to speak. He stuck two fingers in his mouth and whistled. A whinny could be heard in reply, and a bay stallion trotted towards the bastions. Aurelius sprang into the saddle, spurring him towards the rear gate. Vatrenus ordered the doors to be unbolted for just long enough to let out the galloping horse and his rider, then had them closed again immediately.

Vatrenus watched as he rode off into the distance, heading towards the bridge on the Olubria. The squad guarding the bridgehead realized immediately what was happening, as a large group of barbarian horsemen detached from the bulk of the army and raced directly towards them.

'Will he make it?' asked Canidius at his side.

'You mean will he make it back? Yes. Perhaps,' replied Vatrenus. 'Aurelius is the best we've got.' The tone of his voice and his expression told a different story.

He turned back again, observing Aurelius as he raced to cover the open ground between the camp and the bridge. He soon saw another squad of barbarian cavalry emerging suddenly on the left and joining up with the squad arriving from the right, closing in like a pair of pincers to cut short his flight, but Aurelius was as fast as the wind, and his horse devoured the flat terrain between the camp and the river. Aurelius was stretched out nearly flat on the horse's back so as to offer less resistance and less of a mark for the arrows which were bound to start raining upon him.

'Run, run,' growled Vatrenus between his teeth, 'That's the way to do it, boy . . .'

He realized almost instantly that the assailants were too numerous and that they would soon overwhelm the soldiers at the bridgehead. Aurelius needed a greater lead. 'Catapults!' he shouted. The men arming the catapults were ready, and aimed their missiles at the barbarian cavalry converging on the bridge.

'Fire!' shouted Vatrenus again, and sixteen catapults discharged their arrows towards the heads of the two squads, hitting their mark. Those in the lead keeled over while those just behind them tumbled headlong over their fallen comrades. Others were crushed by the weight of their horses, while the archers stationed at the bridge picked off a number of those on the sides. First they sent a swarm of arrows horizontally into the crowd, then flung their javelins high to swoop down in the centre. Many barbarians fell, run through, as more horses stumbled and rolled over, dragging and burying their horsemen beneath them. The remaining comrades continued their charge heedless, fanning out, yelling in fury at this reverse.

Aurelius was close enough so that his companions drawn up on the bridge could hear his voice. He recognized Vibius Quadratus, a tent mate, and shouted: 'I'm going for help! Cover me! I'll be back!'

'I know!' shouted Quadratus and raised his arm to signal the others to open a passage for Aurelius. He shot through the line of comrades like a lightning bolt and the bridge thundered under the hooves of his powerful steed. The garrison closed up compactly behind him, shields clanging tight against shields. The front line knelt while the second stood, only the tips of their spears protruding, shafts planted firmly in the ground.

The barbarian horsemen flung themselves at that little garrison in a blind frenzy, submerging that last bulwark of Roman discipline like a tidal wave. The bridge was so narrow that some of the assailants crashed into each other and were flung to the ground. Others made their way to the centre where they furiously attacked the small contingent. The Romans were pushed back, but held their line. Many of the barbarians' horses were wounded by spears, while others reared up and threw their horsemen, who ended up on the iron spikes. The combat was fierce, man against man, sword against sword. The defenders knew that every instant gained meant ground gained for Aurelius, and this could mean the salvation of the entire legion. They knew what horrible torture awaited them if they were taken alive, so they fought with all their might, loudly urging each other on.

Aurelius had reached the far end of the plain and turned around before bounding into the forest of oak trees before him. The last thing he saw was his comrades being overrun by the relentless vehemence of the enemy.

'He's made it!' exulted Antoninus from the camp's

sentry walk. 'He's in the forest, they'll never get him now. Now we have a chance.'

'You're right,' replied Vatrenus. 'Our comrades on the bridge let themselves be slaughtered so they could cover his retreat.'

Batiatus arrived then from the infirmary.

'How's the commander?' asked Vatrenus.

'The surgeon has cauterized the wound, but he says the pike has punctured a lung. He's coughing up blood and his fever is rising.' He clenched his cyclopean fists and tightened his jaw. 'The first one of them I see I swear I'll butcher him, I'll demolish him, I'll smash him into pieces. I'll eat his liver . . .'

His comrades looked at him in a sort of admiring shock: they knew quite well that his weren't mere words.

Vatrenus changed the subject: 'What day is it today?'

'The nones of November,' replied Canidius. 'What difference does it make?'

Vatrenus shook his head: 'Just three months ago Orestes was just presenting his son to the Senate, and now he already has to defend the boy from Odoacer's fury. If Aurelius is lucky he'll get there sometime in the middle of the night. The reinforcements could leave at dawn and be here in two days' time. If Odoacer hasn't occupied all the passes and bridges, if Orestes has loyal troops he can set to march right away, if . . .'

His words were interrupted by blasts of alarm coming from the guard towers. The sentries shouted: 'They're attacking!'

Vatrenus reacted as if lashed by a whip. He called the standard bearer: 'Raise the ensign! All men at their battle posts! Machines in firing position! Archers to the palisade! Men of the Nova Invicta Legion, this camp is the last outpost of Rome, the sacred land of our ancestors! We shall defend it at all costs! Show these beasts that the honour of Rome is not dead!'

He grabbed a javelin and ran to his place on the bastions. At that very same instant from the hills exploded the howl of barbarian fury, and thousands upon thousands of horsemen made the earth tremble with their wrathful charge. They dragged chariots and wheeled carriages loaded with sharpened poles to hurl against the fortifications of the Roman camp. The defenders thronged the palisade, drawing the strings of their bows, spasmodically clutching at the javelins in their fists, pale with tension, their foreheads drenched with cold sweat.